Blood Divine

Greg Howard

Anakim Press

Edited by Jerry Wheeler and Charissa Weaks

Cover art by Adrian Nicholas

Formatting by Polgarus Studio

Printed in the United States of America

First Printing, 2016

ISBN: 978-0692840498

ANAKIM PRESS
640 S. Lemon Ave. #4226
Walnut, CA 91789

www.greghowardauthor.com

For Steve

We did it.

20 Years Ago

They stood side by side, straddling their bicycles between the two vine-choked, stone columns guarding the entrance to Warfield. The manor house teased them in the distance, the front door a mere speck framed by a cathedral of live oaks dripping with Spanish moss. The deserted plantation was still and quiet, daring them to continue. It was a standoff. Whoever made the first move would lose.

Cooper drew in the thick scent of jasmine and held it in his throat. Beads of sweat formed on his forehead and trickled down his neck. He wiped his brow with the back of his hand and slowly exhaled the nervous energy clogging his lungs. They'd never gotten that far before, and it was nothing like he'd expected. Part ghost town, part sanctuary, Warfield was both creepy and beautiful all at the same time. Like he'd journeyed to hell and felt right at home once he arrived. But being there was wrong. He knew that now.

Kevin rolled his bike forward, calling to them over his shoulder with his trademark sneer. "Let's go, chicken shits."

Cooper glared at the back of his older brother's head and

frowned. Lillie Mae had warned them many times to stay away from Warfield, her eyes cloudy and distant at the mention of the place. The ghost stories and nightmares weren't enough for Kevin and RJ, though. They wanted to see the real thing up close. So there they were, riding right up into Blue's lair. If not for the chance to hang around RJ, Cooper would've stayed behind in the cool of his bedroom, hunkered down under a pile of books and his summer reading list.

RJ glanced over and shot Cooper a smile. "You okay there, Red?"

Cooper's cheeks grew hot. The butterflies in his stomach were back. RJ always had that effect on him. Cooper looked down, pushed his glasses up the bridge of his nose with the knuckle of his index finger and nodded. Easing his bike forward, he cleared the stone gates with Tony riding beside him in silence. A cluster of sagging structures lay ahead, sheltered from the blazing low-country sun by a row of sprawling oaks.

Tony squinted his eyes. "So this is where it happened?"

RJ glanced over his shoulder, one hand resting on the handlebars and the other moving dirty blond locks out of his eyes. "Yep. This is it. This is where it all went to hell."

Everyone knew the legend of Blue. Stories of a murderous slave ghost who roamed the woods around Warfield were standard campfire lore in Georgetown, and the subject of most of Cooper's nightmares.

"Blue got the slaves all riled up one night and they revolted," RJ said, guiding his bike in a circle around the younger boys. "Set the manor house on fire and nearly burned the place down. Killed the planter and his whole family." RJ steered his bike forward, stood on the pedals, and caught up with Kevin in three forceful down-strides.

Cooper studied the sad remains of the slave village. A handful of small cabins lined each side of the road, limp and leaning under the weight of neglect. At the end, on the right, another structure bore a wooden cross over the door. A modest bell tower stood guard next to it. Cooper guessed it was some kind of church, though it looked nothing like the shiny, new Pentecostal one his family attended.

"I don't like it here," Tony said, his voice cracking.

Cooper smiled over at his best friend. "It'll be okay." But he wasn't so sure. Cooper pedalled forward, his insides churning like the drag of his bicycle tires in the soft ruts of the road. Kevin came to a sudden stop and planted both feet on the ground, the bike resting between his legs. He pointed over to one of the cabins.

They all stopped and looked to their right. Cooper's heartbeat quickened, and sweat slicked his hands, making it hard to grip the handlebars. On the porch of the cabin, a rocking chair, rickety and broken, sat empty yet swaying back and forth, the faint creak of rotted wood sounding as it moved. It rocked for a few seconds, then stopped.

Cooper stared at the chair, holding his breath and waiting for it to move again. It didn't.

"It's just the wind," RJ said, dismissing the chair with the wave of his hand. "Let's keep going."

The Spanish moss hanging down over RJ's head was as still as icicles. No wind.

RJ pointed his handlebars back toward the manor house. "Come on. There ain't nobody here. This place has been deserted for years."

Kevin rolled his bike forward, glaring back at the younger boys. "Yeah. Come on, you babies. Or you can go back home by yourselves."

Tony glanced over at Cooper, his brow cocked with anticipation. "Wanna go back?"

Cooper considered the option for a moment, then shook his head and pushed forward. He didn't much like the idea of traveling two miles back down a dimly lit dirt road without the older boys. Besides, his momma wouldn't be waiting for him at home this time with kisses, hugs, and cookies she made special for him. She'd promised she'd never leave him, but she did.

They were halfway down Oak Alley when a foreign sound cracked the silent, crystal blue sky—a desperate clanging that echoed over the grounds. A bell. A big bell. Cooper dropped his feet to the ground. They all looked over their shoulders, searching for the source of the noise, their gazes landing on the bell tower of the chapel. Still, there was no breeze—certainly not one strong enough to cause the bell to swing unattended.

Tony pointed in the direction of the bell tower, panic twisting his face. "Somebody is here!"

Fear clawed at the pit of Cooper's stomach. Kevin and RJ exchanged glances framed with wrinkled brows and foreheads, a sight Cooper had rarely witnessed. Those two weren't afraid of anything.

Kevin yanked his bike around. "Let's get the heck out of here!"

RJ and Tony quickly followed Kevin's lead, creating a tornado of dust in the process.

Cooper righted his bike in the direction of the stone gates and pushed off, his sneakers sinking in the quicksand-like surface of the road. His front tire wobbled through a maze of slick crevices, slowing his speed as they raced back in the direction of the bell tower. They had to. It was the only way out. The clang grew louder with every downstroke of their pedals.

Cooper tried not to look over at the chapel as he passed, but he couldn't resist. He scanned the base of the tower. The rope swung unassisted in perfect rhythm with the badgering noise. With his heart banging around his chest in a wild panic, he looked back at the road. He'd fallen behind. Kevin, RJ, and Tony were several bike lengths ahead of him. Digging into the pedals, he tried unsuccessfully to gain traction on the sandy road.

The first ring of the bell had been jarring, but the final one echoed in Cooper's ears like it was the last sound he would ever hear. Detecting movement to his left, he shot a quick glance over at the cabin with the rocking chair. A mistake. The front wheel of his bike hit a mound of sand, wrenching the handlebars from his grip. Cooper grabbed at them and fought for control of the bike.

A disheartening clanging rattled between his feet, drawing his attention. The bicycle chain buckled up off the sprocket, causing Cooper's breath to catch in his throat.

When he looked back at the road, he barrelled toward the imposing trunk of an oak tree. Slamming his feet into reverse only aggravated the chain's unstable condition. It buckled a final time and left the thread of the chain wheel, the freed pedals spinning wildly between Cooper's feet. Diving off the bike to the left of the oncoming tree, he landed hard on his side, a crash of mangled metal ringing in his ears.

Dazed and disoriented, he lay still on his back, struggling to catch his breath, inhaling mouthfuls of sandy dust into his lungs. He let his heavy head fall to one side and stared at a blurry pile of twisted metal and spinning wheels. Touching his face, he confirmed that his glasses were gone.

Scrambling over on his hands and knees, Cooper ran his fingers over the ground until he felt the wire frame. He shoved his glasses back on and looked toward the stone gates. Kevin, RJ, and Tony zoomed through and disappeared into the cover of the forest, abandoning him to the eerie silence of the slave village. He was alone.

Fighting back tears, Cooper stood with a grunt of pain, slapping dirt off his jeans as a swarm of mosquitoes descended on him. He swatted them away and slapped at his face, but he froze when the low, creaky rumble of wooden rockers rolling over slatted floorboards sounded behind him. Oxygen seizing in his lungs and his heart still pounding, he waited, submitting to an onslaught of mosquito bites, but afraid to move a muscle. The rocking stopped as quickly as it had started, giving him a bit of confidence. Maybe it *was* the wind, like RJ said. He craned his neck toward the cabin behind him and nearly lost control of his bladder.

A massive man sat in the rocking chair, his cold, blue eyes peering through a face riddled with scars. A tattered shirt and mud-caked pants covered the darkest skin Cooper had ever seen. The stranger speared him with a penetrating gaze and the electricity brimming in those peculiar eyes hypnotized Cooper into complete submission. He couldn't run. Couldn't scream. Couldn't cry. A knot of heat formed in his belly and coiled in on itself like a snake agitated by the strange man's presence.

He looked away. Closed his eyes tight. Took two deep breaths and settled his rambling thoughts. Just his eyes playing tricks on him, like his momma used to tell him when he feared shadows in his room at night. If he didn't look, they wouldn't be there. That's what she always told him.

He needed to be sure, though, so he forced his eyes open.

The towering man stood right in front of him, not six feet away, blocking his path to the road. With muscles stacked upon muscles, the man's ebony skin glistened in the sun, blinding Cooper. All the ghost stories he'd heard his whole life came crashing back down on him. There was no doubt who it was. He knew it in his gut. Knew it as well as he knew his own name. It was Blue.

Cooper swallowed hard and managed a shaky step backward. His neck hot and his chest tight, he jabbed his fingers under the rim of his glasses and rubbed his eyes. "It's not real," he whispered. "He's not real. If you don't look, he won't be there." Lowering his hands, he dared to look again.

Blue moved toward him, every step threatening and calculated.

Cooper stumbled back, and something hard pressed against his leg. He lost his balance and tumbled down on top of the bike. Sharp metal stabbed into his back. He winced and stifled a cry. Blue cocked his head to one side and narrowed his eyes so only slits of bright blue peeked through. Rolling off the bicycle, Cooper dug his fingers into the sand and scrambled away from the ghost until his back was against the tree. Blue followed, stretching a broad hand out toward Cooper's throat.

The temperature around him dropped instantly, the humid air turning ice cold and spilling over Cooper's entire body, chilling him to the bone. When Blue finally made contact, it wasn't with Cooper's throat, as he'd feared. Blue covered the top of Cooper's head with his heavy hand, tightening his icicle-like fingers around the skull.

A jolt of current passed from Blue's clammy palm to the crown of Cooper's head, stifling his attempt to scream. The tightly coiled knot in his stomach seemed to burst into a million tiny pieces, and wet heat rushed through his veins like hot candle wax had been spilled all over his insides. The explosion of energy bottlenecked in his fingertips and throbbed for release. Cooper clenched his fists. Tears pooled in his eyes as he forced them closed.

A ringing echoed in his ears, like the sound of the chapel bell, but louder and trapped inside the confines of his brain. An internal, bright light blinded him. His eyeballs pulsed in their sockets from the unbearable pressure.

Determined fingers dug into his skull. He couldn't escape. Blue would crush him with his bare hands, and nobody was around to save him. A single tear pushed out from under Cooper's eyelid and ran cold down his cheek.

Then the darkness came.

CHAPTER ONE

Present Day

A coarse tongue caressed Cooper's jawline with feral precision. Teasing whiskers tickled his skin, gently luring him out of an alcohol-laced slumber. A warm and woolly weight rested on his chest. It shifted and repositioned, emitting a throaty rumble as it moved.

With a measure of trepidation, Cooper eased his eyes open. The incessant licking stopped. A pair of gold eyes peered back at him, brimming with affection and curiosity. Purring with seductive satisfaction, a fat, white cat sat squarely between his bare pecs, like his chest was a mountain peak that had been conquered and claimed.

"Get off me," Cooper scolded in a half whisper. He shooed the feline dominatrix with one hand and wiped his jaw with the other. The animal sized him up with a cocked head, rose, and sauntered off his chest, dropping to the floor with a soft thud.

God, he hated cats. Unfortunately, his true nature was like catnip to them. They sensed things in him that people didn't. Dark things. A draft drifted over his bare skin, sending a chill through him. He propped up on his elbows and scanned his unfamiliar surroundings.

The morning sun slipped through half-open, white plantation shutters, reflecting off white bedding, white walls, a white club chair in the corner—*lots* of white. Where the hell was he? What time was it? And where the hell were his pants?

He eased back down on the mattress, and the naked body lying next to him stirred. Oh, right. *Marco? Matthew? Mario?* Whoever it was, it rolled over and slung a lithe arm over Cooper's chest.

Shit.

He stared up at the ceiling and then closed his eyes tight. If he didn't look, there wouldn't be anybody there. At least that's what he told himself in times like those. He opened one eye and peeked over at sleeping beauty. As usual—still there.

Cooper sighed and studied the angular face of the Latino boy who just a few hours earlier had been priority target number one on his hunt. A nameless, personality-deprived young stud without an intellectual thought in that pretty little head. Just the way Cooper liked them. Easy to bed, easy to leave, and nothing of substance to tempt him otherwise. He reconstructed the events of last night in his head—the thumping music, the gyrating go-go boys, the nagging vibration of the phone in his pocket.

Dammit. The missed calls. *Dis*missed was more like it. What had he been thinking? He ran his hand through his hair and exhaled a quiet sigh. Jesus. He *hadn't* been thinking. Not with his head anyway. Lillie Mae would be worried that he never answered. He needed to call her back.

Sliding his butt stealthily across wrinkled sheets, he edged toward the side of the bed. He was nearly free until the guy's hand fell from Cooper's chest onto the mattress and he opened his drooping, dark eyes.

Let the awkwardness begin.

The guy rubbed his sleepy eyes and directed them at Cooper. "You looking for the bathroom?" The accent was just slight enough to remind Cooper of the desire that had stirred inside him when he first hit on the guy at the bar.

"Actually, I was looking for my phone." And his shirt, and his underwear, and any shred of dignity he had left. Why couldn't Mateo, or whatever its name was, have just stayed asleep? That usually made this part easier on everyone.

"Ah." The guy propped himself up on one elbow and turned his perfectly proportioned body toward Cooper. He ran smooth fingertips over the ripples of Cooper's stomach, reigniting a flicker of desire. "I finally caught the eye of the elusive, hot ginger I've been stalking for a month, and now he's having buyer's remorse." A smirk twisted the guy's lips. "Just my luck." His gaze drifted down Cooper's torso and stopped when it arrived at his exposed morning wood.

Heat rushed to Cooper's cheeks as he pulled the mangled top sheet up over his crotch. "Look...Mattias..."

The guy cocked an eyebrow at him.

"Manuel?" This wasn't going very well.

The guy rolled his eyes, chuckled, and sat up, not

bothering to cover his nakedness. "Really? We talked for an hour at the bar before we left together."

"We did?" Cooper couldn't remember the guy's name, much less the finer points of their no doubt banal conversation. He slipped out from under the sheet and stood with his back to the bed, though it was a little late to play the modesty card at this point. His clothes were scattered on the floor, on a chair, over the lampshade, but his phone was nowhere in sight. Neither was his underwear.

"It's Miguel," the guy said with a huff. Cooper looked over his shoulder. Miguel slung his legs off the bed and scratched his dense, curly mop of dark hair. "It's fine. Your reputation precedes you. I knew what I was getting into." Miguel stood, rubbed his bare ass, and disappeared into the bathroom.

Cooper gave up trying to find his underwear and pulled on his jeans. "What's that supposed to mean?" He scanned the floor. "Where the hell is my phone?" A flash of silver caught his eye just under the side of the bed. Dropping down to his knees, he peeked under the frame. Two familiar, gold eyes stared back at him, just a claw swipe away from his phone, which was partially hidden under his hastily discarded boxer briefs.

Cooper reached a hand under the bed and shooed the cat away. It didn't move. "Beat it, you nappy little pussy." He swatted again. The cat shot out from under the bed with a hiss and disappeared into the front room.

"Cooper Causey..." Miguel called over a healthy jet stream of liquid hitting the toilet bowl. "...a great lay and you don't even have to make him coffee. He'll be gone before the sun's up. That's what they say about you at the bar."

Cooper grabbed the phone and stared at the blank screen, Miguel's words sparking only minor irritation. What the hell did he care? He'd never see this guy again anyway. He got up, sat on the edge of the bed, and held down the power button on the side of the phone. A toilet flushed, and Cooper glanced over his shoulder toward the door.

Miguel ambled into the room sporting a tiny, yet well-filled, black thong. "Don't get me wrong. It was damn well worth the wait."

"I am so glad I don't disappoint," Cooper replied with a sarcasm-laced mumble.

His phone finally came to life. A gray notification box in the center of the blue screen tracked six missed calls and one voice mail, all from the same familiar number. Guilt swelled inside him.

Lillie Mae never liked leaving voicemails, opting to call multiple times to see if she could make a personal connection instead. She'd called three times while he was at the bar before he turned the thing off and shoved it into his pocket and out of his thoughts. But six calls plus a voicemail was not like her, especially since she knew he planned to visit her soon. He'd put it off as long as he could and had run out of excuses. Something had to be wrong.

A pinch of pain shot through Cooper's fingertips, like the simultaneous pricking of a hundred needles. The cat reappeared and weaved in and out of his legs, soaking up the errant discharge. He nudged the cat away with his foot, shook his hands, and looked over his shoulder.

Miguel stared at him with a wrinkled brow and a crooked grin. "You okay?"

Cooper grabbed his shirt off the back of the club chair and slipped it on, stuffing the balled-up boxer briefs in his front pocket. He was definitely not okay. Hadn't been in years.

"Sorry," he said. "I have to get going."

"Oh, right. The dissertation you told me about. Smart and sexy. I am such a sucker for smart and sexy."

God, he needed to get out of there. This guy might actually *like* him. Those were the worst ones. He connected half the buttons on his shirt and sat down to put on his shoes. Before he could get the laces tied, he sensed Miguel hovering over him.

"Not good with personal stuff *afte*r the deed is done are you, Professor?"

"Never going to be a professor unless I get that dissertation done." Cooper paused and looked up, his eyes level with Miguel's bulging crotch. The guy was trying to tempt him with round two. That never worked on him. "Sorry to rush out. Really." Not really. He couldn't get out fast enough. He stood and almost put a hand on each of Miguel's arms in a vain attempt at sincerity. The irritating heat in his palms made him think better of it. He clenched his fists. "I'll call you. I promise." The words rang so hollow in his own ears, he almost choked them back.

Miguel rolled his eyes. "And guys really believe that shit?"

Cooper gave up. This guy didn't know him, and he wasn't worth the effort. He shook his head and made his way toward the front door.

"You can't use that hot body as a shield forever, Cooper Causey," Miguel called after him.

"Whatever." Cooper couldn't help but slam the door behind him when he stepped out of the apartment. He leaned against the door and took a deep breath of fresh Tennessee morning air. The cookie-cutter apartment complex was quiet except for a few birds playing chase in the treetops across the street in Centennial Park.

The phone weighed his hand down. He flipped it over and stared at the screen again, his fingertips still throbbing. A familiar anxiety rumbled inside him as it did every time he made contact with his past. With that place.

He took another deep breath, pressed *listen,* and lifted the phone to his ear.

CHAPTER TWO

Cooper lost traction with the road on the black ice of Sampit River Bridge. With a white-knuckled grip on the steering wheel, he coaxed the SUV back toward the center of the road, his fingers melding to the hard leather like clay.

Straining to see through the persistent barrage of sleet battering the windshield, he spotted a metal sign up ahead. A severely dented post on the right side caused a protracted lean, as if the thing bowed to the majesty of the unusual winter storm. The reflective coating of the letters glimmered under the glare of his headlights.

Welcome to Historic Georgetown

3rd Oldest City in South Carolina

Ghost Capital of the South!

The sign quickly disappeared into the darkness as he passed, and guided the car onto Fraser Street. A single bead of sweat trickled down the back of his neck. The heater had been on full blast since Charleston. Glancing down at the dash, he switched the fan to low and cracked the window for little fresh air.

Grabbing his phone, he checked the screen again. No calls. He'd listened to the voice mail from his grandmother a dozen times between Nashville and Georgetown and speed-dialed her twice as many times to no avail. She didn't own an answering machine. He should've bought her one. He should've done a lot of things. But she was always there. She always answered. Until tonight.

He'd already tried Georgetown Memorial, hoping that if she were hurt, she'd have been able to call 911. No Lillie Mae James had been admitted. All he could think of now was getting to Phipps House and making sure she was all right.

He looked up, and his breath caught in his throat. In the middle of the road, a couple of car lengths ahead, stood the hulking, dark figure of a man. Cooper's foot shot instinctively over to the brake pedal. He yanked the steering wheel hard to the left. The SUV revolted and lunged to the right, skidding to the side of the road and slamming into the thick metal pole of a road sign. Cooper lurched forward, but the seat belt snapped him back. His head bounced off the headrest, and then the car went still.

He rubbed his neck and slammed his palm on the steering wheel. "Fuck!"

The car idled around him, the only sound in the quiet outskirts of the city other than his rapid breathing and the low hum of the heater. He took longer than he should have to open his eyes. He had his reasons.

Finally he turned and scoured the darkness through the back window with only the orange haze of the street lamps to illuminate his search. The road was empty.

Of course it was.

He relaxed his shoulders and ran his fingers through his hair. He needed to get a grip. Needed to shake off what this godforsaken town did to him every time he passed the city limits. Through the ice-speckled windshield, he noted the sign embedded in the grille of the car.

Historic District and Harborwalk

Next Right

Nervous energy coursed down to his fingertips, igniting a tingling sensation he tried his best to ignore. He took a deep breath and wrung out his fingers like a wet dishrag. Focusing on the blinking lights of the instrument panel, he cursed under his breath and jerked the gearshift into park. He needed to see how much damage had been done, but hell if he wanted to get out of the car. He punched the red release button of his seat belt with trembling fingers. Three tries later, he was free.

Jumping out into the harsh reality of the freezing rain and biting wind without a coat was both miserable and invigorating. He sucked in an icy breath of air and looked around, just to be sure he was alone. The combination of dim streetlights and orange dust from the steel mill smokestacks cast an eerie film over the boarded-up shops and offices lining the entrance to the dying shell of a town.

Cooper walked around to the front of the SUV and inspected the damage. The signpost had made a pretty good dent in the grille. Nothing too serious, but the front right tire was flat. Great. Just what he needed.

He looked around to get his bearings and a familiar

landmark caught his eye up the street on the right. With a deep sigh of resignation, he got back in the car, put the gearshift into reverse, and eased the SUV backward. The pole dislodged from the grille with a screech of mangled metal. The drag of the deflated tire lumbered underneath as he pulled into the street, plodding along at a snail's pace.

The lights of the old Ice House gas station and convenience store lit the black sky with garish fluorescence. He pulled into a parking space in the corner of the lot and killed the engine. Grabbed his phone from the center console and hit redial. After five unanswered rings, he shook his head, hung up, and hopped out of the car.

A sudden blast of brittle January air sucker-punched him in the chest. He grabbed his jacket from the passenger seat, pulled it on, and yanked the collar up around his ears. Balancing himself with one hand on the SUV, he made his way around to the back and checked the cargo area. Spare tire? *Check*. Jack? *Not so much.*

The onslaught of freezing rain picked up and sleet stung his face as he carefully navigated the slick parking lot toward the entrance of the Ice House. The bell hanging above the glass door announced his entrance with a jarring clang, shaking cobwebs off long-buried memories in some far corner of his mind. His father used to bring him and his older brother, Kevin, there when they were kids. They'd fill a Styrofoam cooler with ice, bottles of Pepsi, and grab a container of live crickets before heading to the fishing pier off Winyah Bay. The memory no longer seemed like it was his. It belonged to an innocent boy full of life, with a living, breathing family, not to a nearly thirty, immaculately educated yet unemployed English teacher haunted by a clan of shadows.

The store was void of other customers but filled with the pungent odors of raw fish and stale cigarettes. He hurried through rows of potato chips, pork rinds, and beef jerky, making a beeline for the long counter at the back of the store. A man sat hunched over on a stool behind the register, his head buried deep in a rumpled copy of *Field & Stream* and a burgundy Gamecocks hoodie bunched up around his neck.

Greeted with silence and the top of a thick roost of hair the color and texture of dried hay, Cooper glanced down at the counter to a plastic brochure holder housing a bundle of homemade, tri-folded fliers. Scribbled across the front was *Miss Ida's Ghost Tours*. Cooper shook his head. Idiot tourists paid someone to give them a guided tour of the thing he'd run away from since he was a kid.

Annoyed at being ignored, he cleared his throat without trying to sugarcoat his impatience. The guy finally dropped the magazine and looked up. He appeared around the same age as Cooper, and his face was oddly familiar.

With raised eyebrows and a gaping mouth, he looked at Cooper like he'd been raised from the dead. "Cooper Causey?"

A childhood version of the man's face finally popped into Cooper's head. He leaned forward and squinted at him. "Tony? Tony Tanner?"

Tony nodded and looked down, as if he'd been caught doing something he shouldn't have.

Cooper assessed the adult version of the scrawny boy he'd spent so many adventure-filled days with during the long, humid, low-country summers. Tall with a sinewy build, Tony was handsome in that redneck sort of way.

Cooper offered his hand out of habit. "Long time. Ten years at least."

Tony stared at Cooper's hand like it had cooties. After an awkward moment to scrub the inside of his elbow, Tony finally accepted the outstretched hand. Cooper flinched when their palms met. Tony's skin was scaly and cold, like the dead fish resting on ice in the display case a few feet away. His eyes were set deep in their sockets, underscored with baggy dark circles. His face was drawn and weathered, like a crackled canvas of small town history.

"Yeah," Tony said, pulling his hand away after only a couple of seconds. "'Bout that long. Kevin's funeral, I guess."

The reminder stung. Cooper hid behind a stiff smile of well-mannered Southern denial and moved past it. He needed a jack. That was it. Not a walk down memory lane, especially not for those memories.

He pointed over his shoulder with his right thumb. "I hit a sign and blew out a tire. Do you have a jack around here that I could borrow? Or buy?"

Tony nodded to the far right wall before scraping the inside of his elbow again. Probably massaging hungry track marks, because hell if he didn't look like a junkie. Cooper followed Tony's direction to a lone red jack on the bottom shelf, sitting amidst bottles of motor oil, funnels, and gallons of blue windshield wiper fluid.

"Perfect." Cooper walked over, retrieved the jack, and sat it on the counter. Pulling out his wallet and thumbing through the bills, he waited for the inflated price he would be charged for the *convenience* of his purchase. Cooper winced when Tony mumbled the amount, giving him a credit card instead.

Cooper scanned Tony's discarded magazine, mouthing the titles of articles listed on the cover in a vain attempt to avoid small talk while Tony processed the transaction. But guilt and uncomfortable silence prevailed.

"So, you work here now." It was more of a statement than a question, and Cooper hoped that approach would curtail any lengthy answer.

"Sort of," Tony said, looking over Cooper's shoulder.

Why the hell wouldn't this guy look him in the eye?

Tony's voice was flat and distant. "Helpin' out my dad. He bought the place a few years back. Goddamned archaic money pit. Can't make a decent livin' selling ice, crickets, gas, and beer no more."

Cooper really didn't care. He just wanted Tony to process the damn payment so he could be on his way. He rapped his fingertips on the counter as another awkward lull filled the space between them. They both stared down at the credit card machine, Cooper willing it to respond. He probably could make it do so, if he dared.

Tony made no attempt to draw out the small talk either. He obviously wasn't interested in Cooper's life now. Perhaps he carried some shame over what they used to do together as kids when they locked themselves away in the storage room behind Tony's house. He had probably heard rumors about Cooper through the small town gossip mill.

You know that Cooper Causey? Queer as a three-dollar bill. Poor Lillie Mae. Hasn't that woman suffered enough in her life?

The moment Lillie Mae's name drifted into his thoughts, the credit card machine sparked to life and spat out a receipt. Tony slid a pen and the receipt across the counter with overdone caution, like feeding a poisonous snake. Cooper scribbled something vaguely resembling his name on the paper, and they both grabbed the car jack at once.

"Thanks." Cooper pulled the jack toward him by the base. Tony didn't let go, his empty, dead eyes locking onto Cooper's. He closed them and leaned over the counter, taking a long sniff of the air between them.

Cooper froze. He stared at Tony, confused and a little creeped out. Tony's lids fluttered back open, and only the whites of his eyes showed for a split second before dark irises fell back into place. Cooper was sure the guy would pass out.

"You okay?" He let go of the jack and put his hand on Tony's shoulder.

Tony recoiled, stumbling back and crashing into the wall of cigarettes behind him. The whole display nearly toppled over on top of him. He stared at Cooper with a twisted, undecipherable expression.

Fear? Disgust? Desire?

"Sorry," Cooper said, though not sure what he'd done wrong.

Tony didn't respond. Just leered at Cooper like he wanted to slice him up and eat him for dinner. An ice-cold chill ran down Cooper's spine. Something was seriously wrong with this guy, but he had zero time to waste trying to figure out what it was. Cooper grabbed the jack off the counter and backed away. For some reason, he didn't want to turn his back on Tony.

"I've got to change that tire and get over to Phipps House," Cooper said. "Good to see you."

Tony's only response was a silent, unsettling leer.

Cooper turned and hurried for the door, sensing Tony boring a hole through the back of his head the whole way. Tiny beads of sweat broke out along his hairline. His palms prickled, and his fingertips burned with an agitated, preternatural energy. He took a deep breath, clenched his fists, and bolted out the door.

Welcome to fucking Georgetown.

CHAPTER THREE

Phipps House was quiet. Too quiet. No television blaring in the front room. No pots banging around in the kitchen. The monotonous ticking of the antique grandfather clock in the foyer was the only audible disturbance. Cooper let go of the handle on his rolling duffle bag and closed the door. He took off his coat and tossed it over the luggage.

"Lillie Mae?"

He stripped off his gloves, hoping her usually cheery voice would drift down the hall to greet him, but no answer came. All the lights were on. She would never have left the house with all the lights on. Dropping his scarf on his bag, Cooper wiped his shoes on the rug and walked down the hall toward the sitting room.

The house hadn't changed much since his last visit. Outdated, paisley wallpaper peeled in all the same places, and Lillie Mae's eclectic mix of '60s and '70s kitsch fused with the centuries-old antiquities contributed to the schizophrenic personality of the historic, three-story home. Sitting opposite the one hundred-year-old grandfather clock was an *assembly required* Walmart curio cabinet circa 1995. Every glass shelf in it teemed with collectible porcelain dolls, all fat bellies and creepy smiles, purchased from one of those shop-at-home networks that Lillie Mae watched to all hours of the night.

Stepping into the sitting room, Cooper detected movement from the corner of his eye. He snapped his head around and sighed. His reflection stared back at him in the screen of the fifteen-year-old Panasonic television—her first color one—sitting atop an eighteenth century Jacobean server.

Her little sanctuary was so still, so empty. He ran his fingers through his hair and scratched the back of his neck. This was where she spent most of her day. This was where she was supposed to be. Waiting in the silence, he willed her to answer him but heard only ticking. Cooper crossed the room, his chest tightening with every step, and pushed through the swinging door he loved playing with as a child. The kitchen was empty as well. A pot filled with water sat on the stove. A peeling knife and partially cut up potatoes with browned edges littered the counter. Lillie Mae would never have left even a small mess like that. She always took pride in her spotless kitchen.

Cooper scooted around the island in the center of the room and looked out the window over the kitchen sink. The prefabricated carport addition behind the house was an eyesore compared to the stately Georgian architecture of Phipps House. The front of Lillie Mae's twenty-year-old Crown Vic peeked out of the carport, illuminated by a single light bulb hanging over the entrance. A shiny layer of ice blanketed the car's hood and windshield, confirming that it hadn't been driven recently. Not that she should be behind the wheel anyway.

Cooper roamed through the ground floor, opening every door, calling her name, and picking up his pace with every cleared empty room. He didn't need to check the upper floors. Lillie Mae wasn't able to navigate the stairs anymore. She'd moved her bedroom downstairs years ago.

Wind rattled the glass in the sidelights of the front door, drawing Cooper back to the foyer. He stood staring at the door, swallowed hard and pulled it open. A rush of cold air greeted him as he stepped onto the porch. Freezing rain pelted him from every direction, like the storm had skimmed water off the surface of Winyah Bay and slung it recklessly around the neighborhood. He descended the slippery steps, balancing himself with outstretched arms.

"Lillie Mae!"

Jogging around the side of the house, he repeated the call of her name. Frigid air sliced through his thin cotton shirt, making it hard to breathe and antagonizing his already growing anxiety. He stopped and wiped the icy rain out of his eyes with the back of his hand. Turning 360 degrees, he scanned the yard.

His vision waned momentarily and an eerie, greenish glow coated the trees, the house, and the cars parked on the street. Cooper rubbed his eyes, trying to reset his altered sight. He looked up and in all directions. The strange night-vision effect was everywhere. Then it was gone. He shook his head and sighed. Too many hours on the dark road staring at a parade of slow-ass taillights.

He hurried back to the front of the house and down the brick walkway toward the street, wind wailing in his ears and whipping through his hair. Stopping at the waist-high gate, he rested his hands on the tips of the cold iron spires and looked up and down the street. A few porch lights cast a dim glow onto empty sidewalks, but there was no one but him out in the storm.

"Lillie Mae!" The echo traveled down the street, bouncing from one Victorian home to another, never finding its intended target.

Where the hell was she? Maybe she got confused and wandered off. She'd been so out of sorts lately. He'd noticed it getting worse over the past year but figured it was just age. He should have insisted that she see a doctor. Too late now. She could be roaming around in this weather, wearing only her nightgown without even knowing her own name.

With a final glance down the empty street, Cooper stepped back from the gate. He drew a chilly breath into his lungs and exhaled through frosted nostrils. He needed to think. There had to be an explanation. People didn't just up and disappear in Georgetown. Ears and hands frozen, he turned and went back inside the house. He closed the door behind him and leaned against it, letting the frigid night melt away from his bones.

"Lillie Mae?"

He wasn't sure why he kept calling her name. He no longer expected her to answer. He'd had his chance to talk to her; he'd just been too busy chasing tail to be bothered. Some real *World's Greatest Grandson* shit right there. Cooper brushed ice pellets out of his hair and trudged back to the sitting room. Standing in the arched entryway, he scanned the room again. Something was off.

Nibbling on the tip of his index finger, he took tentative steps across the room and stopped in front of the fireplace. Frozen faces, all awkward smiles and heads tilted at odd angles, stared back at him from the mantel. His parents, his brother, Grandpa Joe, Lillie Mae, even his own—all at various ages and stages of life.

A small picture toward the back of the clutter caught his eye. In it, he was eight-years-old, standing in front of their childhood home, posing proudly with sassy hands on his hips and wearing his favorite Wonder Woman T-shirt. Cooper stared at the picture. It had been taken *before*. He didn't know that happy little boy anymore.

A wire stem poked out from behind the frame. He slipped his fingers through the maze of framed memories and pulled out a child-sized pair of glasses. His glasses. Lillie Mae had kept them all those years. As a kid, he'd been practically blind as a bat without them, though he never needed them again *after*...

Cooper shook his head and pushed the glasses back behind the picture, tucking them as far back into the Olan Mills mini-gallery as possible. The last thing he needed was to be reminded of that day. He turned his back to the mantel and scrubbed a hand over his numb face. God, why did he let this place get to him?

Pulling out his phone, he replayed the message on speaker, as if listening a hundredth time might expose some additional information he'd missed. Lillie Mae's voice filled the sitting room, sounding right at home. The anxiety in her crackling voice haunted him, the slight inflection of fear probably noticeable only to him.

When the message ended, he tossed the phone onto the sofa. "Dammit."

The *something off* drew his attention to the coffee table where Lillie Mae's family Bible lay open. It was one of those doorstops of a Bible, with a white *faux* leather cover and gold leaf, indented tabs separating each book of scripture. The thing had never been moved as long as he could remember. She always kept it closed and sitting in the same spot in the corner of the table. Now it was in the center, facing the sofa and opened to the family tree, completely innocuous except for a fresh marring.

Cooper walked over and sank down into the lumpy cushions. His mouth went dry as he stared at it, not believing his eyes. It didn't make any sense. The word written on the page didn't belong in Lillie Mae's Bible. It didn't belong in any Bible. He rubbed his clammy hands on his pants and then pulled the book to him by a tiny corner of well-worn leather with the tips of his index finger and thumb.

A red smudge marked the corner of the page. He focused on the single word scribbled across an otherwise cheerfully illustrated family tree diagram. Dark red letters burned his eyes.

Warfield.

Sweat broke out on Cooper's palms, and the room spun around him. He pushed the book away. A torrent of memories, nightmares, and ghosts he'd been self-medicating away for years flooded back to his mind. Blue, Trevor, that day—all conjured up by just one word. *Warfield.*

Something snagged his attention. A small picture poked out from the gilded edges of the pages. He leaned forward and pulled it out. Another smudge of what appeared to be blood marked the lower right corner, just under the face of a young girl he did not recognize. She wore a long, thick ponytail draped over one shoulder and her blouse buttoned all the way to her jawline. Her tiny freckles framed a pleasant, yet vacant, smile. Anyone other than Cooper might have easily mistaken the girl for a young Lillie Mae. She had the same family freckles, squinted, smiling eyes, and full, round cheeks that he and Lillie Mae had.

He flipped the photograph over, barely able to read the faded ink.

Sally – 1864

Gazing back down at the open Bible, Cooper dropped the picture on the coffee table.

Warfield. It seemed impossible that Lillie Mae could be there. His jaw stiffened, and he gritted his teeth. If that was Lillie Mae's blood on the page, then God help the son of a bitch who wrote it.

Cooper's fingertips tingled with energy. He leaned back, filling his lungs with deep breaths, trying to calm the boiling rage inside. He stared at the ceiling. If he would have just answered her first call, the one that rang the moment he introduced himself to whatever the hell his name is, she might have been safe and sound in her bed right then. He was such a selfish prick sometimes. If anything had happened to Lillie Mae, it was on him.

Cooper shook his head, scolding himself internally. Enough. Every second that ticked by was another Lillie Mae could be hurt, cold, and scared.

At first, he thought he should go to Warfield. Just to be sure she wasn't there. But why would Lillie Mae go there of all places in the middle of the night, or *ever* for that matter? There had to be a rational explanation, unless she was taken there against her will.

Cooper looked down at the phone lying beside him, picked it up, and stood. Standing meant taking control of the situation. At least that's what he told himself.

Staring at the blank screen, he walked over to the front window. Who the hell did he think he was going to call? Lillie Mae was his only family. She'd never been particularly interested in making small talk with the neighbors, even though she'd lived there for almost sixty years. As far as he knew, the woman who came in once a month to set and dye her hair and the cleaning lady that came every two weeks were the only people who saw her on a regular basis.

He pushed back the curtain. The sleet had let up a bit. Front Street glistened in the moonlight, and a thin sheet of ice coated everything in sight. A wave of guilt washed over him. He'd stayed away too long.

He flinched as the grandfather clock sounded down the hall, marking the hour with nine, muffled chimes. On the last one, he pressed three numbers into the phone and hit the call button.

Before the second ring, a disinterested voice mumbled in his ear, “Nine-one-one, what’s your emergency?”

“Hello. I just got to my grandmother’s house, and she’s not here.” He scratched his forehead. “I mean, I think she’s missing.”

“Okay, sir, what is the address, please?”

He released the curtain and walked back over to the sofa. “It’s 42 Front Street, Georgetown.”

“Thank you, sir. That’s 42 Front Street in Georgetown. What is your grandmother’s age, sir?”

“Her age?” Cooper sat and took a moment to think. “I’m not sure.” He didn’t even know how old she was.

Nice, Cooper. Real nice.

He looked back to the Bible resting on the coffee table. Eight reddish-brown letters taunted him. *Warfield.* The word ignited something dark in his very core, something heinous and long forgotten. Or at least long buried. He closed the book with more force than he intended. The coffee table shook.

“Do you have any reason to believe she might be in danger, sir?”

Did he have any reason to believe she was in danger? Hell yes, he did. A message written in blood was a damn good reason.

“Sir? Are you there, sir?”

He curled his fingers into a fist, trying to suppress the nefarious force rumbling around inside him. “Yes,” he finally answered. “She might be in danger.”

CHAPTER FOUR

Cooper paced back and forth across the foyer, the old, wooden floor counting his every step with strained creaks. The constant tapping on the windows along the front of the house grew louder by the minute, a nagging soundtrack to his growing irritation. Pulling back the sheer fabric covering the sidelight, he peeked out. Ice pellets bounced off his SUV in the driveway. He glanced back at the grandfather clock. Where the hell were the police? He'd called them twenty minutes ago. Twenty fucking minutes. No way there was that much going on in this shitty excuse for a town.

After another five laps up and down the hallway, the doorbell sounded a pompous melody about three notes too long for Cooper's agitated state. Without checking the sidelight to see who it was, he pulled the door open.

A tall, broad-shouldered police officer filled the doorframe. A wide smile full of gleaming white teeth lit his face. The uniform threw Cooper for a second, but the pronounced dimple in the chin and the twinkle in those soulful brown eyes were unmistakable, even after all the years that had passed. A silver nametag pinned to the officer's chest bore the name *Collins*, confirming Cooper's slack-jawed assessment.

"Holy mother of hell. RJ?"

The officer gave a slight nod and tipped the bill of his cap. A few stray ice pellets spilled off and hit the doorsill. "Hey, Coop. Yeah, it's me. I go by Randy now." He nodded over his shoulder toward the stormy night. "Can I come in?"

Cooper heard the question and knew he needed to answer. To move. To let the guy in the house and out of the storm, but for the longest of moments, he *couldn't* move. Couldn't speak. RJ Collins, of all people. His brother's best friend and Cooper's first crush. He hadn't seen that face since the day of his brother's funeral ten years ago. Back then, he might have crumbled under a wave of childhood insecurities if he had to face RJ. Probably would have melted into a pile of goo and panted like a lovesick puppy. Not anymore. And certainly not tonight.

A rush of ice-cold wind blew into the house, reminding Cooper they were still standing in the open doorway. He moved to the side. "Oh sure. Sorry. Come in."

Removing his cap, Randy brushed the sleet off before he entered. A woodsy waft of cologne followed him in, tickling Cooper's nose with a decisively masculine scent probably called *Liquid Sex* or something.

Cooper closed the door and faced Randy, his body stiff as a board. "Thanks for coming."

"Sorry it took me a few minutes to get over here. Crazy out tonight. Roads are a mess. We're not used to this kind of weather here. I haven't seen a winter storm like this in years. But you know how it is around here. Could be beach weather by tomorrow afternoon."

Cooper didn't respond. The very last person he'd expected to find behind that door was RJ Collins, and now all he could do was stare. Dirty blond hair cropped close to the guy's head showed signs of premature gray around the temples. Weatherworn creases framed his eyes, aging him more. Other than that and several new layers of expertly crafted muscle, he hadn't changed much. Still had that chiseled movie-star face and that magnetic, boyish smile. Randy offered his hand as an afterthought.

"So you're a cop," Cooper said with a firm shake of Randy's sizable hand. "I didn't even know you were out of the military." It was his second obligatory attempt at small talk of the night. It was jarring to see Randy, but Cooper didn't have the time or patience for idle chatter right then.

Randy stood a good three inches taller than Cooper, his thumbs tucked casually in his duty belt, weight resting on his left side. "Deputy Chief, now. I ended up back here after eight years with the SEALs."

Randy peered over Cooper's shoulder. "Haven't been in this house in a long time. Always was a funny old place. Aunt Mae made it feel homey, though."

Hearing the locals' nickname for his grandmother brought all Cooper's concerns to a hard boil. "Yeah. I'm really worried." Cooper led Randy into the sitting room. "This isn't like her. Her car is outside. Doesn't look like it's been moved in a while. I already checked the house inside and out."

Randy strode over to the wingback chair opposite the sofa and sat without invitation. He didn't remove his thick Gore-Tex jacket. Either that was standard procedure, or he thought Cooper was overreacting and that this wouldn't take too long. Cooper imagined him listening to the call over the scanner and shaking his head. *Just whiney, little Cooper Causey. Panicking as usual. Just like when we were kids.*

Randy cocked his head and leaned forward in his chair. "When's the last time you heard from her?"

Cooper sat on the sofa facing Randy and cleared his throat. "She called a few times last night. I missed the calls. She left a message." Guilt settled in his gut like a rock sinking to the bottom of a river. He pulled his phone out of his pants pocket, pressed a couple of commands into the screen, and handed it over to Randy.

With the phone to his ear, Randy looked down as he listened. Faint traces of Lillie Mae's voice trickled out into the otherwise quiet room. Cooper silently mouthed each word, the message branded into his memory.

Cooper. Listen to me carefully. Whatever you do, don't come home. Stay away, do you hear me? Stay away from Georgetown. He's back, and it's not me he wants, it's—

The abrupt dial tone at the end of the message and the alarm lacing her voice were reason enough to defy her wishes. She'd been scared. And who the hell was this *he*?

Randy handed the phone back to Cooper. "As soon as I got the call from dispatch, I checked the hospital. No luck there."

Cooper flinched at considering the idea of Lillie Mae in the hospital *lucky*.

Randy retrieved a small spiral notepad and pencil from the inside pocket of his jacket. "When's the last time you talked to her?"

Cooper gripped the sofa cushion with both hands and squeezed. "A couple of weeks ago, I guess." Or more. Too long.

Flipping over to a blank page, Randy jotted something down on the pad. "How did she seem the last few times you talked to her?"

"Scattered. Forgetful."

More scribbling in the pad.

Cooper stared down at the well-worn Oriental rug, retreating into its hypnotizing pattern and projecting away his panicky angst so Randy wouldn't see any trace of the scared, flimsy, little boy he once was. That wasn't him anymore, and he'd be damned if he would let a childhood crush shake him up tonight.

He looked up and lowered his voice a notch. "I don't think I'm overreacting here. This isn't like Lillie Mae. Sure she's forgetful, but she rarely leaves this house. A trip to Winn-Dixie would be the highlight of her week."

"Yeah, I see her there sometimes," Randy said, writing something else in the notebook. "Always keeps me up to date on what's going on with you." He looked up, the slightest trace of a smile creeping up on the right side of his mouth. "And I never said you were overreacting."

Cooper's cheeks grew hot. Why couldn't it have been anyone else on the other side of that door instead of the one person who could still reduce his insides to Silly Putty? As much as he hated to admit it, the passing of ten years had done absolutely nothing to diminish the effect Randy had on him. The embarrassment and the sting of rejection that had walloped him that night on the beach now picked at the scab around his heart with needling precision. He didn't need this tonight, and he wouldn't make the same mistake twice with Randy.

Cooper sat up straight. "There's food out on the kitchen counter and a pot of water on the stove. Looks like she was making dinner."

Randy stood, walked over to the swinging door, and peeked into the kitchen. "Maybe she just got confused and wandered off down the street or something. Happens more than you'd think with some of the older folks around here."

"I thought that too." Scooting to the edge of the sofa, Cooper grabbed the Bible and flipped to the page with the family tree, the picture of the young girl still wedged in the fold. "Then I found this." He turned the book around and slid it across the coffee table. Randy walked over, leaned down, and inspected the page, his brow contracting the closer he got to it.

Cooper wondered if same childhood memories flooded into Randy's mind. They likely remembered that day differently. Randy would remember a thrilling adventure, unexplained occurrences, and four kids getting the bejesus scared out of them. Cooper remembered a lot more.

Randy's face hovered just inches above the page. "Looks like blood."

Cooper nodded. "Do you know who owns Warfield now?"

Randy stared at the page like he waited for a secret, invisible message to suddenly reveal itself. "That place has changed hands a few times since we were kids. I'd have to look it up."

"Would you? Seems like the only clue we have."

Randy looked up. "Sure, Red."

Cooper picked up the picture and held it up. "I also found this."

Randy moved around the coffee table, took the photo out of Cooper's hand without asking, and nudged him in the side to scoot over. Cooper obliged and slid to the right. He fought the urge to smile. No need making something out of nothing. The ease with which they moved around each other was just that of childhood familiarity. Nothing more.

Randy studied the sepia image. "This can't be Lillie Mae. It's too old."

Cooper shook his head. "Look at the back."

Their knees and shoulders touched. The casual closeness reminded Cooper of when they were kids, and their appetites for mystery and adventure were as endless as their overactive imaginations.

Randy inspected the back of the picture, ran his thumb over the words written there, and handed it back to Cooper. "Who's Sally? Family?"

"Don't know. I haven't seen it before. Lillie Mae never really talks about her family, though. I don't know anything about them. I found it in the Bible along with that." Cooper pointed to the desecrated page without looking at it. He sunk back into the sofa and chewed on the tip of his index finger.

Looking down at the marred page like it had more clues to offer, Randy patted Cooper's knee and let his hand rest there. "Coop, I know you're worried, but it's going to be okay. We'll find her."

Cooper's heart responded to the physical contact with a heavy thump, which he inwardly cursed. He'd spent his life riffling through a Rolodex of men in search of just one that measured up to this man. Gorgeous, sweet, *straight* Randy. Trace memories of the drunken pass he'd made at Randy the night of Kevin's funeral hung in the air between them with tacit awkwardness. Or maybe that was all just in Cooper's head.

Randy had reacted so kindly that night. After all, Cooper was upset and drowning his grief in a few bombers of Budweiser. After deftly redirecting Cooper's sloppy advance with a peck on the forehead and a brotherly bear hug, Randy had never mentioned it again. Of course, Cooper never saw him again, either. Until tonight. Lesson learned on opening himself up to that kind of rejection. Never again.

Cooper moved his knee away, letting Randy's hand fall to the cushion. That's when he noticed Randy's ring finger was bare. Only an untanned circle of skin remained where a wedding band should have been. Cooper almost asked about his wife—*Renee?*—but he decided against it.

Randy lifted the open Bible and rested it on his knees. His index finger followed a maze of lines and names on the family tree, carefully avoiding the bloody addition. "Check this out."

Cooper leaned in over Randy's shoulder. Only a couple

of entries had been filled in above Lillie Mae's name. A mother, Sarabeth, was listed without a last name. Randy pointed to the scribble on the *Mother* line above Sarabeth's name, faded and barely legible.

Sally P.

The line designated for Sarabeth's father, was blank. Beyond that, no other genealogical entries had been made.

"I guess I've never looked at this very closely. Like I said, Lillie Mae never mentioned her family."

"Well, that solves mystery number one. Sally P. is obviously a distant relative of yours." Randy set the book back down on the coffee table and checked his watch.

Cooper took it as a sign he would be leaving soon. He scooted a few inches away and faced Randy. "So what do we do now?"

"I'll get a couple of cars out around the neighborhood and see if we can lay eyes on her. You know this is a quiet, friendly area. If any of the neighbors see her, I bet they call us or bring her back here. I'll check the restaurants down on the Harborwalk first. Maybe she wandered into one of them."

Cooper pointed to the Bible. "And that?" He couldn't bring himself to say the word out loud.

Randy squeezed Cooper's knee once and then stood. Cooper knew better than to read too much into the intimate, friendly gesture. "I'll ride out to Warfield myself and take a look around, though I think the odds are pretty slim she would be way out there. She might have cut her finger cooking and wrote that in the Bible in a moment of confusion."

Cooper thought of the peeling knife in the kitchen. There wasn't any blood on it. "That's it?" Cooper caught the irritation lacing his voice and dialed it back a notch. "What about the voice-mail message? She referred to someone. She said *it's not me he wants.*"

Randy's lips tightened into a thin line, and he squinted his eyes. "You did say she sounded scattered lately, right? Forgetful. Maybe that's all it was."

Cooper looked away and poked his thumb deep down into the cushion. He didn't buy the Mayberry-esque assessment of the situation. Maybe Randy was too used to dealing with small-town crime to assume the worst like Cooper did. Teenagers drinking beer on the Harborwalk. People peeling out of the Dairy Queen drive-through without paying. Or maybe he just didn't want Cooper to worry.

Randy put a hand on Cooper's shoulder. "Listen, just stay put in case she shows up. I can't make an official report until she's been missing for twenty-four hours, but I'll make certain my people know this a priority." He pulled out his notepad again, scribbled a series of numbers on a page, ripped it out, and handed it to Cooper. "You can call me at this number anytime. Day or night."

Cooper took the paper and nodded, but he knew he couldn't *stay put* with Lillie Mae out there somewhere. He led Randy into the foyer where they shook hands again, and Cooper opened the door for him.

"I'll be in touch." Randy put on his cap and walked out into the chilly night. He paused at the bottom of the porch stairs and turned back, flashing that annoyingly sexy smile of his. "It's really good to see you."

Cooper tried to form words and only succeeded in producing a half wave and a quick nod.

Randy lingered a moment longer, before turning back to the street. He called over his shoulder. "Try not to worry, Red."

Cooper managed to get his mouth open, but still no words emerged. What in the hell was the matter with him?

When the taillights of the police car disappeared down the dark street, Cooper closed the door and stood in the center of the foyer. Alone. The house was quiet again. Only ticking.

Stay put. Not likely.

He had a feeling Randy and his team wouldn't find Lillie Mae wandering around the streets of Georgetown or knocking back a cold one somewhere down on the Harborwalk. He knew in his gut what he had to do, no matter how much he didn't want to.

Ghosts or no ghosts, he was going to Warfield.

CHAPTER FIVE

The sleet had stopped for the moment, and the night sky was the deepest of blues. A showy full moon illuminated blue-gray clouds, and gleaming stars peeked through a three dimensional haze. Cooper's apprehension grew inside him with every passing mile as he fixed his gaze on the shimmering concrete ahead. The heater hummed on low, and he was glad to be locked safely inside his SUV. The image of the defiled family tree flashed in his mind, sending a shiver down his spine. He drew his coat together around his neck. He knew little of his grandmother's past. She had always been tight-lipped about it. He should have talked to her more. He should have asked more questions.

A lump of anxiety clotted in his throat as he searched the right side of the road. The headlights finally cast their beam on the sign. Unassuming and simple, the three-foot-wide white rectangle dangled from a charcoal post. Black letters materialized through the lingering fog like a ghostly calling card written in thin air: *Warfield.*

He took a deep breath and eased the car onto Warfield

Road, if it could be called a road. A two-mile single-lane dirt trail cut through a dense fortress of pine trees was more like it. Cooper hadn't been down that road in twenty years, and he never dreamed he would be back.

Alarm twisted in the pit of his stomach, awakened by an invisible toxic presence as thick and consuming as the fog cloaking the SUV. He tightened his prickling fingers around the steering wheel. It had been more than a decade since he yielded to that side of his nature, and the memory of the destruction left in his wake strengthened his resolve. He inhaled a deep, calming breath, and exhaled the errant energy away. He needed to get a grip.

After two miles of clammy palms and an accelerated heartbeat, the stone gates finally appeared, more crumbled and vine-ridden than he remembered. Darkened gas lanterns punctuated each column. Passing through the gates, Cooper knew he'd crossed the point of no return. He swallowed hard and relaxed his shoulders, which had edged their way up to his ears.

A shadowy collection of dilapidated structures broke through the fog, the ruins guarding the plantation like ancient sentries. The old slave village. A handful of decaying cabins lined each side of the road, anchored by a modest chapel with a free-standing bell tower. It was a sparse reflection of a forgotten community once teeming with more than one hundred fifty slaves.

Twenty feet ahead on the right, the last cabin sat innocuously under the protection of an imposing oak tree. Warped boards coated in green moss broke free of weather beaten walls. The sunken roof had long lost its battle with the elements. Cooper scanned the porch. No rocking chair. No Blue. It was empty. Of course it was.

He focused on a moonlit speck of the manor house in the distance. A somber chorus of Spanish moss hung from the tree limb canopy over the road, waving him forward. Live oaks flanked the road like precisely positioned mile markers measuring his tentative progress to the end of Oak Alley.

He pulled up to the front of the house and shut off the engine. Chilly night air seeped into the SUV, spoiling the illusion of his warm, safe haven. The front door of the manor house sat in the crosshairs of his headlights. Calling to him. Summoning him. The tightness in his chest became a dull ache, and he rubbed it without thinking.

Cooper reached over to the passenger seat and grabbed the flashlight he'd found in a junk drawer at Phipps House. Those heavy black industrial types also made pretty good weapons, if needed. He pushed the button on the side, but nothing happened. He tapped the top of it in his palm, and a dim light appeared, growing into a full, steady beam. Staring up at the house through the sleet-speckled windshield, he took a deep breath, exhaled, and exited the car.

The icy ground crackled under every heavy step, the sound violating the otherwise silent night. He stopped a few feet from the landing of the front door. Under the less than robust beam of his flashlight, the house didn't look as imposing as he feared. Awash in green and black moss and dotted with boarded windows, white paint peeled off the exterior like wet Band-Aids. The house appeared beaten down. Powerless.

Cooper directed the light across the front of the house and sighed. What the hell was he doing? Randy was right. Lillie Mae wasn't way out here.

A voice emerged from some far corner of his mind—distant, hollow, and frail.

Leave, Cooper.

He spun around and cast the beam of light in every direction, nearly losing his balance on the slick ground cover. Though he didn't see anyone, he was sure he'd heard it.

He knows you're here. It's not safe.

Cooper pressed a finger to his temple. He had no doubt. He'd know that voice anywhere. But it had definitely sounded in his head and not out loud.

He peered into the darkness of the yard. "Lillie Mae?"

A wall of icy wind slammed into his chest, filling his lungs with frozen air and muting him.

Please, Cooper. Go now!

Some internal compass guided him around the side of the house. He picked up his pace and headed for a small structure up ahead, inexplicably drawn to it.

Moonlit Spanish moss danced over a clay-shingled roof, and a brick chimney rose from the center of the small building like a miniature steeple. Broken windows and vine-covered walls scarred the insignificant structure anchored by two weather-beaten doors on each end of the façade. The old kitchen house.

Cooper closed his eyes and listened, but he didn't hear Lillie Mae's voice again. Frustrated and anxious, he stared at the building. A barrage of reasons why he should *not* enter it barreled through his mind. That had never stopped him before. Act first, ask questions later—that was his M.O. Besides, if there was even the slightest chance that Lillie Mae was in there, that was reason enough.

As he took a step toward the door, a chill slithered down his neck and back, leaving an army of tiny goose bumps in its wake. Cooper turned and aimed the flashlight back toward the manor house. The beam flickered twice before going out, leaving him stranded and blind with moonlight as his only source of illumination.

Shadows of stunted breath, like dry ice rising up from the bottom of his throat, slipped through his parted lips. Something moved about twenty feet away. He focused on an imposing figure blocking his path back to the SUV. He couldn't determine where the man had come from, though he knew he wasn't there seconds before.

"Hello?" His voice was much less authoritative than he'd intended.

The broad-shouldered man walked forward. No, he *glided.* Without the crunch of frozen grass under foot, he floated like he was standing still on a moving walkway. Cooper shook his head. The weariness of the day had caught up with him, playing tricks with his vision again. He drew back his shoulders and straightened his spine, though his six feet were no match for the man's height.

He stepped to the left, drawing the stranger into the

moonlight. Waves of golden hair framed a pale face that looked carved out of granite. His dark eyes gleamed in the moonlight, set against nearly translucent skin. A white button-down shirt hugged his defined chest, neatly tucked into the narrow waist of strategically wrinkled khakis. Penny loafers topped off the clichéd Carolina college-boy attire. The man stopped ten feet away. His refined beauty momentarily stunned Cooper. He was angelic. And young.

The guy was exactly the type Cooper would target at the bar. He would have immediately zeroed in on a face and body like that. However, the beautiful stranger wasn't right. Something in his eyes was off. They were cold, dead, and tinted with danger. His suspicions resurfaced. What was a guy like that doing lurking around a deserted plantation at night? Maybe he knew something about Lillie Mae. Maybe he brought her here.

Cooper tightened his grip around the cold metal of the flashlight. "Who are you? What the hell are you doing out here in the middle of the night?"

The man smirked confidently, his lips sinuous. "Cooper Causey. So glad you came." His rich, thick voice oozed out of his mouth.

The shock of hearing his own name fall from the stranger's mouth so casually sparked alarm in Cooper's gut.

He moved again to his left, drawing the man's face into the full glow of the moon. "How do you know my name?"

The man eased his hands into his pockets. "Didn't take you long." He stepped to his right, opposite the direction in which Cooper inched, like two boxers circling each other.

The stranger closed his eyes, sniffed the air, and smiled. "My God, you smell amazing. Like honey and cinnamon." His eyes fluttered back open. "I am glad you got my message."

Cooper stopped moving, not sure he heard correctly. "And what message is that?"

The stranger crossed his arms over his chest and widened his stance. "At Phipps House. In the Bible."

Heat flooded Cooper's face. He squared his shoulders, gritted his teeth, and wielded the dead flashlight like a club. "Where the hell is my grandmother? I swear to God, if she has so much as one scratch on her—"

"Ah. Lillie Mae," the young man said with a smirk. "What a difficult creature she is. Always has been, really. Seems she's done a good job of shielding you all these years, with her *enchantments*." The man raised his hands in front of his face and shook them in mock fear.

Enchantments? Cooper had no idea what the guy meant, but it didn't matter. The police could sort it out. He fished his phone out of his pocket and unlocked the home screen with the swipe of a thumb. No bars. He adjusted his grip on the flashlight. It would have to do.

The man curled his lips into a smile. "Calm down, little witch."

Cooper glared at him, the odd moniker singeing his ears.

The stranger raised his eyebrows as he took another step forward, now only ten feet away and blocking Cooper's path to the kitchen house. "Oh. I see. You didn't know that you and your dear old grandmother shared the same peculiar skill set, did you? Thought you were the only one in the world? Now that seems a just a tad self-absorbed, doesn't it?" A pompous chuckle escaped the man's plump lips. "Divinum. What a funny lot you are."

Cooper's head throbbed. Something was wrong, like his brain shared the space with a foreign tenant.

The man sighed and clicked his tongue on the roof of his mouth. "Lillie Mae, Lillie Mae. She really should have done a better job of educating you. All that potential. All those years, just wasted."

Cooper put a hand to his forehead and rubbed his temples. The intruder in his mind was as real as the man standing in front of him, rummaging through his memories, excavating every thought like lost treasure. It was the stranger. Somehow the freak was inside his head.

He raised the flashlight and took a bold step forward. "Where is she? If you don't take me to her right now—"

"You'll what?" The stranger glided forward, breaking up the mist in his path, his eyes as cold as the night itself. "You don't even know *what* you are, much less how to use all that power bottled up inside you."

Cooper stepped back and dropped the flashlight. He opened his palms and raised them at his sides. It was instinct because he didn't know what the hell he planned to do next. The pestilent nature deep inside him rumbled. Percolated in his veins and coursed down his arms. Another second or two, and he wouldn't be able to stop it.

The man raised a hand in the air. "There now. No need for theatrics, little witch."

Cooper took a step forward and flexed his throbbing fingers. He teetered on the perilous edge between control and complete chaos. What else could he do but tempt a dangerous fate? This shit-bag had Lillie Mae. He was sure of it now.

He channeled all his worry, all his fear, and all his anger into his hands. "Take me to her now. I won't ask again."

A scowl spread across the stranger's too-perfect face, and he lifted his eyebrow. His nostrils flared and he moved closer, closing the distance between them. "If you ever want to see her again, you will take a deep breath and calm the fuck down."

Cooper stared the man down, their breath small billowy clouds of condensation mingling in the frosty air between them. The standoff lasted only a few seconds, and then the man's lips tightened and curled up on one side. The smooth skin of his face twisted and melted like soft butter.

Cooper edged back, heart racing and chest expanding. He blinked his eyes, hoping to dispel the impossible illusion.

The man's face morphed back into human shape, taking a new form that Cooper knew all too well. Trevor's.

Cooper stumbled backward, a gasp of chilled breath lodged in his throat. He forced himself to look away. It couldn't be real—a trick of the light or his sleep-deprived mind playing tricks on him. That's all.

After a couple of deep breaths, he dared to look back. Trevor stood before him, dressed in his high school football uniform, holding his helmet at his side. He looked exactly the way Cooper remembered him that night, ten years ago. Curly blond hair, bottomless blue eyes, smooth sun-soaked skin—he hadn't aged a day. Trevor stared at him, the corners of his lips edging down, his dead eyes locked and loaded. Logic told Cooper that it wasn't real. It could not possibly be Trevor. But logic quickly slipped away.

"Well, isn't this rich?" The words came out of Trevor's mouth, but it wasn't the deep baritone voice he remembered. It was the stranger's voice. "What a naughty little witch you have been."

Cooper slowly raised his hands in front of him, his muscles petrifying under his skin. But the innocence in Trevor's trusting eyes transfixed him, dispelling the dark energy solidifying in his veins.

"And he was so beautiful, too. Pity your dark side got the better of you." The face twisted and churned again, morphing back into its original form. Trevor was gone, and the young stranger once again stood before him.

Cooper shook his head, rubbed his eyes, and looked again. The stranger stood nose to nose with him, his breath icy and wet on Cooper's cheeks.

"Now, would you like to see Lillie Mae, or would you rather play judge, jury, and executioner with me like you did with young Trevor?"

Cooper couldn't think straight. Couldn't make sense of what he'd just seen. Maybe the guy was like him. Maybe he was something far worse. In any case, he wasn't 100 percent sure what he was dealing with, and his powers had failed him anyway. He needed to be careful, for Lillie Mae's sake.

He looked up in the man's dead eyes and nodded. "Take me to her."

A one-sided smirk creased the man's lips. He turned toward the manor house and waved for Cooper to follow him. "Shall we? Alexander does not like to be kept waiting."

Cooper stood his ground. "Who the hell is Alexander?"

The stranger kept walking and didn't respond.

Cooper contemplated his options, which were in short supply if he wanted to find Lillie Mae. He wasn't sure what he was about to walk into. Lillie Mae's disappearance was no accident. This asshole had something to do with it, and apparently he wasn't working alone. Reaching into his pocket, he slipped out his phone and unlocked the home screen. Still no bars.

Shoving the phone back in his pocket, Cooper swallowed back his apprehension and followed the stranger toward the manor house.

CHAPTER SIX

A second intruder invaded Cooper's thoughts the moment he stepped inside the house. The new presence was stronger, darker than the blond. It dissected his mind with the methodical finesse of a brain surgeon—analyzing, cataloging, and casually discarding every memory and emotion. He didn't even have a chance to shut it down by focusing on the banal inspection of his peculiar surroundings.

The decaying exterior shell of the house was a complete deception. Inside, the place was pristine, elegant and beautiful. The Victorian-inspired interior with contemporary accents seemed too perfect and sterile to be lived in. A sparkling crystal chandelier hung in the center of the foyer, not a speck of dust marring the translucent baubles. Rich shades of red glistened on freshly painted walls. Intricately carved antiques, all pointy edges and curved legs, filled every room. Cooper felt as if he'd stepped back in time.

The blond man led Cooper down the hall, stepping so lightly that he didn't make a sound as he crossed the black hardwood floors. He carried himself like an underwear model gliding down a catwalk with a stealthy mix of detachment and sensuality. Cooper peered into every room they passed, hoping to find any trace of Lillie Mae and noting all possible exits. They entered a formal sitting room at the end of the hall, and the blond stepped aside, waving him in.

A buttery voice filled the spacious room. "*The blond* has a name. It's Stephen. Stephen Parker."

A man, also unusually tall, stood with his back to them by a floor-to-ceiling window across the room, gazing out into the dark night. "You must forgive us. We sometimes can't help ourselves from taking a look around when such an intriguing mind is available to us." A navy silk shirt stretched across his brawny back. Thick waves of dark hair spilled over his impressively broad shoulders.

Cooper stepped into the center of the room, curling his fingers into fists. "Where the hell is my grandmother? I just called the police outside. They're on the way."

The man turned toward Cooper, projecting a cold, anesthetic gaze. He was also young, with a severe jawline and pronounced cheekbones. Emerald eyes brimming with danger pierced Cooper's steely exterior with laser precision. The man's curling lips told Cooper he'd failed to conceal the lie about calling the police.

With an air of superiority he wore like a warm winter coat, the man cupped a brandy snifter between his middle and ring finger. Dark liquid coated the wide bottom of the glass.

He gave Cooper a slight nod of the head. "Alexander Montgomery, at your service."

The man closed the ten steps between them in three. The unnatural movement unnerved Cooper, though he wouldn't dare show it. Standing directly in front of Cooper, he leaned in and inhaled. The lids of his impossibly green eyes drooped with sensual satisfaction, just like Tony's had at the Ice House.

"Honey and cinnamon," Creepy Underwear Model said from somewhere behind. An unsettling wave of claustrophobia washed over Cooper, reigniting the sour churn of his core.

Alexander smiled. "Yes. Intoxicating. Especially when his power is active."

Cooper didn't have any idea how these two freaks were aware of his condition. He was too worried about Lillie Mae to care, and his patience was waning.

He expanded his chest and widened his stance, his face just inches away from Alexander's. "Look, I don't know or care who you are, but you need to take me to my grandmother. Now."

Alexander peered at him through narrow eyes and eased back. "You thought your grandmother might be here? Why on Earth would you think that?" He shot a chilling glare over Cooper's shoulder in the direction of the blond. "Young Stephen gets a little ahead of himself sometimes." Reproach filled Alexander's voice. He was the guy in charge, though he seemed only a handful of years older than Stephen.

Alexander crossed the room and stood in front of a massive, empty fireplace. On a night like this, a fire should be blazing away in the hearth. Not here. Frost accumulated on the windowpanes. Cooper's breath slipped out of his mouth in small puffs, and he fought back chills. He doubted the house had any heat at all. Yet the two men, dressed in far less than he, seemed unaffected by the cold. Nothing about this was normal.

Alexander swirled the dark liquid in the brandy snifter, gazing down into it like reading tea leaves. "Your grandmother is safe. For now."

Cooper gritted his teeth and took a step toward him. "Where is she?"

Alexander looked up, taking a slow, defiant sip from the snifter.

Cooper opened his mouth to lash out, but Alexander's casually raised hand somehow stalled the words in the base of his throat, like an invisible fist closing around his windpipe.

"You will see her again," Alexander said, lowering his hand. "In due time."

Cooper coughed. Cleared his throat and swallowed. He flexed his fingers as the nefarious force bubbled up inside him. "If you don't take me to her right now."

Alexander's face tightened. "Calm yourself, Divinum." His lips parted into a smile, exposing a glittering array of stark white teeth.

Stephen suddenly appeared by Alexander's side, as if he had been standing in the spot all along. Cooper stared at them both. His eyes were not playing tricks on him. Clearly, the men were not what they seemed. Alexander caressed Stephen's cheek with the back of his fingers, and Stephen leaned into the touch like a submissive kitten, almost purring.

"Lillie Mae's power is fading," Alexander said, staring at Stephen's face like he was admiring a rare painting. "She won't be able to protect you much longer."

Cooper fought to contain his surprise and confusion. Another mention of Lillie Mae's *power.* Could she really be like him? It seemed a ridiculous thought. She'd never once hinted that she might have shared Cooper's curse. She'd given him some probing looks and asked some thinly veiled questions about his life, but he always thought she just suspected he was gay. Obviously, she'd detected something different in him, something different from the rest of his family. Something only they shared.

Alexander sighed. "How little we sometimes know about the ones we hold most dear."

Cooper cursed himself for dropping the defensive shield around his private thoughts. He took a step back. He wasn't getting anywhere, and it was time to go get Randy and come back with the police.

Alexander moved toward him with the slow calculation of a deadly predator. "Lillie Mae is of no use to me." He stopped in front of Cooper. "You leave and she dies. Your choice."

Cooper's heart sunk to the pit of his stomach. The threat was real. "You can't do that." The words sounded hollow and naïve as they left his lips.

Alexander furrowed his eyebrows, and he looked over to the window. Stephen had a similar reaction. They locked eyes, and a silent message passed between them. For the first time, Cooper saw something resembling alarm on their faces. Stephen vanished in a blur of color and light. Cooper flinched, eyes darting around the room, trying to make sense of the visual illusion and sudden disappearance. He couldn't and bolted for the door. Alexander appeared in his path, flashing a patronizing smile, his beautiful face marred by a dark ugliness lurking just beneath his smooth, pale skin.

"Cooper, there is a lot you need to learn of the world you have been shielded from all your life. Lillie Mae did you no favors there." He reached out and touched Cooper's neck with cold, delicate fingertips. Cooper recoiled, tilting his head away from the unwelcome contact. A sudden wave of nausea bulked in his throat. He couldn't move. He tried to look away, but those emerald eyes held him prisoner, filling him with dread and complete submission.

"I propose a trade," Alexander said, his voice a hypnotic melody.

"A trade?" Cooper cursed the whisper of fear seeping into his voice.

"Yes. A simple one. You for Lillie Mae."

Cooper's head ached. Throbbed.

"I will let Lillie Mae go," Alexander continued. "And you take her place, here with me. My work is not yet done, and her seed is diseased."

A wave of anxious heat rolled over Cooper's skin. He was sure he would pass out.

Alexander slid his arm around Cooper's waist and pressed against him, the front of their bodies making intimate contact. "But you, Cooper. Your blood is infinitely more potent. She was right to hide you from me." He sniffed at

Cooper's neck, the tip of his ice-cold nose skimming the surface of the skin. A guttural moan rumbled up from the base of his throat.

Cooper couldn't move. His body wouldn't respond to his simple command to step back.

"Don't worry. It only hurts a little at the start. Relax." Alexander looked into Cooper's eyes, his mouth widening into a smile, revealing blinding white teeth and two unnaturally long, upper canines that extended down into mini daggers.

Cooper stared at them, his heart racing and his brain rejecting the signals sent from his eyes. Those were fangs. Not teeth. The man had fangs, for Christ's sake. He shook his head and finally pushed against Alexander's chest, trying unsuccessfully to free himself of the suffocating embrace.

Alexander leaned in, razor sharp tips grazing Cooper's cheek, down to his neck.

Cooper closed his eyes and held his breath. It couldn't be happening. It wasn't real. There were no such things as *vampires*, but his mind assured him that the sharp pain of forced penetration was imminent.

He closed his eyes. If he closed his eyes, it would all go away.

CHAPTER SEVEN

The pain never came. Cooper opened his eyes.

Alexander drew back, his eyes wild and searching. "I can't…" He pushed Cooper back, holding his shoulders at arm's length. "What has that old witch done?"

An explosion of shattering glass jarred Cooper out of his stupor. Alexander grabbed him by his shoulders, pulled him close, and spun them both around, positioning Cooper's body in front of him like a shield. He closed his right hand around Cooper's throat.

A woman's voice echoed through the room. "Release him!"

Alexander hissed at her, his breath icy on the rim of Cooper's ear. Cooper squirmed and twisted his body, trying to free himself, but Alexander held him fast.

The woman stood in front of the demolished window, dressed head to toe in black. Bitter air spilled into the room, and the little warmth left in Cooper's body quickly evaporated. Gripping sharp objects in each hand, she was both beautiful and frightening. A tallish woman of thirty or so with raven-colored hair spilling down over her shoulders, she scowled at Alexander with eyes full of venom.

"You again," Alexander growled.

"Let him go, Montgomery." The woman's voice was steady, authoritative, and carried not the slightest trace of fear.

Alexander tightened his grip. An icy, wet tongue traveled up from the base of Cooper's neck to the lobe of his ear. Cooper jerked his head away, unable to free the rest of his body.

The woman raised her weapons and took a defiant step forward. "Don't push me, Anakim."

A moment of silent standoff ticked by. Cooper didn't have any idea who had the upper hand, and he wasn't sure one outcome was better than the other. Though he wanted to be free of Alexander, the woman seemed equally dangerous. Alexander shoved Cooper down onto a blue double-ended sofa. Cooper stayed low and scanned the room, trying to get his bearings. He needed to find Lillie Mae and get the hell out of there.

"How did you find us this time, traitor?" Alexander's voice brimmed with contempt.

The woman crept forward. "You know Jericho keeps tabs on every rogue Anakim still in existence, Montgomery."

"Jericho." Alexander spat the word out like sour milk on his tongue. "So earnest and resolute in your holy mission. You already won the war. What more do you want? Still trying to buy your way into heaven with your tiresome, self-loathing righteousness? Spending your years wallowing in pathetic servitude while waging war on your own kind?"

The woman raised the weapons higher. "You are not my kind, you vile monster."

Cooper eyed the door, calculating how long it would take him to cross the room.

Alexander chuckled. "And what are you now? The Jericho sheriff in these here parts?" He spoke with an overdone Southern accent that sounded foreign and silly in his elegant voice.

"Something like that," she responded.

A blur of gray rippling air sailed in through the window behind her. Tiny black particles converged in mid-air and materialized into the form of Creepy Underwear Model.

Cooper stared, transfixed by the spectacle, his grip on reality slipping away with each passing second. Sliding off the sofa, he stayed low and edged back toward the door.

The woman spun around to face Stephen. He hissed at her through bared fangs.

"She got away from me." Stephen seethed at her like he would rip her head off at any second.

The woman's expression when she looked at Stephen was steady and measured. Not the way she'd regarded Alexander with brazen loathing. There was something different in her eyes that Cooper couldn't quite read. Something almost tender.

Alexander bared his fangs at the woman and hunched his shoulders. "Should have known you would show up. With your endless affinity for the Phipps line."

Cooper slowly stood, the name of his grandmother's

house registering. Maybe this woman knew how to find Lillie Mae. Keeping a watchful eye on both Alexander and Stephen, she wielded foot-long daggers in each hand, looking very much like she knew how to use them. Cooper took another step—only a few more to the door.

"If that's the way you want to play this, Montgomery, then fine." The woman moved toward Cooper like a silk sheet billowing in the breeze, slipping right between the two men and floating across the floor. She was like *them.*

Returning to her original form in front of Cooper, she glanced at him over her shoulder while tucking one of the daggers in her belt. Her beauty was without question. With a face as smooth as porcelain and voluminous waves of raven-colored hair dancing around her shoulders, her eyes were so dark they sparkled with the reflection of the lighted chandelier. Her vintage black riding coat could not conceal her warrior figure. The air around her was wet and cold, like it was with Alexander and Stephen. She returned her attention to the two men and reached out to Cooper. He stared at her outstretched hand, reminding himself that if she was like the two men, then she too had sharp fangs, alarming strength, and mind-raping abilities.

She glanced back at him again. "Please. Trust me, Cooper. If you want to get out of here and find Lillie Mae, you must come with me now." Her speech was taut with tension and well-traveled deviations of a subtle Southern accent.

Cooper quickly pondered his options. He could make a run for the door and take his chances with finding Lillie Mae on his own, or take the woman's hand and pray to God she was on his side. At least it appeared she wanted to protect him from Lillie Mae's captors. He looked over at Alexander, who hadn't moved an inch. Either he didn't think he could stop them from escaping, or he knew Cooper and the woman didn't have any chance of getting out of there alive. Cooper took the woman's hand in his. Her skin was cold and chilled his instantly. The touch sent a prickle of anxiety down to his core.

With his shoulders squared and his stance widened, Stephen blocked their path to the open window. "We can't just let her take him." He and the woman stared each other down—her eyes filled with sadness, Stephen's full of rage.

"We cannot take him by force, Stephen. You know that." Alexander relaxed his posture and retrieved his brandy snifter from a side table, as if the bizarre situation was an everyday occurrence. "Don't worry. He'll be back, and he will be more than willing to give me what I want."

Stephen obeyed with a huff and moved across the room to Alexander's side in an instant.

The woman guided Cooper to the window in fewer steps than made sense to him. She slipped her arm around his waist and pulled him close. "Hold on tight."

He barely had a chance to comply before they both shot out of the window and soared up into a cold, dark sky.

CHAPTER EIGHT

Though the face staring down at him was familiar, the fog filling his brain cloaked the name. The man looked down on him. A memorable, woodsy scent peppered the air. As soon as the man smiled, Cooper remembered his name.

Randy.

"Hey, Red." Randy touched Cooper's forehead with the back of his hand. Still in uniform, he looked authoritative and regal. Crinkled lines of worry around his eyes faded. "About time you woke up. I was about to drag your ass down to Georgetown Memorial."

The persistent ticking of the grandfather clock drifted in from the hallway. Cooper massaged his temples and looked around. He was back at Phipps House with no recollection of how he got there. Sitting on the edge of the sofa, Randy pushed up against Cooper's waist, the closeness of their bodies as comforting as it was awkward. He sat up, giving Randy a little more room. No need to make the straight guy uncomfortable.

Cooper circled his temples with the tips of his fingers, his mind a soupy bowl of bizarre memories and images that didn't make any sense. He tried desperately to put all the pieces together and came up empty. It must have been a dream. A really bad dream.

He ran fingers through his tangled hair. "What time is it?"

"It's after midnight." Randy sat up straight. "I was out looking for Lillie Mae. Drove by and saw all the lights on. Knocked, but I couldn't get anybody. The door wasn't locked, so I let myself in and found you here, asleep on the couch."

Cooper slung his legs over the side of the sofa, stood, and went over to the front window. He pulled back the drapes. The SUV sat in the driveway. Maybe it *had* been a dream. It seemed so real. Releasing the curtains, he slowly turned back around.

Randy stood in front of him and raised an eyebrow. "You okay, Red? You look like you've seen a ghost."

Cooper didn't know where to begin. Didn't know what was real and what wasn't. He thought he'd seen freaking vampires tonight, for Christ's sake. He couldn't say anything to Randy that wouldn't sound completely insane.

"No. I'm fine." He sat on the sofa, glancing back over his shoulder at Randy. "I guess I just fell asleep on the sofa like you said."

Randy frowned and pulled back the curtain, peering out into the dark night, like he wanted to see for himself what Cooper had been looking at. "Sorry, but nothing to report on Lillie Mae yet."

A twinge of worry pinched Cooper's stomach. His gut

told him what he remembered was real, not a dream. If that was true, then that freak Alexander had Lillie Mae hidden somewhere at Warfield. He needed to get back and find her, but he didn't want to lead Randy there and risk putting him in the crosshairs of those… whatever the hell they were.

Randy walked back to the sofa and stood in front of him. "I haven't made it out to Warfield yet, but I found something interesting about the place." He pulled the small spiral notebook out of his back pocket and flipped through a few pages. "The current owner is a Stephen Parker."

Cooper looked down, hoping Randy hadn't registered any change in his expression at the mention of Creepy Underwear Model's name.

"Before that," Randy continued, "it belonged to an Alexander Montgomery. Now there's a pompous-ass sounding name."

Cooper looked up at him, careful to keep the muscles in his face relaxed. "Any clue who they are?"

"Negative." Randy sat on the arm of the wingback chair opposite the sofa. "But here's the odd thing, and, granted, the records are pretty old, so this is probably a mistake. It seems that the property has been passed back and forth between Stephen Parker and Alexander Montgomery for almost a hundred fifty years."

The words hung in the air as Cooper processed them. It had definitely *not* been a dream. Of course, he couldn't explain it. It was all too ridiculous to begin with.

Randy closed the notebook. "I mean it obviously has to be descendants of these two guys, though the records didn't indicate that. No *juniors*, no *the second* or *the third*, just those two names."

"Obviously." Cooper entwined his fingers into a ball and rested his elbows on his knees. He stared down at the closed Bible on the coffee table, replaying the night's events over and over in his head. The woman. He needed to find the dark-haired woman. She knew those *men*—Alexander Montgomery and Stephen Parker. She also said she could help him find Lillie Mae. But she was one of them. Like them. He touched his index finger to the spot on his neck where Alexander's teeth—or *fangs*—grazed him and a chill latched itself onto his bones.

"Coop?" Randy's voice lured him back into the moment.

Cooper looked up into Randy's questioning eyes. "Right. Two names. A hundred fifty years. Weird." He knew all he needed to know about the current status of Warfield and its owners. What he needed was to find the woman in black. Go back to the kitchen house at Warfield and find Lillie Mae.

Cooper stood and stretched his arms out wide, forcing a deep yawn. "Man, I feel like I could pass out again." He knew it was a lame excuse. He didn't have time to think of a better one. He just needed Randy to leave. A glint of disappointment passed over Randy's eyes. Cooper could just imagine what he thought.

Your grandma is still out there missing, and you want to go to bed? Wimp.

Randy stood and moved toward the door. "You probably *should* get some rest." Terse disapproval laced his words.

"There's nothing else you can do tonight. I'll be back in the morning to look in on you. In the meantime, I'll check in with dispatch. Make sure there's nothing new on Lillie Mae. Keep your phone close by."

Cooper nodded. "I'll do that." He followed Randy down the hall to the front door. "And thanks, Randy. I appreciate everything you're doing."

Randy grabbed his coat off the rack and pulled it on. "Don't mention it." He flashed a forgiving smile and opened the door. "Get some sleep, Red."

Cooper closed the door behind him and peeked through the sidelight. Randy strode down the walkway to his car without looking back. Letting go of the fabric, Cooper wondered how the hell he would find his mystery woman in black. He didn't even know her name. The hairs on the back of his neck sprang to life. He spun around, his back hugging the front door.

The dark-haired woman stood right in front of him.

CHAPTER NINE

She crossed her arms over her chest and looked at him, no discernible expression on her face. Cooper couldn't even tell if she breathed, for God's sake. Her presence unnerved him. He didn't know exactly *what* she was, but standing only a few feet away from her only confirmed his suspicion that she was *not* human.

"I think that was wise." The woman uncrossed her arms, placed her hands on her rounded hips, and shifted her weight to one side. "And you are *not* going back to Warfield. That is final."

Like hell he wasn't. He cocked his head at her. "Who the hell are you, and what makes you think you can dictate what I can or cannot do?" He leaned in and crossed his arms. "For that matter, *what* the hell are you?"

She sized him up with a single sweeping glance and took a step toward him. "My name is Betsy."

"Betsy?" He huffed. "You don't look like a Betsy."

She shrugged. "What do I look like, then?"

Cooper studied her, from her sure stance to her squared

shoulders to her unusual height. The image of her with those daggers was still in his mind's eye. "I don't know," he said. "But sure as hell not *Betsy*."

She smiled thinly, extinguishing it before it fully materialized. Without a word, she turned on her heel and walked down the hall like she owned the place. Cooper supposed he was expected to follow. He did so with a healthy dose of reluctance. He wasn't used to not being in control of a situation, and he didn't care for the feeling at all.

In the sitting room, Betsy eased around the perimeter, running the tips of her fingers over the wallpaper, like the faded patterns housed some distant memories for her. She stopped in front of the fireplace, gently touching each of the family pictures on the mantel and lingering a moment on each before moving on to the next. It was an odd thing for a complete stranger to do, and also a little creepy. As if she was taking inventory of his life.

Cooper stood at one end of the mantel and waited, his patience quickly waning. "You said you could help me find my grandmother."

Betsy rested her hand on an eight-by-ten sepia-toned portrait of Lillie Mae. She couldn't have been more than nineteen or twenty in the picture. Betsy caressed the glass over his grandmother's face with the back of her hand, as one might on a small child's cheek.

Cooper's uneasiness returned. "Well?"

"Sit down, Cooper." Her tone was calm and even but left no room for discussion.

Cooper shook his head and took a seat in the wingback

chair. If he was going to get the help he needed, it obviously had to be done her way, or no way. All the more irritating.

The woman rounded the sofa and stopped in front of him. "It's good to finally meet you face to face."

Cooper stared up at her, his impatience giving way to impertinence. "Nice to meet you too, *Betsy*. I've never officially met a vampire before. This night is turning out to be a real winner."

If he had offended her, she did not show it. She floated down onto the sofa like a feather drifting to the ground. Leaning forward, she slipped something between her delicate fingers. It was the picture of the young girl he'd found in the Bible. That seemed like days ago, though it had only been a few hours. She studied the image with a melancholic distance clouding her eyes, the same way she'd looked at Stephen Parker earlier at Warfield.

"Do you know her?" Cooper asked, pointing to the picture, not really expecting a straight answer.

Betsy was quiet and pensive, but finally answered. "Her name is Sally Parker."

"As in Stephen Parker?"

She gave a quick nod. "They were brother and sister."

"That picture was taken in the 1800s. There's no way..." He realized how naïve the words sounded as soon as they left his lips. More absurd clichés tumbled around in his brain. Stephen Parker was some kind of freaking undead being. Of course he could have had a sister in the 1800s. Cooper shook his head and ran fingers through his hair. He needed a drink. Or a Xanax. Or both.

Betsy laid the picture down on the coffee table and fixed her dusky eyes on him. "I am not a *vampire*. I am a slayer."

Her response was so matter-of-fact, it was comical. Cooper chuckled. "A *vampire* slayer? Like *Buffy*?"

She crinkled her brow, cocked her head, and then shook it. "Vampire is an insulting word, much like the misnomer, witch. Vampires are the product of legends and fairy tales, a vain human attempt to explain away what they cannot understand." She clasped her hands together in her lap. "I am Anakim. And Anakim, I am afraid, are quite real."

Cooper stared straight through her. There was that word again. She'd called Alexander Montgomery that. "So let me get this straight. You're telling me that you are a vampire-like creature, but you also hunt them down and kill them."

"You make it sound so simple. It is not," she replied. "And why do you sound so incredulous? You have powers that are clearly not of the natural world, do you not? Why is it so hard to believe other supernatural beings are out there?"

She had him there. He'd always known the world was a bigger place than the familiar dimension where most people lived—a dimension of malls, reality television, and smartphones. He'd seen ghosts since he was a kid. He could make things happen with just a thought or the wave of a hand, if he dared. But he'd never considered a race of undead bloodsuckers.

"And the creepy guys at Warfield. Alexander and Stephen. They are vam…Anakim, like you?"

Betsy shifted in her seat and pushed her hair back over her shoulder. "That is correct."

Cooper took a moment to process the insanity. "So you hunt and kill your own kind."

She scooted up to the edge of the sofa, twisting her hands one inside the other. "All Anakim are an abomination, a blight on this world that must be eradicated. But, right now, we must talk about *you*."

Cooper leaned forward in his seat. "Look, my only concern is getting Lillie Mae back home safe and sound." He could live forever not knowing the shit going down in the shadows around him. He stood and paced across the floor, boards creaking under every step. "Damn it. I should've just told Randy the truth. Maybe he could help."

"Chances are he would not have believed you. Besides, I am sure you do not wish to put him in danger, and that is exactly where he will be if you bring him into this. Alexander will destroy anything or anyone that stands in his way."

Cooper looked down at her, his stomach twisting. Her stoic expression told him all he needed to know. "You're serious."

Betsy nodded, her dark eyes trained on him. "It is imperative that you stay away from Alexander and Warfield. No matter the cost."

Cooper was silent. Numb. Her words seared into his flesh like a red-hot branding iron. "No matter the cost? You mean Lillie Mae. But you said if I left there with you, you would help me get her back."

Betsy looked down. She straightened out the hem of her coat and absently brushed unseen lint away. "I would have said anything to get you out of there. Too much is at stake, and you are too important."

Cooper's blood boiled in his veins. "*Lillie Mae* is important. And I know she's there. She called out to me—in my head, somehow. At least for a moment. Then she was gone."

Betsy stood and walked over to him, so close he could feel her frosty breath on his cheeks. "Alexander likely blocked her mental connection to you. He is resourceful and more powerful than we imagined he would be at this point. We have underestimated him."

"So why the hell would Lillie Mae want me to leave her there with him?"

Betsy put a hand on his arm, sending a chill down his spine. "Because she understands the danger you are in, Cooper. She understands the stakes." She bit her lower lip before she finished. "And because she's dying."

Betsy's eyes transfixed him. He searched them for the falsity of her claim, but found none. He stepped back, breaking contact. Lillie Mae had exhibited all the normal signs of declining health for someone her age, but to be told she was dying—from a complete stranger, no less—was like a sucker punch to the gut. She was the only family he had left, and, absurdly, he'd never imagined his world without her in it.

"I am very sorry, Cooper," Betsy said. "I know that must be hard for you to hear."

Her face was devoid of emotion, though her unreadable eyes had softened, as if she shared his pain. As much as he wanted to doubt her, he couldn't.

Betsy closed the gap between them. "I heard her last night as well. I saw into her mind. Yes. She is there at

Warfield. And someone is with her."

Cooper stared at her, dumbfounded. "Who?"

"I don't know. Whoever it is, she cares a great deal for them. Alexander blocked our communication before I could find out who it was, and Lillie Mae was too weak to stop him."

The proximity of their bodies unnerved him, so he edged over to the sofa and sat back down.

He scratched the crown of his head and then slammed his fist down onto the coffee table. "Christ. What's he doing to her?"

Betsy walked over to the mantel, leaned her back against it, and crossed her arms. "My guess is that she is fine for now. Alexander doesn't want her. She is Divinum and special, like you. However, she is old and sick. Her power is fading."

Cooper looked up at her, a word sparking in his brain. "That's what the blond guy called me. Divinum."

Betsy nodded. "It is who you are and why you can do the things you can do."

"Like a witch?"

Betsy sat on the arm of the sofa and flipped her hair over her shoulder with the back of her hand. "Humans call them witches. Another insulting term, if you ask me. Divinum are not your standard variety wiccans or conjurers. Those beings, with their limited and unrefined powers, are the result of the diluted bloodline of true Divinum."

Cooper didn't want to believe anything that came out of her mouth, but damned if every word didn't ring true deep inside.

"The Anakim are nearly extinct," Betsy said. "We only know of a few hundred still in existence. They have been dying off in vast numbers for the last seventy years, but new ones have popped up in Montgomery's wake for years, which should not be possible. Somehow he has been procreating. He has remained strong and virile since the outbreak of the virus, creating a small army he keeps hidden around the world, lying in wait. Biding his time. We could not figure out how he did it until he took Lillie Mae. Then I started putting the pieces together. Alexander must have had a unique blood source with which he has been inoculating himself all these years. A blood source that is linked to Lillie Mae. And to you."

Cooper looked up at her. "You act like I know what the hell you are talking about."

Betsy's mouth pinched at the corners, and her eyes went blank. "The war between the Divinum and the Anakim lasted for centuries and spread across the globe. Anakim numbers had grown to unmanageable proportions. They had set their sights on world domination, no longer satisfied with living in the shadows. They meddled in the affairs of the human world, infiltrating governments and populating armies with their own soldiers. They started wars. Instigated acts of terror. Pitted human against human, all while waiting patiently to make their move to gain the upper hand. It nearly worked. They had decimated our numbers. They were winning. Then Jericho changed tactics and landed the deciding blow in the conflict."

Betsy glanced over at Cooper, no doubt detecting the

maze of confusion twisting his face. She stood and walked the length of the room to the front window, peeking out between the curtains as if she stood watch.

"Jericho is a secret elite army of soldiers and spies made up of mostly Divinum, but also some reformed Anakim like myself. We even have a handful of key human allies sprinkled over the globe. We exist to protect the human race from the Anakim and eradicate them from the earth. We track, hunt, and kill every single Anakim we can find. But their numbers grew faster than ours. The near immortality of the Anakim makes their eradication challenging. They spread their disease through human populations like a plague, creating soldiers by turning humans faster than we could recruit and train our own."

Cooper thought it odd how Betsy spoke of the Anakim with an air of disgust like she wasn't one herself.

She turned back to face him. "Realizing that the only chance we had was to keep them from reproducing, Jericho scientists developed a pathogen. It took years and many failed attempts until they were finally successful with a virus called Sterilus-A, susceptible only to Anakim, that could easily be spread and distributed through their food supply."

Cooper stared across the room, his eyes locked on a homemade clock with a crocheted face plate hanging above the television—the words *I Need Thee Every Hour* expertly stitched above the number twelve. Then it hit him.

"Humans."

"Yes." Betsy crossed her arms and walked toward him. "The virus is not harmful to humans or animals, and is completely undetectable. Almost seventy-five years ago, Jericho dispatched its soldiers around the world, adding the virus to human water supplies. Rivers. Lakes. Wells. Creeks. Purification plants for bottled water. Any human infected with Sterilus-A would carry the virus until death and infect other humans through blood, saliva, all bodily fluids."

Cooper shook his head. He *really* needed that drink. Bad.

Betsy stood behind the wingback chair and slung her sable mane back even though it had not fallen forward. "The Anakim infected themselves when they fed on humans and spread the virus amongst their race as well when they drank from one another—a disgusting habit, often enjoyed during the throes of passion. The virus spread through both the human and Anakim populations like wildfire. It was supremely effective. A real coup for Jericho and a game changer in the war."

Cooper leaned back into the sofa cushion and stared up at her. "*Sterilus-A*. You sterilized them."

Betsy nodded. "When infected, it weakens them, making them much easier to kill. But more importantly, they are no longer able to turn humans." She gripped the top corners of the seatback and shifted her weight. "We stopped their reproduction efforts cold, allowing us to fight them on an even playing field. The surviving Anakim scattered like rats to the far corners of the globe. So now we hunt them. One by one. Ridding this world of their diseased pestilence once and for all."

Cooper stood and went to her side, careful to keep a couple of feet between them. "But you're one of them. So what about you and the other reformed Anakim in this Jericho army? And what the hell does that even mean—*reformed*?"

Betsy's eyes darkened more than Cooper thought possible, sending a chill scampering over his skin. She stabbed the air with a finger pointed only inches from his chest. "We do not feed on humans, for one. Not under any circumstance. We would lose our heads for such an infraction. No questions asked."

"So you get a pass. On the whole eradication of the race thing."

The corners of her mouth edged down and her pointed stare bore right through him. "Of course not. After our work is done, we will present ourselves for extermination and free ourselves of this infernal curse."

Cooper studied her. Searched deep into her bottomless eyes. Resolve etched her face like carved letters on a granite headstone. Her fervor was almost religious. He believed her.

He edged back, giving her space. "If both Lillie Mae and I are Divinum, aren't there others? Why does this freak have such a hard-on for *my* family? Why does he want *me*?"

Betsy glided around the wingback chair, sat, and crossed her legs with the elegance of a supermodel. "You are the last of the Phipps line of Divinum." She said it like she was bestowing some royal honor on him. "And also the last of Sally Parker's seed. Thanks to her, your blood is unique. And without it, Alexander and the entire Anakim race will cease to exist."

CHAPTER TEN

Cooper barely registered the weight of her words. The Divinum part he still had trouble processing, but was no longer a surprise. The Phipps part made no sense at all. As far as he knew, Phipps House had been named after the original owners, who were not connected to his family in any way. Lillie Mae and Grandpa Joe had lived there his entire life.

"The Phipps line can be traced back for centuries," Betsy continued. "The power inside you is unusually potent, and has been altered with other, dangerous properties—a unique mix of meticulous Divinum breeding and dark Vodoun alchemy."

A knot formed in the base of Cooper's throat the size of a baseball. He sat on the sofa, his mind swimming and his stomach churning. He looked up at Betsy. "Voodoo?" God, he couldn't believe the word just came out of his mouth. "Are you kidding me with this shit?"

Betsy gave a curt shake of her head. She uncrossed her legs and slung her silky hair over her right shoulder. "We believe your blood contains the antigen to the Sterilus-A virus. It is the only thing that makes any sense. So far, we think only Alexander and Stephen have discovered this anomaly in the Phipps bloodline, likely due to Stephen's intimate knowledge of the family's history. I have my suspicions about the blood source he has used all these years to start building his army. It makes sense that Lillie Mae went with Stephen when he came for her."

Cooper stared up at the ceiling, organizing his thoughts. He sorted through the impossible barrage of information he'd just been given and applied it to his brief encounter with the Anakim at Warfield.

"Alexander is not interested in just curing his race of sterility, is he?"

Betsy shook her head slowly, leaning forward in her seat. "This is his chance to father a *new* line of Anakim. The *only* line. Generations of monsters loyal only to him. He would be their king, the father of the race. Once the remaining Anakim find out about you, they will hunt you to the ends of the Earth, and Alexander does not like to share."

Cooper sank back into the sofa and rubbed his eyes. It was all too ridiculous for words, or the woman could just be batshit crazy. He'd much prefer that option, though her words somehow rang true to him.

Betsy clasped her hands together and rested her elbows on her knees. "I am afraid it is all true, Cooper. We have been hunting Alexander for decades. He always eludes us. He is descended from an ancient and powerful lineage himself. And his newborns are the worst kind. Alexander turns murderers, rapists, serial killers, you name it. He usually keeps a horde of changelings around him for protection. We have not been able to find their nest here in Georgetown."

Cooper cocked his head at her. "Changelings?"

Betsy shook her head dismissively. "His half-baked little monsters. Just pray you never encounter one."

Cooper's head throbbed. He stood and walked over to the fireplace, massaging his temples. He stared at a framed photo of himself and his older brother on the mantel. It had been taken when they were eight and eleven, both dressed in matching short pants and white T-shirts. It was *that* summer. The summer of Warfield. The summer of Blue. Kevin wore a smile that stretched from ear to ear. Not Cooper. Lines of worry had already defined his eight year-old face.

He looked up and stared at Betsy's reflection in the mirror hanging over the mantel, admittedly surprised he was able to see it. Another old wives' tale, he guessed. "I am no match for Alexander. He's not even human, for Christ sake. If he wants me that bad, how the hell am I going to stop him?"

Betsy stood and eased over to his side. "Your power. You must embrace your power in order to protect yourself from Alexander. It is the only thing that will save you. Or Lillie Mae for that matter."

Cooper's skin soaked up the heat of the room like a sponge. Beads of sweat trickled down his neck, and his throat closed up at the idea of using his cursed magic. It had caused so much damage in the past. The memories made his bones ache.

Cooper shook his head and rubbed his eyes. "I can't do that." His voice was small and beaten down, even though he tried his best to give it weight. "I just can't."

Betsy raised an eyebrow. "Not even to save Lillie Mae?"

Cooper's face flushed hot with anger. He turned toward her, fingers curling into fists at his side. Their faces were only inches apart. "Don't you dare use Lillie Mae for bait, too. I don't care what the hell you are."

He stared her down, but she had him. She knew he would do anything to get Lillie Mae back and he hated her for it.

Cooper relaxed his fists and sighed. "I don't even know if can anymore. I tried to use it earlier tonight at Warfield, and it didn't work. Some kind of mental block." Yeah. A real doozy of one named Trevor. "Besides, I never really knew how to control it anyway."

Betsy put a hand on his shoulder. It was as cold as ice and the chill sliced right through his cotton shirt. "You have to try. Alexander will not stop."

Cooper flinched and pulled away from her touch. The hurt in her eyes was hard to miss. Dropping her hand to her side, she turned and walked back to the front window with slow humanlike steps. She stood with her back to him, as if to make him feel more comfortable that there was plenty of space between the monster and the human. He couldn't have felt more like a dick if he'd tried.

Betsy peeked through the slit in the curtains and then faced him again. "You lost control once. That was a long time ago." Her voice was soft and soothing. "You are older, stronger now."

"Older, yes. Stronger? You don't know that. I could lose control again. What if I hurt someone? Christ, what if I hurt Lillie Mae?"

"Let me worry about Lillie Mae," she replied. "Reinforcements are on the way. We will get her back."

Cooper turned toward her and cocked his head. "Reinforcements. I shudder to ask." He shoved his hands in his pockets and leaned against the mantel. "So… what? I'm supposed to just stay here? Brush up on my wizarding skills and wait for the vampire cavalry to arrive? You said Lillie Mae is dying. I could go back to Warfield and look for her during the day. You people are passed out cold all day, right? Isn't that a thing?"

Betsy crossed the space between them in a fraction of the time it should have taken her. "Yes. The day sleep is a thing. But Lillie Mae would not want you to put yourself in that kind of danger. She warned you to stay away from Warfield because she knows that even if you save her, Alexander will just find another way to get to you. Do not underestimate him, Cooper."

Cooper shook his head in frustration. "I don't believe this." He looked down at his hands, cursed by a *unique mix of meticulous Divinum breeding and dark Vodoun alchemy,* as Betsy so ominously put it. He opened his mouth to protest when a noise sounded on the second floor. The slightest thump—easy to miss. Betsy looked up. She'd heard it too. She stared at the ceiling, putting a finger to her lips. Cooper stood as still as possible, hairs rising up on the back of his neck.

Betsy slipped out of the room and into the hall without the slightest sound, holding firm to the handle of the dagger tucked in her belt. Cooper followed her, poking his head through the doorway. Crouching in the center of the foyer, Betsy held him at bay with her free hand and edged toward the staircase. His curiosity got the better of him, and he took a couple of quiet steps out into the hall. Betsy stopped at the foot of the stairs. Another bump sounded in the darkness above them. Cooper eased down the hall, his back hugging the wall. The floorboards betrayed him with a creak. Betsy shot a frown over at him to which he responded with shrugged shoulders.

She peered up the stairs, and they waited. Nothing. Another few seconds passed. Silence.

"It's probably just a rat," Cooper said in a whisper. "Wouldn't be the first time."

Betsy stared up into the dark, her eyes widening. "Cooper, run!"

He didn't run. He couldn't run. He froze. All of the air rushed out of his lungs as the heavy mass of snapping fangs and clawing talons barreled down the staircase, heading right for Betsy. A tornado of vicious snarls and piercing howls filled the air, ringing in Cooper's ears so loud that he covered them with his hands, but he couldn't look away. He had never seen anything like it before. Never glimpsed anything like it in his darkest nightmares, a grotesque creature formed of rotting flesh, oozing sores, and a misshapen head.

Betsy drew her dagger. "I said run!"

Cooper looked around frantically, searching for anything

he could use as a weapon. The curio cabinet? The coat tree? Anything! An animalistic wail drew his attention back to the stairs.

The deformed shape of what must have once been a human man towered over them with Betsy's dagger lodged deep in its chest. Only momentarily slowed by her strike, the creature clawed the air just inches from Betsy's face with the longest, sharpest fingernails Cooper had ever seen. Open sores and wet, peeling flesh covered its face, hands, and arms. Crazed eyes bulged out of their sockets, filled with rage and hell-bent destruction. Betsy grabbed the thing by the throat with one hand and yanked her dagger out of its chest with the other.

Cooper wished he'd have run when Betsy told him to, if only because his presence was a distraction. She looked over at him as she raised the dagger over her head, but that was all the time the attacker needed to knock the weapon from her hand. It skidded across the floor and bounced off the base of the grandfather clock. The creature slammed into Betsy, knocking her on her back so hard the floor shook. Pinned down with drooling jaws snapping dangerously close to her face, she managed to hold the monster back with both hands wrapped around its fleshy neck.

Shock held Cooper's body prisoner, though adrenaline burned in his veins. Needles of raw, virulent energy shot down his arms, begging for release. He slid down the wall onto the floor and scanned the space. The dagger was too far away. He didn't think he would be able to reach it in time.

The creature bore down on Betsy, and she snapped her

now extended fangs right back at him, not an ounce of fear in her eyes and not giving an inch. Her transformation from warrior princess to crazed beast was immediate and terrifying. The monster had at least a hundred pounds on her and edged closer to her throat with each passing second. Cooper had to do something.

A guttural roar erupted out of Betsy's mouth. She pushed the creature up, away from her throat, inch by inch, putting more space between them. She clawed at the twisted face. Grabbed at a tangled clump of stringy gray hair and ripped it right out of the skull, pulling brain matter out with its roots. Fierce resolve burned in her eyes, like a lioness protecting her young. She would do anything, even sacrifice herself, to save Cooper.

Betsy's fearless resolve triggered something deep inside Cooper. He couldn't suppress it any longer. Having no other options, he released himself to the malevolent rumble in his core, praying it would not fail him this time. The power exploded up from his core, filling his veins with the intoxicating poison he both craved and despised. His fingertips burned with acidic venom. He focused on the dagger lying several feet away and reached out his hand. At first, nothing happened. Then it moved. Twitched. Slid an inch toward him before his mind again filled with the image of Trevor lying on the ground, his neck twisted at a cringe-inducing angle. Motionless. Trying to expel the image, Cooper closed his eyes. He shook his head and opened them again, but the dagger would not move.

Betsy uttered another guttural war cry. The monster's

fangs were less than an inch from her face. Every muscle in her body flexed in resistance. Her extended fangs scraped against the creature's, causing an ear-splitting screech, but her fight was nearly lost.

Cooper scrambled across the floor and over to the dagger. He gripped the handle and jumped to his feet. Without thinking and without a plan, he raised the weapon high in the air and charged the beast, driving the blade down into the back of its sunken skull.

The creature wailed and buckled. Betsy scrambled out from under it. Cooper put all his weight on the blade, forcing it as far down as it could go. Cranial cracks and pops echoed around the room. Cooper released the handle and scrambled backward.

The creature shrieked, twitched, and seized, the fight leaving its body. It rolled onto the floor between Cooper and Betsy. The monster's eyes ignited with blue flames that quickly spread into a small explosion of bone and brains. The creature's body crumpled in on itself and burned until all that remained was a smoldering pile of black and gray ash puddled in thick brown liquid marring the shiny hardwood floor.

Finally, all was silent, interrupted only by the slow, steady ticking of the grandfather clock in the corner.

Cooper drew a deep breath into his lungs and exhaled one long airy stream of relief. Betsy pulled herself up and sat leaning against the wall opposite him, her breathing steady and her pristine appearance now savagely disheveled. They stared at each other in silence for a long time. Betsy's point had been made for her. Loud and clear. Alexander would stop at nothing to get what he wanted, and that included killing anyone who tried to protect Cooper.

He wiped the sweat from his brow with the back of his still tingling hand. "So that was one of Alexander's half-baked little monsters?"

Betsy brushed the palms of her hands together. Pieces of matted hair and bloodied flesh fell to the floor. "Yes. And there will be more."

CHAPTER ELEVEN

The next morning Cooper woke up on the sofa, the sun streaking his face with rays of comforting warmth. He stretched his arms over his head and rubbed his knotted neck as he looked around the room. He was alone. Betsy was gone. Right. The day sleep. His car keys and phone lay on the coffee table. He still wasn't sure how Betsy got his SUV back to Phipps House. He had a hard time imagining her behind the wheel of a modern vehicle. There was something definitively old-world about that woman. On the coffee table, a slip of paper rested beside the remains of his half-eaten ham sandwich. He turned on his side, picked up the note, and read the elegantly scripted words.

Expect visitors this morning. Friends.

Cooper dropped the note and rubbed his eyes. His head was still foggy from the lingering effect of six cups of chamomile tea he'd drunk to help calm his nerves after the attack last night. He hadn't had any luck finding Lillie Mae's secret stash of Jim Beam, and the tea only assisted him in roughly three hours of uninterrupted sleep on the lumpy sofa. He remembered Betsy sitting as still as Phipps House itself, watching over him after she insisted he get some rest. "You'll need it," she'd said in her naturally ominous way.

Letting his head fall to the side, he stared into the empty space of the room, his mind swirling with all that Betsy had told him as well as the questions she'd left unanswered. He wanted those answers. *Needed* them. Anything that would help him save Lillie Mae. The open Bible on the coffee table drew his attention. A pen stuck out under a folded over page. Cooper slid his legs off the sofa and sat up. He reached over and pulled back the page, exposing the marred family tree. The bloody letters had browned and seeped into the thin paper. Fresh blue ink filled the formerly blank lines above and beside Sally Parker's name, names written in the same elegant penmanship as Betsy's note.

Above Sally's name.

Jonathan Parker - Father. Elizabeth Parker - Mother.

And, on either side of Sally's name.

Andrew Parker – Brother. Stephen Parker - Brother

Betsy must have done it while he was asleep, though he wasn't sure why she would. It was like filling in answers to someone else's crossword puzzle uninvited, something that made him crazy. Except for Stephen Parker, they were just more names that Cooper did not know from a distant family he never knew existed just twenty-four hours earlier.

He picked up his phone and unlocked the screen with the swipe of his thumb. No calls. No messages. What he wouldn't give for one of Lillie Mae's rambling middle-of-the-night messages when she'd failed to reach him. How many times had he seen her name on the caller ID and let it go to voice mail? Too busy with his own life to give a lonely old woman who adored him a few minutes of attention and conversation.

He closed the Bible and stared at it. "Just don't fail her again."

Staring back at the home screen on his phone, a search engine icon caught his eye and sparked an idea. He hopped up and went into the foyer, fishing his iPad out of his bag. Hurrying back to the sofa, he opened up a web browser and searched the word *Anakim*. The return of information was shockingly instant. Just under the always-expected Wikipedia result were several biblical source links. He clicked on the first one, an online version of the King James Bible. The screen quickly populated with nine entries. Nine scriptural references to the made-up-sounding word. Five in Deuteronomy and four in the book of Joshua. Cooper's heart thumped noisily against his chest cavity, its beat matching his stunted breathing. He repeated the exercise for the online versions of the Revised Standard and New International translations of the Bible, flipping back and forth between tabs, devouring the results. A few stood out.

> *Numbers 13:32-33 (NIV) And they spread among the Israelites a bad report about the land they had explored. They said, "The land we explored devours those living in it. All the people we saw there are of great size. We saw the Nephilim there (the descendants of Anak come from the Nephilim). We*

seemed like grasshoppers in our own eyes, and we looked the same to them."

Deuteronomy 1:28(KGV) The people is greater and taller than we; the cities are great and walled up to heaven; and moreover we have seen the sons of the Anakim there.

Deuteronomy 9:2 (KGV) A people great and tall, the children of the Anakim, whom thou knowest, and of whom thou hast heard say, Who can stand before the children of Anak!

And finally,

Joshua 11:21 (RSV) And Joshua came at that time, and wiped out the Anakim from the hill country, from Hebron, from Debir, from Anab, and from all the hill country of Judah, and from all the hill country of Israel; Joshua utterly destroyed them with their cities.

Cooper placed the iPad on the coffee table beside the Bible and stared at them both, chewing on the tip of his index finger. Damn if Betsy's story hadn't given credence to a book he'd long ago discarded as a collection of fairy tales. Covering his face with one hand, he desperately racked his brain for the last known location of that bottle of Jim Beam. Who cared that it wasn't even noon yet? Certainly he'd get some kind of pass for apocalyptic biblical revelations. Maybe a hot shower and some caffeine would help. Besides, he needed to get going soon anyway so he could make use of every ounce of sunlight possible.

Cooper stood and drew his elbows behind him, stretching the kinks out of his back. Retrieving his luggage from the foyer, he headed to the guest bedroom. After a quick shower, he pulled on a well-worn pair of jeans and a white button-down Oxford. The scent of clean cotton soothed him, the smell of normalcy in the midst of chaos. He gave himself an once-over in the mirror and styled his damp copper hair with his fingers.

With his index finger, he followed a line of reddish-brown freckles from his cheek down to his neck—to the spot where Alexander had grazed his skin with fangs. He shivered, shaking loose the insane memory.

After scrounging around the sunlit kitchen for a few minutes in search of coffee, he finally found a jar of instant. It was the same brand he'd seen Lillie Mae drink his entire life, with three spoons of sugar and a healthy pour of whole milk. He made quick work of getting a kettle of water heating on the archaic gas stove. His stomach rumbled, and he touched his hand to it. Half a ham sandwich hadn't cut it. A hastily constructed peanut butter and jelly sandwich and three cups of weak coffee later, a woman's voice drifted through the house. No. Two voices. Almost whispers. Alarm prickled the hairs on the back of his neck. He sat the coffee mug down on the counter and eased over to the swinging door that separated the kitchen from the sitting room.

Pressing his ear against the cool wood, he listened.

"Do mind your manners with the boy, Sister." The woman's voice was low and throaty.

"Me? You're the one who unnerves people to no end." The second woman's voice was high-pitched and scratchy. "And he's not a boy anymore, Dora. He's a grown man now."

"It *is* nice to be back at Phipps House, isn't it, Eunie?"

A huff sounded. "The place looks ghastly, if you ask me. Like an indoor flea market. Mother would *not* be pleased."

"Manners, Sister."

Cooper placed a hand on the door and hesitated. Betsy's note said to expect visitors—*friends*—but didn't these people knock first? He finally pushed through the door.

Two elderly women sat in the sitting room, like wax figures in an antebellum museum exhibit. Both wore full-length, intricately laced black dresses with high white collars. One sat on the sofa with her nose in a book and the other knitting in the occasional chair by the window. Their odd vintage attire was identical in design. Mirrored faces bore the same pale skin sprayed with faded freckles, framed under nests of thick red hair awash with light streaks of gray. The only difference in the two women was that the one knitting was rail thin and tightly pulled together, while the other was a bit plump and a little *less* pulled together.

Cooper stood frozen in the doorway staring at them, completely at a loss for words. He'd honestly thought things couldn't get any more bizarre than they had last night. Damn if he wasn't dead wrong. With their matching pursed lips, they glanced up at him like he was no surprise to them at all.

"Close your mouth, young man," Knitting Twin said before shifting her attention back down to the project splayed over her lap. "You'll catch flies."

Reading Twin shot a scowl of reproach at her, then turned back to face Cooper with a warm smile. "Good morning, Cooper." She had a disarming air about her, and Cooper already knew he preferred her to the other one.

"Betsy's friends, I presume?" He stepped into the room, trying to maintain an authoritative edge in his voice. "Break and enter much?"

Knitting Twin snorted without looking up. "Betsy's friends." Another snort and a shake of the head.

"Do forgive our intrusion," Reading Twin said. "I am Eudora Phipps." She nodded over to her counterpart. "This is my sister, Eunice."

Eunice grunted without looking up.

"Please. Come in and sit." Eudora patted the cushion beside her.

Cooper hesitated, sizing her up and taking note of the last name she'd given. *Phipps.* Obviously they had some connection to the house that he was unaware of. Intrigued more than anything, he crossed the space, choosing to sit in the wingback chair opposite her. "Seems there's no need to introduce myself."

Eudora chuckled, her smile widening. "No need at all. It's been a long time, though you still look the same. I would never forget those sparkling hazel eyes and those freckled dimples. You were always such an adorable child. Positively angelic."

Cooper studied her, trying to recall her face. Other than some strikingly similar traits she shared with Lillie Mae, he did not recognize the woman at all. But there was something off-putting about them, something he couldn't quite put his finger on.

"This is not a social call, Dora," Eunice Phipps barked. She trained her antiseptic gaze on him. "We were told you needed our help, and we don't have all day to lollygag around."

Eudora smoothed the wrinkles from her lap and cleared her throat. "My sister is as impatient as she is correct." She looked up at him, her smile failing to put him at ease. Her skin shimmered in the bright sunlight pouring through the windows, so pale it was nearly translucent one moment, then perfectly natural the next. A palpable energy buzzed around the women. He didn't think they were like Betsy, nor did they seem like him. They were different somehow.

He shifted in his seat, sharing Eunice's impatience. He didn't have time for this. He needed to be somewhere. "I'm listening."

"We apologize for barging in unannounced." Eudora inspected the room in a wistful daze. "We lived in this house all our lives. Still feels like home."

Cooper stared at her, words escaping him. He had no clue what she was talking about and didn't really give a shit at the moment.

She leaned forward, her heavy bosom sagging down to her lap. "Betsy said you are having a little trouble accessing your powers. She thought we might be of assistance since we know a little something of the matter."

Cooper leaned forward, mimicking her conspiratorial posture. "Unless you can assist me in finding my grandmother, you're wasting my time."

Eunice snorted. "Lillie Mae. A piece of work, that one. Was always trouble if you ask me. Couldn't keep her legs together long enough to take a piss."

Heat rose to Cooper's ears, and he shot Eunice an icy glare.

No one asked you, Sister!

Eudora's voice rang out in Cooper's head, though her lips hadn't moved. He was appreciative of the rebuke, though unnerved by the delivery.

Yes, Cooper, we shared your gifts, Eudora told him, smiling with her lips closed.

Cooper cocked his head. "Shared?"

"God's balls!" Eunice screeched, dropping her knitting needles to her lap with an overly exaggerated huff. "Before we kicked the bucket, you idiot."

Eudora rolled her eyes at Eunice. "Yes. As my sister said with the refined delicacy of the lady she is…" She cleared her throat. "Before we passed from this world into the half-light of eternity."

Cooper looked back and forth between them, landing on each three times before he broke the awkward silence. "So you're ghosts. Like Blue. You're telling me I am sitting here talking to two dead old ladies." He covered his face with his hands. "Awesome."

"Blue," Eunice huffed. "You can thank that nigra for this mess you're in."

Cooper winced at the archaic racial slur. But she knew about Blue, so he needed to keep her talking. He lowered his hands and looked up at Eudora. "You don't look like ghosts."

"We prefer *spirit. Ghost* is such a trifling word."

"Everybody's so damned sensitive about labels around here," Cooper mumbled.

Eudora raised an eyebrow. "And just how do you think we should look? Like this?"

Her body faded away into a shimmering ripple of light, like the disturbed surface of an otherwise still body of water. Cooper couldn't move. Breathing wasn't an option, either. She'd called his bluff and now she was a freaking wall of light.

Eudora's voice sounded in Cooper's head. *Or should we look like this?*

The wall of light changed before his eyes, forming a fluffy cloud of white smoke.

Cooper dug fingers deeper into the fabric of the armrests.

The apparition rippled again, and Eudora's voice permeated his brain like it was on a loudspeaker. *Or this?*

The white smoke morphed into the decomposing corpse of a woman with stray clumps of hair sprouting out of her skinless skull and sunken black holes where her eyes should be.

Cooper pushed back into the chair, his arms straight and stiff as boards. "Jesus Christ!"

Eunice chuckled from her perch by the window. He shot a glance her way hoping she didn't look the same way. When he looked back, Eudora sat holding the book in her lap, as fully formed and matronly real as she had been when he first walked into the room.

"So sorry to have startled you," she said. "I thought we should get that out of the way so we can get down to business."

Cooper eased his grip on the armrests and took in a deep breath.

"Are you all right?" Genuine concern laced Eudora's eyes. "You look as pale as we do."

Cooper relaxed his shoulders and exhaled. Another insane truth to be cataloged and swallowed away. Eudora and Eunice Phipps were ghosts—*spirits*—whatever the hell they wanted to call it.

They were like Blue.

CHAPTER TWELVE

"Do not concern yourself with Blue right now, Cooper," Eudora said, extracting the name from of his head with all the finesse of plucking feathers out of chicken.

Cooper stood and walked behind the wingback chair, creating a barrier between himself and the women. He scratched the crown of his head, not knowing where to begin. He'd never conversed with spirits before. Not sober, anyway.

"Betsy called or summoned you, or whatever." He gripped the back of the chair like he stood behind a podium. "So, you must know about this Alexander."

"Betsy," Eunice said, punctuating the name with her loudest snort yet.

Eudora ignored her twin and shifted her body toward Cooper. She laid her book on the seat cushion, clasping her hands in her lap as if she was about to tell him a bedtime story.

"*Betsy*. Yes. Troublesome woman, though she was right to call on us in this case. And we have had our past dealings with that devil, Alexander Montgomery, believe you me." She cut her eyes to Eunice as if daring her to add comment. Eunice behaved and remained silent.

"Now. About your power," Eudora said. "Why do you bury it so deep inside you? You have been blessed with the Seraphic gene. You are descended of a storied Divinum bloodline. And with the Vodoun properties mixed in your blood, your potential is immeasurable."

Cooper stared at her with his mouth hanging open, wondering how the hell he was supposed to respond. "Seraphic gene? Vodoun properties? You make me sound like some kind of cursed supernatural test-tube baby."

Eudora stood—or rose, rather—and drifted over to him. He wasn't sure her feet touched the floor under her voluminous skirt, and he was just fine keeping that a mystery. She stopped two feet away from him and again clasped her fingers, resting them on her plump belly.

"Cooper, you are Divinum, like Sister and I were. That means you are descended of the Seraphim. Your power is a gift from God. It is not a curse."

Cooper coughed out a chuckle and walked over to the fireplace. He stood with his back to them and caught his own reflection in the mirror hanging over the mantel. "Angels? A gift from God?" He coated the words with a thick layer of sarcasm and turned to face them. "Is that right?" He looked Eudora in the eye. "I have a hard time believing this is a gift from God. This *thing* inside is not angelic. It's evil. I've *hurt* people."

Eudora took a step toward him. "It's true. You have the

potential to be wildly powerful, but you must learn how to balance the light as well as the darkness inside you. That is your unique challenge."

Cooper hung his head, the nagging heat of shame filling his cheeks. *Challenge* was right. He'd lost that battle between light and darkness more than once with horrendous results.

Eudora placed her hand on his shoulder, though Cooper barely felt the contact. "Tell us about him. Tell us about Trevor."

Cooper looked up and reared his head back like she'd thrown a punch at him. He stuck a shaky index finger directly in her face. "Stay out of my head!"

Eudora raised her hands and withdrew, retreating to her seat on the sofa.

Cooper scrubbed a hand over the day-old stubble on his face. Eudora had no idea how many demons he had locked away. So many parts of his past *and* his present lay hidden behind forbidden doors. He wasn't ready to peek behind any of them. Who knew what he might find?

Keyed up and irritated, Cooper barreled through the swinging door into the kitchen. He noisily pillaged around in the walk-in cupboard for several minutes in a frantic search for his grandmother's whiskey. With no luck there, he tried the kitchen cabinets, riffling through an unorganized maze of pots, pans, and oversized serving utensils. He slammed a cabinet door above the stove, and turned to find Eunice's rail thin frame poised in the center of the kitchen, not a foot away him.

He flinched and stepped back. "Jesus Christ! Don't do that."

With arms crossed over her chest, every muscle in Eunice's face turned down in reproach. "If you ever take that tone with my sister again, I will skin your hide so bad you will have to shit standing up for a month. Do you hear me?"

Her narrowed eyes and pursed lips told him that she was dead serious. Heat flushed his cheeks, and he simply nodded.

Eunice planted a hand on her bony hip. "What my sister was getting at, Mr. Einstein, is that your powers are blocked by your guilt over what you did to Trevor. And Betsy said you shot blanks last night."

Cooper had to process her words a moment before realizing she referred to his less than stellar performance during the zombie-vampire attack in the foyer.

"You must get past this mental block before you get not only yourself but everyone around you killed. This is no game, Cooper Causey. Your life is not the only one at stake here."

Cooper shoved his hands in his pockets, shrugged his shoulders, and sighed deeply. "Trevor was just someone I knew in high school. I haven't even seen him since that night."

"The night you hurt him." Eunice's words were flat and void of consolation, not that he deserved any.

All Cooper could do was nod. He moved over to the sink, filled a glass with water, and downed the whole thing in one gulp. He sat the glass on the counter and looked back at her.

Eunice clasped her hands in front of her and cocked her head at him. "Were you close to him?"

A sigh passed through Cooper's half-parted lips. "About

as close as any two people can possibly get. At least *I* thought we were."

He waited for Eunice to say something. She didn't. Apparently, she wanted more. He leaned against the kitchen counter and ran fingers through his hair. "We met around the same time I discovered my… what I can do." He and Trevor had shared some good times, and the thought made him smile. "We were eighteen. And I was a mess." A closeted freak with unexplained power shooting from his fingertips was even dangerous before you added teenage hormones to the mix.

Eunice rolled her eyes, as if it pained her to participate in such sentimental recollections. "So you cared for him a great deal. Then what?"

Cooper turned away from her a little, leaned his hip into the counter, and peeked out the kitchen window. The sky was clear, the sun bright. The freak winter storm had fizzled as quickly as it came on.

"I cared for him more than I should have. I let my guard down, and he betrayed me. He denied what we had and made me the laughing stock of the whole school. And I made him pay for it." He faced Eunice, not meeting her eyes. He'd said too much already. It didn't matter, though. She plundered his brain like a nosy neighbor until she gathered all the pertinent facts she needed.

Eunice moved toward him at a slow and unnervingly fluid pace. "You know, I had a friend like that once—well, I *thought* we were friends. I adored her. I wanted her to like me, to accept me so badly. She betrayed me too, and I exacted my revenge much like you did. And my Divinum blood is not even tainted with malevolent properties like yours.

"Still, I *wanted* to hurt her. We all make choices. We all make mistakes, whether there is inherent darkness in you or not. You can control it, if you try. You can choose light over darkness or love over hate." He looked up at her and caught a brief glimpse of tenderness. She blinked it away and rolled her eyes. "God's balls. Lillie Mae should have prepared you. She understood your internal struggle as well as anyone."

"That was a bad time for Lillie Mae." He closed his eyes and pinched the bridge of his nose. "We lost my brother that year."

Cooper stared down at his feet. The motorcycle accident. He'd always assumed he'd been responsible for that too, though he'd never been sure. He and his brother had fought that day, and he'd wished Kevin dead. Six hours later, he was.

A suffocating sadness fell over him, the kind he'd become so good at keeping at bay with a revolving door of beautiful and disposable men. He'd lost nearly everyone—his parents, his brother, and Grandpa Joe. All gone. Lillie Mae was all the family he had left. A tinge of resolve formed in the pit of his stomach. He could not lose her, too. He *would not* lose her. Eunice's face was as blank as a clean chalkboard, not a flicker of emotion in her eyes.

"What time is it?"

Eunice narrowed her eyes on him. "Almost ten o'clock. Why?"

Cooper stood up straight. To hell with Betsy's warnings. "I can't just stay locked up here and do nothing."

Eunice clicked her tongue on the roof of her mouth three times and shook her head.

Cooper dismissed her disapproval and headed for the hallway, but she planted herself in front of him with her hands on her hips, blocking his path. Cooper stepped around her, wondering for a moment if he could have just walked right through her.

"Go see him, Cooper," Eunice called behind him. "Go see Trevor. You must confront your demons in order to exorcise them. You will need your powers to survive this, and that's the only way to get control of them."

He shot her a glance over his shoulder. "No. I've done enough damage already using *my power*. I won't take the chance of hurting Lillie Mae, too. I'm going back to Warfield to find her."

Eunice threw up her hands in a huff.

Cooper didn't care. He hurried down the hall to the guest room to get his shoes. Although he had plenty of time, he didn't want to waste one more minute of daylight.

CHAPTER THIRTEEN

Sunlight broke through the threadbare branches of majestic pines that cloaked Warfield Road. Though the road was much less intimidating in broad daylight, still a knot formed in the pit of Cooper's stomach as his tires churned down the slushy lane. He kept his speed steady, his fingers sealed around the steering wheel, and his eyes alert.

His plan was simple. Get to the plantation during broad daylight, go directly to the kitchen house to find Lillie Mae, and get back to Phipps House before dark. Simple. He even went so far as to check the exact time the sun would set. *6:58 PM.* He glanced at the digital clock on the console. *10:36 AM.* Plenty of time.

After passing through the stone gates and into the cover of full sun, he stared straight ahead, ignoring the cabins of the slave village surrounding him. If any stray spirits were hanging out on the crumbling porches, he didn't want to see them. Two in one day were plenty, thank you very much.

Brilliant streaks of sunshine mapped his trek down the oak-lined drive. A few straggling clumps of Spanish moss clung onto bare branches for dear life, determined to survive the winter. It reminded him of the way Lillie Mae hunkered down and rode out threatening hurricanes over the years.

Just a little rain, she'd say. *Nothing to get all in a tizzy about.*

The manor house appeared innocuous enough. Of course, now he knew that was just an external illusion. Emboldened by the cloudless blue skies and beaming sun, Cooper continued around the corner, driving right up to the kitchen house. He stopped the SUV ten feet from the building, got out, and inspected the modest structure. It looked just the same as it had last night, but in the almost cheery sunlight, it exuded a significant dose of charm.

Cooper walked up two steps to the front door, placed a hand on the coarse rotted wood, and pushed it open. A daunting, extended creak invited him in. He slipped inside.

Sunlight peeked through cracks in the walls, casting long streaks of light and shadow across the length of the small room. A crumbling fireplace anchored the back wall. A long wooden table sat in the middle of the room, covered with a thick layer of dust. Outlining half the room, a wide L-shaped counter topped empty shelves underneath. Uneasiness permeated the dismal little space from the dust-covered floors to the cobweb-coated ceiling, as if the spirits of the imprisoned souls that once worked in the room were there with him, warning him to leave while he still could.

A vibration on Cooper's hip made him jump a little. He fished his phone out of the front pocket of his coat and looked down at the screen. Only half of one service bar was lit, sending the incoming call straight to voice mail. Randy was probably checking on him. Cooper didn't think he'd have anything new to report in the search for Lillie Mae, because she was here somewhere. He could feel her. He tucked the phone back into his pocket as a pinch of guilt formed in his gut. As much as he would have liked Randy by his side at that moment, he couldn't risk dragging him into this after what he had witnessed last night. Too dangerous.

Though he could scan the entire space standing in one spot, Cooper moved around the room at a reverent pace. He inspected every crevice in the ceiling, looking for an attic door. Nothing. Crouching down, he ran his fingers along the dusty floorboards. He finally saw it near the back wall. Two rusted hinges bolted to the floor. He scrambled over to it and dropped to his knees, running the palm of his hand over the cracks between the boards. Cold air tickled his skin, igniting a flicker of hope in his chest. He brushed dust away from a two-by-two square patch of board outlined in the floor. A cellar door. His heart raced. He wedged his fingertips into the widest crack in the seam and pulled, but it had been nailed shut.

His body temperature rising by the second, he shed his coat and cast it aside. He jammed his fingers into a crack between the boards and pulled with every ounce of strength he could summon. Lillie Mae was down there. He knew it in his bones. When he opened his mouth to call out her name, a blanket of ice-cold air spilled over his entire body. The already chilly room dropped twenty degrees in an instant. He froze. Deep, raspy breaths sounded behind him, their clammy residue singeing the rims of his ears. Every muscle in his body contracted with fear, paralyzed by a foul presence filling the room. He was too afraid to look. He knew what he would find.

Close your eyes. You can't see him if you close your eyes.

But he couldn't close his eyes. He had to see, had to know for sure. He forced himself to turn and peek over his shoulder, if only to bolster his case that nothing was there. A pair of azure eyes stared back at him. Blue. The massive man towered over him like a dark, threatening storm cloud. Ebony skin shimmered in streaks of sunlight. A milk-chocolate scar etched the left side of the leathery face. Eyes full of death and malice locked on to him.

Bile crept up in Cooper's throat, and his hands slicked with sweat. He scrambled around to face the spirit, his hands planted onto the floor and fingertips digging into the splintered wood. Blue moved toward him, the floorboards creaking under his heavy steps. Cooper shook his head and scooted back to the wall. The hinges of the cellar door pressed into the seat of his pants. He pulled at the loose boards underneath him. His quickened heart rate and erratic breathing sparked something deep in his core. Blue reached a massive hand out for him, the same open palm he remembered from their first meeting twenty years ago.

Cooper dug his fingers into the floor. The power inside him swelled, as if agitated by Blue's presence. It spread up through his torso and down into his arms. The tips of his fingers, like ten short-fused firecrackers sprouting from his hands, exploded into the wood. A loud crackle sounded, and the cellar door gave way under his weight. For a moment, he floated face up on a cloud, cascading downward in dreamlike slow motion. Then his body made contact with hard and pointy edges. He flipped over, completing an unintended somersault. Wood cracked as it snagged his shins. Sharp pain shot up through his legs. He landed on a hard, unforgiving surface with one more blow to the back of his head.

Cooper lay still—disoriented, bones aching, vision hazy. He gasped to refill his lungs and moaned through the pain when it returned. He blinked twice, trying to dispel the blur from his eyes. A face loomed over him, fuzzy at first and then familiar for a split second before fading into darkness.

Lillie Mae.

CHAPTER FOURTEEN

A whispered voice sounded in his ear. "Lie still."

Cooper opened his eyes to see her face inches away from his. Faded traces of copper hair overtaken by a nest of gray spilled unkempt around her shoulders. Deep wrinkles creased the pale skin of her face like a maze of family secrets and canyon-sized heartaches. She dabbed his forehead with a damp cloth. Bruises circled her wrists, and a square bandage covered the side of her neck. He resolved to make Alexander pay for what he had done to her.

A sharp pain stabbed through Cooper's head like someone had rammed a hunting knife into the base of his skull. He winced and closed his eyes. Oh right. He had just fallen through a hole in the floor of the kitchen house. He was *not* dreaming. He pushed through a throb of pain and raised his heavy eyelids. Lillie Mae sat beside him, a weary smile etching her face. Damn, it was good to see her.

He swallowed a mouthful of dank air. "Are you okay?"

She brushed her soft crinkled fingers over his cheek and

shook her head. "You shouldn't have come here. You should have listened to me."

Her tone was thick with disapproval, and all Cooper could think was how this was not the time for her to reprimand him for finally being a good grandson.

He raised his head, and the world spun around him. "Can you get on to me later? We have to get you out of here."

"Lie back." Lillie Mae pushed him back down by his shoulders. "You took a terrible tumble down those stairs. But I don't think anything's broken."

Cooper's back ached, and his head throbbed. He surveyed his grandmother's prison as the room finally slowed its spin. A steep wooden staircase with several missing steps anchored the corner of the dimly lit room. Earthen walls framed a smooth dirt-packed floor, twenty feet wide and thirty feet deep. Carved into the earth on the back wall was a four-foot wide tunnel, pitch black beyond the entrance. Candles positioned around the perimeter of the floor provided some meager lighting. It was more like a dungeon than a typical cellar. And God only knew where that tunnel led. At least he didn't see any sign of Blue. Cooper wondered if the spirit waited for him at the top of those broken stairs.

He looked to his left and focused on the surreal image of a woman lying deathly still on a cot just four feet away. He'd never seen her before. She was old, though not as old as Lillie Mae. Her skin was so pale she looked like she'd been beaten down with a sack of flour. A thick patchwork quilt covered the lower half of her body. With eyes closed, her chest barely moved at all. A long tube taped to the inside of her arm ran red and up to a plastic bag resting near her waist. The bag was half full of dark liquid he assumed was blood.

He glanced up at his grandmother. "Who is that?"

Lillie Mae turned toward the ghostly patient and smiled. "Charlotte."

He decided to forgo the next question since Lillie Mae offered no further information. "What's wrong with her?"

Lillie Mae sighed and looked down, a stray tear trickling out of the corner of her eye. "She's dying."

"Dying?" God. There was that word again.

Lillie Mae nodded and wiped her cheek with the tips or her fingers. "She's been drained of blood for so long, little by little her whole life. Her poor body can't take it anymore."

Everything she said produced a dozen more questions for Cooper. He pushed them aside and eased up on his elbows. "Those… men. Did they hurt you?"

Lillie Mae folded a damp rag in the lap of her soiled floral-print housedress. She reached up absently to the bandage on her neck. Cooper's stomach twisted into a knot of rage. That sick bastard had bitten her.

She shook her head. "I'm fine now. When Stephen came for me, he stared at your picture on the mantel for a long time. That's when I knew what they really wanted. I convinced him to let me collect some of my things and called you from my bedroom."

A familiar pang of guilt settled in Cooper's gut. Lillie Mae had been abducted by freaking vampires while he was out drowning himself in a sea of vodka and go-go boys. She gave a quick shake of her head again. Dammit. She'd probably heard his thoughts.

"Stephen desecrated the good book with his own bloodied finger." Lillie Mae placed her cold hand on Cooper's cheek. "Why didn't you listen to me, son?"

Cooper cupped her hand as if it would break in two with too much pressure. He didn't regret his decision to defy her wishes for a second.

Lillie Mae dropped her hand in her lap. "He didn't force me to come here. I came willingly. I had no choice when he told me that Charlotte was alive and here at Warfield. I had no idea. After all these years…" She stared off, swallowing back errant sobs.

Cooper placed a hand on her knee. "You had no idea of what?"

She looked back at him. "It doesn't matter now." She dismissed the subject with the wave of her hand. "I never wanted you involved in any of this. I tried to protect you from it. Tried to shield you from this world."

Lillie Mae patted his hand once and then stood, her creaking bones announcing every move. She teetered over to the second cot, stood at the end of it, and looked down at the woman.

"They used Charlotte to lure me here, and then used me to lure you." Quivers of regret shook her thin voice. She looked over at him. "The veil of protection I placed on you when you were a child allows for free will. They know that now."

Cooper didn't know how to respond. Nothing she said made any sense. A veil of protection? He sat up slowly and slid his legs over the side of the cot.

Lillie Mae tried to stop him, but he waved her off. "I'm okay. I've got to find us a way out of here." Cooper stood, shaky at first. He fished around in his pants pocket for his phone and came up empty.

He sighed. "Dammit." It was in the pocket of his coat on the floor of the kitchen house above them. With Blue. Terrific. The situation just got better and better. Cooper walked over to the staircase. Several steps were missing, and the ones left didn't appear very sturdy.

He looked back at Lillie Mae and gave her a forced smile of false hope. "I think we can make it to the top, if we're careful."

She shook her head and another tear trickled down her cheek. "You don't understand, sweetheart. It's too late."

"It's not too late." Cooper grabbed the railing along the staircase and inspected its sturdiness with a firm shake. The boards jostled around. Not very promising. He looked back at Lillie Mae and plastered on an artificial smile. "We have plenty of time to get out before the sun goes down."

Lillie Mae looked down at Charlotte. "I can't leave Charlotte here. I won't. I left her once, and God will never forgive me for it. I can't abandon her again."

Cooper looked from Lillie Mae to Charlotte and back, his mind a mess of throbbing pain and confusion. She'd veered into the land of nonsense again. He'd witnessed it before. Clear as a bell one minute and nearly incoherent the next.

He walked over and put a hand on her arm, keeping his voice steady. "We'll go and get help, and then we'll come back for her, I promise. She doesn't look like she should be moved anyway."

Lillie Mae covered his hand with both of hers and squeezed, something she always did when she really wanted his attention. "Didn't you hear me, son? It's too late."

The clarity in her gray eyes startled him. Cooper swallowed hard and willed the impatient tone from his voice. "We have several hours of daylight left. We'll be okay. Now, let's go." He put his arm around her shoulder and nudged her toward the stairs. She wouldn't budge.

"You don't understand." The words slipped from her lips in a strained whisper, dragging down the corners of her mouth. "I couldn't wake you."

A sliver of panic caught in Cooper's throat. "Wait. How long was I out?"

Lillie Mae's eyes pooled with tears. "Hours."

CHAPTER FIFTEEN

Cooper stood just inside the opening of the tunnel and peered into the darkness. Sour air drifted from its depths, singeing his nostrils with the smell of death. He didn't know where the passage led, but he knew in his gut it was not their path to freedom. He had no sense of time, though if he'd been out for *hours* as Lillie Mae said, the sun would set soon, if it hadn't already. He had to get Lillie Mae out of there before Alexander and Stephen returned.

Cooper backed out of the tunnel and crossed the room, glancing over at Lillie Mae and her mysterious patient as he passed. A flicker of candlelight glistened in Lillie Mae's eyes as she nursed the woman on the cot, both sweet and a bit unsettling. Her touch was so gentle, so familial, the way his mother used to nurse him when he was a kid home sick from school. The doting, the tender touches, the eyes full of love and concern, Lillie Mae gave all of it to a complete stranger. *Charlotte.* The woman never once responded or even opened her eyes. The rise and fall of her chest was nearly imperceptible.

Cooper stopped in front of the unstable staircase from

which he'd made his less than graceful entrance and peered up. Running his hands over the rotted boards, he applied pressure cautiously to see if it would hold. He glanced over his shoulder at Lillie Mae. She'd said she wouldn't leave without Charlotte, but he would throw her over his shoulder and carry her out kicking and screaming if he had to. They would send the police back for the woman.

Lillie Mae looked up and flashed him a reproachful glare. He quickly diverted his attention back to the staircase, wondering if she had been peeking around in his head like that his whole life. Scary thought. He went back to formulating a plan. He could probably get himself up onto the lowest remaining step. If he pulled the empty cot over, Lillie Mae could stand on it, and he could pull her up. He didn't know if the stairs would hold up under their combined weight, but he had to try.

Heavy footsteps plodded overhead on the floor of the kitchen house. Cooper looked back at Lillie Mae and raised his index finger to his lips. Her eyes grew wide as she nodded. Easing around to the side of the staircase, Cooper picked up a loose board—one of the steps he'd taken out during his fall. Gripping it with both hands, he stepped back into the shadows. He took a deep, silent breath, readjusted his grip on the board, and raised it over his right shoulder, ready to strike whoever or whatever the hell came down those stairs.

The footsteps above moved toward the cellar door. A moment of silence passed before a heavy boot landed on the first step. The wood structure creaked in protest. Black boots eased down onto the third step. The board could not withstand the weight and snapped in two. A jumble of arms, legs, and curses spilled down the remaining steps, taking a few more out along the way. A man landed on his stomach with a hard thud at the foot of the stairs.

Cooper couldn't tell which one of Lillie Mae's captors it was and didn't care. He stepped out of the shadows and brought the board down hard on the back of a man's head. The rotted wood cracked and split into pieces upon impact.

The intruder rolled over onto his back. "Son of a goddamned bitch!"

Cooper's heart sank. "Randy?"

Randy sat up, rubbing the back of his head. "Jesus H. Christ, Cooper! What the fuck?"

Cooper sighed and helped Randy to his feet. He was out of his police uniform, looking oddly casual in a red flannel shirt and leather bomber jacket. Faded jeans hugged every bulging curve of his lower half.

"Sorry." Cooper ran his fingers through the hair on the back of Randy's head, pushing it clear of the scalp. No blood. "How the hell was I supposed to know it was you?"

Randy slapped red clay off his legs and ass. When he looked up, he stared at Lillie Mae standing at the foot of Charlotte's cot. His eyes lit up.

He hurried over to her with Cooper close behind. "Oh thank God, Aunt Mae." But when he looked down at Charlotte, creases of confusion formed on his dirt-smudged face. "What the…" He walked around to the side of the bed, leaned down, and put two fingers to the side of her neck.

"This woman barely has a pulse. Who is she?" He looked up at Cooper but didn't wait for an answer. "We have to get them both to a hospital right now."

Cooper nodded over his shoulder at the stairs. "You may have just destroyed our only exit."

Randy scanned the room with narrowed eyes. "What the hell is this place?" He looked toward the tunnel opening.

"That's not the way out," Cooper said, resting his hands on his hips. "Trust me."

Lillie Mae stood behind Randy and touched his shoulder. "You shouldn't have come here."

Randy stripped off his leather jacket and draped it carefully around her shoulders. He ran fingers over her face and limbs. "Are you hurt, Aunt Mae?" Taking her by the arm, he led her over to the empty cot and helped her sit. She murmured some unintelligible explanation of her appearance. Touching her hair. Smoothing the wrinkles from her dress. Her eyes grew cloudy. She was fading again.

Cooper stepped up to him, fueled by a combination of panic and relief that Randy had inserted himself into the dangerous situation. "What the hell are you doing here? How did you find me?" He hadn't meant to sound reproachful, but it spilled out before he could stop it.

Randy turned and frowned at Cooper. "I told you to stay put."

Heat flooded Cooper's face. He never liked being told what to do or scolded when he invariably did the exact opposite.

"And what am *I* doing here?" Randy poked a finger in

the center of Cooper's chest. "Looking for you, that's what. I've been calling you all day. I went back to Phipps House, but you weren't there. I figured your stubborn ass would come here even though I already told you I would check it out. Your damn car is parked right out front, and your coat is up there on the floor by the cellar door, Sherlock." Randy shook his head and went over to Charlotte's cot. He ran his thumb and index finger over the tubing that led from a needle taped against her arm to the bag full of blood. "I don't think we should move her. We need to call EMTs."

Cooper gave a curt nod, his cheeks tingling from the lingering sting of Randy's admonishment. "Good luck getting cell service down here." He sat down beside Lillie Mae and put his arm around her, rubbing her shoulders. She fidgeted with her hands, growing agitated.

Randy shoved a hand in the front pocket of his jeans and pulled out a phone. He stared at the screen. "Shit. You're right. No bars."

Lillie Mae reached over and clutched Cooper's forearm, her eyes clear as crystal again. "Cooper. Please. They'll be here soon. You have to go."

Cooper patted her hand. "I'm not leaving you. We're going home. Together."

Randy stepped in front of them. "Who's coming? Does she mean the people who brought her here?"

Before Cooper could explain, Charlotte's eyes shot open, searching and full of terror. Her chest heaved, drawing in a desperate gasp of air. Lillie Mae tried to stand but required Cooper and Randy's assistance getting to her feet. They helped her over to Charlotte's cot and sat her down on the edge.

"It's okay, sweetheart," Lillie Mae whispered through her tears. "I'm here. I won't leave you again. I promise."

Her mouth agape, Charlotte's eyes froze in place, and her body fell eerily still. A final whisper of breath slipped from her mouth. Lillie Mae stared down at her, tears spilling down her cheeks. She laid her head on Charlotte's stomach, her shoulders shaking with silent sobs. Randy touched his fingers to Charlotte's wrist and glanced over his shoulder. He shook his head at Cooper.

Lillie Mae?" Cooper put his hand on her back as gently as he could. "I'm sorry. She's gone now, and we have to go. We have to get you to a hospital."

He put his arms around her and pulled her to her feet, the slight weight of her frame melting into him. Randy took the other side, draping her arm around his neck. She hung between them like a scarecrow as they eased her over to the stairs.

Cooper nodded to a spot against the dirt wall. "Let's sit her down. We'll get you up there, and then I can lift her up to you."

Randy's brow crinkled, and he shook his head. "I hope that thing holds."

They lowered Lillie Mae to the ground, and Cooper looked back at the still body of the mysterious old woman on the cot, wondering whom they were leaving behind. A frigid gust of air billowed out of the tunnel and passed over the candle flames. They danced and flickered in wild patterns around the room. Cooper's pulse quickened, and his throat tightened as a toxic presence closed in on them.

"Come on," Randy said behind him. "Help me up."

Cooper couldn't tear his eyes away from the tunnel, Lillie Mae's earlier words solidifying in his mind. He repeated them under his breath. "It's too late."

CHAPTER SIXTEEN

Alexander Montgomery emerged from the tunnel as if he'd materialized right out of the shadows, his black attire accentuating his already menacing presence. Leather pants stretched over muscled thighs, and a crewneck tee hugged every curve of his torso. His heavy boots raised a cloud of danger in the dirt floor. The unnerving glimmer of his impossibly green eyes exposed the malignity lurking just underneath his carefully constructed image of seductive aggression. He locked eyes with Cooper, and his lips parted slightly, exposing the tiniest glimpse of his fangs. If Cooper hadn't been looking for it, he might have missed it.

"Leaving so soon?" Alexander's voice traveled around the room with a low and steady rumble that almost sounded like a growl. Stephen Parker appeared out of the shadows and sidled up to him.

Randy took a step forward, staring at the pair with suspicious disdain, as if their coiffed hipster appearance offended his masculine sensibilities. "Are these the perps that took Lillie Mae?"

Alexander smiled widely, his gaze drifting down the length of Randy's body and back up again. Cooper wished to God Randy hadn't drawn Alexander's unwelcomed attention.

The Anakim expanded his chest and widened his stance. "I have not yet had the pleasure of meeting you, my friend. I am sure I would have remembered."

Randy huffed. "Friend? Pleasure? I am the fucking deputy chief of police. In case you hadn't noticed, we're standing in the middle of a dirt dungeon with one dead body and a kidnapped woman."

Lillie Mae mumbled something unintelligible behind them. Cooper glanced back at her and then whispered over to Randy. "Be careful. They're not what they seem."

Alexander moved half the length of the room and stopped at the foot of Charlotte's cot. He glanced down at the body and back up, as if the dead woman was of no consequence to him. "Lillie Mae came of her own free will, as I am sure she will attest. No one kidnapped her." He waved a hand over Charlotte's lifeless body. "How could a mother resist rushing to the bedside of her dying child?"

As much as the revelation rattled Cooper internally, he wasn't about to let it show. He stood close enough to Randy that their shoulders touched in a show of solidarity.

Randy stared Alexander down and rested his hands on his hips. "I don't know what's been going on here, but from where I'm standing, things aren't looking too good for you right now, *friend*. And we'll talk about whether or not Lillie Mae came here of her own accord down at the station. Now. You want to do this the easy way, or the hard way?"

The grin on Alexander's face implied he was both amused and charmed by Randy.

Stephen moved to Alexander's side and snarled at Randy through gritted teeth. "Let me rip this idiot hick's throat out."

Randy squared his shoulders and edged forward. Cooper held his arm out, blocking his advance. "Don't get any closer to them." He knew Randy had no clue who, or what, he was dealing with here. His badge and his brawn meant nothing to those creatures.

Randy pushed Cooper's arm away and walked right up to the Anakim, his six feet four inches of muscled mass nearly matching Alexander's. "Here's what's going to happen, Princess. First we're going to get Lillie Mae out of this hellhole. Then I am going to call this in, and my officers will be here in a matter of minutes to personally escort you and Pretty Boy there down to the station."

Cooper didn't know what was about to happen, but he was relatively sure it wasn't going to go down the way Randy had just mapped it out. His chest tightened, and he flexed his fingers at his side. He had to do something before Randy got them all killed. Their options dwindled fast.

Alexander chuckled and backed away with his arms raised in mock surrender. "Of course, you are free to go, Officer. You can even take Lillie Mae with you, if you like. She has outlived her usefulness, much like Charlotte here." He narrowed his eyes on Cooper. "But he stays. You will stay, won't you, Cooper?"

The threat was obvious and real. Stay, and Randy and

Lillie Mae might get out of there alive. Leave, and all bets were off. Cooper only had one alternative left, and he prayed it worked this time.

Randy huffed. "The hell he's staying. Let's go, Cooper." Randy turned his back on Alexander. A mistake.

Alexander twisted his face and extended his fangs as he left the ground.

Cooper shoved Randy out the way. With a quick, deep breath, he corralled all the anxiety, fear, and anger in his core. He opened his mind to the darkness lurking deep inside him and released himself to it. The dark power answered his call, burning like steel rods under his skin. As Alexander lunged forward, a jolt of electrical current seized Cooper's body and expelled itself through the tips of his burning fingers. Alexander received the full impact, sailing backward and taking Stephen down with him. They both slammed hard against the dirt wall and fell face-forward onto the ground.

Cooper's heart pounded in his chest. His ears burned, and his skin tingled all over. He looked down at his still throbbing hands. He'd done it. Unleashed the beast—in front of Randy, no less. Shit. Cooper peered over his shoulder, a sliver of panic catching in his throat. Randy stared at him, eyes wide with a mixture of shock and fear. Cooper looked back at the two downed Anakim bodies. He didn't know how long they would stay that way.

Ignoring Randy's frozen state, Cooper hurried back over to Lillie Mae. "Help me get her up those stairs."

Randy stood motionless, gaping at Cooper.

Cooper draped Lillie Mae's arm over his shoulder and lifted her, emboldened by the successful exertion of his power but with no time to relish in the small victory. "Randy. *Now!*"

As if on autopilot, Randy walked over with glazed eyes and took Lillie Mae's other arm. They moved her gently toward the stairs. A cool breeze tickled the rim of Cooper's ears, and the hairs on the back of his neck sprang to attention. Never a good sign when you're trapped in a dungeon with supernatural creatures. He stopped and craned his neck around. Alexander stood with Stephen at his side, his face twisted into a menacing scowl.

"Bravo, Cooper. You finally embraced the demon inside you. Makes you an eminently more interesting companion. Too bad your friend will suffer for your insolence."

The blatant threat to Randy made Cooper's blood boil in his veins. He shifted all of Lillie Mae's weight over to Randy and took a step toward the two men. He would show those toothy motherfuckers what the demon inside him was capable of, and he wouldn't hold anything back this time. He would send those bastards up in flames if he had to. In truth, he wanted to feel that intoxicating combination of surrender and dominance again.

Stretching his arms out in front of him, he pointed his fingers at the Anakim. "Go back to whatever hell you crawled out of, you son of a bitch."

But the expected rush of burning magic coursing through his veins never came. The room around him vanished. Cooper looked down. At his feet lay Trevor's body, fully uniformed and twisted at an impossible angle. Cooper stared down into those vacant eyes, and the horror of what he'd done paralyzed him once again.

Randy's voice echoed from somewhere behind, dragging him back into the moment. "Cooper! Look out!"

Cooper looked up. Alexander had closed the distance between them, his mouth twisting into a sneer. "Your parlor tricks are amusing but quite unreliable, it seems, Divinum." Alexander's fangs glistened in the candlelight, completely transfixing Cooper. Randy had to have seen them that time. "So. What will it be? You?" He nodded over Cooper's shoulder. "Or them?"

At a loss for words, Cooper stood there, gaping. He couldn't put Randy and Lillie Mae's lives at risk. But Betsy's dire warning about what would happen if Alexander got hold of his blood plagued his conflicted thoughts.

A small tornado of black smoke surged down through the cellar door with an ear-shattering howl and swirled around the room. Randy shrank back and pulled Lillie Mae close to him. The dark mass knocked Cooper to the ground and settled right in front of Alexander, solidifying into the shape of a woman. Betsy. With squared shoulders and a dagger raised in each hand, she glared at Alexander. Stephen crouched defensively and hissed at her through bared fangs.

"Holy mother of God," Randy's voice echoed from behind. "What the hell are these people?"

Cooper scrambled over to Lillie Mae and Randy, leaving the supernatural creatures to their standoff. He got to his feet and draped Lillie Mae's arm over his shoulder. "Randy! Let's go!" Randy finally moved and helped him carry Lillie Mae over to the stairs. Cooper kept a watchful eye on the three Anakim the whole time.

Stephen made his move. He leaped and was instantly behind Betsy, knocking the dagger out of her right hand and drawing her focus. Alexander rounded on her and sunk his teeth into her neck. Betsy cried out—a shrill wail that dropped Cooper's heart in his chest. She drew her left hand up, driving the second dagger into Alexander's stomach and ramming her elbow into Stephen's face.

"Cooper!" Randy said, demanding his full attention. He shifted Lillie Mae's weight over to Cooper. Standing facing the broken stairs, Randy jumped up, catching hold of the lowest and sturdiest looking step. The whole staircase wobbled and creaked in protest, but Randy managed to pull himself up. They would be lucky if the whole structure didn't crumble.

Cooper tried his best to ignore the grunts, hisses, and wails behind him, lifting Lillie Mae's frail body high enough for Randy to get his arms under her shoulders. Her head bobbed from side to side. She was completely out of it. Only after Randy had safely navigated her up the broken maze of stairs, did Cooper dare to look behind him again.

Betsy crouched in front of Alexander and Stephen, successfully holding them at bay for the moment. Alexander held his stomach and hissed at Betsy. Thick black liquid seeped through his fingers. He looked over and leveled a threatening glare at Cooper. His head fell back and lips peeled up over his fangs. A primal screech emanated from his throat and grew louder by the second, the pitch rising higher and higher. A chorus of reciprocal screeches echoed from somewhere deep inside the earthen walls around them. Cooper's blood turned to ice in his veins.

Betsy looked back at him, her eyes wild. "Cooper, run!"

Before he could comply, a rumble sounded from the depths of the tunnel, like a charging herd of cattle. The floor shook. Dirt trickled down the walls all around the room. Cooper couldn't tear his eyes away from the tunnel. He wished he had. One ghastly changeling after another spilled out of the tunnel. Rotted skin hung off exposed bones. Empty eye sockets oozed black blood. Jaws full of razor-sharp fangs snapped at the air. Daggerlike fingers clawed their way over each other. Cooper turned back to the staircase. Randy stood on the top step, holding onto Lillie Mae, staring back at the horde of monsters wide-eyed and slack-jawed.

"Cooper, go!" Betsy barked behind him.

When he looked back, a dozen monsters had circled her, sizing up their prey. One charged her from behind. Cooper snapped to his senses. Without thinking, he threw out his right hand toward the monster. Nothing happened. No jolt of power seized his body. No rush of heat flooded his veins. Only Trevor's vacant eyes clouded his mind.

Betsy spun around, nailing the attacker square in the chest with a dagger. It wailed and fell back, twisting on the ground in a puddle of the black tar that poured from its wound. She fought off three other changelings at once, as even more emerged from the tunnel. The room filled with monsters so fast that Cooper lost track of Alexander and Stephen.

Randy's voice came from above. "Goddammit, Cooper, get the hell out of there!"

Cooper looked up. Randy stared down at him through the cellar door on his hands and knees, reaching down for him.

Cooper jumped up and grabbed onto the closest step. It held. He pulled himself up on the staircase, the entire structure moving under his weight. Another step and his left foot sank through a rotted board. He steadied himself and wriggled free. Only three more steps to go. The moment he made contact with Randy's outstretched hand, the structure gave way under him. With a grip around Cooper's wrist, Randy pulled him up and through the cellar door. They both scrambled away from the opening and over to where Lillie Mae sat on the floor by the front window. Though her eyes were wide and clear, Cooper doubted she truly understood their situation.

Randy panted beside him. "What in holy hell are those things?"

Out of breath himself, Cooper couldn't speak. He shook his head.

Betsy flew up out of the cellar door, landing hard in the center of the room. Her hair was wild around her face. Deep gashes littered her clothing, exposing ripped flesh and oozing, black blood. "Get to your car and go straight to Phipps House," she said in a steady and sure tone. "Once you are back there with Lillie Mae, you'll be safe. I'll hold them off as long as I can."

Randy scrambled to his feet and pointed at Lillie Mae. "She needs a hospital!"

Betsy leveled a steely glare on him. "I said straight to Phipps House." The not-so-subtle growl in her throat shut Randy down cold.

Cooper gathered up Lillie Mae with one arm behind her head and one under her legs and stood. Randy grabbed Cooper's coat from the floor, like it mattered, and led them outside to the SUV, primal howls and piercing screeches chasing them the whole way. Without giving his pristine red pickup a second look, Randy opened the back door of the SUV. Cooper eased Lillie Mae onto the seat, gently laying her on her side and closing the door. He jumped into the driver's seat and fumbled around in his pants pocket for the keys. Randy slid into the passenger's seat without looking at Cooper, adding a chilly layer to the already heightened anxiety inside the car.

After three failed attempts getting the key inserted into the ignition, Cooper finally rammed it in and turned. The engine instantly roared to life. Shoving the gear stick into reverse, he pressed the gas pedal all the way to the floor and spun the tires in the sand before finally gaining some traction and rocketing backward.

Randy shot a look out the back window. "Tree!"

Cooper glanced up. The imposing trunk of live oak filled the rearview mirror. He slammed on the brakes and yanked the steering wheel hard to the right. The SUV lurched and slung them both across the cab, stopping with a jerk just inches away from the massive live oak. As the car settled, they both stared out the front windshield. Betsy charged out of the kitchen house door, frantically waving them away. Cooper wasted no time getting the gear stick into drive and flooring it. They sped down Oak Alley, the backend of the SUV weaving a path from side to side in the sand. They headed for the dim outline of the stone gates in the distance, and a tiny flame of hope ignited inside Cooper. He had Lillie Mae back, and they just might live through the godforsaken night.

Randy twisted in his seat, looking out the back window. "Christ almighty."

Cooper glanced up at the rearview mirror, which framed the shrinking moonlit image of a woman. A warrior. Alone. She did not run. She stood facing the kitchen house, a dagger raised in each hand as a swarm of changelings poured out of the door, heading straight for her.

CHAPTER SEVENTEEN

"Cooper? Is that you, honey?" Lillie Mae's voice crackled. She opened her drooping eyelids for the first time since they'd made it safely back to Phipps House.

Cooper sat beside her on the lumpy down-filled mattress, wiping away the final traces of dirt from her face with a damp cloth. "I'm here."

It had been a night straight from Hell. Though he didn't understand the magic that protected Phipps House, Betsy was right. The second he stepped inside its walls with Lillie Mae in his arms, he knew it in his bones. They were safe. He laid the cloth on the side table and pulled the quilt up to her neck to shield her from the random pockets of cold air drifting around the drafty bedroom. Even covered by Cooper's coat and with the heater in the SUV going full blast, she'd shivered all the way home. Randy hadn't looked at or spoken to Cooper the whole time. After he helped Cooper get Lillie Mae in bed, he had left the room without a word. Cooper had no idea what Randy thought of him after all he'd witnessed.

Cooper stroked Lillie Mae's hair. Once a majestic crown of copper glory, it was now wet and matted with sweat—coarse, stringy, and the color of Spanish moss after a full day of rain. The skin on her face drooped over her cheek and jawbones. She looked so frail it broke Cooper's heart to meet her eyes.

She's dying. Betsy's words echoed in his brain.

He forced a smile. "Everything's okay. We're safe now." He wasn't sure which one of them he was trying to convince.

Lillie Mae gave a slight shake of her head, and her eyes sagged. "Not okay. Not safe. My power is fading. I can't protect you much longer."

He didn't know what to say, so he just rubbed the back of her hand and looked down. He'd spent a few peaceful moments while Lillie Mae slept, thinking they were out of danger and that the nightmare was over. Lillie Mae was back, and Alexander would just go away and leave them alone. He knew in his gut that was foolish thinking. Now that Charlotte was gone, he was Alexander's last hope for creating his army of bloodsuckers. It wasn't over. Not by a long shot.

"Charlotte?" she asked, as if he'd spoken the name aloud.

"I'm afraid she didn't make it. Remember?"

The clarity in Lillie Mae's eyes waned, the sedative he'd given her taking effect. He might not have much time before she faded away again.

Cooper squeezed her hand. "Alexander called her your child."

Lillie Mae managed a weak smile accompanied by a long wispy sigh. "She was my daughter. Before Mary."

The simple mention of his mother's name silenced Cooper. He could count on one hand the number of times Lillie Mae or Grandpa Joe had spoken Mary's name since her death over twenty years ago. She was their pride and joy, their only child, and a rare beauty inside and out. Her death nearly destroyed them. A devout Christian her whole life, Lillie Mae had never again set foot inside a church. In stark contrast, Grandpa Joe stopped his notorious drinking cold and started going to church for the first time in his life. Never missed a Sunday after that until the day he died, believing his daughter's death was punishment for his abuse of alcohol and the many betrayals of his marriage vows.

"You never mentioned having another daughter. Not in my whole life can I remember you or Grandpa Joe or even Mama mentioning her."

"Joe wasn't her father, and your mama never even knew about her. And I... well, I thought she'd died when she was just a baby."

Cooper picked at a loose thread in the seam of the quilt. "He had her? All this time?"

The soft lines on Lillie Mae's face petrified in an instant, and her eyes grew cloudy. "Yes. He took her. That monster stole my baby and used her up all these years. Her blood was special, like yours and mine."

Cooper leaned forward, hoping to hold her attention. "Alexander, you mean."

She looked up at him. Something akin to fear filled her eyes. "Terrible thing I did, son. Horrible thing. That thing inside you. That darkness. It'll make you do terrible things.

And God made me pay for it. He gave me the cancer. Gave it to your mama, too. Then he took Joe from me, and your brother. Now he's taken my only living child away before I even had a chance to know her."

Cooper leaned back and relaxed his shoulders. It was the first time she'd ever mentioned the dark nature they shared.

"You have to leave here, Cooper." Lillie Mae touched his face with arthritis-twisted fingers. "He'll take you, too. To make me pay for the horrible things I've done."

Cooper wasn't sure if she meant God or Alexander, but it really didn't matter. She was confused again. He stroked her hair. "You haven't done anything horrible. You're a good person. Best person I know. Everything is going to be all right now."

She took his hand in hers, a sadness brimming in her eyes. "No, son. It's not going to be all right. I wish it could be. Promise me you'll leave here, Cooper. Promise me you'll go as far away as possible." Her eyes clouded over again. She used to be sharp as a tack but had grown more forgetful over the years, maybe more than he realized. Did she even know what she was saying? He couldn't make her a promise he knew he wouldn't keep.

"It's late. Get some rest." He touched her cheek with the back of his hand. "We'll talk in the morning." He stood up and brushed the wrinkles out of the quilt where he'd been sitting.

"RJ was there," Lillie Mae whispered with half-raised eyelids.

Cooper leaned over her and pushed the hair off her

forehead with his fingers. “Yes, he was. I think he’s still here.” At least Cooper hoped he was.

“He’s such a sweet boy,” she said. “Thinks the world of you. Asks about you all the time.” She closed her eyes and released a breath of sleepy air through her slightly parted lips.

Cooper didn’t know how to respond, so he didn’t. Instead, he leaned over and kissed her forehead, trying not to put too much stock into her ramblings. But he warmed at the idea of Randy asking about him. After all these years, he still thought of Cooper.

“Go talk to him,” Lillie Mae whispered as she drifted off. “He must be confused. And scared.”

She was right. If Randy was still around, they had a lot to hash out. He tucked the quilt snug around her shoulders and headed toward the door.

Mumbled words from Lillie Mae made him pause and look back. “What was that?”

Her words were thick with the slur of sleep. “Good people can do bad things.”

CHAPTER EIGHTEEN

Cooper double and triple-checked the lock on the front door, as if a simple oak door could stop Alexander and his minions. Betsy insisted they would be safe there. Some kind of *veil of protection spell* Lillie Mae cast over Phipps House. As long as she was in the house, nothing got in that wasn't invited. He hoped to God Betsy was right, and that she made it out of Warfield alive.

Cooper pulled back the sheers and peeked through the sidelight, Lillie Mae's words haunting him.

Good people can do bad things.

Releasing the fabric with a slight shudder, he ran his fingers through his hair. No way could his grandmother's past sins be as bad as his. He shuffled down the hallway toward the kitchen, his wool socks slipping on the slick hardwood floor. Randy's voice drifted out of the kitchen. Cooper had to face him. The things that happened at Warfield, the things Randy saw him do… he couldn't imagine what must be going through the guy's head. The sound of Betsy's voice quickened his heartbeat and slowed his steps. She'd made it. He stood just outside the doorway and listened. A noticeable edge laced her tone.

"If Alexander knows how you feel, he'll use it against Cooper," she whispered. "Your presence puts him in danger."

The breath caught in Cooper's throat, and he was careful not to move on the creaky hardwood. Randy offered no response. Betsy likely detected his presence and silenced Randy on purpose, so Cooper exhaled and went in.

They hovered over the distressed wood island in the center of the room but dispersed like rats the moment he entered. Betsy crossed her arms and leaned against refrigerator. She didn't have any particular expression, like she was neither happy nor sad to see him. You would never have known she'd just fought off a small army of monsters. Randy rested his butt against the sink and stared at the floor. Tension hung thick in the air between them.

Cooper stepped into the middle of the room and looked at Betsy. "You made it." He sounded more astonished than he'd meant to and hoped she wasn't offended. A deep cut ran from under her mussed hair down the side of her neck. He cocked his head at her. "Do you need a doctor?"

A scowl of disapproval crossed her lips, and she raised an eyebrow. "Really, Cooper?"

He shoved his hands in his pants pockets and rocked forward on his toes. "Right. Guess I should've seen that one coming."

She grinned a little. "From a mile away." She touched the gash. "It will heal soon. Just a little scratch. Besides, it was worth it. I managed to take out at least a dozen of those nasty bastards."

"Yeah," Randy huffed. "You should have seen all of the other little scratches, cuts, and bruises she had when she showed up out of nowhere a few minutes ago. They just disappeared one by one. Like they were never there." He shrugged his shoulders at Cooper and rolled his eyes. He wasn't taking this well.

Cooper considered crossing the kitchen and giving Betsy a hug. She had, after all, saved the two most important people in his tiny little world tonight. He chose words instead.

"Thank you," he said, the corners of his eyes moist and itchy. Damn that was annoying. "If it wasn't for you, we wouldn't be standing here right now."

"Damn right you wouldn't." A glaze of scorn coated her eyes. "What the hell were you thinking going back there, Cooper? I told you it was too dangerous. Don't you understand what's at stake here?"

She glared at him a moment before her eyes finally softened. She walked over and touched his arm. Though her fingertips were like five tiny ice cubes searing through his shirt to his skin, she squeezed him gently. Maternal, even. Her fingers lingered a second too long for his guarded comfort level. He stepped back, pulling away from her touch.

"This is all very sweet," Randy said, disrupting the awkward moment. "But will one of you kindly explain what the hell happened back there? Because I feel like I'm trapped in an episode of the motherfucking *Twilight Zone* here."

He had lost the professional reserve of their earlier meeting. This was the Randy that Cooper remembered from their youth, and the familiarity comforted him.

"What the hell were those things?" Randy demanded. "And who were the two fancy boys with the jacked-up dental work?"

Cooper and Betsy exchanged glances. How much should they tell him?

Randy pointed to Betsy. "Don't even get me started on Xena, Warrior Princess over here. And the two creepy old ladies I met in the front room who said they lived here a hundred fifty years ago?" He threw up his hands and let them fall with a loud slap against denim-clad thighs. "Hell, I must be as crazy as they are, because after everything I saw tonight, hell if I don't believe them!"

Cooper sighed. He'd forgotten all about the twins.

"And you, Cooper." Randy shook his head.

Cooper stared at him, a little put off by Randy's tone.

Randy squinted. "What did you do to them? With your hands? It was like you shot them with invisible bullets or some shit. I mean, Christ almighty, Coop. What the hell was that?"

Overwhelmed by Randy's completely valid questions, which really only scratched the surface, Cooper didn't know where to start. He peered up at Betsy. "Help me out here, will you?"

She uncrossed her arms and stepped up to the island opposite Randy. "My name is Elizabeth Parker."

Cooper leaned in, confused. "Elizabeth Parker? You wrote that name on the family tree in Lillie Mae's Bible."

She nodded and looked down.

"You're Sally Parker's mother? My..." Cooper tried counting back the generations in his head but quickly gave up. This just kept getting better and better. Now he had a freaking vampire granny.

Betsy returned her attention to Randy. "The young blond man with Alexander is my son, Stephen. He and Alexander are both Anakim."

Randy's mouth hung open. "Ana-who?"

Still a little jarred by Betsy's familial revelations, Cooper redirected his focus on Randy. "*Anakim*. Betsy is one too, but she's also a slayer." He nodded and crossed his arms over his chest, as if the information he'd just imparted sounded completely sane and reasonable.

Randy stared at him. "A slayer?" His voice was barely more than a whisper. "Like Buffy?"

"Yes! Like Buffy."

Betsy rested her hands on the island and cocked an eyebrow. "Who the hell is this Buffy person? And this Princess Xena? I think I would very much like to meet them."

Cooper shook his head at her. "Skip it. Trust me."

She shrugged and pushed her thick, wavy hair over her shoulder.

"Yes, like Buffy, *sort of*," Cooper said to Randy. He looked over at Betsy. "Those creatures that attacked us at Warfield? They were like the one that was here last night. Changelings, right?"

Betsy looked at him and then to Randy. Cooper knew she was wondering if Randy would be able to handle any more reality-dismantling tonight. He gave Randy a quick glance and knew instantly his childhood pal would be fine. Tonight was probably the most fucked-up night in Randy's entire life, but he was a rock. Always had been. Cooper nodded for her to continue.

"Yes, they were changelings." She let the words hang in the air a moment. "When Anakim drain humans to the point of death, we have the power to turn them into our kind after their heart stops beating. If this process happens within a matter of a few minutes after death, the human will transform into Anakim, looking much like they did before they died. Better even. Taller, stronger, faster. They will have the same memories, the same qualities, and traits. They will basically be the same person, though an enhanced version of that person with a few unfortunate peculiarities."

Randy stared at her like he'd just been told the Easter Bunny and Santa Claus were completely real. He rubbed his eyes. "Please tell me I'm dreaming."

Betsy shook her head. "The longer the Anakim waits before turning their kill, the less they will resemble their human selves after the transition. Our blood is poison. It's harmless enough in small doses—restorative even, but the decomposition process goes into overdrive if an Anakim drains you completely and too much time passes. The brain gets scrambled. Rage and hunger become the only motivation, and you get what Alexander has created—walking corpses with fangs and enhanced strength but no capacity for reason. Well, none other than an innate and complete loyalty to their maker. Alexander has created a changeling army from the dregs of society to protect himself. All mutated versions of their former selves. Think of them as overripe vampires."

Randy's eyes were blank. "Overripe vampires." He covered his face with his hands and exhaled slowly.

Cooper and Betsy exchanged glances and waited, giving Randy a second to process the insane information.

"If I hadn't seen it for myself..." Randy lowered his hands and shook his head. "And what does this Alexander creep plan to do with his army of zombie vampires?"

Betsy moved toward Randy, and he stiffened. He stood completely erect, with his shoulders back and his fists clenched, like he would lay her out if she got any closer, fanged supernatural creature or not. Betsy took a respectful step back. She told Randy about Jericho, the war, and the Sterilus-A virus while he stared at her blankly. Cooper didn't see the need to reveal the biblical implications he had uncovered. No sense in completely deconstructing Randy's worldview all in one conversation.

When Betsy paused, Randy threw up his hands and shrugged. "So why imprison two helpless old ladies in a dungeon?"

Betsy walked over to the sink and peered out the window. "The blood of my daughter's descendants contains unique mystical properties and dark power. Alexander needs their blood because it can reverse the effects of the sterility virus. Without it, he cannot build his army of Anakim followers and changelings. Cooper is now his last and only source for it."

Randy scrunched up his dirty blond eyebrows. "How is Cooper the source...?" Randy peered over at Cooper. "Wait. Your daughter's descendants. Aunt Mae? That woman with her in the dungeon?"

Cooper shifted nervously. "That woman was Lillie Mae's daughter. She was like Lillie Mae. Like me."

Randy's focus drifted back to Betsy. "Do you mean witches?"

Betsy stood silent with her back to them.

Randy raised his voice a couple of decibels. "Aunt Mae and Cooper are goddamn witches?"

Betsy turned on her heel to face them. "Not witches. Divinum. The seed of the Seraphim, with powers you cannot begin to imagine."

Randy stared at Cooper, his eyes blank and unreadable.

Cooper's muscles grew rigid under the intense inspection. He couldn't imagine how Randy must see him now. As his best friend's whiney little brother? Or the monster he really was?

Betsy slung her hair over her shoulder. The scar on her neck had vanished without a trace. "When Lillie Mae is gone, Cooper will be the last Divinum of the Phipps line and the last descendent of my daughter, Sally. Lillie Mae has cancer. Her blood is tainted, and she will die soon. She is no good to Alexander. Charlotte carried the anomaly in her blood but did not have the Seraphic gene. There was only so much he could do subsisting on her blood all those years. Now that she is gone, Alexander will stop at nothing to get at Cooper. He has both the Seraphic gene and the mutation in his blood. If Alexander has a lifetime supply of his blood, the human race will never be safe again. People would be nothing more to him than a food supply and potential soldiers. Slaves."

Cooper's body went numb, realizing what Alexander meant by *stay with me*. A blood slave. He rubbed his itchy eyes. He wanted to get away from this madness. Just take Lillie Mae and run. Take her to the farthest corner of the world where Alexander would never be able to find them. Let this insane war run its course without him. But he knew that wasn't an option anymore. Not if he was Alexander's last hope of building his army. They would never be safe as long as Alexander lived. Randy would never be safe either.

Cooper stood in front of Randy, fighting the urge to put a hand on his shoulder. "I know this is all a lot to take in, but now you understand why we can't just call your police buddies like you wanted. They would be slaughtered before they could draw their weapons. And Alexander could unleash those monsters on the town for sport." Cooper took a step back and squared his shoulders. "Look, I don't want you getting involved any more than you already have. And I know what I am must disgust you, frighten you. Hell, I don't blame you for that. I scare the shit out of myself sometimes. So just go, okay? You shouldn't be here." He walked around to the opposite side of the island, putting a barrier between them to make Randy more comfortable.

Randy flashed him a chilly glare. "Can you give us a minute, Xena?" His steady, authoritative voice was back.

Betsy was gone before Cooper could glance her way, only the slight rock of the swinging door left in her wake.

Randy stared at the door and shook his head. "Damn, that's creepy." He walked around the island and stood beside Cooper. They both leaned forward against it, side by side with their arms touching and looking straight ahead. Neither said anything for a solid minute. The silence unnerved Cooper.

Randy finally nudged Cooper's arm gently with his elbow. "So, that's why you've been acting weird since we left Warfield?"

Cooper looked over at him. "*Me* acting weird?"

Randy shook and lowered his head. "Coop, you really believe that I think you're disgusting because of what you did tonight?"

Cooper ran his fingers through his hair nervously. "The look on your face in that dungeon when you saw what I could do. I thought..."

Randy shook his head and released an extended sigh. "Cooper, tonight I saw three vampire *things* trying to rip each other's throats out, a horde of demonic-looking zombie fuckers charging out of a hole in the ground trying to rip our faces off, and two old lady ghosts sipping tea in the front room. Yeah. Seeing you do your John Wayne-voodoo shit was the icing on one really fucked-up cake."

A moment of silence passed before they both shook with stifled laughter. It felt good to laugh in the midst of all the chaos. Cooper searched Randy's honey-brown eyes and saw that flicker of something tender again. His knee-jerk reaction was to shut it down. Batten down the hatches around his heart. But this was Randy, for Christ's sake. Not some nameless mark at the bar.

Randy faced him. "Look, I don't understand what you can do, Red. And yes. At first, it freaked me the hell out. But I think it's amazing. Freaky as hell, for damn sure, but amazing. That's not why I couldn't look at you in the truck or why I couldn't talk to you when we first got back here."

"It's not?" Jesus Christ. He sounded like a lovesick puppy. He needed to get a grip. This was *not* what he thought it was.

Randy's smile faded, and he broke eye contact. "It's just that… when I looked down through that cellar door and saw those vampire-zombie things swarming around you, I thought it was over. I thought you were gone. Forever this time."

A single embarrassed tear scurried down Randy's cheek and ran to hide under his jaw. Cooper was stunned into silence. He looked at Randy, staring up at his stubbled jaw and waiting, his lungs working overtime for oxygen.

Randy rubbed his eyes with the tips of his fingers. "I know we haven't seen each other in a long time, but it always made me feel good knowing you were out in the world somewhere, living life on your own terms. Happy. You're so brave, Coop."

Happy? Brave? Randy obviously didn't know him very well. Turmoil glazed his friend's eyes. Cooper wanted to reach out and touch his face. He wanted to hug him, to hold him. Jesus Christ, he wanted to kiss him so damn bad. He needed to get hold of himself, but years of unrequited pining boiled over inside him and before he knew what he was doing, he leaned in. Target locked. Randy's lips.

The moment changed from tender to awkward in less than a second.

Randy turned his head away right before Cooper made contact. He wiped his eyes with the back of his hand and stepped away from the island, like he hadn't even seen Cooper's advance. Of course, he had. Cooper winced. That familiar knot formed in his stomach, and he snapped back to reality. Blood rushed to his cheeks.

"Wow," Randy said, looking down at his watch. "It's after eleven. I have to be at the station at six."

Cooper didn't respond. Even though he knew that only made Randy more uncomfortable, he couldn't help it. He seethed inside, his anger directed both at Randy and himself for opening his heart and making such a dumbass move. *Again.*

All signs of vulnerability had vanished from Randy's face. He smiled the good-buddy smile. The childhood-friend smile. Invisible walls flew up all around him, shutting Cooper out completely.

"So. Do you feel safe here, now? Like Buffy said?" Randy moved toward the back door, putting even more space between them.

Cooper nodded and looked down. He wasn't used to having his advances rebuffed. He should have known better, having been down the very same road once before with Randy years ago.

Randy cleared his throat and tucked his thumbs in the pockets of his jeans. "Good. All this *vampire-witchy* stuff—I need some time to get my head around it, if you know what I mean."

Cooper looked up, heat rising on his neck, his words pointed. “I know exactly what you mean.”

Randy inched toward the back door, finally making contact with the knob. “You have my number if you need anything, right?”

Cooper plastered on a fake smile. “Don’t worry about me. I’ll be fine. I’m always fine.” His insides burned. He curled his fingers inside fists. A familiar rumble churned in his core.

“Bye, Coop.” Randy nodded, lowered his head, and walked out the door.

When the reverberation of the glass panes in the door stilled, the kitchen was silent. Cooper stood staring at everything and at nothing. Alone. The raging darkness inside him his only refuge.

CHAPTER NINETEEN

Cooper entered the sitting room and ran smack into an icy wall of silence. Betsy stood regal and on guard at the front window. Eunice knitted in the occasional chair by the fireplace. Perched in the center of the sofa, Eudora's nose was so deep in a book that he couldn't even see her eyes. None of them looked his way.

Betsy spoke with her back to him. "He could be dangerous."

"Who, Randy?" He walked over to her.

She faced him. Her eyes were like two black pebbles resting at the bottom of a shallow creek bed, shimmering in the light but cold and hard just the same. "Yes," she said. "Randy."

"Very handsome, that one," Eunice mumbled, still focused on her knitting. "They certainly did not build young men like that back when I courted."

Betsy took a graceful step toward him. "He has feelings for you. Alexander will pick up on that if he hasn't already. He will use Randy against you, and we can't afford to give him that kind of leverage."

Cooper stifled a chuckle. "Okay, let me just stop you right there. I think you are confused about something. Randy may be sweet, sensitive, and gorgeous, but he's about as heterosexual as they come. Trust me. I know firsthand. He was married for fifteen years. The boy is as straight as I am gay. The only feelings he has for me are as a close friend of the family."

She studied his face for a moment. "Are you trying to convince me or yourself?"

Cooper dismissed Betsy's musings with the shake of his head. He could never bring himself to hope for such a thing. The potential disappointment was far too great.

"This word, *gay*," Eudora said, lowering her book. "I think I am missing its contemporary meaning."

Eunice huffed and looked up. "God's balls, Dora! It means he prefers men to women. Even I know that." Her voice was so thin and piercing Cooper winced.

He walked over, rested his hands on the back of the sofa, and glowered at Eunice. "It's an *orientation*—not a *preference,* or a *choice* for that matter. Like how even though I would *prefer* not to be sitting here talking to dead people, I apparently don't have a *choice* in the matter."

Eudora craned her head around to him, her eyebrows rising until they nearly reached her hairline. God. Now he was arguing with dead witches over proper homosexual terminology. He'd officially lost it.

Cooper looked at Betsy and leaned against the back of the couch. "In any case, I don't think Randy will be around much anymore."

Betsy nodded. "Good. Reinforcements should be here tomorrow morning."

Cooper crossed his arms and cocked his head at her. "Reinforcements?"

"Jericho." She mumbled the word as if it was of no consequence. "The Manheeg insisted."

She obviously was in no mood for chitchat. That or she was hiding something. Cooper wasn't having it. He was tired of being kept in the dark when he was the one supposedly in so much danger. "The Manheeg?"

Betsy glanced up at him, waving her hand in dismissal. "The leader of the Jericho army."

Cooper dropped it and sat in the wingback chair opposite the sofa. He rubbed his eyes and then stared from one Phipps twin to the other. For a moment, neither of them regarded him at all, so he cleared his throat. They both looked up at him with simultaneously raised eyebrows and tightly pursed lips. The mirror effect was damn creepy.

"I just wanted to make sure you were really here," he said, scratching the back of his head. "I feel like I'm going a little nuts."

"Well, where else in the world would we be, dear?" Eudora said with saccharin sarcasm.

"This *is* our house," Eunice said under her breath.

Eudora glanced over her shoulder at her sister. "Not anymore, sister."

"It's Lillie Mae's house," Cooper said definitively. "Lillie Mae is still around. Don't forget that. You are in her house, though I don't have the slightest idea why."

"We left Phipps House to Lillie Mae in our wills," Eudora said, as if it was the most obvious thing in the world. "She was the only living Phipps heir at the time. When she is gone, it will be yours."

Cooper leaned forward in his chair. He didn't care about the house and certainly didn't want to discuss what would happen when Lillie Mae was gone. But he had to admit he was curious about the remaining blanks in his family tree. "Lillie Mae's maiden name is Carter, not Phipps."

Eudora sat her book down on the coffee table. She picked up the picture of Sally, still stained with a bloody thumbprint. Betsy looked over Eudora's shoulder at the picture, bit her bottom lip, and retreated back to the front window.

"Your grandmother," Eudora said, "was only raised by the Carter family. She was not born a Carter."

"Thank God for that at least," Eunice said through a series of overdone snorts. "Nothing more than a pack of wild animals, if you ask me."

Eudora stared at the picture. "Lillie Mae's mother was Sarabeth."

Betsy physically winced at the mention of the name he recalled from the family tree in the Bible. "I will check around the house." In a whirl of thick black smoke, she disappeared from the room.

Eunice coughed twice and waved her hands around. "God's balls, I wish she wouldn't do that. You know what they say about second-hand smoke!"

Eudora smiled. "The subject of Sarabeth is a mite tender for our sister."

Cooper sat straight up in the chair. "Your *sister*? Betsy?"

"Hard to believe, isn't it?" Eunice said with an overdramatic roll of her eyes.

Eudora nodded. "Yes. Elizabeth is our older sister. She was Elizabeth Phipps before she married Jonathan Parker. They had three children, Andrew, Stephen—"

"And Sally." Cooper finished her sentence, his familial connection to the Phipps name finally solidified in his mind. "Betsy wasn't like you, was she? With the magic? Or Divinum stuff, I mean."

Eunice huffed. "No. Elizabeth was a *huge* disappointment to the family when she turned eighteen without exhibiting any Divinum power. The Phipps line was nearly as powerful as any pure-blood Divinum. She, however, got none of it." Eunice stared at her knitting needles and scraped them together like she was sharpening knives. "She was *still* Mother's favorite, however."

"My sister is not wrong there," Eudora said with a raised eyebrow.

"When we were young, beauty, poise, and social graces were Elizabeth's strong suits. Eunice and I always played second fiddle to her with Mother and Father, even though she was not born with the Seraphic gene."

Cooper nodded and clasped his fingers together. "My mother never showed any signs of it either, though I was really young when she died."

"Sometimes it skips a child or even a whole generation." Eudora wrangled a stray strand of hair and tucked it behind her ear. "While it always flows through the original ancient bloodlines, the Seraphic gene is as particular as it is potent. It skipped Elizabeth, your mother, and your brother, just as it skipped Lillie Mae's daughter, Charlotte, and her mother, Sarabeth."

"Half-negro, that one," Eunice barked without any hint of social grace.

Cooper craned his neck around and gawked at her. "What did you just say?" He shook his head. "The term is mixed or biracial, if you don't mind."

Eunice held her hands up and shrugged. "That's what I said! She was half white and half Negro. Same thing. You and your fancy modern terms." She huffed and went right back to knitting.

Cooper couldn't help but chuckle, but not at Eunice. He had mixed race blood in his ancestry, too. Didn't see that one coming, but it was South Carolina, after all. Plantations of the antebellum South were not safe places for enslaved women of color.

Cooper shifted in his seat and leaned forward. "By the looks of her in that picture, Sally Parker was a rich white girl. If she was Sarabeth's mother, then who was the father?"

Eudora eased back into the cushions of the sofa, crossed her arms over her healthy bosom, and cocked an eyebrow. "You are correct. Sally was about as fair as they come and a plantation princess. Jonathan Parker owned one of the richest estates in the county."

Cooper shook his head as puzzle pieces finally slipped into place. "Warfield."

"Yes," Eudora said. "Sarabeth's father was a slave at Warfield."

Cooper stared at her, dumbfounded. He scooted to the edge of his chair and entwined his fingers. "Lillie Mae's grandfather was a slave? Who was he? What was his name?"

Betsy's voice drifted into the middle of their conversation like a falling feather. "You know him as Blue."

Cooper snapped his head around and stared at her, standing over his shoulder by the fireplace. The ticking of the grandfather clock counted down the five seconds it took for her words to register in his brain.

He stood and faced her, his knees nearly buckling under him. "Blue?"

Betsy nodded.

Cooper walked over to her. "You mean Blue, the ghost..."

Eunice cleared her throat.

"I mean... *spirit*," he continued, "who has given me nightmares my whole life?"

"Yes," Betsy said. "That Blue."

"His birth name was Gazini Mutamba," Eunice said. "The slave traders gave him that silly nickname for obvious reasons. I'll never forget those unsettling eyes. A mark of the devil if you ask me."

Betsy crossed her arms. "More like creative breeding."

Cooper had to move. The walls were closing in on him. He circled the room, rubbing his eyes with his thumb and his index finger without saying a word. It made no sense to him. Blue. His ancestor. Un. Freaking. Believable. He made himself dizzy pacing, so he went back to the chair and sunk down into it.

He looked up at Betsy. "I saw him tonight. At Warfield. He was there in the kitchen house, right before I fell through the cellar door." He couldn't stop shaking his head. "Blue and your daughter?"

"Sally fell in love with Blue the moment she saw him." Betsy paused and smiled, her eyes glazing over. "She had such a capacity for pure, blind love and compassion. She was also naïve to the ways of this world. She was a wondrous and magical creature from another time and place." She fell silent, seemingly adrift in a sea of memories from which she didn't want to be rescued.

"Different times, back then," Eunice added. "Not anything goes, like you people these days."

Eudora leaned forward like the wise old sage who was about to enlighten him. "The Phipps line is one of the oldest and purest of all Divinum bloodlines. The power flowing through your blood is legendary in the heavenly realm." She was practically salivating. "And Blue was an incredibly powerful Houngan."

Cooper shrugged at the unfamiliar term.

"He was born of the Bokor," Eudora explained. "The Vodoun high priests of the dark magic, very powerful and dangerous. That is the origin of your dark side. The mixing of two such powerful and diverse bloodlines is unprecedented."

Cooper stood and rested hands on his hips. "So you're telling me that I am descended from a powerful witch and some badass, evil voodoo priest."

Eudora shrugged. "*Evil* is a relative term. Not all darkness is evil."

"If all this is true, then why has Blue tormented me all my life? Why did he scare the hell out of an eight-year-old kid at Warfield that day? What was he doing at the kitchen house tonight or standing in the middle of the road when I drove into town?"

"He was likely trying to warn you," Betsy said, standing beside his chair. "To stop you from putting yourself in danger like you did in the kitchen house. You were always Divinum, Cooper. You were born that way. All those years ago at Warfield, when Blue touched you, he simply awakened the dark side of your powers—his Bokor seed in your blood—for your own protection."

Eudora straightened her spine and brushed the wrinkles from the lap of her gown. "Betsy is right, dear. He was never your tormentor. You created that in your own rather overactive imagination." She cocked her head, one eyebrow creeping a little higher than the other. "Blue is your guardian."

CHAPTER TWENTY

The next morning, sunlight slipped in through the cracks of the curtains, casting bright horizontal lines across the width of the bed as Cooper woke. He'd managed about five hours of uninterrupted sleep, after lying awake pondering Betsy and Eudora's seemingly implausible revelation. Blue. His ancestor. And some kind of damn voodoo high-priest, guardian angel.

The information was hard to get his head around after twenty years of thinking Blue was just a malevolent spirit hell-bent on scaring the crap out of him. Apparently, he'd been trying to protect Cooper all those years. It made little sense in the absence of caffeine. He pushed the muddled thoughts from his mind, slid his hand under the pillow, and touched the cold blade of the dagger Betsy had left with him just in case. Grabbing his phone from the nightstand, he unlocked the screen with the swipe of his finger. No calls from Randy, not that he really expected one after their awkward encounter last night. He just hoped Randy was safe.

The familiar sounds of the creaky old house soothed him as he lay there pondering his next move. He needed to know how to kill an Anakim, if it was even possible. He couldn't ask Betsy. She would never let him get within a mile of Alexander again. He could think of only one other person in Georgetown who might know.

Cooper threw back to the covers, sat up, and stared at the pile of clothes on the floor beside the bed. He didn't even remember taking them off. Old habits. At least he wasn't doing a walk of shame this time. That old life of his seemed pretty lame now since becoming aware of the dark world around him.

After a quick shower, he pulled on some jeans, his navy Vanderbilt sweatshirt, and ambled down the hall to check on Lillie Mae. Turning the doorknob as quietly as possible, he cracked the door open and peeked in. She lay on her side facing him, emitting a low, steady snore. The creases in her timeworn face had smoothed, and a nearly imperceptible smile curled her lip. Maybe she was lost in a beautiful dream. He hoped so. He pulled the door closed.

She would be out for a while, and it was morning. Phipps House had its veil of protection, and he would be back soon. Still, he felt guilty for sneaking out.

Old habits.

CHAPTER TWENTY-ONE

Prince George Winyah Episcopal Parish was a regal battleaxe of a church at the corner of Highmarket and Broad streets. Having endured over two hundred fifty years of wartime occupations, fires, and hurricanes, the church stood in the heart of Georgetown's historic district as a beacon of spiritual perseverance and fortitude. A third generation recovering Pentecostal, Cooper always found the quiet reverence and dignity of Prince George Parish alluring. If Lillie Mae ever minded his preference for the liturgical, she'd never said so.

He stood on the sidewalk, staring up at the belfry and rubbing his hands together. The temperature had risen almost fifteen degrees since yesterday, so nerves chilled him more than the cold. He hadn't stepped inside a church for almost a decade, and he was sure the walls of the historic landmark would crumble around him the moment he darkened the doorway. He'd nearly convinced himself to turn around and walk the ten blocks back to Phipps House, when a rotund figure sporting salt-and-pepper hair and a clerical collar barreled around the corner of the building.

"Cooper Causey! I thought that was you." Wayne Johnson was cherry-cheeked and a little grayer on top, but no worse for the wear. The rector of Prince George had been a high school buddy of Cooper's dad and a close friend of the family since before Cooper was born. Not only an eloquent speaker, Wayne was the foremost biblical scholar in the state, versed in a variety of subjects ranging from Old Testament history to demonic possession. If anyone in Georgetown—any *human* in Georgetown—could help him, it was Wayne.

Cooper pushed through the iron gate and extended his hand. "Good to see you, Reverend."

Wayne looked down at Cooper's hand with a frown and pulled him into bear hug. "Reverend, my big fat patoot. Don't sass me, boy." Wayne slapped Cooper's back and squeezed his shoulders. "Your daddy gave me carte blanche to bend you over my knee whenever necessary."

Cooper chuckled and looked down, flustered by the brazen display of affection. "Sorry, Wayne."

The rector draped an arm around Cooper's shoulder and centered his eyes on him. "How is Aunt Mae?"

Cooper forced a smile, choosing to omit any mention of Lillie Mae's recent dungeon imprisonment. "She's okay. Gettin' up there. You know how it is. She's asleep right now, so I thought I'd take a walk. Can't stay long, though."

Wayne pulled back, holding Cooper at arm's length and staring at him with a raised eyebrow. "You always were a piss poor liar, just like your daddy. Get your tail inside where it's warm and tell me what really brings you here."

Stepping inside the church was like stepping back in time. A vast cluster of original colonial-style boxed pews sat in the center of a room awash in white walls and dark woods. Wayne pushed through the knee-high wooden gate of a pew box near the back of the nave and waved Cooper in. They sat side-by-side on the wooden bench facing the altar, exchanging a few meaningless pleasantries about Cooper's life in Nashville and his snail-paced graduate work at Vanderbilt. Wayne was genuinely interested. Cooper was not. He had more pressing things on his mind. Even with the safety of daylight, he still didn't want to leave Lillie Mae alone for too long.

"I need your help with something, Wayne." Cooper leaned forward and clasped his hands together in front of him. "Jesus, this is going to sound crazy."

Wayne stopped smiling. "What's wrong? You sure Aunt Mae's okay?"

Cooper waved a hand in front of him and fought back tears. The words *she's dying* refused to form on his lips. He sucked back the sudden wave of grief and looked up. "That's not it. I'm… in some trouble." He hadn't rehearsed what he'd planned to say, and now he wished he had.

"Trouble?" Wayne said. "What kind of trouble? Boy trouble?"

Cooper shook his head. "Oh, God no. Although I could really use some absolution for some recent indiscretions."

"Wrong church." Wayne smiled and pointed his thumb over his shoulder. "St. Mary's is right across the street."

Cooper released a nervous chuckle. "Sorry. I just don't know how to say this."

Wayne rested his arm on the back of the pew and smiled. "Cooper. It's me. I changed your diapers and bought you your first pack of condoms. What is it?"

Exasperated, Cooper didn't try to edit himself and just spat out the words, a little louder than he'd intended. "I need to know how to kill an Anakim." His voice echoed through the nave, the word *Anakim* bouncing around the room as if repelled by every wall in the holy place.

Wayne's face sagged, and his eyes instantly lost their cherubic sparkle. He stared at Cooper. "What do *you* know about the Anakim?"

Cooper held his palms up. "Just what I read in a few Bible scriptures."

Wayne cocked his head at him and furrowed his brow. "That's basically all there is—in the standard translations, that is. Why the heck would you need to know how to kill one? Something for your dissertation?"

Cooper's breath caught in his throat. Why the hell didn't he think of that? "Exactly. My dissertation."

Wayne tapped his index finger to his lips, staring Cooper down out of the corner of his eye. "Like I said. Piss poor liar." He dropped his hand to his lap and sighed. "Okay, I'll play along." Shifting in his seat, he faced Cooper and crossed his legs, ankle to knee.

"According to biblical lore, and I lean heavy on the word *lore* here, the Anakim were a race of giants that lived thousands of years ago. They were an ancient evil people—

multiplied like rodents, killing humans and somehow recreating their victims into their own image. Playing God, basically. The Anakim were a plague of death and destruction on the human world. Some believe they even subsisted on the blood of humans. The city of Jericho was one of their strongholds. An entire city inhabited by those foul devils."

Cooper wiped a hand over his face and massaged his temples, his head throbbing. "But the Israelites defeated the people of Jericho, right? It's in the Bible. *Joshua fit the battle of Jericho* and all that."

Wayne peered at him. "Well, if that's what the Bible says, then it must be true, right?" He shook his head and chuckled, running his fingers over the top of his head like a comb and then resting his hands on his belly. "Some believe a different version of that story, one that rarely gets shared—a version in which Joshua and Caleb didn't lead the Israelites to victory that night, but to slaughter."

Cooper swallowed hard and shifted in his seat, his suspicions confirmed.

Wayne loosened his clerical collar and unfastened the top button of his shirt. "They had no idea of the evil that awaited them when the walls of the city came down. Some believe the Anakim captured Caleb and transformed him into one of them, that he developed unquenchable bloodlust and even betrayed his closest friend and leader. Supposedly, he drained Joshua right in front of the surviving women and children of the Israelite camp before he murdered them all. Caleb rose up in the ranks of Anakim society and leadership.

After a few centuries passed, he became their most ruthless king." Wayne paused and flashed Cooper a conspiratorial smile. "But that wouldn't have been an appropriate Sunday school story for the kids, now would it?"

Cooper shook his head. He ran his index finger along the edge of the pew, the wood smooth and cold under his touch. "Where did they come from?"

Wayne picked up the burgundy hardcover Bible sitting beside him on the pew and flipped absently through its pages. "The Anakim were the children of the Nephilim."

Cooper nodded. He remembered that word from his years of forced Sunday school attendance. "Nephilim. The sons of God and the daughters of men. The unholy seed of the fallen angels of Heaven when they came to Earth and procreated with humans."

Wayne smiled, seemingly pleased with Cooper's recall of biblical knowledge. "The Nephilim were an abomination, just like their mutant offspring, the Anakim."

The weight of Wayne's revelations pressed down on Cooper's chest, constricting the flow of oxygen. The origins of the Anakim and the Divinum were closer than he had imagined—the Divinum descended from righteous angels of heaven and Anakim from the fallen. He was part of a Seraphic lineage with a cataclysmic sibling rivalry that could destroy the human race, and he was their pawn. Cooper stood and crossed the four-foot pew box, wondering how much he should share with Wayne. He could use all the allies he could get.

He turned toward the rector. "I think I believe the lore

over the scriptures. I don't think the Anakim were destroyed by the Israelites at Jericho. In fact, I know they weren't, because I've seen them here in Georgetown."

Wayne stared at him, his chubby cheeks sagging. The corners of his mouth curled down. The heat of Wayne's judgment warmed Cooper's cheeks. He couldn't blame the guy. He knew he sounded certifiable.

Cooper shook his head and turned away. "Never mind. Just forget I brought it up."

Wayne spun him around with a hand to the shoulder and stood in front of him. His usually sparkling eyes dark with worry. "Come on. I want to show you something."

Wayne led Cooper through the side door of the nave and out into the church's graveyard, one of the oldest in South Carolina. Majestic oaks draped with a protective canopy of Spanish moss over uneven ground littered with headstones, some pristine and new, but others ancient and crumbling.

Cooper followed him through a maze of graves into the center of the yard where Wayne stopped and pointed down. "Two nights ago, I saw a woman dressed all in black standing right here looking down at those headstones. She was tall. Like really tall for a woman. Late twenties, maybe early thirties. Beautiful. I'd been working late and saw her through my office window. I came out and asked if she was all right. You know, did she want to come inside out of the cold and talk. She didn't answer, so I got a little closer and asked her how she knew the deceased. She mumbled something like she belonged with them."

Cooper stared down at the overgrown headstones of

Sally, Andrew, Stephen, Jonathan, and Elizabeth Parker, the date of their deaths identical except for Betsy's, which showed five years earlier than the others. He wondered whose remains, if any, rested under the markers for Stephen and Elizabeth Parker.

Wayne tugged at his clerical collar. "I turned away for just a second, and when I looked back, she was gone. Vanished. I nearly messed myself right here. I thought I'd seen a ghost. Wouldn't be the first time around here, but she was different somehow."

Cooper shook his head. "She was no ghost."

Wayne circled the Parker graves and stood behind the headstones, facing Cooper. "Something about that woman stuck with me. Something dark. Made my skin crawl. Barely got a wink of sleep that night."

"And she's supposed to be one of the good ones." Cooper scanned the graveyard from one end to the other. The burn of invisible foreign eyes was distinct and unsettling, unless it was his overactive imagination. "There are others like her who are dangerous. *Extremely* dangerous." He looked back at Wayne. "So back to my original question. How do you kill them?"

Wayne chuckle-snorted and wiped his nose with the back of his hand. He strolled back around the Parker family plot and stood beside Cooper. "You can't kill them, Coop. They're like cockroaches."

Cooper crossed his arms and widened his stance. "There has to be a way."

Wayne reached down and picked up a small rock from

the ground. He rolled it around in his palm and then stared at it. "God banished the Anakim to eternal darkness. Sunlight renders them paralyzed and defenseless. Scrambles their brain or something. But his attempt to rid the earth of them failed."

Cooper cocked his head at Wayne, not following his meaning.

The rector looked down, dropped the rock, and shook his head. After a silent moment, he looked up, genuine fear pooling in his eyes. "God tried to kill them once. Remember the Great Flood? It didn't work. They survived."

CHAPTER TWENTY-TWO

Cooper sat in the Boston rocker by the window in Lillie Mae's room, absently picking at the edges of a stale cinnamon roll he'd found in the cupboard on his third failed quest to find the elusive Jim Beam. Staring out the window onto Front Street, he reflected on his conversation with Wayne, and a pang of hopelessness gnawed away at his insides.

He considered leaving without Lillie Mae in an attempt to draw Alexander away from her. But the thought of abandoning her now, when she only had God knows how long left to live, made him sick to his stomach. No. He couldn't leave her. He wasn't going anywhere. Betsy and the twins were right. His less than reliable power might be his only hope, if he could ever get it under control.

Movement on the sidewalk across the street drew his focus. Cooper recognized the burgundy Gamecocks hoodie right away. Tony Tanner walked with his head down, and his hands shoved into his pockets. He casually glanced over at the front of the house as he passed. Cooper pulled back the sheers to get a better look. Tony must have spotted him because he stared down at the sidewalk and picked up his pace, disappearing around the corner. Cooper wondered if it could have been Tony he sensed in the churchyard. What the hell was the guy doing? Stalking him? Looking for a little down-low afternoon delight?

He shook his head, released the sheers, and glanced over at Lillie Mae propped up in the bed by a small mountain of fluffy down pillows. The soft purr of a snore slipped through her parted lips. The doorbell woke her. She opened her eyes.

"I'll go see who it is," he said, putting the half-eaten cinnamon roll on a napkin on the seat of the rocker. He went over and squeezed her hand. Color had returned to her face, but the ordeal at Warfield had taken an obvious toll on her already weakened body.

"Be right back," he said, with the most reassuring smile he could muster.

He slipped out of the bedroom and down the hall to the front door. A quick peek through the sidelight revealed an odd trio of strangers awaiting him on the porch. He was hesitant to open the door. However, the safety of sunlight and Betsy's nine-inch dagger tucked under his shirt finally gave him the courage to do so.

A stunning dark-skinned woman stood in the center, her arms crossed, and her weight resting on her right side. Wide-set eyes and long, dark hair pulled back into a ponytail accentuated her angular face. A broad-shouldered man of some exotic Pacific Islander variety stood to her right. A dazzling smile stretched across his handsome face, anchored by a set of ridiculously pronounced dimples. His body looked like he had just stepped off the cover of *Men's Fitness* magazine, ripped to Photoshop perfection. Another man—an absurdly tall and thin albino stood behind the man and woman, towering over them. Cooper had never seen an albino up close before, and he couldn't stop staring. The woman cleared her throat, drawing his attention. Her frozen facial features told him she was all business and this was not a social call.

"I am Odessa. We are Jericho agents." She stated it as casually as if she'd just introduced herself as the Avon lady. "Betsy sent for us. Are you going to let us in, or are you just going to stand there gawking at us all day?"

Cooper was so mesmerized by her beauty, her petulance didn't even bother him. She was around his age, maybe a little younger, and nearly as tall. A shapely, statuesque body begged to be released from the confines of a fitted leather jacket and tight pants neatly tucked into knee-high leather boots. Her milk-chocolate skin was impossibly smooth. A perfectly formed chin and mile-high cheekbones led up to probing black eyes that peered out from under long lashes thick with mascara. The effect was haunting and beautiful.

She tapped the toe of her boot and raised a precisely penciled eyebrow. "Well?"

Cooper stared at the group for another moment, sizing them up. They were Divinum. That much he knew. Their raw magical energy leaped across the threshold and latched on to his with awkward familiarity. He peered into three sets of distinctly mesmerizing eyes, probing their open minds.

He couldn't see anything clearly. He would need to work on that. But he sensed that he could trust them.

He finally stepped out of the way and waved them in. "Sorry. Come in, I guess."

Fitness Model Guy gave Cooper a quick nod as he followed Odessa inside. "Name's Rafe." His thick mane of black hair danced around the top of bulky shoulders, and he flashed Cooper an overly confident smile filled with sparkling white teeth. He offered his hand with a flirtatious twinkle in his eye Cooper knew all too well. Hell, he'd mastered it himself.

Cooper shook his hand. Rafe didn't ping on his gaydar, but Cooper got a definite vibe from him. Mostly straight but needs to be desired by everyone, male or female. And very sexual. Wouldn't even require a six-pack. Cooper knew the type well and had bedded his share of them.

Rafe stepped inside like he owned the place. Filling the foyer with a musky air of testosterone and masculine bravado, he looked like he'd just hopped off a Harley. He slipped out of his black leather jacket, exposing a ridiculously carved chest and rippling abs veiled only by the thin cotton of a tight white tee. Snug black leather pants hugged his muscled ass and bulging crotch like they had been painted on. After his quick inspection of the foyer, Rafe's leer traveled down the front of Cooper's body and stopped just below his waist.

"Nice blade." He winked at Cooper.

As hot as the guy was, Cooper couldn't help being annoyed by his off-the-charts cockiness. Cooper lifted his shirt and withdrew Betsy's dagger. He eyed all three of them with a healthy dose of suspicion, trying to become comfortable with his decision to trust them. He looked at the dagger and finally laid it on the antique telephone table by the door.

The albino man did not offer his hand but gave a slight bow as he entered, his long white hair falling forward into his pale face like strands of fine silk. His movements were so fluid, he looked as if he were skimming the surface of the floor rather than taking actual steps. A white trench coat flowed open behind him. As he passed, a warm wave of calm spilled over Cooper's body from the top of his head down to the tips of his toes. He felt like he'd just woken up from a long nap, refreshed and peaceful. The albino man made him feel that way, though he didn't understand how.

Hello, Cooper. I am Lex.

The man's internal voice didn't sound intrusive like the others Cooper had recently heard in his mind. It was lyrical and melodic. Even soothing.

"Lex is a pure-blood. And mute," the woman said behind him. "He only communicates with his mind. You heard him, right?"

"Yes. I heard him." Cooper nodded to the albino, looking up at the light fixture above the man's head to make sure he would clear it. He did, but just barely. Lex stood like a granite statue with no visible signs that he even breathed. He patiently allowed Cooper to gawk at him. One of the twins had mentioned the term. Cooper looked back at Rafe and Odessa. "Pure-blood?"

Odessa planted a hand on her hip. "A direct descendant of the Davidic dynasty. The Divinum line of David. The most pure of heart and powerful of our kind."

"That's right." Rafe reached up and put his hand on Lex's shoulder. "Pure-bloods are rare as fuck, and we got one!" He nudged Cooper's arm with his elbow. "Old Lex here is pushing four digits. And more powerful than frickin' Moses."

"Wait. *Moses* was Divinum?"

Rafe snickered. "Well the Red Sea sure as hell didn't part itself."

Odessa turned on her heel and walked straight down the hall to the sitting room as Rafe and Lex fell in behind her. Cooper followed them, feeling more the visitor than the host.

"We're here to extract you and relocate you to safety," Odessa said as soon as he stepped into the room. "Get your things. We leave immediately."

"Extract me?" Cooper's blood came to an instant boil in his veins. Damn if he wasn't tired of supernatural beings, dead and otherwise, telling him what to do. "Look, I am not in the mood to be ordered around by complete strangers. I'm not going anywhere without Lillie Mae."

Rafe chuckled and plopped down in the wingback chair. "Oh, this is going to be good." He slung a meaty thigh over the armrest. His T-shirt rode up, and he laced his fingers together over the ripples of his tanned lower stomach. Lex stood by the door, unnaturally still. Cooper never saw him blink, never saw his chest move with the normal flow of oxygen. His presence was disconcerting, yet oddly comforting.

Odessa circled the room with the calculated steps of a lioness stalking her prey. She stopped in front of Cooper. "The Manheeg has decided it is not safe for you here, and we are to remove you. That is all you need to know at this point. Go pack a bag."

Cooper walked right up to her. "Betsy said reinforcements were coming, not a damn moving van. And this Manheeg guy might be *your* leader, but he sure as hell isn't mine. Like I said, I'm not going anywhere without my grandmother, and she's in no condition to travel."

"She'll be dead soon," Rafe interjected like he was commenting on the weather. "Her spirit is already fading. When she's gone, you'll no longer be safe in this house. You're coming with us, like it or not."

A spit of rage flared in Cooper's gut. He walked over to the chair and knocked Rafe's leg off of the armrest with his hand. "Watch yourself, Fabio. That's my grandmother you're talking about. And that's her chair you're treating like a damn barstool."

Rafe raised an eyebrow, and a crooked smile formed on his lips, like he was slightly turned on by Cooper's display of aggression. Speechless, Cooper crossed the room shaking his head. Lex met him by the front window, emitting waves of compassion and reason that spilled over Cooper like an invisible rain shower. His anger toward Rafe dissipated in seconds, Lex's voice in his head only calming him more.

Cooper, please forgive our intrusion and the disrespectful tone of my colleague. We are only trying to protect you. It is imperative that we get you somewhere safe where the Anakim cannot find you. Once they discover you, as Montgomery has, we will not be able to guarantee your safety.

Cooper faced the window, rubbing his eyes. How did everything get so screwed up? His life was spinning out of control. Was this his new normal?

"He's right, Cooper," Odessa said from behind. "And we hear you do not have complete control of your power. It is erratic and dangerous. You will not be able to protect yourself *or* Lillie Mae like that."

Betsy's betrayal stung. She had not been too impressed with his haphazard displays of magic, but he couldn't really blame her. If he didn't get past the Trevor mental block, he would never be able to keep Lillie Mae safe. He took a deep breath and turned back to face them. Odessa stood by the fireplace with her arms crossed and one eyebrow raised. She was the one he had to convince. He walked over and stared into her bottomless gray eyes. They were cold, but not completely lacking traces of humanity.

"Look, I get it, okay? Alexander is a monster, and my blood is like crack to him. It could cause some real balance of nature shit if he gets it." The tinge of sarcasm in his voice was hard to resist. "But I can't—no, I *won't* leave Lillie Mae. You may be right about her dying, but that's all the more reason why I won't go. So you can either help me deal with Alexander here and now, or you can try to take me by force, and I will show you just how *dangerous* and *erratic* my power can be." He crossed his arms, mirroring her domineering stance, and hoped she didn't call his bluff.

Odessa stared through him for a solid minute, her face

blank and unreadable. The room was silent and thick with tension, but Cooper would not back down. She finally let out a sigh of resignation, rolled her eyes, and looked over at Rafe.

"Check the house."

CHAPTER TWENTY-THREE

Rafe sprang up out of the chair and went over to the wall opposite the fireplace. He put both hands on it and closed his eyes.

Cooper shook his head and mumbled under his breath. "Great. Now we're praying for the damn house."

Lex drifted over to Odessa, his hands clasped in front of him.

The Manheeg gave specific instructions, O. We are to remove Cooper and take him to one of our safe houses across the sea.

Cooper focused on Odessa and peered inside her head. The ease with which he accessed her thoughts surprised him.

I know what the Manheeg said, Lex. But we can't take him if he doesn't want to go.

Lex raised an eyebrow. *Well, in fact, we could.*

Cooper's muscles stiffened. He'd been bluffing before. He couldn't count on his power to stop them if they tried to take him by force. All he had was a dagger he'd never used and ten itchy fingers, against the three of them. He didn't like his odds.

Lex touched Odessa's shoulder, likely pure-blood strategy to calm her. *I know it is in your nature to go on the offensive rather than retreat, but we do not know how many changelings Montgomery has created or where they have nested. Best to heed the Manheeg's instructions until we know more.*

Odessa pushed his hand away and narrowed her eyes on him. "You will remember, Lex, that I am the ranking agent on this mission. Your fabled origin is of no consequence in this matter, and you *will* do as I say."

Without expression or protest, Lex gave her a slight nod and took a visible step back. The woman didn't play. Not even with a pure-blood.

Rafe walked the perimeter of the room, running his hand along the wall. "The enchantment is weakening, O. It's bound to the old woman's life force. As she fades, it fades. It should hold well enough, though, as long as she's alive and here in the house."

Odessa stood in front of Cooper, her finely crafted nose just inches from his own. He kept his arms crossed between them as a barrier, not about to let the emanating force of her Divinum power intimidate him.

"Lex is right about one thing. Jericho will never be able to get close to Montgomery unless we first eradicate his changelings. Finding and destroying their nest would take precedence over a VIP security escort. Any ideas on the location of the nest?"

Cooper glanced at Rafe and Lex before shaking his head. "I only found out last night what the hell a changeling is. How would I know where they nest? They came out of a tunnel under the kitchen house. Except for the one that attacked Betsy here. Somehow it got into the house."

Odessa paced in a circle, staring at the floor with one hand planted on her hip and the other propping her chin. "Did you see where this tunnel led?"

Cooper shook his head. "No. But according to local lore, there's a labyrinth of tunnels under Georgetown dating back to the Revolutionary War. Supposedly they were used for sneak attacks on the British, getting booze into town during Prohibition, and even to smuggle slaves out to the harbor during the Civil War. But those are just old wives' tales."

Odessa nodded. "The nest would be underground, and if there is an entrance close enough for one of the changelings to get into this house, other access points must be scattered around town."

A knot formed in the pit of Cooper's stomach. If Alexander unleashed those monsters, Georgetown would be decimated in minutes. Hundreds, even thousands of people would die. And he had a feeling the Anakim wouldn't stop with Georgetown.

Odessa pressed the tip of an index finger to her lips. "If we find the nest and destroy the changelings, it will significantly weaken Montgomery's defense. We could get to him then. The Manheeg should be pleased enough if we are successful."

Rafe strutted over to her. "We going hunting, O?"

Odessa gave him a quick nod.

"Fuckin' A!" His grin was as mischievous as a rowdy frat boy.

Lex stepped between them with raised eyebrows and a finger in the air. A cold glare from Odessa shut him down before he could protest. She paced with long, elegant strides, looking more like a high-fashion runway model than a lethal weapon. Rafe and Lex were silent, watching her, apparently awaiting instruction.

She stopped in front of Cooper. "Montgomery must have a day soldier who keeps tabs on you during the day sleep. Have you seen anything unusual or met anyone lately who seemed strange to you?"

Cooper rubbed his forehead with the tips of his fingers. He hadn't really seen anyone since he returned except for Randy and Lillie Mae. And Tony. Talk about strange.

He looked up at them. "Yes. I have. A guy. He was my best friend when we were kids. Tony Tanner. I ran into him the first night I drove into town, and then I saw him again in front of the house earlier looking kind of sketchy. Jesus, it was right before you got here."

Rafe bolted out of the room, nearly taking the front door off the hinges from the sound of it.

Odessa was in Cooper's face again. The woman had no sense of personal space. "What did he say to you?"

"Not much. He acted really strange when I first saw him at the Ice House," Cooper said. "All twitchy and distracted. I thought maybe he was strung out on something. He didn't try to hurt me or anything. He actually seemed kind of repelled by me."

Odessa gave a quick nod. "Montgomery would not have wanted him to hurt you. Just to keep an eye on you. Report back if people like us showed up."

Cooper looked at her sideways. "Tony is one of *them*?"

"Not likely since you saw him this morning in broad daylight." She rolled her eyes like his ignorance was a waste of her valuable time. "It sounds like Montgomery got to him, though. Gave him a taste of Anakim blood. Given in small doses, their venom can be quite effective in controlling humans. It connects their minds. The day soldier will crave more of it and will do anything to get it. He's Montgomery's slave now."

Rafe rumbled back into the room. "Nothing. He's gone."

Cooper scratched the back of his neck. "Alexander couldn't have known that Tony and I knew each other, though."

Lex glided over to him, his nearly translucent skin accentuated by his all-white attire. If he dressed that way to tone down the haunting effect of his skin, he failed.

Human scents are like Anakim radar, Cooper. No matter how long it has been since you last saw this man, he will always carry traces of yours on him. That's how the Anakim knew you were connected. This friend of yours was likely the first Alexander encountered here carrying your scent. It could have been anyone that knew you.

Odessa tapped a toe on the floor. "Do you know where this guy lives?"

Cooper shrugged. "No clue. Why?"

She tapped the tip of her index finger to her bottom lip. "He may know where the nest is."

Rafe plopped down on the sofa and picked up Cooper's

iPad from the coffee table, handling it like it belonged to him.

Cooper leaned in over Rafe's shoulder. "Tony Tanner."

Rafe typed the name into a search engine, mumbling to himself. "Tony Tanner. Georgetown, South Carolina."

Odessa sat on the arm of the sofa and peered in. Cooper looked up to find Lex suddenly standing right beside him. Damn, that was creepy.

"Got him." Rafe held the tablet out at arm's length so they all could see.

He looked over his shoulder at Cooper. "Do you know a place called Harmony Hills Mobile Home Park? Map shows it off Montford Road. Near the…"

"Near the Pennyroyal Cemetery," Cooper said. He knew the place all too well, having buried his entire family there. It was also just down the road from the Waccamaw Rehabilitation Center and Nursing Home. He'd avoided Montford Road like the plague for over a decade.

"I guess you do," Rafe said with a raised brow and then looked up at Odessa. "What do you want to do, O?"

Odessa stood and cupped her shapely hips with her hands. She sauntered over to the fireplace, Rafe's leer following her ass with brazen lust and appreciation.

Turning on her heel, she tapped her fingertips together. "Let's pay this day soldier a little visit. See what he knows."

Lex moved to her side. *Odessa, Betsy said—*

She shot him a glare full of daggers. "You think I care what that infernal Anakim bitch said?"

Lex stared at her, eyes wide. *Betsy is a loyal and dedicated Jericho soldier.*

"Perhaps." Odessa balled her right hand into a fist at her side. "But if she doesn't do the deed when the time comes, I will gladly do it for her."

Lex raised an eyebrow at her. *And will you do the same to the Manheeg? Or is it his fondness for Betsy that fuels your impertinence?*

Odessa shoved her index finger up into his face. "You are out of line, Lex. I suggest you stop now before I lose my temper."

Lex stood his ground for only a moment, then drifted backward, easing the suffocating tension in the room. The retreat was odd. Something about Lex made Cooper think Odessa's Divinum power was no match for the pure-blood, yet he obeyed her anyway.

"Lex, you will stay here with Cooper and Lillie Mae," Odessa announced with renewed authority.

Lex gave her a protracted nod, as if to reinforce his submission to her commands.

"No chance in hell," Cooper said. "I'm coming with you." He expanded his chest with a deep breath, preparing for Odessa's wrath. "If Tony knows something, there's a better chance that he would tell me than you. We've known each other since we could walk. Besides, my gut tells me my methods would be a little more humane than yours."

Odessa cut her eyes at him, but he didn't back down. He would go with them whether she liked it or not.

Rafe dropped the iPad on the coffee table just hard enough to make Cooper flinch. "We doing this or what?"

Odessa's glare faded a little too quickly for Cooper's

comfort. He'd expected more of a fight. "Don't be surprised if he isn't as receptive to you as you think. Trust me. He's changed." She looked over at Rafe. "He's with you. Transportation?"

Rafe stood. "Already taken care of." He walked around the sofa and slapped Cooper on the shoulder. "Let's roll, Ginger."

Cooper shot him an icy scowl. He'd always hated being called that. The idea of leaving Lillie Mae with a stranger—a very *strange* stranger—unnerved him. Looking up into Lex's peaceful white eyes, a sudden wave of reassurance spilled over him.

Lex's smile warmed Cooper to the bones. *She will be safe with me, Cooper. You have my word.*

Cooper believed him, and he followed Odessa into the foyer with Rafe close behind. An imposing figure filled the sidelight of the front door, its rugged, handsome face peering in through the glass. Randy. Cooper sighed, grabbed his coat, and reached for the doorknob, pulling it open before Randy had a chance to ring the bell and wake Lillie Mae again.

Looking smart and fit in his uniform, a puffy breath of cold air slipped out between Randy's parted lips. He looked over Cooper's shoulder to the odd cluster of guests standing behind him. Wrinkles formed in the corners of his eyes, and his chiseled jawline stiffened.

"Sorry. I didn't know you had company."

Cooper avoided those eyes and kept his voice even. "Randy. Hey." His heart thumped hard against his chest, and he silently cursed it for doing so. Hell if he would let this guy get to him again. His heart was not available to the unavailable, and Randy had made it perfectly clear last night that he was *not* available. At least not to Cooper.

Rafe cleared his throat from behind, prompting Cooper to move it along.

"We were just leaving." Cooper clenched his fists, quelling the hurt and anger churning in his gut.

A disingenuous smile formed on Randy's lips. "You going to introduce me to your friends?"

Cooper nodded over his shoulder. "That's Odessa, Rafe, and Lex."

Randy pointed his thumb over his shoulder toward the street. "There are only two bikes."

Cooper peered around him. Two tricked-out black Harleys sat the end of the driveway. He wondered where the hell they had come from, because he certainly hadn't heard them pull in. Rafe must have conjured them up to provide a more traditional mode of transportation for the newbie.

He looked back at Randy. "Lex is staying here with Lillie Mae."

Rafe stepped up beside Cooper and put a hand on his shoulder. "And Cooper is riding with me." The jerk winked at Randy, as if trying to make the situation even more uncomfortable than it already was. He was probably getting off on it.

Randy's raised eyebrows implied that he wanted more of an explanation, but Cooper didn't offer any. He was too busy rebuilding the fortress around his heart and systematically shutting down his emotions. The sting of Randy's rejection was still fresh.

Randy abandoned his line of questioning and leaned in. "I wanted to talk about last night. I could come back later if that's okay." He lowered his voice to a whisper. "I just want to make sure things are square between us."

Cooper chose his words carefully. "There's really no need. Everything is fine. We're *square.*"

After a momentary silent stare down, Randy sighed and moved aside. Stepping out onto the porch, Cooper let Odessa and Rafe pass. They regarded Randy like he had leprosy as they passed him. The heels of Odessa's boots punctuated her displeasure with the delay in a noisy clatter of clicks and scuffs down the front steps. Cooper closed the door behind them and strolled down the walkway, leaving Randy standing on the porch alone. His heart sank, and he sighed. What the hell was the matter with him? It was Randy, for Christ's sake. He glanced back over his shoulder. Randy stood with hands on his hips, shoulders back, and a laser glare shooting down the walk at Cooper like an arrow.

Rafe shuffled up beside Cooper and flashed him what his brother used to call a *shit-eatin' grin*, a reference that he never quite understood. Why would someone grin if they ate shit?

"That your man?" Rafe jabbed a playful finger in his side.

Cooper flinched and pulled away, heat rising in his cheeks.

Rafe let out a throaty laugh and threw a thick arm around his shoulders. "What? He's one sexy motherfucker. Hell, I'll do him if you don't." Rafe slapped him on the ass and sprinted ahead to the bikes.

Cooper lowered his head and kept walking, too mortified to look back at Randy.

CHAPTER TWENTY-FOUR

Harmony Hills Mobile Home Park was an eyesore of Southern Americana. Established before it was in vogue to add porches or decks to your doublewide to give the feel of a traditional brick and mortar home, the trailers at Harmony Hills looked like they had been pulled in, lined up side-by-side, unhitched, and forgotten. Narrow sandy paths connected by a black asphalt road bore names like *Recital Road*, *Symphony Circle*, and *Refrain Lane,* and were all that separated the endless rows of rusted hurricane bait.

Rafe deftly guided the Harley down Harmony Hills Drive. Cooper sat behind him, straddling the rumbling machine, plastered against Rafe's warm body, his hands resting on the guy's meaty upper thighs. He fit nicely between Cooper's legs and smelled of leather and finely aged scotch. Any other time, Cooper would've been turned on. He would've taken Rafe's initial flirtations and handed a few of his own right back. Rafe was his type—a pretty face, nice ass, and all man. He was perfect for a great romp between the sheets if that's all one was looking for. Cooper bet the body beneath that leather had pleasured many men and women alike. But like all the other men Cooper had been with over the years, Rafe was not Randy. Not even close. He wished like hell Randy wasn't even around. His presence only made Cooper more acutely aware of what he would never have.

Rafe turned left onto Treble Trail and stopped the Harley a couple doors down from Lot #14. Killing the motor, he hopped off. Odessa pulled up next to them and did the same. She removed her helmet and her long sable locks fell obediently into place over her shoulders. She didn't even have to shake it out. Rafe released his wavy mane from under his own helmet and leered at Odessa with an ear-to-ear smile. The guy didn't even *try* to hide his lustful desires. Odessa didn't give Rafe a second look, which he was probably used to if she had a thing for this Manheeg person as Lex had hinted earlier.

She sashayed over to Cooper, her rounded hips punctuating every step. "This shouldn't take long. Stay here with the bikes."

"Don't think so." Cooper removed his helmet, and a cold blast of wind walloped his bare cheeks. He balled his hands into fists and blew warm breath on them. Odessa cocked her head and raised an eyebrow at him. She was obviously not used to being defied.

Cooper slung his leg over the bike and sat the helmet on the seat. He stood and returned her penetrating gaze. "Don't even try that intimidation crap. And sorry, but your ass doesn't have the same effect on me as it does on him." He nodded over his shoulder at Rafe who snickered like a twelve-year-old boy.

Cooper pointed a finger in the direction of Tony's trailer and edged forward. "That guy in there was my best friend from the time I could talk until I graduated high school. We learned how to hunt, fish, ski, and masturbate together. I don't know what's wrong with him, but whatever it is, it's not his fault. He doesn't deserve to be treated like an animal or a criminal."

Odessa shrugged and pushed past him. "Suit yourself, rookie."

She plowed a path through the sand toward the trailer. He didn't quite trust her. She definitely had her own agenda.

Tony's trailer had no skirting, deck, or awning, just five wooden steps right up to the door. A few dark windows dotted the façade, and the vinyl siding wore a thin coat of orange cancer dust, courtesy of the Georgetown Steel Mill. Cooper eyed the residue and shook his head. He never understood why people stayed in this deathtrap of a town where cases of cancer outnumbered Palmetto trees. It had claimed both his parents and his grandfather, and now had its clutches around Lillie Mae's neck as well.

Rafe marched up the steps and stopped at the top of the landing. He held his hands up in front of him and the door exploded inward with a thunderous blast of aluminum and metal.

"Holy hell," Cooper mumbled with an honest dose of wonder and respect.

"Jesus, Rafe." Odessa mounted the steps and crossed the threshold. "Ever consider knocking first?"

Rafe shrugged. "Not as much fun."

Cooper took the steps two at a time and followed Rafe inside, sidestepping the downed door. A ratty sofa, a camouflage-patterned recliner, and a sixty-inch wide-screen television anchored the room. A messy combination of cardboard and spray paint blacked out the windows.

Heavy footsteps from the back of the trailer drew their attention. Tony barreled down the lone hallway into the kitchen, wearing only a pair of white briefs, his morning wood, and a sizable Confederate battle flag tattooed across his otherwise smooth chest.

"What the fuck?" His darting glare landed on Rafe and Odessa first, then Cooper standing behind them. He turned and bolted back toward the hallway.

"Tony. Wait!" Cooper started to go after him.

Rafe blocked him with an outstretched hand. "She's got this."

Odessa held her arm straight out in front of her, pointing her long index finger at the center of Tony's back. He screamed and froze. His whole body shook like he had been electrocuted and slid backward toward them. He dug the tips of his toes into the linoleum, grabbing at chairs, counters, and walls. None of it helped. Odessa guided his body over to the couch while he screeched like an angry cat. Kicking the door out of her way, she finally released her captive with the flick of her finger. Tony hit the cushions and bounced only once before Rafe was on him, all of his weight behind the knee he drove into Tony's stomach. Tony buckled over, gasping for air.

Cooper stepped forward and tugged on Rafe's shoulder. "You don't have to hurt him. He hasn't done anything. He's just scared."

Rafe pinned Tony's wrists to the top of the sofa. Small red holes dotted the inside of his arms. They were too big to be needle marks. Alexander's handiwork, Cooper supposed.

Rafe reached down between Tony's legs, grabbed his fading hard-on, and squeezed. "Well, hell, Sweet Pea. What's the matter? Not feeling sexy anymore? And here I thought you were happy to see me."

"Quiet, Rafe," Odessa commanded, slinking over to the sofa.

Cooper felt sorry for the guy. "And let go of his dick."

The sound of Cooper's voice drew Tony's attention and the fear in his eyes turned to rage. He hissed at Cooper, exposing a normal set of ill-managed, yellowing teeth, which he bared as if they were something much more threatening. If Cooper had come here alone, it would not have been pretty. He stepped back. Maybe Odessa and Rafe *were* better equipped to deal with this than he was.

Odessa gave Cooper a satisfied *I told you so* look. "He's mimicking Anakim behavior, but he's relatively harmless." She leaned over Tony, one slender hand on the back of the ratty couch, the other wrapped around his throat. "Now listen up, day soldier." Her tone was calm, yet thoroughly menacing. "We're going to have a little chat, and you are going to answer all of my questions until I am completely satisfied." She glanced down at his shrinking crotch and smirked. "And it takes *a lot* to satisfy me. You cooperate, and

Rafe here might not be inclined to rip your spine out with his bare hands."

Tony's eyes grew wide, rage returning to fear.

Rafe grinned and winked at him, like this was all just fun and games. Cooper knew that it wasn't. The crazed twinkle in Rafe's eye told him Rafe could and would do it without a second thought.

Odessa cocked her head. "What are your orders?"

Tony sealed his lips into a pale, thin line. Odessa gave her command with a simple nod. Rafe looked into Tony's eyes. Something happened behind them that could not have felt good. Tony's eyeballs bulged out like they were trying to escape their sockets, and he gave a blood-curdling scream. Rafe clamped his open palm down over Tony's mouth. The agonizing, muted screams sent a chill down Cooper's spine.

After thirty seconds of Rafe's eye-fuck thing, Cooper couldn't take it anymore. He stepped in and pushed hard on the Divinum's shoulder. "That's enough, Rafe! Let him talk!"

The instant Rafe looked up at Cooper, the screaming stopped, and Tony gasped for air under the firm cover of Rafe's hand.

Cooper kneeled down beside Rafe. "What the hell did you do to him?" The possible answers terrified him.

Rafe shrugged. "Just made him feel like his brain was on fire is all. I went easy on him."

Cooper shook his head and nudged Rafe aside. "Let me try." He kneeled in front of Tony and looked him in the eye. "Tony, look at me. It's me, Cooper Causey. You've known me your whole life. You have to tell them what they want to know, okay? Do that, and they'll leave you alone. They won't hurt you anymore. I promise."

Rafe removed his hand, and Tony clamped his mouth shut. Rafe raised a threatening eyebrow at him, which seemed to give him the needed motivation.

Through shallow breaths, Tony looked down at Cooper. "He told me to watch you during the day and warn him if freaks like these two come around. That was the day I saw you at the Ice House. Somehow he knew you were coming to town. I didn't know what he meant until you showed up."

Odessa rested her foot on the edge of the sofa and leaned forward. "What have you told Montgomery about Cooper?"

Tony looked over at Rafe. "Just what he does during the day—where he goes, who he talks to. That's all. I swear."

Cooper tapped Tony's knee once to get his attention. "Did you tell him anything about Randy?"

Tony stared at him, his top lip twitching. "Just that he's been to Phipps House a couple of times since you got back. That he's a cop and we all used to be friends when we were kids." Tony scowled. "And that you was always sweet on him."

Cooper stood up. "Dammit!" Heat flooded his face. "You put a target on his back, you dumb son of a bitch."

Rafe curled his fingers around a clump of Tony's coarse hair and yanked his head to the side. "Where is the changeling nest, Jethro?"

Tony winced and shrugged his shoulders. "How the hell should I know? He doesn't tell me nothing. Just calls me out to Warfield every night for my report and then makes me drink from him. That guy scares the shit out of me. I can feel him in my head all the time, like he's watching me from inside. He'll know I talked to you. You fuckers are gonna get me killed."

Cooper's patience was gone. "*We* are going to get *you* killed? Jesus Christ, Tony." He punched the back of the sofa. "You're the one that's going to get us all killed!"

Odessa nudged Cooper aside and pressed her index finger into Tony's chest, right in the center of the Confederate flag tattoo. "The tunnels under the kitchen house at Warfield. Where do they lead?"

Tony chuckled and glared at Odessa. "Are you deaf or just stupid? I said he doesn't tell me nothing, you dumb black bitch."

Rafe punched Tony in the stomach so hard that he doubled over onto his side, gasping for air.

Odessa kneeled in front of Tony's crumpled body and playfully outlined the tattoo with the tip of her fingernail. "Rafe, take Cooper and wait for me outside."

Without hesitation or question, Rafe hopped up and nudged Cooper toward the door.

Cooper considered resisting but knew it would be futile and allowed himself to be guided down the steps. "What's she going to do to him?"

Rafe snickered and sauntered toward the bikes. "She's going to take a peek around inside his head. Find out what he's not telling us. Trust me, you don't want to see it. It's not a pretty sight, especially when she's pissed off."

Cooper caught up to him. "Jesus. Is she going to hurt him?"

A piercing shriek echoed from inside the trailer.

Rafe laughed and looked over at him. "Well, it doesn't sound like they're swapping recipes, does it?" He leaned against the seat of his Harley, crossed his legs at the ankles, and grinned. "I don't think she liked his tattoo very much."

CHAPTER TWENTY-FIVE

Bitter cold wind sliced its way under the face shield of Cooper's helmet as they traveled down Montford Road away from Harmony Hills. Odessa had emerged from Tony's trailer after a five-minute scream and profanity littered interrogation, looking all too pleased with herself. She hadn't shared any of the information she'd gleaned from Tony's head. Cooper noted she didn't like secrets being kept from her, but she had no problem keeping her own.

Rafe seemed happy enough to follow Odessa's blind leadership, and she wouldn't allow Cooper to go back inside to check on Tony. More disturbing was her reasoning.

He likely won't remember you now, anyway, she'd said. Cooper shuddered to imagine what that meant.

His muscles stiffened at the sight of the road sign barreling up on the right. Without thinking, he gripped Rafe's hips a little tighter, likely sending mixed signals to his cocky Divinum escort. He always looked the other way so he didn't see the sign, and the turnoff would be so easy to pass. That's what he'd done every time he'd traveled that road in the last ten years. Not this time, though. Not after everything that had happened in the last two days. As Eunice had instructed, if he had any chance of getting control of his powers, he had to get beyond the mental block that made them go haywire. He had to face the past.

Cooper tapped Rafe on the shoulder and pointed to the road marker ahead. Rafe glanced back and hesitated only for a second before nodding. Cooper looked behind and saw that Odessa had followed them on their detour, no doubt filling her helmet with a myriad colorful curses. A few more taps, points, and turns, and Rafe guided the bike into a parking place at the side entrance of the Waccamaw Rehabilitation Center and Nursing Home.

Odessa pulled up beside them, killed her engine, and yanked off her helmet. "What the hell is *this*?"

"*This* is something I have to do." Cooper dismounted and tossed his helmet to Rafe who caught it with one hand. "I won't be long. Just wait here."

Before she had a chance to protest, Cooper sprinted across the parking lot. The moment he passed through the door, a nose-hair curling odor of piss, shit, and ammonia assaulted his senses. A hefty, middle-aged white woman wearing blue scrubs sat behind a reception desk in front of him. Her head was buried behind a computer screen, and she tapped away on the keyboard, not noticing him *or* the smell.

When Cooper cleared his throat a second time, she finally looked up at him with a disapproving scowl. "Can I help you?"

He looked down and fidgeted with a fat pink pen tied to a clipboard resting on the desk. "I'm visiting a friend."

The nurse shoved a pencil into her wiry nest of brown hair and scratched. "Sign in, please. Name of the patient?"

His breath caught in his throat. He had to say it out loud. "Stone. Trevor Stone." He exhaled. There. It was out, and it hadn't killed him. He scribbled his name on the clipboard, feeling mildly emboldened. The nurse couldn't have been less interested in his emotional breakthrough. She held a sheet of paper fortified inside a clear plastic page protector, and she ran a cherry-red one-inch fingernail down columns of names, numbers, and germs, all while smacking the hell out of some Juicy Fruit.

"Room 110," she finally announced, dropping the paper on the desk and returning her attention to the computer screen. "Go to the end of the hall. Turn left. First room on your right."

Cooper forced a smile and set off down the hall to face his sins.

Pushing through the heavy oversized door of Trevor's room, he wasn't prepared for what he found. Lying on a bed in the center of the sterile white room was a pale shadow of his first boyfriend, the once-strapping star quarterback who had been at the top of the recruiting short list for every collegiate football program in the Southeast. Now, Trevor stared up at the ceiling. Vacant eyes. Sealed lips. A tube emerged from under the sheet. Cooper stood motionless just inside the door, staring at his handiwork. He wanted to curl up and die.

A rail-thin nurse in her sixties wearing a crooked blonde wig bent over, tucking the sheets under the foot of the mattress. Leathery skin hung from her face like used-up chewing gum. Pursed ruby-red lips formed a permanent cigarette-holding pucker in her mouth.

She looked up at him and smiled. "Hey there, hun. You a friend of Trevor?" Her voice was smoky and too loud for the small room.

"Yes." The lie sizzled on his tongue. No friend could have done this. He half expected Trevor to look over at him and call him out for the fraud he was. He should just turn around and slip quietly out the door. The nurse seemed to detect his hesitation and cocked her head at him.

"Well, come on over," she said. "He won't bite. Couldn't if he wanted to." She giggled a little, which seemed inappropriate in the weighted atmosphere of the room.

Cooper took small calculated steps toward the bed, as if he was walking through a field of land mines. In theory, he was. It took him less time to cross the minefield than he'd hoped, and he found himself at the side of the bed, staring down at his judge, jury, and executioner.

Trevor's trademark thick blond hair had been buzzed away. His face was pale and gaunt. Dead eyes clung to stained and speckled drop-ceiling panels.

"Can he hear us?" Cooper used a library-grade whisper and hoped the nurse took his cue.

She adjusted knobs on the monitors beside the bed. "Oh, sure he can."

Still too loud.

"Go ahead and talk away. If you don't mind one-sided conversations." She let out another unfortunate cackle as she moved a chair to the side of the bed for him. There was no need. He wouldn't be there long enough to sit.

"He hasn't talked in ten years. But there's always hope." She gathered up a tray full of pill cups. "I run out of things to say pretty fast. Find myself asking questions I know he won't answer or telling him all my problems. He's a good listener. Makes me feel a little crazy sometimes, though. Enjoy your visit." She turned and disappeared into the hallway without another word. Thank God. The door closed behind her in ominous slow motion.

Cooper stared over his shoulder at the door. He could still bail. He had no right to be there, anyway. How selfish could he get? And just what did he expect? Some kind of absolution? Permission to fully awaken the part of him that put Trevor there in the first place? He looked back down at Trevor's face. Dark brown irises stared back at him, haunting, cold, and empty.

"Trevor?"

Trevor's eyes were cloudy, aware of the world around them but locked inside an unresponsive body. If Trevor was glad to see him, Cooper couldn't tell. If the sight of Cooper disgusted him, he couldn't tell that, either. Cooper stood there, gripping the side rail of the bed so tight his knuckles whitened while trying to compile the random words rolling around in his brain into complete sentences.

Sorry. Such a piss poor excuse for a word. Would Trevor even understand what he was apologizing for? He likely had no memory of what happened that night at the football game. But Cooper needed Trevor to know so he could move past it. Once again it was all about him.

He decided to start small. “Hey.” He caught a glimpse of his own reflection in Trevor’s glassy eyes. Clearing his throat, he gave it another shot. “I hope you don’t mind me coming here.

The steady beep of a bedside monitor mapping Trevor’s vitals was the only audible response in the room.

“I was in town and wanted to come by and see how you were doing.”

If he could have sucked the words back into his mouth, he would have. How the hell did it look like the guy was doing?

Cooper glanced down at Trevor’s exposed hand. That hand had touched him so many times when they were young, caressing every inch of his body. But when the rumors started, Trevor betrayed him. Denied their love and joined in the public ridicule aimed at the pathetic redheaded queer pining away for the quarterback.

In a brazen move, Cooper touched the back of Trevor’s hand with the tip of his index finger. Just testing the waters. The pale hand trembled at the touch, and Cooper froze. Before the shock of the movement could register in Cooper’s brain, Trevor curled his brittle fingers and clamped down on Cooper’s hand like a vise. His heart thumped against his chest. Involuntary reflexes. He’d read about it. That’s all it could be.

A jolt of hot energy ignited in Cooper’s core and rushed

down to his fingertips, fusing their skin together. Panic washed over him as Trevor tightened his grip. It shouldn't be possible. He shouldn't be able to do that. Cooper reached for the call button hanging above the headboard, but Trevor applied more pressure. The force deep inside Cooper bubbled and pooled in the tips of his fingers. He clenched his jaw and fought to hold it at bay. Using his free hand, he tried to peel Trevor's fingers off of him. He would not hurt this man again.

Trevor's eyes pinged from side to side like pinballs. Cooper gasped, and his whole body went numb, as if he had no control over its function. The room spun around him, and he closed his eyes, trying desperately to calm the erratic beating of his heart. Memories of that night played in his mind's eye like a bizarre movie trailer. A series of images, one frame after another taunting him. His head throbbed, like his brain was locked inside a pressure cooker and would explode soon if he didn't get away. His muscles seized, expelling everything boiling inside him out through his fingertips. Finally, Trevor's grip eased, and the room stilled. Cooper opened his eyes.

Trevor stared back at him with renewed clarity and life brimming in his eyes.

Yanking his hand away, Cooper stumbled back. He had awakened something long dormant in Trevor, like their spirits had entangled into one. Trevor knew what Cooper did to him. The memories he'd just witnessed were not his own. He'd relived the events of that night through Trevor's eyes. Saw what he saw. Felt what he felt. And Trevor didn't have a trace of the anger or judgment Cooper had expected. Only regret. Trevor's previously unreadable eyes danced with a new kinetic vigor, bright and full of life.

Cooper leaned over the bed. "Trevor?"

A gurgle of sound spilled from Trevor's mouth. His moist eyes were fixed on Cooper's. "I…"

Cooper's heart skipped a beat at the long forgotten sound of Trevor's voice, now raspy and thick with the labor of speech. He lowered his ear to Trevor's mouth. "What? What do you need?"

A moment of silence passed, and Cooper thought he'd imagined it. Two strained and whispered words slipped from Trevor's lips. "Loved. You."

Cooper straightened his spine and stared down at him, unable to process the simple words that hung in the air between them.

Trevor's lips twitched and struggled to part once more. Two new words came stronger—desperate and earnest. "Forgive. Me."

Cooper's heart sank to the pit of his stomach, and his mouth went bone dry. After all the pain he'd caused this man, Trevor wanted *his* forgiveness. Those wet and glassy eyes reflected the forgone absolution of Cooper's sins, something he'd never even considered possible.

The nurse barreled through the door. "What happened? His heart rate spiked on the monitors."

"I… I don't know," Cooper stammered, easing backward to the door.

Another blur of a nurse whizzed by him, over to Trevor's

side and picked up his hand. “Oh my God. His fingers are moving. His toes. Call Dr. Baker!”

Cooper pulled opened the door and looked back at Trevor’s newly flushed face one last time. Trevor held his gaze, a single tear trailing down his cheek. If Cooper hadn’t known better, he would have sworn Trevor’s lips eased into the faintest of smiles.

CHAPTER TWENTY-SIX

All the way back to the parking lot, Cooper's steps were lighter than they'd been in years. He'd gotten what he came for and somehow jump-started Trevor's broken body in the process. The crushing heaviness that had weighted his chest for a decade was gone. He was free.

Rafe held his hands up, halting Cooper's advance. "Whoa, whoa, dude. Take a beat before you hop on. You are pinging off the freakin' Divinum charts. You'll send us sailing into a ditch or something with all that juice flowing through you. What the hell happened in there?"

"Doesn't matter," Cooper said, breathing without obstruction for what felt like the first time in his life. He paced back and forth in front of Rafe. He couldn't stand still. "I'm good now. Let's go."

"Seriously," Rafe replied, putting a hand on Cooper's shoulder. "Just calm down a minute before you get on the bike."

Odessa leaned against the seat of her Harley with her long, shapely legs crossed at the ankles. "Rafe's right. Your power is brimming and reckless. It's untamed. Triggered by your emotions. That is dangerous. Take a minute to get it in check."

Cooper stopped pacing and stood beside Rafe's bike. He leaned forward with both hands on the seat and lowered his head, drawing in deep, calming breaths. He knew they were right, and *brimming* was as good a word as any to describe what he felt. His skin teemed with goose bumps, and his ears rang. His fingertips burned, and blood surged like hot lava in his veins. He was no longer afraid of his power, but he still needed to control the dark side of his nature. That would be the tricky part because it was stronger than he wanted to admit.

He stood and shook his fingers, expelling the nervous energy. "I'm fine now. Really." He looked over at Odessa. "Where are we going?"

She eyed him with a healthy dose of suspicion and threw a lithe leg over the seat of her bike. "*We* are going to the clock tower. You know it?"

Cooper took the helmet Rafe offered him and pulled it on. "Of course I know it. Everyone does. It's at the Rice Museum on Front Street, just down the street from Phipps House. And what exactly did you do to Tony?" Cooper eyed her through the cocked open visor of his helmet. "He'd better be okay."

"He'll be fine." She stood and balanced the Harley between her legs "But he's in no shape to alert Montgomery of our visit anytime soon."

Cooper shook his head, and he threw his leg over the seat of Rafe's bike.

Odessa shrugged. “And as long as he doesn’t turn, he’ll be allowed to live. Just don’t be too offended if he doesn’t remember you the next time you run into him.”

Rafe stood between the two bikes, a goofy grin twisting his face. “Hold up. Hold up. Let me get this straight. There’s a museum about fucking rice?”

Cooper snapped the chinstrap of his helmet in place. “Not fucking rice, just rice. In the 1800s, Georgetown produced one-half of the total rice crop for the entire country. So yes, we have a museum about rice.”

Rafe cocked an eyebrow, nodded, and then looked back at Odessa. “What of it, O?”

“According to the day soldier, that’s where the changeling nest is located.” She slung her hair back and pulled on her helmet. “So that’s where we’re going.”

Rafe slid his leg over the seat, inserting his bubbled ass between Cooper’s legs. “Let’s drop him off with Lex and then hit it.”

Cooper planted his feet into the pedal rests and gripped Rafe’s waist. “I’m going with you.”

Odessa looked his way, glaring beneath the visor of her helmet. “I don’t think that is a good idea. You’ll be safer back at the Phipps House with Lex. We don’t know how many creatures are in the nest. It could get ugly.”

Cooper nodded and looked straight ahead. “Exactly why you need me. Don’t worry. I think I can handle myself now.” This would be as good a time as any to see if the mental block was really gone. The magic pooling in his fingers throbbed for release, yet he still silently cursed himself for leaving Betsy's dagger on the table by the front door of Phipps House.

Rafe shook his head. "I don't think the Manheeg and Betsy would like it, O."

"The Manheeg put *me* in charge of this mission, Rafe. You let me worry about him. And I don't answer to his Anakim bitch." She looked back at Cooper and studied him a moment. Her unreadable eyes gave him pause. "You can come with us. But you stay right on Rafe's ass."

Rafe shrugged and pulled his helmet over his thick head of hair. "I don't think that will be a problem. He certainly knows where my ass is. Been staring at it all day."

Cooper eased his grip on Rafe's hips. "Just because you have a dick doesn't mean I'm into you, asshole. You're not my type."

Rafe chuckled and kicked life into the bike. "I'm everyone's type, Ginger."

The raw power of the Harley's engine fusing with the heat coursing through his veins only intensified Cooper's need for release. Anticipation and anxiety made for a savory stew of dark urges deep inside him. His newfound clarity of mind assured him the mental block was gone. The next time he used his power, he would know exactly what he was doing. He would hold nothing back.

CHAPTER TWENTY-SEVEN

The street-rumbling wail of the Harleys shattered the sleepy charm of Georgetown's historic business district. They passed tight rows of buildings dating back to the 1700s, which would have been forgotten by time if not for the presence of their gentrified new tenants. Over the decades, the locals had slowly abandoned the downtown area, leaving the city no choice but to take one last stab at survival and relevance by reinventing itself as a charming historic tourist stop on the way to the gaudy glitz of Myrtle Beach.

They passed *Harborwalk Books*, a quirky gem of an independent bookstore that oozed local personality and charm. The front window displayed a collection of required reading on the infamous ghosts of Georgetown and a poster touting *Miss Ida's Ghost Tours.* Apparently the bookseller was adept at playing up the local lore to lure in tourists.

Diagonally across the street, the Strand Theater stood as a beacon of fond childhood memories for Cooper as well. Somewhere along the way, the Strand had been transformed from a movie theater into a community playhouse. Red block letters adorned the rusty marquee announcing the next production.

Swamp Fox Players present

A RAISIN IN THE SUN

March 1-3

It was a bold theatric choice for a small town that masked its deep-seated racism in a cloak of Southern charm. Like referring to the Civil War as *The War of Northern Aggression*, or *The Recent Unpleasantness*.

Rafe and Odessa guided the bikes into two empty parking spots directly in front of the clock tower of the Rice Museum and killed the engines simultaneously. A few tourists stopped and gawked at Cooper's odd-looking companions to the very limit of Southern hospitality. He had to admit that his Divinum friends could not have looked more out of place if they tried. Odessa turned the most heads when she hopped off her bike and stretched her legs in those tight leather pants, which clung to her body like a second skin.

Before Cooper and Rafe had a chance to dismount, a police cruiser pulled into the empty space beside them. Randy hopped out of the driver's side and rounded the front of the car, looking like sex on a stick in his neatly pressed uniform. Cooper looked away. Dammit. He didn't need that kind of distraction, and he still felt like a grade-A asshole for giving Randy the cold shoulder earlier. He removed his helmet, peeled himself from the back of Rafe's body, and slid off the bike. Randy glowered at Rafe, who could not have been more oblivious to the open show of disdain.

Rafe pulled off his helmet and flashed Randy a mischievous

grin. "Officer Thor! Nice to see you again, dude."

Cooper knocked Rafe's arm with the back of his hand and shot him a reprimanding glare.

Rafe held up his hands. "What? He looks like Thor." He dismounted and hustled over to an unamused Odessa, Randy's contemptuous glare following him every step of the way. He looked like he wanted to bash the back of Rafe's cocky head in. If Cooper didn't know better, he'd think Randy was jealous. But he knew better.

Cooper walked over to Randy with the intention of being direct but cordial. He struggled to keep his internal swamp of murky feelings in check. He needed to stay focused. "What are you doing here? I'm fine. Really." Not bad. He'd even managed to sound a tad annoyed, a nice touch.

Randy cocked his head at Cooper. "I saw you turning onto Front Street. Thought you were heading back to Phipps House, so I followed. Surprised to see you pull up here. What's going on, Cooper? Surely your *friends* are not that interested in the history of Georgetown's rice culture."

It was a fair question. His whole life, Cooper had never once set foot inside the Rice Museum. Most locals hadn't, either. Not unless they were on an elementary school field trip. Cooper looked over to Odessa for help. She offered none, leaning against the brick wall of the clock tower with her arms crossed. She wasn't tapping the toe of her boot on the sidewalk, but she might as well have been. She obviously didn't like interruptions or detours derailing her plans. Cooper knew she couldn't care less what he told Randy, as long as he got rid of him.

He turned his attention back to Randy. "It's a long—"

"Doesn't matter," Randy said, cutting him off. "I followed you because I need to talk to you. About… all of this… shit."

Cooper sat his helmet on the seat of the bike and sighed. "All of what shit, Randy? You mean like how I led you into that clusterfuck last night that almost got you killed? How I opened your eyes to things no one should ever have to face? Or is it how I made an idiotic move based on a pathetic childhood crush and tried to kiss you? All *that* shit?"

Randy's cheeks reddened, and he clenched his jaw. "Well. When you sum it all up like that, it does seem to beg for a follow-up discussion, don't you think?"

The sarcasm in his tone stung, though Cooper knew he deserved it. He took a deep breath and absently ran his hand over his hair. "Look. I'm sorry. You're right. We probably should talk. It's just not a good time right now."

Randy glanced over his shoulder at Odessa who gave away nothing with her eyes. He then eyed Rafe with a healthy dose of mistrust. "Just tell me what the hell you're doing here, Coop."

When he didn't immediately answer, Randy stepped so close to him that his minty breath chilled Cooper's lips. He breathed in Randy's woodsy scent and exhaled it in smoky breaths of his own, his brain instantly turning to mush. Goddamn that cologne. Taking Randy by the arm, he led him down the sidewalk, out of earshot of Odessa and Rafe.

"Listen. It's just something we have to do, okay? For me, for Lillie Mae, hell, maybe even for you and the rest of the world for all I know. Alexander. The guy from last night. He's up to some really bad shit and has to be stopped."

Randy shook his head defiantly. "Coop, I don't care if they're cooking meth out there at Warfield. I'm not letting you get anywhere near those psycho-fag vamps again."

The slur slapped Cooper hard across the face, causing him to physically flinch. Randy noticed.

"Dammit. I'm sorry, Coop," he said, his tone and eyes softening. "I didn't mean—"

Cooper shot his hand up, silencing Randy cold. They'd never discussed the drunken kiss on the beach the night of his brother's funeral or how long that kiss had lingered before Randy put a stop to it.

Cooper scratched the back of his head and raised his index finger in the air at Rafe and Odessa, silently requesting another minute before turning back to Randy. "It's fine. Nothing I haven't heard before. Now, I really need to go."

He turned and joined Odessa and Rafe near the front entrance of the Rice Museum. A firm hand on his shoulder spun him around, and he came face to face with Randy again.

"Red, listen—"

"What?" Cooper was exasperated and tired of being on a confusing emotional rollercoaster ride with the guy.

The corner of Randy's mouth twitched. "Is it dangerous? What you're doing?"

Cooper stared at him and sighed. "Couldn't be any more dangerous than living an honest life. I'm so brave that way, remember?" He didn't know why he said it. Didn't know why he poured on the retaliatory sarcasm. But, damn it felt good. The sting of betrayal in Randy's eyes confirmed Cooper had made his point. All too well.

Rafe stepped between them, posturing his muscular build and swagger to match Randy's. It was a full-on man-off. Cooper half expected them to whip out their dicks and engage in an actual pissing contest right there on the sidewalks of Georgetown.

Rafe's face and his tone hardened. "We've got him."

The scowl on Randy's face was no joke either. "You know what douche dick? *I've* got him. Whatever shit you're about to drag him into, I'm coming with you."

After an uncomfortably long ten seconds, Randy won the stare down. Rafe shrugged. "Suit yourself. I just hope you've got a big one."

"What the hell did you say to me?"

Rafe grabbed the buckle of Randy's utility belt and gave it a firm tug. "A gun, you hot-headed hick."

Randy's top lip tightened into a sneer. Cooper was sure he would lay Rafe out cold. He took a step toward them, ready to jump into the middle if needed, like that would do any good.

Randy pulled his jacket open. A large service revolver hung from his shoulder holster. "That big enough for you, Princess?"

Rafe glanced down at the gun and then just below Randy's utility belt. "That should do just fine." He looked up with a smirk and walked away, leaving Randy speechless and scowling.

With her thumbs tucked into her back pockets, Odessa actually tapped the toe of her boot on the sidewalk. "If you boys are finished measuring your cocks, we've got work to do." She walked up to Randy and planted a hand on her hip. "You can come, but you're on your own down there, cowboy." She nodded over to Cooper. "*He's* our number one concern."

Randy got so close to her that their noses almost touched. The threat lacing his words made Cooper's heart skip a beat. "No, lady. If anything happens to him, *I'm* your number one concern."

CHAPTER TWENTY-EIGHT

Closed for renovations.

Cooper stood in front of the group, staring at the white paper sign taped to the inside of the glass door. "Follow me."

He led them around to the back of the building with Randy on his heels, searching windows and doors that looked accessible. He was on a mission, the need to release the dark power inside him reaching a dangerous boiling point. Odessa and Rafe followed his lead for a change. Maybe they were finally starting to trust him.

When they reached the back door of the museum, Cooper pulled on the handle. "It's locked."

Randy stepped in front of him and dangled a daunting ring of keys in his face. It looked like he had a key to every business in the historic district and most of the houses.

Rafe slapped Randy on the back. "Nice, Officer Thor."

Randy rolled his eyes and fiddled with the key ring until he found the right one. "It's a small town. I have keys to most municipal sites." He shoved the key into the hole and looked back at Rafe. "And please, *please* touch me again, so

I'll have a legitimate excuse to break your fucking hand."

Rafe raised both hands in the air like he was being arrested and grinned. If he only knew how serious Randy was, he wouldn't be grinning. Randy turned the key, pushed the door open, and held it for Odessa and Rafe. Cooper followed them, but Randy stopped him with a hand to the shoulder.

"Hey," Randy said in a whisper. "Your boyfriend in there is a real prick, you know that, right?"

Cooper cocked his head. "My boyfriend?"

Randy nodded over his shoulder in Rafe's direction. "Diesel meat. I mean, I know he's got the face, the muscles, and a sweet-ass Harley, but other than that, I can't for the life of me understand what you see in him."

Cooper stared at him, horrified. The blood drained out of his face, not only because Randy assumed he was *with* Rafe, but that they were having the discussion at all. "Rafe is *not* my boyfriend."

Randy raised his eyebrows and tucked a thumb in his utility belt. "He's not?"

"No." Cooper ran nervous fingers through his hair. "I don't have a *boyfriend*." The word sounded foreign on his tongue. He couldn't ever remember having a boyfriend. Not since high school. Not since Trevor.

"Oh. Sorry. I just thought—"

Cooper shook his head and pushed past him. "You thought wrong."

"Well, okay," Randy stammered, sounding almost relieved. "Good."

Good? Cooper wasn't at all sure of Randy's meaning. Good that he didn't have a boyfriend, or good that it wasn't Rafe? He let it go and walked into the center of the room. It was warmer inside the museum, though there was very little light. The place was a maze of Georgetown history. Large sheets of plastic protected antebellum artifacts and machinery from dust. Placards lined the walls and the bases of the table displays, filled with a lot of information about rice cultivation.

Cooper unzipped his jacket, allowing the warmth to reach his body. He rubbed the back of his neck, kneading his fingers into the base of his skull. His muscles had been bound in tense knots for the last two days with no relief in sight.

Randy moved to the front of the eclectic group. He was obviously used to being in charge. Problem was, so was Odessa. And Cooper was never fond of playing follow the leader either, so they all jockeyed for position as they explored the room.

Randy eyed Odessa. "So? What are we looking for?"

Odessa nodded up. "How do we get to the base of the clock tower?"

Randy pointed over his shoulder to a door at the far end of the long rectangle-shaped room.

Cooper walked over to the door and tried turning the knob. "It's locked."

Randy moved in front of him, holding up the same key that gained them access to the rear entrance. He opened the door, stuck his head inside, and looked up. "I doubt anyone ever comes in here unless they have to do repairs on the clock or something. It's just an access space."

Cooper slipped around him into the four-foot wide space. A cool draft caressed his cheeks. He got down on hands and knees, brushing away the thick layer of dust covering a slatted wood floor. Unlike the kitchen house, there wasn't a trap door, which didn't make any sense to him.

"What are we looking for anyway?" Randy asked, hovering over him.

Cooper scanned the floor around Randy's feet. It creaked when he shifted his weight. "Step back a sec."

Randy looked down and then moved to the side. Cooper ran his fingers along the seam between two of the boards where Randy had stood. He finally found a crack wide enough to slip his fingers into. He tugged, but the board wouldn't move.

"Hang on." Randy kneeled down beside him and found another crack in the same seam. With their combined strength, the board popped up.

Cooper caught a shiny glimpse of what he'd been looking for and went to work on the rest of the boards with Randy's assistance. Within a couple of minutes, they had most of the floor removed, exposing a rusted silver latch and hinges in the center of the room. Odessa leaned in over Randy's shoulder, her relaxed expression hinting at something like approval.

Cooper looked over at a frowning Randy. "That's what we're looking for." He curled his index finger through the metal ring recessed in the wood and pulled open a two-foot square section of the floor. A wave of putrid air rushed up from the dark hole and blew over his face, triggering his gag reflex.

Randy crouched and peered down into the opening. "Great. Another dark-ass hole in the ground." He'd read Cooper's mind.

Cooper stood and looked at Odessa. "You really think the nest is down there?"

She stepped up to the edge, turned around, and stuck her right foot down onto the top rung of a wooden ladder. "Only one way to find out." The top of her head quickly disappeared into the darkness below.

Rafe had already descended waist-deep down the ladder when he looked back up at Cooper and Randy. "Remember, aim for the head." He flashed a crooked grin and then disappeared within seconds. Cooper knew what he meant from his encounter with the changeling at Phipps House. Rafe obviously found exploding zombie brains infinitely amusing.

Cooper moved toward the opening, and Randy stopped him with a firm grip on his bicep. "Are you sure you can trust these people, Red? How do you know they're not leading us into a trap?"

Cooper forced a reassuring smile. "I know they're odd, but yes. I trust them."

Randy shook his head. "I don't know. Something doesn't feel right."

"They're Divinum, like me." Cooper cupped Randy's elbow in his palm. The Gortex jacket was cold and scratchy to the touch. "Remember those… things, the changelings we ran into at Warfield last night?"

Randy peered down into the black hole. "Those demonic-looking zombie fuckers?"

"Yes. We have to find their nest and eliminate them so Rafe and Odessa's friends can get to Alexander." He squeezed Randy's elbow until he'd regained his attention. "You really don't have to come with us. In fact, I would feel better if you didn't. We're not sure what we'll find down there. Or how many of those things there might be."

Randy cocked his head. "You think I'm scared?" He huffed and rolled his eyes. "Look, I wouldn't mind taking out a couple of those nasty fuckers myself. But more importantly, you're not going down there without me. So stop trying to get rid of me, already. I'm not going anywhere."

Cooper's cheeks flushed with heat. If he could have formed a coherent response, he would have. Instead, he nodded, stepped down onto the top rung of the ladder, and descended into darkness.

CHAPTER TWENTY-NINE

The waning light from above provided little assistance in the frigid black void that enveloped Cooper at the bottom of the ladder. He couldn't see a damned thing, and the foul odor had intensified with every step of his descent. He stood cupping his nose and waited as Randy stepped down off the ladder.

"Jesus!" Randy's feet hit the ground, and he waved a hand in front of his face. "Smells like the asshole of death down here."

"It's the changelings." Odessa's voice drifted over from somewhere in the darkness. "The nest must be close."

A light flickered on. Randy held the flashlight from his utility belt in his left hand, the beam illuminating the backs of Odessa and Rafe.

Odessa turned and squinted into the light. "Oh, right. You *do* need that."

Cooper cocked his head at her. "And you don't?"

Odessa looked back down the tunnel. "Neither do you, Cooper. Just keep your eyes open and focus. You'll see."

Cooper stared at the blinding wall of darkness in front of him and focused his eyes, straining to see. At first, he saw nothing. Then goose bumps popped up on his arms as shapes outside the bounds of Randy's flashlight beam took form in a haze of greenish illumination. It was like wearing night-vision goggles, or like the green glow he'd experienced the first night he arrived at Phipps House when he was outside looking for Lillie Mae. It wasn't perfect, but he could see.

The tunnel was five feet wide, with no sign of any human presence. No crumpled soda cans, beer bottles, or cigarette butts littered the ground. Ahead, the outline of Rafe's sizable green frame emerged, looking like the Incredible Hulk.

Cooper eased forward, running his hand along the dirt wall. "This is so freaky."

Rafe looked back at him with glowing green orbs for eyeballs. "See what you've been missing out on, bro?"

Rafe and Odessa continued, their backs fading into the void. Cooper struggled to recalibrate his vision. It flared full blast one minute and waned the next. Something heavy scrambled over Cooper's foot. He jumped and kicked at the dirt.

"Holy hell!"

Randy shined his light down at Cooper's feet. "What?"

Grabbing Randy's hand, Cooper aimed the light down on the ground in front of him. A fat rat scampered through the beam and back down the tunnel. Randy laughed softly as Cooper sighed and let go of his hand, suddenly too aware of the contact.

Odessa had stopped ahead. She held a hand up to halt them and peered down the dark tunnel, craning her neck. Waiting. Listening. She looked back at them and whispered, "We are close."

The pungent smell grew stronger with every step. Cooper struggled to maintain his night vision. At the moment, though, he flew blind. He would have to work on that. With eyes peeled to the beam of Randy's flashlight for guidance, he mapped their path in his head, imagining what sat above their location. The tunnel was more like a maze, and he couldn't tell exactly where they were. They could have been going in circles for all he knew. Randy slipped his hand just under the hem of Cooper's jacket, touching the small of his back and sending shivers down his spine. It remained there only a few seconds. Then he dropped it.

In front of them, Odessa and Rafe came to a sudden stop, which halted Cooper and Randy as well. A cool breeze swirled around them, tickling the rims of Cooper's ears and filling his nostrils with the unbearable acrid odor. As best as he could tell, they had emerged from the tunnel into a large open space. Cooper followed the beam of Randy's flashlight, inspecting their surroundings as they edged forward. The area was at least double the size of the space under the kitchen house at Warfield. A dozen tunnel entrances dotted curved clay walls leading in all different directions. One of them to Warfield, he supposed, and one of them toward Phipps House.

Odessa moved from one tunnel entrance to the next, inspecting each and sniffing the air until she had circled the entire perimeter. Rafe stood in the center of the room, chest puffed out like a shield and staring up the walls to the ceiling.

Randy covered his nose with the back of his hand. "What the hell is this place?"

Rafe's hand shot straight up to silence Randy, his head back and eyes peeled on the ceiling. Cooper's breath caught in his throat. Something was wrong. Very wrong. Rafe pointed up.

Cooper looked up, a knot of dread forming in his stomach as he did. He focused his eyes on the darkness above and concentrated. The night vision kicked in again, and green shapes materialized about thirty or forty feet above them. A mass of twisted bodies tangled in knotted clumps of decomposing flesh hung from the ceiling, moving in waves of labored breathing. Cooper's heart pounded in his chest so hard, he was sure the sound would wake the sleeping monsters. Palms and fingers burned with blistering heat like they were being held over an open flame. Randy innocently raised his arm and pointed the flashlight up at the ceiling, its searing beam landing right in the middle of the nesting horde.

Cooper wished to God he hadn't done that.

CHAPTER THIRTY

A bulbous head snapped backward, unnaturally so. Beady green eyes locked onto Cooper. The creature's jaws parted in jerky slow motion, like it was about to vomit. What came from its mouth instead, was an ear-splitting shriek that reverberated through the cavern.

"Fuck me," Randy muttered, gazing up in a trancelike state.

Odessa backed toward them with her eyes peeled to the ceiling. "They are waking up."

"Yeah. No shit," Cooper replied, trying to keep his voice steady and low as he edged closer to Randy.

A chorus of cracking bones and ripping flesh trickled over the ceiling as the changelings untangled themselves and woke one by one. Dozens of them slithered over one another and hissed at the intruders. Odessa and Rafe closed in around Cooper, circling with their backs to him. The pale-skinned changeling that started the battle cry dropped to the floor only a few feet away from Odessa. Dirt bounced up around its feet upon impact. It crouched and hissed at her.

Odessa threw a hand out in front of her and the creature sailed backward, slamming hard into the dirt wall thirty feet away. Odessa curled her fingers into a tight ball. The changeling screamed and writhed around on the ground. The cry was somewhat human, but amplified tenfold and laced with a piercing cadence that started a chain reaction of equally shrill cries above them.

Two changelings hit the ground in front of Rafe. He drew daggers from somewhere inside his leather jacket and charged the beasts, spinning away from their grasps and driving the blades down into the center of two hairless skulls. The bodies exploded, flesh, bone, and brain matter shooting in all directions. Cooper edged back, wishing to God he still had Betsy's dagger, or Betsy herself for that matter. They needed all the help they could get.

Randy jumped in front of him, aiming his gun over Cooper's right shoulder. "Get down!"

Cooper dropped to his knees. The gunshot blasted in his ears, echoing through the room. He hoped Randy had gotten one, but he had no time to check. A linebacker of a changeling barreled toward him, snarling at him with a dislocated jaw. A mass of pointy teeth snapped as it advanced with surprising speed. Adrenaline burned in Cooper's veins, and a surge of destructive power rumbled deep inside him, like molten lava erupting from his core. With slight trepidation, he allowed his instincts to take over.

Springing to his feet, he threw his hand straight out in front of him and released the power percolating inside him. He wasn't sure what he did, but the creature wailed and fell back, tumbling several times over itself until it slammed into the wall. It rolled over and sat up. Shook its head—dazed, but not dead. He didn't have time to relish in his minor success. More changelings dropped from above and surrounded them. Escape through one of the tunnels would be hard-fought, but it was their only chance. Cooper eased back and looked over his shoulder. Randy held his gun out in front of him in one hand and wielded the flashlight in the other.

"We have to get to one of the tunnels," Cooper yelled over the deafening screeches. His night vision was a shaky mess of green monsters and a hundred bright orbs of sinister eyes. He'd lost track of Odessa and Rafe, and his clarity of vision waned once again.

Another gunshot exploded from behind and a shriek sounded right in front of him. Panic solidified in his gut when the faint green glow of light illuminated a changeling rushing straight for him, its teeth gnashing and its claws reaching out for him. Cooper spun around, crouched, and sliced a hand, palm up, through the shrinking space between him and the charging monster. His fingertips sizzled, releasing a sharp spasm of power that took his breath away.

The creature stopped in its tracks, a howl of pain roaring from its mouth. A straight line across its fleshy stomach opened up, like a zipper in his skin had been yanked back, purging its contents in a gush of foul-smelling innards and thick steaming blood. The creature's mouth hung open as it looked down and inspected the front of its body. It looked back up at Cooper, lingering a moment before melting onto to the ground into a pool of blood and entrails.

The stench of rotted intestines burned Cooper's nasal passage. He stared down at his hands, momentarily oblivious to the chaos around him. He'd killed one and couldn't believe how strong the instincts were, how precise the execution. And how good it felt. No images of Trevor had clouded his laser focus. He hadn't hesitated. And he was ready to kill again. He jumped to his feet and spun around. Randy stood staring at him, eyes wide, and mouth agape, no doubt wondering who was protecting whom.

Odessa rebuffed a charging changeling with her invisible force-field punch and yelled over to them. "There's too many of them! Get out of here!"

She stared at Cooper, as wide-eyed as Randy. Apparently she had witnessed his first kill as well. A cluster of creatures focused their attention on the two Jericho soldiers. Randy and Cooper were momentarily in the clear.

"Get back up top. Back to the sunlight!" Odessa shouted while circling an agitated and severely decomposed monster. She waved Cooper and Randy off. "We'll draw them away. Go!"

Odessa and Rafe put down changeling after changeling. Rafe sailed over the creatures like gravity was a matter of choice and not scientific fact, and drove his dagger down into the crown of one's head, setting off another grisly explosion of flesh. Odessa somersaulted through the air, landing on the shoulders of a heavy-set creature and plunged her dagger deep into its chest. But the monsters kept coming. A dozen changelings blocked their path to the tunnel Cooper thought led back to the clock tower. Another gunshot rang out close to his ear. He ducked and looked over his shoulder. A dark-skinned creature dropped not two feet away from him. He hadn't even seen it coming, but Randy had. They needed to move. Now.

Cooper scanned the perimeter of the space and noticed movement at a tunnel entrance on his right. He strained his eyes and focused into the black hole. The blurred green shadow of a hulking figure appeared just inside the opening. Though the broad face was hazy, the imposing shape and domineering posture was undeniable. It was Blue. Cooper swallowed a lump back down his throat. He hoped to God Eudora was right about Blue being his guardian. He was about to either lead them to safety or to their demise. They were completely out of options.

He grabbed Randy's arm. "This way!"

They ducked and dodged several oncoming attacks as he led Randy in the direction of Blue's tunnel. Every few steps, a changeling landed in his path and charged. Each time, Cooper knocked it out of the way, sending it flying in the air with the flick of his wrist, like swatting flies. He barely had time to think about it. Just reacted as his body commanded. Randy stumbled, trying to run while guarding them from behind, firing off rounds that Cooper prayed hit their intended targets.

They finally made it to the tunnel. Cooper stayed close to Randy, wanting an ally if he did come face to face with Blue. To his relief, the tunnel was empty. He looked back. Rafe and Odessa stood in the middle of the cavern, surrounded by the attacking horde and fighting for their lives. He didn't want to leave them, but he had no choice. He had to get Randy out of there. Odessa spotted him through a sea of snapping jaws. She pulled Rafe toward a tunnel on the opposite side of the cavern. They plowed a path of carnage through the monsters to get there, drawing as many of the demons away from Cooper and Randy's direction as possible, but not all of them.

Cooper had no time to wait and see if they made it or not. He and Randy ran down their new path of darkness, Randy guided by the beam of his flashlight, Cooper with a tenuous hold on his night vision. He shot a glance over his shoulder. Three changelings were in pursuit. Randy reached back and fired but missed.

Cooper made a left turn. He wasn't sure why. It just felt right. He didn't have any idea where they were headed; he just hoped they could find a place to emerge from this hellhole and into the safety of sunlight. His vision faltered again, as if his internal batteries were low, and then it went completely dark. After a few seconds of running blind, he smashed head on into a wall of hard clay. Randy careened into him, and they both tumbled to the ground. The flashlight rolled out of Randy's hand and flickered off, abandoning them in an abyss of darkness.

Cooper quickly righted himself and leaned against the wall, heaving desperately for air. They were in total and complete darkness. He couldn't even distinguish the outline of Randy's body, and the shrieking in the distance told him the creatures couldn't be far behind. He willed his night vision to return, and it denied him once again.

Randy pressed his shoulder up against Cooper, and the heat of his body calmed Cooper's breathing. "I think we lost them."

Cooper leaned forward and ran hands over the ground searching blindly for the flashlight. "Not likely." He kept his voice to a whisper and finally gave up his search. "I can't see a damn thing. This night vision is—"

Randy touched his face, interrupting his train of thought. The rough skin of his palm scraped Cooper's cheek and sent a rush of electricity over his body. Worse timing for this could not exist, but Cooper couldn't stop himself from wanting to absorb the moment. Randy found Cooper's mouth and pressed a finger over his lips. It wasn't an affectionate caress in the dark. Of course it wasn't. It was a silent warning to shut the fuck up.

Labored wheezing sounded a few feet away in the darkness, and a rancid stench sizzled the hair of Cooper's nostrils. He closed his mouth for fear he might gag. He slid his hand over the surface of the ground again, hoping to find the flashlight. After a few unfruitful seconds, he finally made contact with cold, hard metal. He coiled his fingers around the cylinder and lifted it off the ground. It flickered to life, the beam shooting out in front of them and exposing the misshapen forms of two approaching changelings.

A female crawled on hands and knees toward Randy. She snarled at him, snapping impossibly long fangs in the air. Clumps of long matted hair sprang randomly out of her bashed-in skull. She threw her head back. Her mouth stretched open wide, well beyond what her human form would ever have been able to do. She unhinged her jaws with spine-tingling snaps and pops, and her jagged fangs extended even more. Before she could alert the rest of her herd, Randy filled her mouth with the heel of his boot, knocking her back several feet. She crashed into the wall opposite them and fell still on the ground.

Standing ten feet away from Cooper, the second changeling reared its head back and howled. Randy reached for his gun, and Cooper aimed the beam on the creature's bulbous eyes, blinding it with a flood of light. Two shots rang out. The changeling lunged forward. Jumping to his feet, Cooper dropped the flashlight and stretched his hands out at the charging monster. A rush of hot energy discharged from his fingertips, ejecting a softball-shaped flame from each hand. The fire orbs landed squarely in the center of the changeling's chest, igniting into an explosion of burning flesh and ear-piercing shrieks.

Cooper stumbled back in shock. He dropped to the ground and scrambled away from the flailing ball of fire. It collapsed in on itself a few feet away, the fire dissipating, as there was less and less flesh and bone to feed on.

Randy grabbed the flashlight, the shaky beam illuminating eyes wide as golf balls. "Holy shit. Red. I didn't know you could do *that*."

Cooper crawled over to him, shocked and a little impressed with himself. "Neither did I."

They sat side by side in silence, catching their breath and basking in the bliss of momentary safety. Randy lifted his arm and draped it loosely over Cooper's shoulders. Cooper knew better than to read too much into the casual, friendly gesture, but he soaked up the physical contact all the same. He remained perfectly still, knowing any sudden move would likely end with Randy shifting away from him. He knew it was only a fantasy, but he wanted to stay like that forever—tucked safely in the arms of the only man he wanted to comfort him that way. The only man who could wear down his defenses with a wink and a smile. For once, he loosened the tight reins of control and allowed himself to be protected. Cared for. Even though he knew it was all in his head, in that moment, it felt real. And he savored it, even with the corpses of two flesh-eating monsters a few feet away.

Randy turned to him. "You ready to find a way out of this hellhole, Red?"

Cooper wiped the sweat from his brow with the back of his hand and looked back at him, their faces only inches apart. "I think we circled back at one point. Best I can tell, we shouldn't be too far away from the clock tower."

Randy stared into his eyes, and Cooper's breath caught in his throat. He held it there, afraid to move or breathe.

Randy peered over Cooper's right shoulder and squinted. "What the hell is that?"

CHAPTER THIRTY-ONE

Randy grabbed the flashlight from Cooper's hand and scrambled to his feet. Cooper jumped up and followed him down the tunnel toward faint illumination forty feet away. Dim light trickled down from somewhere above, projecting a square outline on the ground. A way out. Cooper had no idea where it led, but almost anywhere was better than where they were.

Standing directly under what looked to be another trapdoor, Randy bent over and laced his fingers together, creating a makeshift step. "Come on. I'll hoist you up."

Cooper hesitated. He looked up and then back at Randy. "You sure you can hold me?"

Randy cocked his head and raised an eyebrow, like his manhood had just been called into question. "Cooper, I've lifted you up into trees since you were six years old. I know I'm a lot older and more decrepit now, but I think I can still manage."

Cooper ran his fingers through his hair and sized Randy up, comparing their height and weight. The guy had nearly four inches on him and at least ten to twenty more pounds of solid muscle.

"Maybe I should help *you* up first. I think I would have a better chance at *pushing* you up, than I would *pulling* you up."

Randy stood up straight and planted his hands on his hips. "You sure?"

Cooper leaned down and entwined his fingers. "Positive."

Randy shrugged. "Suit yourself." He placed his right foot into the handmade step and gripped the crown of Cooper's head, pushing himself up.

Straining under the weight, Cooper managed to ease him up a few inches.

"Almost there," Randy said, reaching up. "A little more."

Every muscle in Cooper's body protested. "Jesus! What have they been feeding you around here?"

"Shut up and lift, Red." Randy pressed his open palms against the trapdoor. "The son of a bitch is stuck or sealed or something."

Cooper locked his muscles in place and straightened out his spine, maximizing each of his six feet of height. Fatigue set in quickly, and sweat stung his eyes. He cursed himself under his breath for going easy at the gym. Too much time spent studying physiques other than his own.

Randy beat against the door with his fist and then looked down at Cooper. "Is there anything you can *do* to get it open? You know, that hocus-pocus shit of yours or something? Christ almighty. I can't believe I'm saying this."

Cooper wasn't sure he was capable of any hocus-pocus shit at the moment. However, a chilling moan from somewhere down the tunnel behind him gave him the needed motivation to try.

Without acknowledging the oncoming intruder, Randy pounded the wood with a heightened sense of urgency. "Goddammit!"

Cooper fought to keep his arms locked into place and focused on the trapdoor above. He took a deep breath, his leg muscles twitching and buckling under Randy's weight. A spark ignited immediately in the pit of his stomach, like the strike of a match. The prickle in his palms returned and spread down to his fingertips, lightening his load a little. He willed the trapdoor to open, and it did—in a small explosion of splintered wood.

Randy flinched and covered his eyes with his forearm, causing Cooper to nearly lose his balance. After a quick, appreciative glance down at Cooper, he reached up and grabbed onto the ledge, pulling himself up through the opening with relative ease. An ear-splitting shriek sounded right behind Cooper. He spun around. The female changeling stumbled toward him. Cooper made a quick mental note. *Boot-to-mouth. Not entirely effective.* It reached out for him with twisted claw-fingers, snapping its dislocated jaw.

Randy reached down to him with an outstretched arm. "Jump up. Now!"

Cooper did as he was told and caught hold of Randy's firm grip. He peered over his shoulder. The female was only a couple feet away. Her crooked fangs dripped with brown saliva. She swiped at his dangling legs. He kicked, catching her jaw, and ascended into the air with a powerful yank. He hooked his elbows over the ledge as Randy grabbed the waist of his pants and pulled him the rest of the way to safety. Scrambling to their feet, they both looked down into the tunnel. The female hissed at them before she dug her claws into the dirt wall and climbed.

Cooper scanned the room and quickly spotted a massive cedar wardrobe against a nearby wall. Randy was on it before Cooper could communicate to him. They each took a side. Edged it away from the wall one corner at a time. It was heavy as hell, but with their combined strength, they finally managed to tip it over. The impact of the solid piece of furniture hitting the concrete floor echoed through the room, covering the trapdoor.

Cooper dropped to his knees, his heart pounding away in his chest. Minimal streaks of sunlight from two small windows close to the ceiling broke through the shadows of the cluttered and dusty room. He didn't know where they were. All he knew was they were safe—at least for the moment.

"I hope Rafe and Odessa made it out."

"They looked like they could take care of themselves down there." Randy squatted beside him, wiping sweat from his brow with his forearm. Dirt smudged his face, his usually pristine uniform soiled and ripped in several places. It was the most disheveled Cooper had seen him since they were kids.

Cooper looked around the room through a thin cloud of suspended dust. Racks of colorful costumes lined the walls.

Shelves housing archaic projection equipment stood in the center of the room. Movie posters dating back as far as *On the Waterfront* sat in stacks on the floor.

A large metal film canister sat on the floor beside him and he touched it. "I think we're in the basement of the Strand Theater." He glanced up at the small rectangular windows near the ceiling. Though he couldn't gauge the exact time of day, the dim sunlight told him they needed to get back to the safety of Phipps House soon.

Randy stood and offered his hand. The exertion of his power had left Cooper physically drained, so he accepted the assistance getting to his feet. They stood face to face, their proximity much closer than Cooper had intended. He expected Randy to quickly release his hand and step back, but he didn't.

He looked into Cooper's eyes, then reached up and cradled his face in his hands. Oxygen stalled in Cooper's lungs. He couldn't move. Nor did he want to. Randy's lips parted, like he was about to say something. Something that would, no doubt, steal this moment away from Cooper forever. Something that would once again wring his heart out like a dishrag. But Randy didn't say anything. He closed the gap between their faces, planting his moist, hungry lips on Cooper's.

A shudder ran the length of Cooper's spine. A toxic mix of shock, relief, and pure pleasure paralyzed him. The kiss was hard and rough, laced with an urgent passion that Cooper had never experienced. Without hesitation, he welcomed Randy's thick, probing tongue with equal hunger, his skin tingling all over. He'd fantasized about that moment all his life, and it was nothing like he'd ever imagined. It was unpolished. Clunky. And perfect.

Slipping his arms around Randy's waist, Cooper pulled him closer. He wanted to feel the heat of that hard body against his, and he stiffened instantly when Randy's thickening crotch pressed against him. He let his hand fall down Randy's back and rest on the cleft of his muscled ass. A mistake. Because as suddenly as the kiss had started, it stopped.

Randy pulled back. Stared at Cooper with moist red lips, his eyes glassy and unreadable. He put hands on Cooper's shoulders and held him at arm's length. Cooper's heart sank, and he dropped his hands to his side. Shit. Here it comes. Another cut and run. And damn if he didn't deserve it for letting his defenses down so easily. How could he be so weak?

As Randy opened his mouth, Cooper lifted a hand to halt his words. "No need to say anything. It's okay. Heat of the moment. All this pent-up anxiety, that's all. I get it. No harm, no foul."

Randy's grip on Cooper's shoulders tightened. "No, asshole. That's what I was trying to tell you earlier, only you wouldn't give me a chance. Before all the exploding skulls, disembowelments, and fireballs shooting out of your ass. *That's* what I wanted to say to you." He paused and shrugged. "Well, that, but with *words*."

Slack-jawed and speechless, Cooper stared at Randy and let the words sink in, analyzing them internally for any signs of a *gotcha!* moment lurking just around the corner. He detected nothing other than complete sincerity.

He eased his hands back onto Randy's hips and exhaled for what felt like the first time in his life. "Wow. Actually, I… kind of *love* the way you finally said it." He put a hand on Randy's thick bicep. "And just for the record, the fireballs shot out of my fingers, not my ass."

Randy's mouth slowly curled into a smile. They chuckled and rested their foreheads against each other. Cooper took a deep breath of Randy's cologne into his lungs and allowed himself to let his guard down and relax a second. It felt good. He felt safe. For a moment, he actually thought everything was going to be okay. The moment was brief, interrupted by the chilling scrape of claws against the bottom of the overturned wardrobe.

CHAPTER THIRTY-TWO

With a sudden, hammering blow, the wardrobe rose three feet into the air and landed just to the right of the trap door. A twisted hand emerged, clamping its claw like fingers onto the floor. A spasm of panic seized Cooper's muscles. He scanned the room and immediately found cause for hope. A staircase. At the opposite end of the basement. He pushed Randy into the middle of the room where there was more sunlight and pointed. "The stairs. And stay in the light!"

Cooper glanced over his shoulder as they crossed the room. The female changeling dug her claws into the concrete floor and pulled herself out of the hole. She crouched like some giant mutant spider, her stomach and face low to the ground with elbows and knees extended above her back. A broken bone protruded through the ripped flesh on its leg and oozed with thick brown blood. The creature advanced but made the mistake of crossing a stream of sunlight in its path. With a piercing wail, it shrank into the shadows by the wall.

Randy spun around and drew his gun. Pointed it at the

creature and fired. Only the hollow click of an empty chamber sounded. "Fuck me!"

The female inched along the wall, hissing at them but staying clear of the streams of light separating them. Cooper kept an eye on the creature's position as they hurried over to the stairs. Another mangled arm rose out of the hole in the floor. Then another. Two new changelings crawled over one other, pulling themselves up into the room. The taller one had dark skin dangling from its face in crudely torn strips. The shorter, stocky one's tattoo-riddled skin hung loosely from its bones, making for a splotchy patchwork of ghoulish art. With eyes black and menacing, the creatures widened their dislocated jaws, releasing ear-splitting shrieks. A reciprocal chorus of war cries sounded from the tunnel below. More of them would soon emerge.

At the base of the stairs, Cooper pulled on Randy's arm. "We have to get outside."

He took the stairs two at a time and burst through the door at the top with Randy right on his heels. Sprinting around the thirty-foot-high projection screen, they skidded to a stop in the center of the empty stage to get their bearings. A single fluorescent light above them provided the only illumination in the theater other than the red glowing exit signs mounted along the wall in the back of the auditorium.

Randy tugged on Cooper's arm. "Come on. There's got to be a stage door somewhere closer."

They turned and froze. The three changelings from the basement rushed onto the stage, blocking their path. The creatures spread out and circled them like a pack of wild animals stalking their next meal. Cooper and Randy exchanged glances, but neither offered a plan.

A crackled voice sounded from behind the screen. "Who's there? Theater's closed." A lanky older man shuffled out onto the stage wearing coveralls and a tool belt. "How the hell did you people..." The man froze when he saw the changelings. "Jesus, Mary, and Joseph."

Cooper waved him off. "Get out of here!"

The tall changeling was on the old man before he could move an inch. It snatched the back of his head with its claws, jerking the skull back in a ninety-degree angle. The sound of snapping bones and ripping flesh made Cooper's stomach lurch. He edged forward. Randy grabbed his sleeve and held him back. The old man's eyes bulged from their sockets as the creature sank its fangs into his neck and gnawed right through to the spine in seconds. A bone-chilling crack echoed across the stage and a violent spray of blood spewed out of the man's neck as the changeling chewed his head completely off his body. The headless corpse crumpled to the floor. The changeling held the decapitated head at its side like a bloodied bowling ball, two fingers thrust inside the eye sockets and one inside a hole where the man's nose used to be.

Randy sidled up to Cooper. They stood shoulder to shoulder, facing down their attackers, the two sides each waiting for the other to flinch as new screeches and wails echoed through the basement door. They didn't have much time. The female was the first to charge.

Cooper jumped in front of Randy, shielding him from

the attack. The creature was on him before he could even raise his tingling hands. He expected to feel her claws ripping into him at any second. He didn't. Instead, the creature hesitated and stared at him with the slight cock of her head. She swung a bony but powerful arm at him, knocking him to the floor with surprising force. He landed hard on his back and lay there stunned, gasping for air and ears ringing from the blow.

The changeling grabbed Randy's shoulders. She widened her jaws and yanked him toward her. Breaking the monster's grip with a quick spin of his body, Randy rammed his fist into the center of her face. The blow broke straight through bone and rotting flesh, his fist disappearing deep inside the decaying skull with the sound of ice being crushed in a blender.

Randy stared wide-eyed at his hand lodged inside the skull, then jerked it back in disgust. It was stuck. "Jesus H. Christ!"

Cooper scrambled to his feet and kicked the female in the stomach, dislodging Randy's hand. The monster stumbled backward toward the projection screen with a fist-sized hole in her face. The tall changeling dropped the dead janitor's bowling ball head on the floor. It landed in messy splat and rolled off the front of the stage. The creature cocked its head and moved toward them slowly, its fangs drenched in the old man's blood.

Randy's whisper was hot on Cooper's ear. "We have to make a run for the stage door."

Cooper shook his head and stared the monster down.

Running had gotten them nowhere, and he wanted to kill again. Needed to kill again, or the power would boil over inside him and explode. He lowered his head and closed his eyes. Summoning all of the erratic energy pinging around inside him, he commanded it to consume him. The power responded instantly, as if it had been waiting for his call. He opened his eyes and looked up. The female was back on her feet and heading right for them.

Randy shook him by the arm. "Cooper, what the hell are you doing? Run!"

Cooper ignored him, turning his palms forward and bracing for the impact. The virulent force rushed up from his core, a hot electrical current running down his veins. Golden orbs of fire formed on his palms and shot out of him with the jarring kick of a double-barreled shotgun. The female received the full brunt in the center of her chest. Somehow howling through the gaping hole in her face, she flew backward, exploding into flames as she slammed into the projection screen.

"Holy. Fucking. Shit," Randy murmured behind him.

Cooper couldn't agree more, but he had no time to survey his handiwork. The tall changeling was only a few feet away. Cooper aimed and released two newly formed fireballs at the monster and his squatty partner. The fireballs hit both targets dead-on, sending them to the same blazing end as the female demon. All three changelings burned into the giant screen. Their almost human-sounding cries echoed through the hollow theater, rattling off the walls and rolling over the tops of rows of empty red velvet seats. The stifling stench of burning flesh filled the room and settled in depths of Cooper's lungs. He and Randy stood gawking at the grotesque display as if it were a surreal 3-D horror film. The screen quickly caught hold of the flames, the fire consuming it like it had been doused with gasoline.

Cooper grabbed Randy's arm. "This whole place is going to go up. Let's go."

Randy moved a little too slowly for Cooper's comfort. A high-pitched bell alarm sounded as Cooper guided him to the stage door, pushing through it and stumbling out into the alley. Once they were clear of the building, Cooper dropped to his knees and drew clean, icy air into his lungs, the chill of it stinging his insides as his momentary relief quickly dissipated. They'd made it out and were safe for the moment, but the Strand Theater was on fire and Odessa and Rafe were lost in the tunnels trying to protect him. He hadn't even acted quickly enough to save the poor janitor inside.

On hands and knees beside him, Randy panted and coughed. "That zombie bitch didn't kill you when she had the chance. She knocked you away and came after me."

Cooper struggled to catch his breath and just nodded. He'd noticed the same odd behavior of the changeling and didn't understand it either. Coughing smoky bile out of his lungs, he looked up as the final traces of sunlight slipped out of the sky.

CHAPTER THIRTY-THREE

A cacophonous choir of sirens echoed in the distance and dusk settled in around them, the combination coating the air with an ominous sense of doom. Cooper sat leaning against the building several feet away from the stage door. The sun had set, and they were sitting ducks. They needed to get back to Phipps House, but he was so physically spent he could barely move a muscle.

Randy rested his hands on his hips. "Sounds like they're sending everything Georgetown has with a siren attached. We need to get away from the building. You okay?"

Cooper rubbed his palms on his thighs, still working to steady the rhythm of his own breathing. He looked up at Randy and caught a glimmer of reproach staring back at him.

Randy kneeled in front of him. "Don't you ever do anything like that again, Cooper Causey."

Cooper shrugged his shoulders. "What? I saved our asses, didn't' I?"

"Don't get cocky, Red. You could've gotten yourself killed

in there. No offense, but that hocus-pocus shit of yours hasn't been 100 percent reliable."

Cooper touched Randy's shoulder. "I knew what I was doing. Trust me. I can control it now. Well… mostly."

Randy stared at Cooper, his eyes softening, and the creases in his face easing. He leaned in, and Cooper's heart thumped hard against his chest cavity. Awkward and tentative, Randy tilted his head to the right before he stopped and then tilted it to the left instead, as if he really wanted to get it right this time and not rush it like before. Finally, he parted his lips, and they landed on Cooper's. The scruff of his late-afternoon beard scraped against Cooper's skin. He pushed his fingers into Cooper's hair, lacing them through locks thick with sweat. When he pulled away, Cooper's lips ached. He wanted more.

Randy stared down and him and cocked his head. "Do you know how long I've wanted to do that?"

Cooper had to clear his throat before he could speak. "I'll bet not as long as I have."

"That's a bet you'd lose, Red."

Cooper studied his face—the burly, rough-around-the-edges interpretation of rare angelic beauty with pools of dark honey for eyes. The woodsy scent that followed Randy everywhere drifted into Cooper's nose, expelling the lingering stench of smoke and burning changelings from his nostrils. A hundred questions swirled around in Cooper's head, but he pushed them all away. But after years of wondering, he had to ask one question right then, while he still had the courage, the building burning behind him be damned.

He looked up into Randy's eyes and took his hand. "That night on the beach after Kevin's funeral. You wanted that too?"

Randy looked down and squeezed Cooper's hand. "Like I'd never wanted anything so bad in my life. But the timing was all wrong. We had just buried your brother. You were shit-faced and a mess, if you remember. But mostly, I was just a fucking coward. Then before I knew it, you'd left for college and that was that."

Cooper had to be sure, before he even considered the foreign possibility of surrendering his heart to another man. He pushed a little farther. "But you married your high school sweetheart—your first love."

Randy's gaze pierced right through the residual armor around Cooper's heart. "No, Coop. Renee wasn't my first love. You were."

Cooper stared back at him, completely at a loss for words. His usually boundless knack for defensive barbs and sassy retorts had completely abandoned him.

Randy peered down the alley. "I've pushed these feelings so far down inside me for so long, it threw me for a loop when I saw you at Phipps House the other night. All those old memories and feelings came rushing back to the surface. I didn't know how to deal with it." Randy glanced down at the ground in front of Cooper. "I guess I didn't handle it very well. I'm sorry."

Cooper touched his cheek and scraped his thumb across the stubble. "It's okay. I get it. Everything is fine now."

Randy looked up and kissed Cooper gently on the

forehead. "Well, not quite everything. I need to get to my car and check in. I'm sure they need me, and I lost my radio down in those godforsaken tunnels."

"I'm fine," Cooper said. "Go. I'll be right behind you. Just need to catch my breath."

Randy stood and nodded. He turned and sprinted down the alley, disappearing around the corner. Cooper sighed and looked back toward the theater. Blue-gray layers of smoke seeped out from under the stage door, the only visible sign of the fire raging inside. He needed to get farther away.

He pushed his back against the wall and edged his way up to his feet, but his legs wobbled under him. The exertion of his power had left him weaker than he realized. He lumbered down the alley, his muscles aching with every step. When he turned the corner onto Front Street, another fire alarm sounded in a nearby building. He walked a few steps up the sidewalk toward the entrance of the Strand, drawn by the need to see the damage he'd done to the beautiful old building.

Smoke billowed from the roof of the building, cloaking the already dusky sky over Front Street with a fresh blanket of unease. Flames danced over to the rooftops of adjoining buildings on either side of the theater. Businesses rumbled with activity, expelling their human contents into the middle of the street in various states of disarray and confusion. Patrons flocked out of coffee shops, cafes, and other businesses to see what the clamor was about. Cars emptied out of parking spaces in front of the theater. Store clerks and restaurants servers escorted customers out of their doors in as orderly a fashion as possible.

Exhausted, Cooper stopped walking and leaned against the front window of a flower shop. Randy stood wedged in the open door of his police cruiser across the street barking into the handset of a radio, the long-coiled cord stretched to its limit. After all that time lost in the maze of underground tunnels, they'd emerged a mere fifty yards away from where they started, thanks to Blue. Just as he was starting to relax, a fresh wave of chills rolled over Cooper's body. The hair on the back of his neck sizzled and sprang to attention. He heard the disapproving clack of someone's tongue behind him, and he turned around.

"Cooper, Cooper, Cooper," Alexander said, his voice oozing with malice and mockery. "What rueful calamity have we caused now?" With his granite face frozen into a rigid mask of rancor, the Anakim took a fluid step toward him. Cooper squared his shoulders and straightened his spine. Though he might not be able to kill the immortal psychopath, surely he could do some serious damage. But too many innocent people were around. Alexander would have no problem sacrificing any or all of them.

"You've had quite the busy day meddling in my affairs—harassing my day soldier, slaughtering my children." Alexander stared down the sidewalk toward the theater. "I will require your blood now more than ever to replenish my army and defeat the Jericho soldiers you have attracted."

Cooper stared into the Anakim's eyes and fought internally to keep his voice low and steady. "That's never going to happen, you psychotic fuck. I've learned a few tricks since we last met that I'm just dying to try out on you." Cooper forced himself to smirk.

The Anakim was on him before he could inhale another breath of charred air. Pressing his cold, hard body against Cooper, Alexander leaned down and hissed in his ear. "You have experienced firsthand what my children are capable of. Give me what I want, or I will release them on this pathetic excuse of a town and do the world a favor by wiping it off the fucking map."

A fist-sized lump hardened in Cooper's throat. He knew the threat was real.

Alexander leaned back and smiled wider. "Take your time making up your mind. I can see plenty of locals to amuse myself with while I wait."

Three fire trucks screamed down Front Street and jerked to a stop in front of the Strand. Cooper glanced across the street and settled on Randy a moment too long.

"Ah, yes. I think I will start with that one. Excellent choice." Alexander was suddenly in front of him, a salacious grin stretching across his face exposing sparkling fangs. "I cannot wait to taste him."

A stew of rage bubbled over inside Cooper. Georgetown, he could sacrifice. Randy, he could not. He curled his fingers into fists at his side, the darkness pooling in his fingertips. "If you touch one hair on his head—"

Alexander shoved him so roughly against the flower shop window, the back of his head bounced off the glass. He felt Alexander's icy fingers close around his throat. "You will what?" His jawline petrified, and his voice dropped to a near hiss. "I *will* have your blood, Divinum. If I have to kill every person you love, every Jericho solder that tries to protect you; if I have to reduce this town to ashes, you *will* give yourself to me." Alexander's voice increased in volume with every word, each syllable punctuated by the tightening grip around Cooper's throat. "The Anakim will be legion again. We will be a race of kings as we once were. As we should be."

Cooper struggled to breathe. He clawed at Alexander's fingers to no avail. He thought he would pass out, but the Anakim released his grip and Cooper gasped for air. Alexander slid the tip of his index finger down Cooper's neck, igniting a multitude of chills on his skin.

Blood rushed back into his cheeks and oxygen back into his lungs. "Don't you mean a race of slaves? With you as their master and king?"

Alexander ignored the barb. He closed his eyes and leaned in so close their noses almost touched.

With eyelids fluttering, he breathed in Cooper's scent and pressed his mouth to Cooper's ear. "I will save them from extinction. Repopulate the race and deliver them from the cursed existence imposed by your ineffective god and his precious Divinum seed. The Anakim will rule this pathetic human world he tossed aside so long ago. That's *your* god, Divinum. I would never forsake *my* people. *I* am their messiah."

Cooper drew strength from the darkness churning in his core. But before he could focus its release, Alexander was behind him. He twisted one arm up Cooper's back until he thought his shoulder would jump out of its socket, and then he spun Cooper around to face the clock tower and purred in his ear.

"There will come a time when you beg me to drink from you."

Cooper watched Randy across the street, searching up and down the sidewalks, his face flushed. He turned and spotted Cooper and Alexander, His eyes widened. Cooper's heart surged in his chest. No. Not now. Randy moved toward them anyway with a determined and angry expression. A flurry of thick gray smoke encircled him before he stepped off the sidewalk, stopping him in his tracks. The dark cloud dissipated, and Stephen Parker materialized behind Randy. Cooper's heart sank. God. Please. No. Stephen grabbed a handful of Randy's hair and jerked his head back. Struggling to free himself, Randy elbowed and kicked at his captor. His efforts had absolutely no effect on Stephen.

Cooper twisted his body, struggling to free himself of Alexander's iron grip. "No!"

With his free arm, he rammed his elbow into a rib cage of steel. Searing pain shot through his arm. Alexander pulled up on his pinned arm, and Cooper cried out. He was sure his arm would twist clean off his body at any moment.

Alexander hissed into his ear, his icy lips tickling the edge of the lobe. "Perhaps next time we meet, you will be more cooperative."

Cooper stared across the street as Stephen Parker easily subdued Randy, the crook of his elbow wrapped tightly around Randy's neck. The color quickly drained from Randy's face, and the fight left his limbs. There was too much chaos and focus on the burning buildings for anyone to notice the attack.

Cooper swallowed hard and whispered. He knew that even though a sea of noise separated them, Stephen could hear him. "Please. Don't."

Stephen grinned at him. He wrapped his arm around Randy's waist and dissolved back into a swirling mass of gray smoke. The whirlwind engulfed them both and rose into the darkened sky, disappearing from view. The sidewalk was empty. Alexander released his grip. Cooper dropped to his knees and hugged his numb arm, staring at the spot in front of the clock tower where Randy had stood just seconds before. Itchy tears stung the corners of his eyes, and his resolve solidified.

Alexander moved in front of him with deliberate human speed. He looked down and dusted himself off, like Cooper's Divinum essence had soiled his clothing. "Do the right thing, and you will be reunited with your man." He narrowed his emerald eyes on Cooper, a sneer twisting his lips. "Don't and I will drain him in front of you. That is a promise."

With that, in a shimmering ripple of color and light that shot up into the sky, Alexander Montgomery was gone.

CHAPTER THIRTY-FOUR

Cooper leaned against the iron gate in front of Phipps House, out of breath, his chest pounding. He'd run all ten blocks down Front Street, haunted every step of the way by the look of panic on Randy's face right before he disappeared. His legs were numb, and his lungs heavy with smoke. An ashy film coated his tongue. He stared up at the house, glowing against the dark backdrop of a starless sky. Light illuminated nearly every window, and the house buzzed with internal activity. Something was wrong. Concern for Lillie Mae spiked in his gut, and he sprinted up the walkway. Took the porch steps two at a time. The door swung open before he could touch the knob, and he stopped dead in his tracks.

Betsy stood staring at him and holding the door open, her eyes filled with relief. "Cooper."

He pushed past her. "Lillie Mae—"

Lillie Mae is fine. Lex drifted into the foyer and stopped in front of him. *She's safe and resting.*

A wave of relief spilled over Cooper, but he wasn't sure

if it was genuine or manufactured by Lex. Likely the latter. Betsy closed the door and stood in front of him with hands resting on her hips. She looked slightly different than the last time he saw her. She had more color in her face, and her eyes sparkled with life. The effects of the day sleep and a recent feeding, he supposed.

She leaned into him. "Where the hell were you?"

Cooper peeled off his coat and threw it on the coat rack. "I'm fine."

She crossed her arms. "Rafe and Odessa?"

"I don't know. We got separated in the tunnels when the changelings attacked."

Betsy's face hardened. Her eyes clouded with anger. "Tunnels? Changelings?"

Cooper paced the width of the foyer, rubbing his forehead. "Odessa, Rafe, and I. And then Randy showed up. We went looking for the changeling nest. Odessa said if we destroyed the nest, Jericho would be able to get to Alexander." He scratched the back of his head. "Well, we found the nest all right, and a shit ton of those nasty bastards. We had to split up. Barely made it out. And then… Randy…" His voice cracked, and he swallowed it back. He looked up into Betsy's eyes. "Alexander took him."

Betsy's face softened just a little. "Montgomery has Randy?"

Cooper nodded. "He said he'd kill him and unleash those monsters on the town if I don't surrender myself to him."

Betsy turned her back to him and cursed under her breath. "I knew he would use that boy against you." She turned on her heel and faced him, her nostrils flaring. "I told you that, Cooper. I told you not to get him involved."

Cooper took a step toward her. "You think I wanted this? You think I wanted him involved in any of this?"

Betsy looked away and slung her raven mane over her right shoulder but did not respond.

Cooper held his ground. "I am going back to Warfield to find him."

"The Manheeg will never allow that."

Cooper rounded on her, jabbing a finger in her face. "I don't give a shit what your *Manheeg* says. I won't play with Randy's life. So either help me get him back or stay the hell out of my way."

He turned and crashed squarely into a wall of girth and hard muscle. Massive hands gripped his shoulders and steadied him. Momentarily dazed, Cooper stared up into ancient black eyes. The man's dark skin was smooth and oddly flawless. A pattern of geometric lines had been shaven into his buzzed hair, and a close-trimmed goatee framed his sculpted face. Standing more than a head taller, the man peered down at him. Cooper's Divinum reflexes reacted to the man's Anakim nature before his brain did.

He backed away and squared his shoulders. "Who the hell is this? He's—"

"Anakim. Yes. That I am." The man's accent wasn't easily placed. Certainly not American South. Hell, not even American-American. Middle Eastern, perhaps, peppered with a hint of British sophistication.

Betsy placed a hand on Cooper's shoulder from behind.

"Cooper, this is the Manheeg."

The Anakim giant looked Cooper up and down, his right eye twitching and the corner of his mouth pulled tight. He finally offered his hand with a slight grunt. "I have heard much about you, Cooper. I am glad we finally meet. I am Joshua."

CHAPTER THIRTY-FIVE

Cooper stared down at the broad hand before he finally accepted it, the cylinders of his brain firing in all directions. Joshua. *The* Joshua. He appraised the much-lauded Manheeg with a bit of wonder and a healthy dose of suspicion. The guy had to be pushing seven feet tall, and he was as solid as a brick wall. His eyes were unreadable, a trait that Cooper did not appreciate in this fucked-up new world he'd been sucked into, where he wasn't altogether sure who he could trust.

"Come, Cooper. You should meet the others." The voice was deep and round, soothing and dangerous all at once. "We have much to discuss."

"I don't have time for a social visit." Cooper kept his voice even and stared up into Joshua's blank eyes. "My friend has been taken by a blood-sucking psychopath. One of you."

Without another word, Joshua turned and walked down the hall, disappearing into the sitting room.

Cooper turned on his heel and faced Betsy. "*The* Joshua?"

She crinkled her eyes and nodded.

Cooper shook his head. "But he's Anakim. Like Alexander. Like you—no offense."

Betsy nudged him toward the sitting room with a hand on his back. "He is here to help and has come a very long way to meet you."

Cooper walked down the hall toward the sitting room. "Yeah. Around three thousand years, by my calculations."

When he entered the room, over a dozen eclectic strangers looked up at him and extinguished their hushed conversations. The crowd was mostly Divinum with a few Anakim sprinkled in. A variety of ages, sizes, and colors were represented, all sporting serious expressions. Eunice and Eudora sat side-by-side on the sofa, holding court. Eudora smiled warmly at their unexpected guests. Eunice openly scowled at them.

Eudora beamed and slapped her hands on her lap when she spotted Cooper standing in the doorway. "Oh, thank heavens you're all right. We were all so worried."

Cooper looked around the room again. He doubted *all* of them were so worried about him.

Eunice rolled her eyes at her sister. "God's balls, Dora! He's not a lost puppy, for Christ's sake. He's a Phipps man and perfectly capable of taking care of himself."

Cooper nodded their way, hopelessness gnawing away at his insides. If this was the extent of the famed Jericho army, the world was in deep shit.

"Everyone." Joshua's resonant voice quieted the room in an instant. "This is Cooper Causey, the carrier of the mutation."

Cooper cocked his head at Joshua. "Really? You're calling *me* the mutant here?" He scanned the room, receiving a dozen chilly stares and a few audible grumbles in return.

Betsy cleared her throat, silencing them.

Joshua continued. "Cooper is the last of the Phipps line."

The weight of those words knocked the breath right out of Cooper. Lex had said Lillie Mae was safe.

Joshua looked over at him and raised an eyebrow. "I am sorry, Cooper. I misspoke. Your grandmother still lives. For the moment."

Cooper left the room. He didn't have time for this. He needed to see Lillie Mae. In the hallway, Lex touched him on the small of the back, but it didn't startle him. Raw magical energy sizzled through the fibers of his shirt where the pure-blood touched him, sending waves of comfort through his skin and down to his core. He assumed that was Lex's intention, and he didn't mind it at all.

She has visitors. A holy man and her friend.

Cooper stopped in front of Lillie Mae's door and stared up at Lex. "Lillie Mae doesn't have any friends. And she hasn't set foot in a church since my mom's funeral twenty years ago."

Lex opened the door for Cooper but did not follow him in.

The holy man was Wayne Johnson. That made more sense. Wayne practically grew up with Cooper's parents, and he adored Lillie Mae. He sat in the Boston rocker by the window, leaning forward and resting his elbows on his knees, eyes full of worry. He nodded once at Cooper and then looked down. He'd likely seen and heard more in one evening than his well-educated brain could process.

An elderly woman sat on the edge of the bed holding Lillie Mae's hand. She wore a pale blue antebellum-era apron gown with a white lace collar and cuffs. She tucked stray strands of silver hair up into the bun pinned at the back of her head and looked like she had stepped right out of the pages of *Gone with the Wind*. Her face was familiar, but he couldn't readily place her.

Wayne rose and walked over to Cooper, putting a hand on his shoulder. "I came a little while ago. I've been sitting here with Miss Ida and Aunt Mae. She's been asking for you."

Miss Ida, of Miss Ida's Ghost Tours. Of course. She lived a few doors down, though Cooper never knew she and Lillie Mae were friends. He studied the rector's weary eyes. Wayne's faith had either been fortified tonight or shaken to its very core. Cooper could relate.

"Thanks for coming, Wayne. Are you okay?" He nodded toward the door. "With all that out there?"

Wayne's brow furrowed even more. Before he could answer, Lillie Mae called out in a broken voice. "Cooper? Is that you?"

Miss Ida gave him a warm smile and stood, motioning for him to take her place.

He sat, took Lillie Mae's hand, and cupped it in his own. Her crackled skin was cool to the touch and her bones brittle in his grip. "I'm here now."

Lillie Mae relaxed and smiled. She squeezed his hand with failing strength.

"How are you feeling?"

She coughed and then cleared her throat. "I ain't dead yet, son. Lex and Ida have been taking real good care of me. And Wayne came to see me."

"I see that." Cooper looked over his shoulder at Miss Ida standing at the foot of the bed. She beamed at Lillie Mae, her eyes sparkling with affection. He was still a little puzzled by her presence.

Ida smiled at him. "You'll have to forgive my attire, Cooper. I gave a tour earlier today and came over right after."

Lillie Mae patted his hand. "Ida is my dearest friend in the world." She craned her head toward the door. "Is Randy here?"

Cooper looked down at Lillie Mae's hand. He didn't want her to see the tears pooling in his eyes. He brushed them away with the back of his hand. "They took him. The Anakim."

When he looked back at Lillie Mae, the dark circles around her eyes had deepened. "That demon will do anything to get to you, Cooper. Once I'm gone, my wards on you and this house will be broken. He'll just take you. Like he took my Charlotte when she was just a child."

Lillie Mae looked over to the wall, and she went quiet, fading away for a moment. "The Jericho soldiers came back. They can help you save Randy, if they will." She looked back at him. She reached out and touched his face. Her skin was dry and clammy, but he relished her gentle touch. "I know you won't leave now without him. I wouldn't ask you to."

Cooper shook his head and looked into her eyes. "He's too important to me. Now more than ever."

Lillie Mae looked at Ida and smiled. "I understand completely, dear."

Cooper picked at a fraying seam in the quilt. He didn't think she did. Not really. And he didn't want her to die with secrets left between them. He had chosen to shut her out all those years, assuming she wouldn't accept him without giving her a chance to prove him wrong. He'd wasted years hiding who he was from her. He tried to formulate just the right words. Lillie Mae beat him to it.

"I remember how you used to look at him when you were just children."

Cooper's breath stalled in his throat. He stared down at her, stunned.

Her eyes softened. "Nobody chooses who they love, son, especially not a child that young. He just loves, natural and pure. As everyone should."

Cooper adjusted the pillow under her head. "I had no idea you knew."

"And all those times Randy asked after you, I could see it in his eyes, too. He was lost without you. You two were always meant to be together."

He smoothed out the quilt square he'd been picking at and returned her smile. "I never in a million years thought Randy felt the same way, or that he even *could* feel the same way. But he does."

Lillie Mae squeezed his hand. "You hold that love in your heart, son. You are going to need it now more than ever."

Though he wasn't completely sure of their meaning, her words resonated inside him.

Lillie Mae reached up and touched his cheek. "Don't waste another second being apart. You'll never get those years back, son. Trust me. I know all too well."

Her eyes were moist. Ida eased around to the opposite side of the bed and sat, taking Lillie Mae's free hand in hers. The two women stared at each other for several quiet moments, like Cooper wasn't even in the room.

Lillie Mae took his hand again. "I am just so happy that the two great loves of my life are here with me now."

If he didn't know better, he'd think he was hearing things. He glanced over at Wayne, who just smiled at him like he was amused it took Cooper so long to figure things out.

He turned back to Lillie Mae. "You? And Miss Ida's Ghost Tours?"

Miss Ida chuckled, and Lillie Mae coughed up a laugh.

Cooper cocked his head at Lillie Mae. "But you were married to Grandpa Joe for fifty years." He couldn't believe the ignorant-ass words came out of his mouth. He, more than most, should've understood.

"I loved your grandfather for every one of those fifty years. Ida came into my life before I met Joe. But I was afraid. Thought I had to be a certain way to make it in this world. She, on the other hand, waited for me for all those years. Never married, no family."

Cooper shifted on the mattress, tucking his leg underneath him. He could not have been more surprised by the revelation. He was also sad for Lillie Mae and the love she sacrificed. Sad for Miss Ida, a lonely old woman living just a stone's throw away, watching her one true love raise a family with someone else.

"Don't feel sorry for me," Lillie Mae said. "My regrets pale in comparison to the overwhelming joy in my life. I have known great love, and it's your love for Randy that will save him. That and your divine gifts."

Cooper looked down at his hands. "My power has proved less than reliable. Besides, Wayne said the Anakim are immortal."

Lillie Mae's eyelids drooped. She needed to rest. He squeezed her hand and stood, but she didn't let go. "Even immortality has its limits, son. But you have to convince them to help you. I just hope it's not too late."

CHAPTER THIRTY-SIX

Cooper stepped out into the hallway and into a rumble of agitated voices echoing from the foyer. Rafe and Odessa stood surrounded by Joshua, Lex, and Betsy, and he was even more relieved to see them than he expected. Clothes soiled, hair askew, and eyes weary, they looked very different from the picture of perfection he'd first met. But they'd made it out alive. A haze of tension hovered over the group of warriors, so thick you could almost see it. He eased down the hall, his steps light and his back hugging the wall.

"We acted on the day soldier's information." Odessa's tone was sharp and defensive. "But it was one of the largest nests I've ever seen. There were too many of them. We were not able to exterminate them all."

Betsy rounded on Odessa and cold-cocked her square on the jaw, knocking her back into Rafe's arms. Cooper threw a hand over his mouth, stifling a gasp.

The veins in Betsy's neck throbbed. She shoved a finger in Odessa's face. "How dare you take Cooper down there? He could have been killed!"

Odessa regained her footing and lunged at Betsy like she wanted to rip her throat out. Cooper thought she just might until Joshua stepped between them, and she backed away from Betsy.

Odessa rubbed her jaw and caught sight of Cooper. "Well, maybe that wouldn't have been altogether bad." She glared at him. "At least then the Anakim wouldn't be able to use him against us."

Heat rose into Cooper's cheeks. He closed the distance between them and went right up to Odessa. "Is that why you wanted to split up in the tunnels? Were you hoping I wouldn't make it out alive?" He straightened his spine, emboldened by the sting of her betrayal. "Sorry to disappoint you, but I did."

Odessa cocked an eyebrow, crossed her arms, and leaned into him. "If I had wanted you dead, you would be."

Betsy hissed at her.

"Enough!" Joshua's thunderous voice rumbled through the house.

Cooper seethed through gritted teeth. He finally took a step back.

Rafe put a hand on his shoulder and whispered into his ear. "She didn't mean it, bro. We would have gotten you out of that hellhole if we could have. I'm glad you made it out."

Cooper looked at him and nodded. He believed Rafe's sincerity, but he wasn't sure Rafe and Odessa were on the same page.

Joshua pointed down the hall. "Elizabeth. Cooper. Kitchen. Now."

With a final fang-laced snarl at Odessa, Betsy stalked down the hall, the heels of her boots doing some serious damage to the hardwood floor. Cooper fell in behind her and glanced back over his shoulder. Joshua was in Odessa's face, every muscle in his face strained. A part of him wanted to see Odessa get her ass handed to her, but he had no desire to witness an example of the Manheeg's wrath, so he quickly looked away.

In the kitchen, two impressively muscular women stood opposite each other with their arms crossed, whispering at the island in the center of the room . Cooper remembered them from the sitting room earlier. Standing a good two to three inches taller than him, with dark brown hair, wild and wiry, they were clad from head to toe in brown leather. Tight pants and an array of straps covered *most* everything up top. Other than the scar that marked one on the side of the face, they looked almost identical—sisters for certain, likely twins. They greeted Betsy and Cooper's intrusion with uninterested nods. An empty Jim Beam bottle and two glasses sat on the island between them.

Cooper picked up the whiskey bottle and held it up to them. He didn't even try to mask the annoyed sarcasm in his voice. "Please, make yourselves at home."

They both scowled at him and pushed through the swinging door into the sitting room.

Betsy took a glass out of the cabinet, filled it with water from the sink, and offered it to him. "Drink this."

He sat the whiskey bottle down with a hard clank and accepted the glass. He drank it all down in one gulp, not realizing how much he needed the hydration. Refilling the glass himself, he downed a second one. He knew he would have a better chance saving Randy with Jericho's assistance, and his best chance at getting that was through Betsy. She obviously had a *special* relationship with Joshua.

He sat the glass down on the counter and turned to her. "I can't get Randy out of there by myself. I need your help. I need Jericho's help."

Betsy crossed her arms and shook her head. "Cooper, the Manheeg will never allow you to get anywhere close to Alexander."

Exasperated, Cooper slammed his fist on the counter. "Dammit, Betsy. He will kill Randy if I don't go to him." He paused, sighed, and lowered the escalating volume and resonance of this voice. "My power is more reliable now. I can feel it. The mental block is gone. The more I use it, the more I'm able to control it, but it's not 100 percent yet. I can't take the chance of facing down Alexander and Stephen on my own and failing. Not with Randy's life on the line."

A voice crackled like thunder behind him. "Elizabeth is right."

Cooper turned as Joshua entered the kitchen with Odessa and Rafe following close behind. "We cannot take the chance of Alexander getting your blood. Rafe and Odessa will complete the mission they were given and will escort you to a safe house far away from here."

Cooper straightened his spine. "Like hell they will."

"We need to hide you, Cooper." Joshua's piercing black eyes were absolute in their resolve and indicated that this was yet another subject that was not up for discussion.

Cooper crossed his arms over his chest in defiance. "The only place I'm going is to Warfield to get Randy."

Joshua's nostrils flared, and his right eye twitched. "Cooper, I don't think you understand—"

"What I understand is that Alexander has Randy, and I am not leaving him there."

Anger flashed in the Manheeg's eyes, as he drew forward and towered over Cooper, standing much too close for comfort. "Cooper, there are forces at work here that you cannot begin to comprehend. You will leave this place. Now. *We* will handle Montgomery." Joshua turned his back on him and walked away.

Cooper clenched his fists. "If you *could* handle him, then why haven't you already?"

There was a little more volume to his voice than he'd intended. Joshua stopped in his tracks. The room fell silent, no doubt from the shock of blatant challenge to their Manheeg. He didn't blame them. Joshua slowly turned to face him, mouth tight, eyebrows raised. The guy likely wasn't used to being defied. Cooper didn't care, but Lillie Mae always said you catch more flies with honey.

He took a deep breath and lowered his voice a notch, evened it out and continued. "Look, I might not understand everything that's going on here. Hell, I'm sure I don't. But you can bet your ass that I will not be carted off to some safe house out in the middle of nowhere and just hope that Randy makes it out of this alive. Somehow, I don't think his safety is your number one priority. And the Anakim already kicked your ass at least once at the battle of Jericho, or you wouldn't be one yourself."

Cooper matched Joshua's chilly stare, willing the muscles in his face to remain frozen and hoping the Anakim blinked first. He knew he'd stepped over the line. He just hoped it didn't cost him Randy's life.

Cooper relaxed his shoulders a little and took a step toward the Manheeg. "I can help you get close enough to Alexander to end him for good."

Joshua squinted at him. "And how might *you* be able to accomplish that?"

Cooper leaned against the island and cupped his hands on the corners. "The changelings won't hurt me. I could walk through an army of them, right up to Alexander and spit in his face."

Betsy touched her chin and looked up at Joshua. "He's right. When the changeling attacked here, it came after me—not him."

Cooper nodded. "And in the tunnels, they charged, screeched, and pawed at me, but when one had the chance to kill me, it knocked me out of the way and went after Randy instead."

Joshua exchanged glances with Odessa and Rafe. He turned away from them and walked the length of the room and back before he responded. "Of course. You are no good to Montgomery if the changelings deliver you to him in pieces. He needs you alive. He would never allow them to harm you."

Betsy shook her head. "Joshua. No."

Joshua ignored her. "It is actually a perfect way to get close to Montgomery and to distract him while we fight through his horde of changelings."

Betsy walked over and stood beside Cooper. "It's too risky, Joshua."

Emboldened by his small victory and annoyed by Betsy's obvious lack of faith in him, Cooper turned to her. "I can take care of myself." He shot a glance at Rafe. "Right?"

Rafe nodded. "The guy has some killer moves. I saw it firsthand. He held his own with me and O against those things."

Odessa threw her hands up. "He nearly got us killed, you idiot."

Joshua stared back at Betsy with a tiny glint of tenderness in his eyes. "We *could* use him, Elizabeth. We can keep him safe."

Betsy squared her shoulders and stepped up to him. "Cooper is my family. He is the last of the Phipps line. I will not allow you to put his life in danger."

Joshua gritted his teeth, and Cooper couldn't help notice the way Odessa seemed pleased with the rift forming between her Manheeg and Betsy. Her mouth eased into a smile as she watched them staring down one another.

Betsy faced Cooper, resting one hand on his shoulder. He could have sworn he caught the trace of a tear in her eye. "You don't have to do this, Cooper. It's not safe. None of this is your fault, and you are not responsible for fixing it. You can leave here tonight and live the rest of your life in peace. And we will do everything in our power to save Randy."

"It's his choice, Elizabeth," Joshua said, his voice commanding and firm.

Cooper peered into Betsy's eyes. Though he barely knew her, he already felt such deep affection for her. He knew she meant what she said. She *would* do everything in her power to save Randy. That just wasn't good enough.

"I'm sorry. I have to do this. For Randy. And so I *can* live the rest of my life in peace. I can't keep running from them." He looked up at Joshua. "I'll do it. Under one condition."

The Manheeg lowered his eyebrows and clenched his jaw.

Cooper stepped up him and pointed a finger in his chest, which was like poking a concrete slab. "You guarantee Randy's safety."

Joshua's nostrils flared, and then he finally nodded once. "Agreed."

Cooper stared into Joshua's eyes a moment longer. He wasn't sure he trusted the man. Lillie Mae's words rang in his ears.

Even the immortality has its limits.

He rested his hands on his hips and shifted his weight to one side. "And you have to tell me how to kill Alexander. I want to be the one to do it."

Odessa huffed and slapped her hand on the counter. "There's no room for error here. We only get one shot at Montgomery. The only way to kill an Anakim that old and powerful is to remove his heart. Even if you make it past the changelings, what makes you think you will be able to do that?"

Cooper couldn't argue with her. Slicing open a walking corpse was a little different than cutting the heart of a powerful Anakim like Alexander. He wasn't a hundred percent sure he could do it either.

"There is a way."

Heads turned toward the doorway where Miss Ida stood, her slight countenance engulfed by the space as Wayne peered in over her shoulder. She clasped her hands together in front of her dress. Everyone in the room stared at her in silence, waiting for her to speak again.

Her voice was small and thin, but resolute nonetheless. "It's extremely dangerous. But there is a way."

CHAPTER THIRTY-SEVEN

"Clear your mind, Cooper." Miss Ida covered his hands with hers. "Relax and breathe."

They sat side by side on the edge of the guest room bed. Wayne leaned against the closed door, arms crossed. Cooper knew the rector wasn't totally on board with the plan, but he wanted to be there in case something went wrong. Cooper wondered how long Wayne had known about his abilities. And for that matter, who else knew? Had his parents known?

"Cooper," Miss Ida said firmly. "Focus."

He did as he was told and cleared his mind. He wasn't altogether sure what was supposed to happen next. Miss Ida hadn't explained anything in front of the group in the kitchen. She'd just led him into the room and sat him down on the bed.

"When you are back at Warfield and you are in danger, Blue will appear as he always has."

Cooper nodded. She had that right. He'd always thought Blue's presence was something else—something more sinister. All along the spirit was only trying to warn him or protect him. He could have saved a shit-load in therapy bills if he'd figured that one out a little sooner.

Miss Ida squeezed his hands. "He's your guardian, and you are the last of his Houngan line. But he can only do so much from the half-light of eternity. He will need your body as a vessel. At the moment when you need Blue the most, open your soul to him. Allow him to embody you, just as your grandmother once did."

Cooper lost his concentration. "Wait. Lillie Mae let Blue possess her? Why would she ever do something like that?"

A shade of sadness passed over Miss Ida's eyes. "She had her reasons. Just as you have yours. Now focus."

Cooper let it go. "How do I let him in or embody my vessel or whatever?"

"I don't know how to tell you to do that. I have never experienced possession firsthand. You will have to find your own way. But once he does, you will no longer have control of yourself. You will see what he sees. Feel what he feels. He alone will determine your physical actions, and you may be shocked by what he makes you do."

Cooper swallowed hard. "Well, I don't think I like the sound of that."

Miss Ida looked down at her dress. "It was hard on your grandmother, the things Blue made her do. Even though the outcome was as she wished."

Cooper would have pressed her on that any other time, but not now. Saving Randy was his primary concern.

"Just remember. The origin of all magic, even in its

bastardized and watered-down incarnations, is divine power. Never forget you are descended from the Seraphim, the holiest of the angelic hierarchy." She touched the palm of her hand to his heart. "You are *good*, Cooper. No matter what Blue makes you do. You are good."

Cooper shifted his weight on the mattress and nodded, a lump forming in his throat. He looked over at Wayne. The rector rested his chin on the tips of his index fingers. With eyes closed, his lips formed words of silent prayer that Cooper couldn't hear, but comforted him nonetheless.

Miss Ida sat up straight. "Now. Close your eyes and concentrate."

Cooper drew in a deep breath and closed his eyes. Clearing his head of the clutter and stress of the last couple of days wasn't easy. Memories and images came to the forefront of his mind, and he extinguished them, one by one, until nothing was left but an empty void.

"They are always around us," Miss Ida said. "You just have to open yourself up to their presence."

He waited for what seemed like minutes, and nothing happened. As his patience waned, so did the tenuous hold on his concentration. Then Miss Ida's voice sounded farther away than it should have, even though he knew she hadn't moved an inch. The change in his senses refined his focus. Two vertical streams of light formed in his mind's eye. They wavered and floated toward him, growing brighter the closer they got to him. Somehow he knew them. He wasn't sure how because they had no human form. They were nothing more than raw energy, souls—the souls of Eunice and

Eudora Phipps. Eudora was the stronger of the two because her resistance to him was formidable. Eunice's soul was more easily manipulated. Though she fought him, she complied when he willed her to come closer.

"*Invite* her in, Cooper. Don't try to force her." Miss Ida squeezed his hands. Their physical connection was obviously some kind of window into his soul, and he knew that she saw what he saw.

Cooper focused on the stream of Eunice's soul and implored her to help him, to show him. After a few more seconds of struggle, the spirit relinquished a bit of control. It was only a brief wave of awareness and foreign imagery. She refused to fully embody him, but finally a small part of her passed through him, seizing up in his throat. He tried to raise a hand to his mouth to steady a wave of nausea, but trapped inside his own body, he was unable to control his limbs.

His eyes opened, though he never gave his body such a command. Wayne stood by the door with his head down, praying. He looked to his right, and Miss Ida stared back at him, her smile fading. He didn't feel his arm move at all, so he could hardly believe his eyes when he raised it and slapped her hard across the face.

Miss Ida's hand flew up to her cheek, her eyes wide and mouth agape. Cooper's throat closed up, and his chest tightened into one giant knot. Eunice's soul left him instantly of her own accord, in another wave of nausea and expelled oxygen. He no longer felt her presence in the room. Eudora was gone as well.

Wayne was by Miss Ida's side. "Cooper! What the hell?"

Horrified by what he had done, Cooper grabbed the old woman's hands. Fucking Eunice.

"Miss Ida," he stammered. "I don't know what to say. I am so incredibly sorry. I don't know what happened. I didn't even know that was coming, or I would've stopped it."

Miss Ida shook her head, and the lines in her face softened. She offered him a weak smile he knew was meant to make him feel better for the red handprint scarring her face. She was a tough old broad. She and Lillie Mae were perfect for each other.

"You don't have to be sorry, Cooper. You couldn't have stopped her if you tried." She ran a hand over her the top of her head and tucked stray silver strands behind her ears. "That was Eunice, not you. When I looked into your eyes, I saw her staring back at me."

"But she made me hit you!"

Miss Ida patted his hand. "I think Eunice was trying to help in her own special way." She chuckled and coughed into her fist. "She wanted you to fully understand how out of control of yourself you will be when Blue possesses you. But don't fight him." She leaned in closer to him, and flashed him a conspiratorial smile. "I also don't think she liked that I encouraged you to do that to her in the first place."

Wayne kneeled down in front of him and balanced himself with one hand on the side the bed. "Cooper, what did it feel like? What did you see?"

Cooper lowered his head and tried to reassemble the

experience into some kind of relatable example. "It was like being a living puppet. I saw Eunice's memories. I felt her pain and her anger. I had no idea she was going to hit Miss Ida. I just saw it happen and couldn't stop it."

Wayne reached up and touched his shoulder. "Did you have any trouble getting her out?"

Cooper shook his head. "All of a sudden, she was just gone."

Miss Ida stood and brushed the creases out of her dress with her hands. "That's because Eunice was an unwilling subject. Blue will be quite different. I am not nearly as concerned with Blue's ability to get *in* you as I am of getting him *out* of you."

Cooper stared up into the woman's deep-set gray eyes. "So how do I get him out if he doesn't want to leave?"

Miss Ida clasped her hands in front of her. "The Bokor power inside Blue, inside *you*, feeds on hatred and rage. When he was alive, everything he loved was taken from him. He suffered grave injustices. He has spent over one hundred fifty years trapped inside a dark and troubled soul. The only chance of getting back to yourself will be to repel that darkness with love." Miss Ida smiled and touched his shoulder. "The great love your grandma had for baby Charlotte once gave her the power she needed to expel Blue, but she was too late to save the child from Alexander's clutches. Find and embrace the great love inside you, Cooper. Hold on to it for dear life and don't let go." She poked her finger in his chest. "*That* will restore your soul."

Cooper ran his fingers through his hair. After a decade of

pushing people away and building up walls of emotional defense, he prayed to God he really *did* have that kind of love inside him. He wasn't so sure. But if anyone could pull it out of him, it was Randy.

Cooper stood up and faced her. "One more thing. How can you be so sure that Blue will use me and my power to go after Alexander?"

Miss Ida clasped her hands together and looked up at him with a raised eyebrow. "You've probably heard all your life about how Blue led a slave rebellion at Warfield and set the manor house on fire, killing Sally and her family."

Cooper nodded. "Sure. Everyone around here has heard that ghost story."

"That's the thing with ghost stories. They're never as scary as the truth."

CHAPTER THIRTY-EIGHT

Cooper checked in on Lillie Mae a final time before leaving her in the care of Miss Ida and Wayne, and he joined the others in the sitting room. Joshua stood in front of the fireplace with his eclectic group of soldiers gathered around him, looking very much like the God-ordained prophet he once was. Betsy and Odessa flanked the front window, tension thick between them. One of the Amazon twins from the kitchen sat in the blue wingback chair, the other stood behind it. Eudora and Eunice were nowhere in sight. He'd likely pissed them off royally with his little possession experiment.

Rafe stood by the back wall. Cooper sidled up next to him and leaned in to whisper in his ear. "I need you to do something for me tonight. At Warfield."

He leaned in close, and Rafe scrunched his face as Cooper whispered his request. He glanced over at Joshua and then back at Cooper before finally nodding in agreement. Joshua surprised Cooper by waving him to the front of the group. He crossed the room and stood beside the Manheeg.

Joshua cocked his head at him. "Well, are you ready to share this plan of yours with us?"

Cooper nodded and faced a roomful of icy stares. "The changelings won't hurt me. They will charge me, try to frighten me, even knock me out of the way, but Alexander won't let them kill me. I am the only one here who can get past them and close to Alexander."

The Amazon twin in the chair leaned forward. "They may not be able to kill you, but they could take you."

"No. Thanks to my grandmother's wards of protection, they can't do that either. Not against my will." Cooper crossed his arms and widened his stance. "I can take care of myself with the changelings, trust me." He looked into a sea of unconvinced eyes. "When I get to Warfield, Alexander will pick up my scent. He'll think I have given up and come to trade myself for Randy. You guys need to stay back until I get close so he won't detect an ambush. I'll need all of you to keep the changelings busy while I get in and take care of Alexander."

Odessa strode forward and stopped behind the sofa, directing an icy glare at him. "And if you fail? What then? We'll all be sitting ducks."

Cooper shoved his hands in his pocket and stared at her. "I won't fail. I know what I have to do to kill him. It won't be easy, but I think I can do it."

Betsy moved around the sofa and stood beside Joshua. "Not good enough." For once she and Odessa agreed.

Cooper shrugged his shoulders. "Like I said, you are going to have to trust me. I am the only one here who can get close enough to Alexander to end him once and for all."

Odessa threw up her hands and stalked back over to the window, cursing in some foreign tongue he didn't recognize.

Joshua edged forward and took over with resolute authority in his voice. "Lex will transport Cooper to Warfield." He looked at Cooper. "Lex will be your fastest mode of transport, and we want your scent to distract Montgomery from ours right away. We will be right behind you."

Cooper nodded. He knew he was the catnip to keep Alexander distracted while the Jericho soldiers fought through the changelings. Bait.

Joshua pointed to Odessa who stepped forward and took center stage. "Rafe and I discovered tunnels that run from the harbor to all the plantations in the area. We were lost down there for a while, but we think we found the one that leads to Warfield. The changelings have plowed quite a path back and forth in that one."

Cooper shook his head and rolled his eyes. Oh. So she and Rafe discovered the tunnels—all by themselves. How clever of them.

Odessa sauntered over to the fireplace and stood on Cooper's left. "Half of you will come with me through the tunnel that leads to Warfield. There's a large changeling nest down there. We eliminated a lot of them, but we don't know how many are left, so keep your eyes open and watch your backs."

Joshua pointed to a young blond Divinum boy leaning against the back wall. With his stringy bleached-blond locks, torn jeans, and tie-dye T-shirt, he looked like he would be more at home riding the waves at Myrtle Beach.

"Taj, you and Rafe will enter the plantation grounds from the rear by way of the canal behind the manor house." He nodded over to the Amazon twins. "Daria and Marissa will lead the rest of you through the woods and flank the property."

All the point leaders nodded obediently.

Joshua shifted his weight and scanned the room. "Betsy, Lex, and I will cover Cooper until he gets into the house." He glanced over at Cooper. "You'll be on your own in there until we can put down the changelings and join you."

Cooper swallowed hard and nodded.

Joshua looked back at his soldiers. "Any questions?" The room was silent. Things always seemed to be definitive around Joshua, so not surprisingly, no one had questions—only murmured, small group discussions about their orders.

The Manheeg faced Cooper and crossed his arms over his mountain of a chest. "Rafe says you do not need a dagger."

Cooper didn't know what to say. He was a little flattered by Rafe's confidence in his Divinum combat abilities. He shook his head and straightened his spine. "I did okay without one."

Joshua took his hand and placed one of Betsy's daggers in it. "Well, I would feel better if you kept one on you this time around."

Cooper turned the cold blade over in his hand and grabbed it by the handle, surprised by how good it felt in his grip. He looked up into the Manheeg's black eyes. "Obviously you didn't die at the battle of Jericho. And for some reason, I don't think it was you who slaughtered the surviving women and children of the Israelite tribe."

Joshua's nostrils flared, and he looked down. "Caleb would have killed me too, if the Anakim of Jericho had not already turned me. I was a coward. I ran. I didn't understand what had happened to me—what I'd become or why God had so infinitely abandoned me. I deserted my tribe, and Caleb slaughtered his own people. Feasted on them all over the course of a night. Not one innocent soul survived his bloodlust. So I built this army to atone for my sins and make the Anakim pay for theirs as well."

Cooper nodded. The distant shadow passing over Joshua's eyes told him that was all he was willing to share. He looked around the room and glanced in the faces of each Jericho soldier, counting them silently, small as they were. Less than twenty. Holy hell. Randy's life hung in the balance, and this had all the makings of a pitiful bloodbath.

"Seems like we will be seriously outnumbered out there," Cooper said to Joshua, trying not to sound disrespectful. "Do you have more soldiers on the way or something?"

Joshua looked around the room. "This is it, I'm afraid. At least all we could spare for this mission. There are still a few hot spots around the world with rogue Anakim activity. At the height of the war, our numbers topped half a million strong. Now, with the success of the Sterilus-A virus and advances we made in the war, there are only a few hundred of us left to hunt the remaining Anakim. To be honest, we weren't prepared for this kind of situation." He looked back at Cooper. "No matter our numbers, we *must* prevail here."

Cooper nodded. "We will."

Gliding forward with eerie grace, Lex stopped in front of Cooper and extended his hands.

Are you ready, Cooper?

Cooper glanced over at Betsy, who stood guard by the front window with her arms folded over her chest. Her eyes, thick with worry, made him think she was hiding something. He knew she was the only one in the room who really cared if he or Randy made it out of this alive. So he had no choice but to trust her. He nodded at her and she back at him. Cooper reached out and took Lex's nearly translucent hands in his. When their skin touched, a hot surge of energy passed through Lex's palms into his. Cooper flinched and tried to pull away, but the albino's grip was tight.

Don't fight it, Cooper. Close your eyes and relax. We will be at Warfield momentarily.

Cooper looked up at him. "Don't fight what?"

A low hum emanated from the center of Lex's chest and grew in Cooper's ears like the rumble of an oncoming train. The floor spun under his feet, getting faster by the second. Lex's chest glowed through his robe like his insides were on fire under his skin. His whole body lit up—a seven foot tall statue of glowing light. Cooper looked down at their fused hands, Lex's skin melting into his. It was the way he felt inside, all of his internal organs becoming one. His vision blurred as the Jericho army, the sitting room, and Phipps House all slipped away.

CHAPTER THIRTY-NINE

Everything was still. Cooper and Lex stood facing each other, hands clasped together. A chilly draft brushed Cooper's cheeks and ears. The room was mostly dark, lit only with streaks of moonlight creeping in through the cracks of warped boarded walls and gaping windows. The cold night air spilled in, chilling him to the bone. He hadn't thought to put on his coat before they'd disappeared from Phipps House. He peered up at Lex who posed like a flagpole in front of him.

"How did you…" The question seemed silly at this point, so Cooper stopped and rephrased it. "Can all Divinum do that?"

Lex shook his head and released Cooper's hands. *Only pure-blood Divinum are capable of teleportation.*

Cooper nodded. "Teleportation, huh? I'll bet that comes in handy." He could have saved himself the embarrassment of a few early-morning walks of shame with a talent like that.

He looked around. Four windows anchored the barren space, two on each sidewall. Leaves, sticks, and a few traces of man-made debris like crushed beer cans and cigarette butts littered the wood floor. At the far end of the room, an unassuming wooden pulpit stood elevated on a six-inch raised platform. A simple cross hung on the wall behind the pulpit. Tilted lower on one side than the other, it looked slightly sacrilegious. Like something unholy announcing it had the upper hand there.

Cooper knew the place from his childhood memories and nightmares. They were in the old slave chapel at Warfield Plantation. An unexpected wave of sadness washed over him as he stood wondering how the hell a hundred fifty slaves managed to cram into that small room. Or why they would even *want* to worship a god that had forsaken them so. Cooper swallowed hard, his eyes edging with tears. He swiped them away with the back of his hand. Another icy chill gripped his bones, and he shuddered.

Allow me. Lex put a pasty white hand on his shoulder, penetrating his chilled skin with a jolt of ancient power. A wave of heat spilled over Cooper's entire body, warming him down to his bones. The bitter wind swirling around him had no effect, though it no doubt picked up his scent and delivered it to Alexander Montgomery. That was the plan.

"Thanks," he said, eyeing Lex with wonder. The albino gave a slight bow of his head.

The others will be here soon. Follow me. The Anakim will know you have arrived, but my scent is undetectable to him.

Cooper's legs responded before his brain had a chance to, and he followed Lex out the door of the chapel down two rickety wooden steps. The bell tower loomed in the moonlight to his right, a muted ring sounding out as the wind jostled the bell around. A flood of anxious childhood memories rushed into his mind. The ringing bell. The rocking chair. Blue. His ancestral guardian had awakened the dark power inside him for his protection that day. It had taken him a lifetime to finally feel grateful for that burdensome gift. It just might save his ass tonight. And Randy's.

Sensing Anakim presence behind him, Cooper spun around and crouched defensively. A swirling cloud of black smoke billowed with a soft rustle of fabric and sand. Betsy and Joshua appeared.

Joshua gave the slave village an uninterested glance and moved toward them. "The others are in place." He looked at Cooper. "Montgomery will have picked up your scent by now. Are you ready?"

Cooper nodded and scanned the length of Oak Alley. It seemed much longer than he remembered. "Ready as I'm going to get."

Betsy stepped up to him and put her hand on his arm. "You're sure about this?"

Cooper swallowed hard and nodded. There was no room for mistakes tonight. Randy could wind up in the cross hairs.

Betsy's dead black eyes transfixed him. "If you run into trouble, we can get to you in seconds. Lex even faster."

Cooper took a deep breath. It would only take a changeling half a second to rip his throat out if they wanted to. He hoped to God he was right about being immune to their attacks.

Lex appeared at Betsy's side. *With any luck, Odessa's team will clear the tunnels of changelings before Montgomery summons them. Stay focused and alert.*

Cooper turned to Betsy and Joshua. "And Randy?"

Betsy rested her hand on the handle of a dagger tucked in her belt. "We'll find him."

Cooper nodded, shrouding his thoughts from them. Hell if he would leave Randy's fate in their hands. He would find Randy himself. He faced the long, lonely trek ahead before him. The enormous oak trees lining the road waved spidery branches at him, limbs creaking under the weight of dead Spanish moss, beckoning him down the road to the manor house. He took a deep breath and walked forward, coaching himself with every step. One foot in front of the other. Slow and steady. Betsy had his back. Lillie Mae's veil of protection would keep him safe. Randy was in there somewhere. He had to end this tonight.

The urgent bark of a dog echoed somewhere in the distance, and the wind howled through the spindly branches. Just keep moving forward, he told himself. A tight fist of anxiety gripped his heart and squeezed. He rubbed his chest without thinking. The manor house drew him forward. He was halfway there. A rustle sounded in the branches above him. He froze, not daring to look up. It stopped a moment later. Must have been the wind. He exhaled and took another step forward. Again, tree limbs above him crackled. Again, he stopped. Slipping a hand under his shirt, he gripped the handle of the dagger tucked in the waist of his jeans. Wood snapped and splintered overhead. His heart raced, and the breath caught in his throat. No way that was the wind.

His instincts told him to make a run for the manor house, but his feet did not respond quickly enough. A rabid changeling dropped out of the trees with a chilling thud just three feet in front of him.

CHAPTER FORTY

The creature was enormous. Rotting flesh and tattered rags of clothing hung from exposed bone. Blood red eyes oozed dark fluid from the corners of their sockets. Long, crooked teeth jutted out of its mouth like a handful of razor-sharp ice picks, and the right ear dangled from the side of the monster's head, attached only by a flimsy tag of flesh. The changeling crouched and hissed at Cooper. Mirroring the creature's stance, he stared it down, not quite sure what the thing was allowed to do to him. Maim him? Break a few bones? He didn't want to stick around long enough to find out. He was just steps away from the manor house—and Randy. The standoff continued, one waiting for the other to blink.

Then the thing lunged at him.

Cooper didn't hesitate. He spun on his heel and kicked his right leg high in the air. The pointed toe of his boot caught the creature squarely in the jaw. Bones crackled, and the changeling stumbled back, momentarily stunned. The grotesque thing could not have been any more stunned than

Cooper. He'd never been in a physical fight in his life and had no idea he could kick like that.

Emboldened by his successful first strike, Cooper reached for the dagger tucked in his jeans, closed his fingers around the handle, and pulled it out. The changeling shook its head and wobbled on its feet. Cooper charged, drawing the dagger underhanded and up into the beast's stomach. The entire length of the dagger and Cooper's whole hand sank deep into fleshy bowels.

He yanked his hand away, leaving the dagger submerged inside. The changeling staggered back, eyes bulging out of their sockets, and crumpled down to the ground in front of him. Cooper stood over the remains of the dead changeling and wiped his soiled hand on the leg of his jeans—disgusted, yet feeling a little more confident than he had when he'd started the trek. The branches above him came alive with movement from the first tree to the last, running the entire length of Oak Alley. Cooper peered up, a wave of dread washing over him. The trees were full of them, every branch occupied with the slithering, snapping monsters. Alexander knew they were coming, and he'd already assembled his army.

Changelings dropped all around him, first like walnuts shaken loose by the wind, then like a sudden, violent hailstorm pummeling the ground. Each landed with claws drawn in the air and fangs extended. They surrounded him. The first creature to advance on him tossed its head back and wailed a piercing war cry, setting off the entire horde. Cooper winced and covered his ears with his hands, shielding them from the deafening chorus. The monster licked what was left of its lips and stared him down, but it didn't charge him. Though relatively confident that the creature wouldn't harm him if he tried to walk past it, each monster he left standing was one more that would attack the Jericho soldiers.

A swirl of black smoke descended from above and landed beside him, Betsy's form emerged from the vaporous mist. She stood next to him without glancing his way. The beasts snarled at her, seemingly more agitated by her intrusion than his, which was likely her plan. Two changelings charged her at once. She reared back and head-butted one of the creatures, knocking it on its ass. The second monster's neck met her vicious fangs. She ripped out what remained of its throat and spat the vile contents on the ground.

Cooper shot a look back down the sandy road to Joshua and Lex. A dozen changelings circled them, and the warriors put them down one by one, Joshua with sheer strength and a dagger and Lex with barely the wave of his hand. But, the creatures' numbers grew every second. They fell from the trees above them and poured out of the slave cabins behind them. It was a complete ambush.

Betsy let out a guttural cry behind him, drawing his attention. A changeling almost twice her size lifted her off the ground with its claws wrapped around her throat. A dark spit of rage rumbled inside Cooper, igniting the power in his core.

He stepped forward, savoring the darkness and welcoming its intoxicating mettle. "Put her down. Now!"

His voice was no more than a growl and sounded foreign to his own ears. He didn't know what the hell he was thinking, trying to talk to the creature. He wasn't sure these former humans understood language anymore. The changeling regarded him as it dangled Betsy in the air. She wrestled for her freedom, clawing at the monster's grip around her throat. It appeared unfazed by her struggle. Cooper caught Betsy's eye and thought he understood what she wanted to do. His fingertips sizzled, and he thrust his hands out in front of him.

Betsy swung a leg back and brought her foot up hard into the creature's groin. It wailed, and released its grip on her. The moment she was clear, Cooper released the dark energy surging through his veins like a bolt of lightning. He sliced his open hand through the air like a sword—just as he had in the nest—missing actual physical contact with the changeling by at least four feet. The thing froze in place and stared at him. No wound peeled open like a zipper this time. Cooper's heart sank. He'd failed, and the monster would surely finish Betsy off.

The changeling looked down and touched its crooked fingers to its stomach. A thin line of dark liquid seeped diagonally across its midsection as the top half of its body slid at a downward angle and splattered onto the ground. The lower half of the changeling's severed body stood upright, blood and entrails protruding out. A wretched odor of feces and bile assaulted Cooper's nostrils, triggering a dry heave gag.

Betsy was on her feet, blocking the path of the oncoming horde. "Go while the way is clear!"

Cooper took a last look down Oak Alley. Though greatly outnumbered, Joshua and Lex appeared to be holding their own. Movement at the treeline on both sides of the yard caused Cooper a moment of hesitation, fearing more changelings were on the way. Figures formed in the moonlight and a surge of hope shot through his body. Daria led a team of Jericho soldiers on one side and Marissa on the other. Relieved that reinforcements were on the way to assist Betsy and the others, and alarmed by the shrinking patch of clear road that separated him and the house, Cooper gave a last appreciative glance to Betsy.

Growling and hissing at a cluster of approaching changelings, she charged them—creating just the window of cover he needed.

Cooper turned and bolted toward the manor house.

CHAPTER FORTY-ONE

If not for the piercing shrieks of the changelings outside, the house would have been completely devoid of sound—perhaps even peaceful. It looked pretty much the same inside, yet not so brightly lit as it had during his last visit. Flickering candlelight and low-flamed oil lamps muted the dazzling luster of the pristine Victorian décor. Cooper stood in the foyer, feeling naked and exposed. Thankfully, no one probed around in his head this time. Retracting his impulse to call out Randy's name, he moved with quick and quiet steps, heartbeat pounding, fingertips still sizzling from his attack on the changelings.

He peeked inside the candlelit dining room on the left. A dark walnut table stretched from one end of the room to the other and was set for twenty people with the finest china and silverware he'd ever seen. He eased down the hallway, his back pinned to the wall and hair standing at full attention on his neck. The Anakim presence in the house was as thick as tar. It needled at his Divinum nature, like the hatred between the two races was inherent and nonnegotiable.

Something caught his eye at the top of the staircase.

An ornately framed portrait hung atop the landing. He'd missed it the last time he was there. The young woman in the painting was instantly recognizable from the blood-stained photo in Lillie Mae's Bible. Sally Parker. The princess of Warfield. Blue's Sally. She looked so young and innocent—alabaster skin dotted with freckles, copper hair cascading down around her shoulders. Her features were so similar to what he imagined of a young Lillie Mae. The Phipps family resemblance was undeniable. He moved cautiously up the staircase, Sally's haunting dark-brown eyes luring him every step of the way.

At the top of the landing, Cooper looked to the right, then to his left. Identical doors stood closed at each end. A random step took him left, but he changed course when a muted cry sounded to his right. The floorboards betrayed him, creaking under his cautious steps and urging him to pick up his pace. He needed to find Randy and get him clear of the house before he dealt with Alexander. He finally reached the door, turned the knob, and peeked in.

Cooper's heart lurched in his chest. Randy lay sprawled on a high four-post bed—bound, gagged, and naked save for a white top sheet resting low on his hips. A jerk of his head in Cooper's direction revealed wide eyes filled with alarm. Cooper slipped through the door and eased it closed behind him. He hurried over to the bed and removed the wadded cloth from Randy's mouth. Gasping for air, the ripples of Randy's sun-bronzed stomach stretched and expanded as he replenished his lungs. Blood trickled down his neck and over his heaving chest. His wrists had been tied to the bedposts behind him and his ankles bound at the bottom of the bed.

"Fuck, am I glad to see you, Red," Randy whispered. "Untie my ass."

Cooper was so happy to see him that he didn't even know what to say. He went right to work, freeing Randy's wrists and ankles while he untangled his tongue.

He eyed two bloody holes in the side of Randy's neck. "Are you all right?"

Randy's eyes were wild, and his short hair spiked with sweat. "Those sick sons of bitches bit me and sucked on me, like I was some kind of goddamned human buffet."

Cooper's gaze drifted down and back up Randy's body, hoping he didn't find bloodstains or wounds below the neck, or the waist. "Did they do anything *else*?"

Randy shook his head, understanding Cooper's meaning immediately. "No. Just stripped me down and gawked at me. Fucking vamp pervs."

Cooper couldn't suppress a relieved smile. He was so glad to see him alive and still so *Randy.* Before he could stop himself, he draped his arms over Randy's shoulders and rested the side of his face on the hairy contours of his chest. An unexpected tear slipped out and fell onto Randy's skin. What in hell had happened to him? Here he was acting like a sixteen-year-old girl, crying and shit, though he couldn't make himself care. Gone were the days of one-night stands and going-nowhere relationships. Randy had changed everything. That much he knew. Their lives would be different now. If they got out of there alive.

Randy wrapped his arms around Cooper and kissed him lightly on the forehead. "I'm okay. I'm fine, Coop. I promise. You got here just in time. You saved my ass *again*, which is getting pretty damn annoying."

Cooper sat up, the urgency of their situation crashing down on him. "Get dressed. I don't know how long the Jericho soldiers will be able to hold off the changelings."

Randy gripped Cooper's arm. "You know it's not me he wants. You shouldn't have come here."

Cooper stood and glanced back at the door again. "I can handle Alexander. I just need to get you out of the house first. Come on. We don't have much time."

Randy hopped out of the bed, not bothering to take the sheet with him for cover. He gathered his clothes from a nearby chair. After a moment of gawking, Cooper averted his eyes, but he'd already glimpsed a heavenly blur of naked bronze skin and thick muscle. Walking over to the door, Cooper put an ear against the cool wood and listened. No sound of movement outside, but he knew Alexander was aware of his presence. He glanced over his shoulder to check Randy's progress.

Randy stepped into his uniform pants and pulled them on. He shoved bare feet inside his boots. "Freaks took my gun and radio." He pulled a white cotton T-shirt over his head.

Cooper whispered over to him. "The front yard is full of changelings. We'll need to get you out through a back door."

Randy stared back at him. "Me? Don't you mean us."

Cooper met him in the middle of the room and took his

hands. “Rafe will meet you at the back of the house down by the canal and get you back to Phipps House. You’ll be safe there.”

Randy’s nostrils flared, and he shook his head. “Oh, hell no, Cooper. I’m not going anywhere without you.”

Cooper stepped back and scrubbed a hand over his face. “Dammit, Randy. We don’t have time for this.” He planted his hands on his hips. “Alexander’s never going to let me go, don’t you understand that? He’ll never stop hunting me. And when the rest of the Anakim find out what my blood can do…” Cooper shook his head and locked eyes with Randy. “I have to stop him. End him. Tonight.”

Randy took Cooper’s face in his hands and ran his thumb over Cooper’s wind-chapped lips. A sly grin twisted his lips. “This Rambo shit is really turning me on right now.”

Cooper pushed Randy’s hand away and ran fingers through his hair, his chest tightening. “Goddammit, this is not a joke.”

Randy’s smile faded instantly, and he pointed over to the blood-stained sheets on the bed. “I’m well aware that it’s not a joke. Those fuckers are crazy and dangerous.”

Cooper placed a hand on each of Randy’s bulky biceps. “Alexander can’t hurt me. He can’t keep me here or drink from me unless I allow him. Lillie Mae did something to protect me. *A hedge of protection* or something.”

Randy rolled his eyes. “Unless you allow him? Why the hell would you do that?”

Cooper shrugged. “That’s just it. I wouldn’t.”

Randy pursed his lips and exhaled through his nose.

"Listen to me, Cooper Causey. I've waited for you my whole life. Pined for you. Dreamed of you. Thought about you every day since you left town. When I had sex with my wife, I imagined I was with you just so I could get the job done, which is a little fucked-up if you ask me. Hell, I couldn't even grieve for my own best friend at your brother's funeral because I couldn't take my eyes off you. You looked so lonely. So lost. All I wanted to do was march down that aisle in front of the whole goddamned town, take you in my arms, and hold you. Never in a million years did I think that I would finally have you, or that you would ever love me. But I do have you now. And you *do* love me. I know you do. I won't let you do this alone. Understand? So, either we leave together or we go vampire hunting together. Your call."

Cooper had no response whatsoever, overwhelmed by Randy's words. He pulled Randy into his arms, and they held each other tight for a silent minute, their bodies fitting together like they were born that way. After all the years of nameless tricks, he had the only man he ever truly wanted right there in his arms. The decision was easy. No way in hell he would let Randy get caught in the crosshairs of his mission. First, he would deliver Randy to Rafe, and then he'd face Alexander—alone. He would have to keep the plan to himself. Randy would never agree.

Cooper took a step back. "Okay, then. Let's get the hell out of here."

Randy smiled and nodded.

Cooper crossed the room with Randy right behind him. He eased the door open, praying it wouldn't creak, and slipped out onto the landing. He looked both ways. The coast was clear. Nodding for Randy to follow, he moved toward the staircase. They weren't alone in the house, he knew that much. His mind was in a foot race with his heartbeat.

At the bottom of the stairs, they were met with the sounds of the ongoing battle on the other side of the front door. Unearthly shrieks and bone-chilling war cries echoed through the night. Cooper couldn't imagine the carnage, or which side had the upper hand. But he couldn't worry about Jericho right now. He had to get Randy out the back door and safely to Rafe.

Leading Randy away from the front door, he glanced over his shoulder and pointed down the hall toward the back of the house. He faced forward again and found Alexander standing in their path not six feet away, a smug, self-satisfied grin on his angular face.

Cooper froze. Randy did not. He pulled Cooper by the arm in the opposite direction. Stephen Parker glided out of the dining room and blocked their path to the front door. Randy looked back and forth between Alexander and Stephen, likely wondering which one he had a better chance against. Cooper took a deep breath and put a hand on Randy's arm to settle him. If they resisted, it would get ugly fast, and he couldn't risk Randy getting hurt.

Cooper faced Alexander, who had closed the distance between them and stood only a couple feet away. His form-fitting black leather pants and a tight black T-shirt indicated that he'd dressed for battle. Cooper glanced up into his shimmering green eyes and fought their alluring pull on his dark side.

Alexander's lips tightened into a thin line. "We've been waiting for you, Cooper. Your friend here kept us aptly entertained." With a not so subtle taunt, he wiped the corner of his mouth with his thumb and leered at Randy's crotch.

Randy rushed forward, roaring with the fury of a caged lion. Cooper turned and held him back, which was no small feat.

Alexander sneered at Cooper. "Settle your man, Divinum, before I snap his neck."

Randy seethed through gritted teeth. "Do it now, Red! Zap the motherfucker!"

Alexander chuckled at Randy's outburst and stared Cooper down. "What'll it be, Cooper? A polite negotiation between two gentlemen, or this one's beautiful head separated from that delicious body?"

The darkness inside Cooper stirred. Hatred oozed from every pore. He was so enraged he felt he could destroy Alexander even without Blue's help. But something checked in his spirit, disrupting his rage. A spasm of pain cut through him, and a light went out somewhere deep inside. Cold and empty, he froze and processed the internal revelation, insulating his mind so the Anakim would not discover it.

Lillie Mae was dead. And gone with her, the veil of protection around him.

CHAPTER FORTY-TWO

Cooper sat on the edge of the sofa in the same room where he'd first encountered Alexander Montgomery. Building an impenetrable wall around his brain brick by silent brick, he kept all thoughts of Lillie Mae locked away in a deep dark corner of his mind. He would use that later to fuel his revenge when he ended the Anakim for good. For the moment, he had to be careful. Randy could get hurt.

Alexander stood in front of the empty fireplace, leaning on the mantel with thumbs lodged in his pants pockets. He stared at Cooper with his signature condescending smirk etched into his granite face. With his relaxed yet seductive posture, he looked like he was posing for *GQ*—some bizarre article like *Stylish and Sexy: Maniacal Monsters of the Deep South*.

"I assume the traitor, Joshua, has been filling your head with all manner of malicious lies about me."

Cooper cleared his throat. "I don't know what you are talking about. I came here alone." Stephen had Randy pinned to the wall with a pit bull-like grip around his throat.

His body stiff and rigid, Randy was uncharacteristically silent at the moment, likely realizing any masculine bravado would only stoke Alexander's wrath. He looked around the room, no doubt preoccupied with finding any and all options for escape, biding their time as well.

Alexander chuckled. "Come now, Cooper. No need for lies. I can feel you pushing me out of your head as we speak. I know what's going on outside. Once I sifted through your ridiculously alluring aroma, I sensed their presence. Especially Joshua's. I'd know that traitorous mongrel's stench anywhere. He and my father go way back, you know."

No. Cooper didn't know. A tinge of suspicion gnawed at his insides. He'd sensed earlier that Joshua held something back. Apparently, he had a personal connection to Alexander. What else could the Manheeg be hiding from him?

Cooper forced his facial features to soften and tempered his voice with contriteness. "Please. Just let Randy go. I'm the one you want. He's got nothing to do with this. He can't help you."

"Oh, I beg to differ," Alexander said, walking over to Randy and Stephen. He touched Randy's chin. "It might be fun to have him around."

Randy spat and glared at him like he wanted to rip the guy's head off. The discharge hit Alexander just under his right eye. Stephen grabbed a handful of Randy's hair and yanked his head back. He hissed, his open mouth hovering only an inch over Randy's neck.

Cooper sprang to his feet. "No!"

Alexander gritted his teeth and wiped the saliva from his face with the back of hand. He turned to Cooper. The green hue of his eyes went instantly dark, filling Cooper with an overwhelming sense of dread. "*You* will pay for that, not him."

Randy swung a fist at Alexander. Missed him by more than a foot. "You touch him, and I will rip your fucking—"

Stephen gripped Randy's throat and lifted, instantly cutting off his words.

Randy struggled to breathe, clawing at Stephen's hands and kicking his legs wildly while dangling inches above the floor.

Alexander glided over to Cooper and smiled. "Your friend here, with his small-town charm and manners, has proven to be quite the effective motivation for you, which is precisely why I brought him here. I think we will keep him. His presence may help you stay focused and malleable."

Cooper shook his head. God, this was going from bad to worse. He pointed at Randy. "At least let him breathe! He'll behave. I promise."

Alexander nodded over his shoulder to Stephen who lowered Randy to the ground and loosened his grip. He buckled forward, gasping for air.

Alexander leaned in and sniffed Cooper's neck. He brushed Cooper's skin with chilled lips, igniting a spasm of quivers through Cooper's body. "Such a fascinating blend of the Bokor and Divinum. Your internal battle between light and dark power must be endless."

Alexander regarded him a moment and then turned away. "The Seraphim High Council had big plans for your ancestor, Sally. She was to be a great weapon against the Anakim," Alexander said. "Too bad the poor girl didn't live long enough to fulfill her lofty destiny."

Stephen glared at Cooper. "That cursed Negro slave killed her and set this house on fire. If Alexander hadn't found me and pulled me out, I would have perished right along with my sister, brother, and father."

Cooper's mind raced. Stephen had just handed him the ammunition he needed. He tucked it away, along with his grief over Lillie Mae, behind the fortified wall around his mind.

It was an inopportune moment for Randy to lose the battle to hold his tongue. "Does this story have a point?"

Stephen's grip tightened around Randy's throat, producing a muted wince of pain.

Alexander ignored Randy and kept staring at Cooper. Madness flashed in his eyes. "You're much stronger than Charlotte ever was. With your blood, I will make this world my own."

Cooper raised an eyebrow at Alexander, his blood beginning to boil. "You will never have me. And I will never help you breed more of your abominations." He embraced the rage churning inside him. "I will send you straight back to whatever hell you came from." Cooper's fingers tingled, and he curled them into fists, triggering a smile on Randy's face.

Alexander walked over and assessed Randy from head to

toe. "We can do this the easy way or the hard way, Cooper." Alexander smiled at Stephen. "He would be even more spectacular after the change, don't you think?"

Stephen sneered at Cooper and hissed in Randy's ear. "Yes, he would. Everything would be enhanced. He would be an Anakim god."

Randy gritted his teeth and twisted his body under Stephen's iron grip, trying unsuccessfully to free himself.

Alexander looked back at Cooper, danger lacing the emerald sheen of his eyes. "Give me what I want, or I drain him in front of you here and now. Your choice."

Cooper's blood rumbled through his veins like molten lava. He searched deep into the black void of his mind, releasing all his rage and fear out into the spirit realm. But Blue had yet to make his presence known. Cooper played the only card he had left.

He took a step forward. "Just like you drained Sally the night she died?"

The room fell silent. The twitch of Alexander's cheek was the only indication Cooper's suspicions were correct. He could only imagine Stephen's confusion.

He seized the moment and pushed forward. "You were hunting Divinum blood that night, weren't you? That's why you came to Warfield. Like you said, Sally was very powerful. Her scent must have been incredibly alluring. You tracked her here, snuck into her room, and drained her. Then you left her for dead and escaped with a pretty blond souvenir."

Stephen shifted his weight, loosening his hold on Randy.

He stared wide-eyed at Cooper, the cocky swagger quickly fading from his eyes.

Randy raised an eyebrow, and an impish grin crept across his face. "Well, this is awkward."

"Don't listen to his desperate babbling, Stephen," Alexander said, his countenance turning more threatening by the second.

"No." Stephen's voice was small. With eyes full of doubt, he stared at his lover and dropped the hand from Randy's throat. "The slaves revolted. Blue killed Sally and set fire to the house. Alexander saw the flames from the distance and rushed in to help. I was the only one he was able to save."

Cooper's brazen streak held firm. He moved toward Stephen. "A powerful Vodoun Houngan like Blue would have been able to detect an Anakim presence. He wasn't trying to kill Sally, Stephen. They were in love. Blue was trying to protect her from him," Cooper said, pointing at Alexander. "Those slaves died that night trying to save your family from the devil himself."

Stephen stared at Alexander, eyes wide and full of pain. Alexander's silence spoke volumes.

"Alexander." Stephen's voice was barely a whimper. "Tell me this isn't true. Please."

Alexander looked away. "Ridiculous lies. Don't listen to him." His words held not a trace of conviction.

Stephen stumbled back, bewilderment twisting the muscles in his face. "Then why can't you look me in the eye?"

Randy drew in a deep breath and exhaled through pursed

lips. "Well. Sounds like you two fellas have a lot to talk about. I would suggest couple's counseling, but it didn't work for shit with me and the ex-wife."

Anxiety clicked in Cooper's core. He couldn't wait for Blue any longer. They were distracted. He had to end Alexander now while he had the chance, before Randy got hurt. He inhaled through his nose and held it inside, letting the darkness fill him.

Alexander must have sensed his intentions because he sailed across the room. He grabbed Randy by the throat and spun his body around in front of him, holding it there like a shield. Randy struggled under Alexander's grip, but he was no match for Anakim strength.

Suddenly Stephen was behind Cooper with an arm wrapped around his neck, applying instant pressure against his windpipe.

He hissed into Cooper's ear. "You're lying. I don't believe you. Tell me it's not true."

Cooper gasped for air and clawed at Stephen's arm. He focused all of his residual Divinum power into penetrating Stephen's mind. *Why was he here that night? You think he just happened to be close by and saw the fire? He killed Sally.*

Stephen tightened his grip, and Cooper knew he wasn't yet convinced.

"Don't listen to his Divinum lies, Stephen." Alexander stood five feet away, holding Randy up in front of him. "Hold his arms down, Stephen. Now!"

Stephen hesitated a few seconds but finally obeyed. He let Cooper go and bound his hands behind his back. Cooper lunged forward, but Stephen's grip was relentless.

Alexander glowered at Cooper over Randy's shoulder. "I am done playing games with you, Divinum." His lips parted. His mouth twisted unnaturally, and his fangs extended.

Randy widened his eyes, and for once Cooper saw real fear in them. This was it. Randy would die at any moment if he didn't so something. But Blue had forsaken him, he couldn't access his powers, and he wouldn't risk hurting Randy anyway. His only currency was the blood running through his veins.

"Wait!" Cooper cried out in a panic. "I'll do it! Whatever you want. You can drink from me. I will stay with you, just let him go." Tears edged his eyes. "Please. Don't hurt him."

Alexander looked up at Cooper, his face contorting into a sadistic leer. A second of anticipation hung heavy in the air between them, and the tiniest bloom of hope opened in Cooper's chest. He allowed himself to believe Alexander might accept his offer and spare Randy after all. But the evil fixed in Alexander's eyes was absolute and unforgiving. He unhinged his jaw and ripped into Randy's neck with the violent hunger of a starving wild animal.

A bellow, primitive and guttural, erupted from the base of Cooper's throat and rang in his ears as if it didn't belong to him. He squirmed and twisted in Stephen's grip to no avail. Hot tears sizzled on his cheeks. Randy's eyes, protruding and wild, searched for him as Alexander tore deeper into his flesh.

The energy drained from Cooper's limbs as fast as the blood left the side of Randy's neck and flowed into Alexander's insatiable mouth. He was powerless. He could do nothing other than watch the vulgar feasting. Cooper collapsed into his captor's cold, steely arms. A waterfall of gut-wrenching grief poured over him, pelting his body with relentless, painful blows as the life evaporated from Randy's terror-stricken eyes.

CHAPTER FORTY-THREE

Stephen released his firm hold, and Cooper sank to his knees. He stared at Randy's lifeless body, lying ten feet away, just out of reach. His eyes were blank with certain death. Blood trickled down his neck and disappeared into the dark, intricate patterns of the rug. He finally raised his head and stared up at Alexander.

The Anakim strolled over to the fireplace, wiping the corners of his mouth with a handkerchief, like he'd just finished a lovely meal and had retired to the sitting room for some brandy and a cigar.

Stephen crossed the room and stood in front of Alexander. "What he said about Sally. He was lying. Tell me he was lying, Alexander."

Cooper crawled on hands and knees over to Randy's side and gaped at the carnage. Glaring back at the Anakim monster, darkness heated him from within. Alexander would pay for what he'd done.

Alexander touched Stephen's cheek and kissed him gently on the lips. "Of course he lied."

Stephen didn't respond, but the cold mask of skepticism on his face spoke volumes.

Cooper peered back down at the lifeless body before him. He touched his fingers to Randy's eyes, closing the lids. The sounds of a hard-fought battle raged outside the window. Changelings screeched. Jericho soldiers grunted and released fervent war cries. They were too late. Randy was dead.

Alexander eyed the window. "We don't have much time."

Cooper stood with some effort. His body was completely numb except for the hot energy pooling in his hands.

Alexander had the nerve to smile at him. "Decomposition sets in rather quickly after the draining. The longer he's dead, the more likely he will arise a changeling. I'm sure that is not what you want."

A cold chill ran the length of Cooper's spine. Alexander had played his trump card. Cooper had no choice now. He would have to let the monster drink from him so he could bring Randy back. As Anakim, but he would be back. And he needed Cooper's blood to do it. The devil had won.

Cooper's mind raced with a ramble of conflicting thoughts. Was that really saving Randy? Doomed to a life of darkness? Subsisting on human blood? Would Randy even want that? He closed his eyes and lowered his head. He had to decide before the only option other than final death was transformation into a deranged vampiric zombie. His choice was a selfish one. Some version of Randy was better than no Randy at all. Cooper looked up at Alexander with fire erupting in his core. He crossed the room, each step more determined than the last.

His approach silenced the two Anakim. He kept his voice low and assured. "Do it."

Stephen stood at Alexander's side, his face marred with lines of doubt and mistrust.

Alexander's grin made Cooper want to rip his face off. He restrained himself. He had to be patient and hope Blue had not completely abandoned him.

Cooper tilted his head to the side. "I said do it."

Alexander cocked his head and raised a brow.

"Drink, goddammit!" Cooper straightened his spine. "And if you don't turn him immediately, I will bring the wrath of God down on you."

Alexander's smile faded. "Watch yourself, Divinum. I will do what pleases me. Luckily for you, the thought of having your man under my control, day and night, is tremendously appealing."

The thought of it made Cooper's stomach turn. Shattering glass sounded somewhere in the front of the house. Alexander did not appear concerned that the Jericho soldiers were advancing on him. With the tip of his index finger, he traced a vein down the side of Cooper's neck. The touch ignited an army of tiny goose bumps across Cooper's body. Though it was not a complete shock, he still flinched when Alexander was suddenly on him. He felt cold fingers wrap around the back of his neck. The Anakim parted his lips, exposing fangs that were forever seared into Cooper's memory.

Cooper clenched his jaw, his words masked in a murderous growl. "Get it over with, you sick son of a bitch."

Alexander lowered his head, slow and taunting, as if leaning in for an intimate kiss. The razor-sharp tips of his fangs grazed Cooper's neck, seeking the most desirable point of entry, leaving a thin trail of chills in their wake. Cooper's whole body shuddered with an avalanche of ice rushing through his veins. The baneful power in his core seized in on itself, and he fought to hold it at bay just a little longer.

He was unprepared for the sheer force of the penetration when it finally came. Alexander drove his fangs deep into the side of his neck. A shock of pain blistered at the insertion point and rushed through Cooper's entire body. He instinctively tried to push the monster away, but with little effect. A flow of hot liquid spilled down his neck. He wasn't sure if it was his blood or some vile poison originating from the rabid jaws clamping down on him like an angry pit bull.

The dark force churning deep inside did not rush to assist him. Alexander consumed it. The Anakim drew it out of his flesh with primal, erotic groans. The sound sickened Cooper and the room spun around him. An all-encompassing pain commandeered his body, seeping into his pores and coating his muscles in agony.

Then it changed.

The pain eased. The ice running through Cooper's veins heated into steel rods, which burned under this skin. Anakim poison, he surmised. The sensation was too much. He flexed his fingers, feeling as if he might explode from the inside out. He struggled to keep his eyes open and his mind under his own control. But it drifted, succumbing to the brutal domination with which Alexander held him captive.

Cooper fought it, but he was no match for the ancient Anakim. He finally stopped pushing Alexander away and leaned into him. He dropped his hands to his side, reluctantly giving the monster easier access to take what he wanted.

Alexander groaned, twisting his fingers through Cooper's hair. He pressed their bodies together as close as they could get and gave a long, intense pull of blood from Cooper's jugular. His cock hardened against Cooper's thigh, throbbing and hungry. He slid his probing fingers down the front of Cooper's body, gripping him roughly through the front of his pants, stroking him like an impatient lover. Cooper's stomach lurched at the Anakim's lascivious touch, but he had no energy to pull away.

His body melted against the cold, marble-like statue of a man as the last shreds of his consciousness faded away.

CHAPTER FORTY-FOUR

Cooper's cheek pressed against the cold hardwood floor. He wasn't sure how long he'd been out, but his bones ached and his muscles felt stiff. He opened his eyes and peered across the floor. A motionless body lay a few feet away. Someone hovered over it, shoulders hunched with predatory menace. Randy. Alexander.

Cooper tried to make sense of the ghoulish scene. Beads of dark liquid fell from Alexander's neck and landed on Randy's parted lips like the first gentle raindrops before the storm. Randy's torso buckled with a sudden, violent heave. His chest rose. Fell. And rose again. Thank God. He was alive. His eyes were glassy and wild, darting around in their sockets like frenzied pinballs. The muscles in his face twitched with confusion. He licked his lips, sampling the foreign liquid spilling into his mouth.

Cooper propped himself up on his palms and dragged the dead weight of his legs across the floor, inching closer. He needed to touch Randy. Needed to know this was real. He was only an arm's length away when Randy looked up at

Alexander leaning over him, reached up, and yanked Alexander's head down to him with shocking force. He clamped his mouth down over the open wound on the Anakim's neck and drank.

Cooper froze, shocked by the disturbing image. The irrational heat of jealousy burned his cheeks as Randy suckled Alexander's neck like the starving newborn he was. Randy sat up as he drank at the fountain flowing from Alexander's neck. The Anakim craned his head back, giving his newborn easier access. His Adam's apple plunging up and down, and the feasting grew more impassioned by the second. Randy moaned as he consumed every ounce of Alexander that was offered him. The sound sickened Cooper. His stomach churned. Acid pooled at the base of his throat.

Cooper couldn't take it anymore. He crawled closer, a wave of panic rushing over him. What had he done? "Randy. Stop!"

Stephen stood over him. "If he does not drink Anakim blood, he will die."

Randy worked Alexander's neck like a starving wild dog gnawing on a fresh animal carcass. His eyes closed into tight slits, as if he was either enduring excruciating pain or lost in complete and total ecstasy. Cooper feared it was the latter. He knew it was.

A wave of nausea chilled Cooper's body from within, and a determined knot of bile rose up from the pit of his stomach, lurching in his throat. This time, he couldn't force it back down, and he scrambled up on hands and knees. All of the anxiety, fear, and despair that had been knotted in the pit of his stomach for the last three days emptied out onto the hardwood floor in a rancid puddle, every strained muscle in his body assisting with the expulsion.

When it finally stopped, he stared down at the floor, panting. He closed his eyes and inhaled deeply. A stream of light formed in the dark void of his mind. It was far away at first, then it grew closer and stronger by the second. Cooper's heart thumped hard against his chest. The light filled his mind, blinding him from within before it dissipated completely. Cooper opened his eyes and raised his head. A shadow in the corner of the room drew his attention.

Alexander and Stephen remained focused on Randy, seemingly unaware of the new presence in the room. Cooper wiped his eyes with the back of his hand and peered into the shadows by the window. The dark mass solidified into the form of a man. Electric blue eyes seared Cooper's skin. Commanded his full attention. A nearly imperceptible nod of Blue's head calmed him, then the form dissolved. Cooper finally understood. Blue had been there all along, lying in wait for Alexander to reach his weakest, most vulnerable point. But Blue's cold calculation had come at a price. Randy's life.

Cooper's empty stomach expanded, the contents he'd just expelled replaced with a heavy clot of death and darkness. It filled his lungs and his veins, bullying its way inside through every available pore and orifice. *Blue.* The spirit had taken up residence, claiming Cooper's broken shell as its own.

He opened his mouth, and a deep, unexpected roar pushed itself out, followed by prickles of movement edging up his throat, over his tongue, and finally onto his parted lips. With his last ounce of self-control, Cooper slapped at his face, trying to extinguish the disturbing, tingling sensation. He wiped his lips with the back of his fingers, pulled his hand away, and stared at it. A slimy swarm of maggots scurried over his palm, lacing through his fingers. He gagged and shook his hand like it was on fire. His mouth still tingling, he spat out the remaining intruders. Tiny, muculent creatures fell to the floor and scuttled away.

If he would have still been in control of his body, he might have retched again at the sight. His senses were numb, his limbs no longer his own. The darkness that had resided inside him all his life embraced the dreaded new occupant with excited familiarity. His detached gaze traveled around the room without mental instruction as if taking in the scene for the first time. Alexander and Randy were a few feet away, still locked in their sickening embrace and oblivious to his internal transformation.

Someone grabbed him by the shoulders and pulled him up. He was almost grateful since he couldn't seem to do it on his own. He'd forgotten how to control his limbs. Stephen faced him and gripped his wrists, regarding him with suspicion.

A missile of pain detonated in the base of Cooper's neck and splintered up to his temples. An assault of incoherent images exploded in his brain, filling every cerebral nook and cranny. A bizarre movie began to play on the back of his eyeballs, full of vivid and intense memories, as if they belonged to him, but they didn't. He was lost in a parade of unfamiliar scenes viewed through someone else's eyes.

Warfield teeming with nocturnal activity. Frantic shouts and cries of desperation fill the air. An angry mob of dark-skinned men in tattered clothing, holding axes, pitchforks, and torches surrounding him. He looks down at the axe in his own grip, hanging by his side. He leads them as they storm up Oak Alley toward the manor house, words like 'devil', 'demon', and 'blood-sucking monster' echoing through the dark night.

A spine-tingling scream calls from somewhere inside the manor house. They pick up the pace and burst through the front door. He rushes up the staircase and pushes into the room where he found Randy.

The red-haired girl from the picture in Lillie Mae's Bible, Sally Parker, lies there in the bed, a swath of blood pooling between her legs. Her face is fraught with fear. A tall man hovers over her. It is Alexander. His deadly jaws are on her neck, his mouth pulsating as he sucks out her life in vulgar gulps of aggression.

He rushes Alexander, knocking him off Sally with the clumsy swing of the axe and a roar of unbridled rage. He looks down at Sally. Touches her neck. It's too late. She does not breathe.

Field hands fill the room and surround Alexander, circling him, wielding their torches like swords. The Anakim is too fast for them. He disappears and a swirling dark cloud envelops the room, weaving through the men like an anaconda of black smoke. The men scream out in pain, dropping to the floor one by one, their throats being ripped out by unseen hands. They grab at their necks, trying to keep their heads from being severed completely off their shoulders.

Their lit torches fall and roll across the floor. The curtains are on fire. The black cloud is evaporating. The men are dead, Alexander gone. The fire spreads over the walls. The ceiling.

He drops to his knees and slips his arms around Sally's lifeless body, cradling her, swaying back and forth with the rhythm of his guttural wails. He is distraught, overcome with grief, and he cries out in agony as flames dance high around him.

He hears a gurgled cry across the room, so he lays Sally's body gently back down on the bed and walks over to it. He sidesteps the body of a plump dark woman lying in a pool of blood, a chunk of flesh missing from her neck.

In the basin on the dresser is a caramel-colored baby. A girl. Her face slipping under the waterline. He draws her out of the basin and peers down at her. She is breathing. She is alive. This baby. He knows her intended name because he chose it. Sarabeth. This child will one day become Lillie Mae's mother.

He looks up and catches a glimpse of himself in the dresser mirror. It is not his face he sees in the reflection, it is Blue's. Hardened and cragged, filled with lines of all-consuming grief.

The house erupts in a quick blaze of flames.

He clutches the baby tight in his arms and flees the room. Angry flames chase him all the way down the stairs and out the front door. Betsy is standing in dark shadows under a tree. She watches the house burn with thick red tears falling down her pale face. She is not human.

"I am too late," she cries. "My husband. My children. I am too late."

He places the naked child in her arms.

One final scene filled the virtual movie screen of Cooper's mind.

He is roused by the ferocious snarl of a large dog nipping at his feet. He looks up. A large section of the big house smolders in the distance as men douse it with buckets of water. Dead bodies dot the front yard. The morning sun greets the grisly scene with irreverent splendor.

Searing stripes of pain burn into the flesh of his back. Angry white faces scream at him from below. His body sways in the breeze, cold and choking. The dog rips into the flesh of his dangling feet. He swings from the drooping branch of a spindly oak tree, a thick rope cutting into his neck.

Wind blows Spanish moss over his face like a death shroud as he releases the defensive tension in his muscles and drifts into an all-consuming black void.

CHAPTER FORTY-FIVE

Stephen stared at him, mouth agape and eyes wide with shock. He released Cooper's wrists, breaking their cerebral connection. Shoving Cooper away, he stumbled back. He had seen it, too—all of Blue's memories that Cooper just relived. Stephen saw all of it.

Cooper turned his head, although he gave his body no such mental command. Blue was in total control, the spirit's strength grew stronger by the second. Cooper did not panic. Instead, he released himself completely to the malevolence rumbling in his core. Submitted his will completely to Blue's dominance.

He looked down at the entwined bodies of Alexander and Randy, their arms wrapped around each other in a lover's embrace. Alexander dug his fingernails into the bare flesh of Randy's back, creating multiple rows of seeping blood. Randy clamped down on the Anakim's neck, sucking. Devouring Alexander's essence.

Cooper was powerless to stop them. Blue had other priorities.

Alexander's eyes drifted open and rolled back in his head. "Enough." The sickening heat of desire laced his whisper.

Undeterred from his feast, Randy continued.

"I said enough!" Alexander pushed him away with one hand.

Randy's body sailed across the room and slammed into the wall beside the fireplace just steps away from Cooper. He sat up, unfazed by the crash. Licking the last remaining drops of Alexander's blood from his lips, he pushed himself up against the wall. Inches taller than before, the bronze skin of his naked torso glistened like it had been recently oiled. His muscles were bigger. Bulkier. His shoulders were wider, and his facial features more defined. He gawked at Cooper with wild, hungry eyes, as if he didn't even recognize him. A tinge of fear sparked in Cooper's gut. Never in his life did he imagine being afraid of Randy, but he was terrified of him in that moment. Blue, however, was not. He looked over at Alexander and rage heated him from within.

Alexander stood, rubbing the side of his neck, dabbing his own blood on the wounds. All physical traces of Randy's attack faded at his touch. He swayed, visibly weakened by Randy's feasting. Just the way Blue wanted him.

Alexander glanced up at Cooper. "He is not done yet. He needs human blood to complete the transition."

The words were a jumbled mess, knocking around in Cooper's head. Did Alexander mean him? No. He didn't.

Tony Tanner lumbered into the room, his aimless eyes sunken in their sockets and devoid of coherence. A wide swath of skin was missing from the center of his chest where his Confederate flag tattoo once was. He passed in front of Cooper and gave him an uninterested glance without registering an ounce of recognition. Odessa had really done a number on that guy. Tony crossed the room and stood in front of Alexander, like an obedient dog awaiting its master's command.

The Anakim nodded toward Randy. "Anthony, you will give yourself to my newborn and allow him to drain you."

Tony nodded and walked over to Randy without hesitation, passing Stephen and Cooper without a glance.

Cooper willed his arms to block Tony's path to certain death, but his body would not respond. Tony stood in front of Randy and cocked his head in compliance. Randy stared at the offering, his eyes filled with hungry desire.

No. Randy. It's Tony. Don't you see? It's our friend, Tony Tanner! None of the words actually made it out of Cooper's mouth. They just rattled around in his head, searching for the nearest exit as the muscles of speech eluded him.

Randy opened his mouth, and Cooper saw ivory fangs sprouting, heralded by the sound of crackling bone—the hideous bloom of Alexander's seed. Tony stood motionless as Randy locked onto its unblemished target. With shocking ferocity, he drove his sparkling new blades deep into Tony's neck.

No! The silent word shot through Cooper's mind and bounced off empty walls as the man he loved devoured their childhood friend.

Randy showed no mercy, gnawing into Tony's neck with voracious hunger, holding back none of his newborn strength or appetite. It lasted only a few moments. Tony's body seized with violent spasms, and his eyes drifted closed. He wilted in Randy's clutches, finally slithering out of his grip and onto the floor into a spiritless pile of human debris. Randy had just killed Tony, and Cooper was powerless to stop him.

Losing the last shred of control he had over his eyes, Cooper looked away from the horrific scene, his sights again set squarely on Alexander. Both Blue's and his own rage ignited a fire in the center of his being. His anomalous Divinum power churned inside him. His fingertips blistered, aching for release.

Alexander moved to the window where the fading sounds of battle seeped in. He pulled the curtain back and looked out. "Jericho soldiers will be here any second." He turned to Stephen, who had literally backed himself into the corner. "We will leave at once."

Stephen stared back at his maker with a mix of fear and judgment clouding his eyes. He shook his head slowly.

Alexander released the curtain and turned toward him. "For God's sake, Stephen, pull yourself together. We do not have time for your pathetic sniveling."

Cooper took a surprising step toward Alexander and opened his mouth. Blue's deep baritone emerged. "You will have no more of my children, Devil."

Alexander looked at Cooper like he noticed him for the first time. Muscles in his face stiffened with recognition. He had his clutches around Cooper's neck before Blue could command his body to react. A roar sounded behind them. Randy's roar. He tackled Alexander, taking Cooper down with him.

The two boulder-like bodies landed on top of Cooper with blunt force. Pinned under a heaping pile of Anakim flesh and muscle, Blue made quick work of regaining control of him. Cooper wiggled out from under Alexander and Randy and sprang to his feet. Randy rolled off of Alexander, leaving him exposed and vulnerable. Blue kept Cooper focused on Alexander. He stood over him and stretched his arm out. His hand shook as he pointed down at the Anakim, his nefarious power and Blue's dark rage solidifying as one in his core.

A cloud of black smoke roared into the room and instantly took Betsy's form. Her hair, matted with blood and changeling guts, hung wild over her face. Her eyes were wide and panicked.

She held her hand out toward him. "Cooper! Stop! Don't do it."

Cooper stared at her, confusion clouding his vision. Her eyes widened as she peered into his. A flurry of footsteps drew Cooper's attention to the door. Joshua, Rafe, and Taj bounded into the room and froze, scanning the scene with hands and daggers raised.

Without a glance at her distraught son cowering in the corner of the room, Betsy eased toward Cooper like she approached a coiled snake. "Blue. Listen to me. Let us handle Montgomery. He will pay for what he did to Sally, I swear to you. Please. Don't do this to Cooper."

Joshua's voice echoed across the room. "What the hell are you doing, Elizabeth? Let him finish the monster."

Betsy scowled at him. "You know what will happen to him if he does this!"

Cooper looked back and forth from Betsy to Alexander. Everything inside urged him to kill Alexander. He couldn't understand why Betsy wanted to stop him. Lex appeared in the doorway, flanked by Marissa and Daria. Joshua disappeared in a blur and reformed beside Betsy, his powerful arms binding her to him. She struggled, pushing him away and hissing, but she was no match for the Manheeg.

Joshua looked at Cooper and nodded down to Alexander. "Do it. End him now!"

Propped up on his elbows, Alexander glared at Joshua. "The traitor returns. My father should have killed you in the beginning, when he had the chance. I will finish the job for him." He opened his mouth and released a shrill wail that lasted for several seconds.

A reciprocal war cry sounded from somewhere behind the walls. Chair legs bounced off the floor. The baubles of the crystal chandelier clattered above them, swinging back and forth with wild agitation. Alexander reached over and pulled a silver lever at the base of the fireplace. The entire wall behind the hearth shook and swung forward, creaking open into the middle of the room.

Cooper stumbled back and peered into the dark tunnel. A surge of dank air rushed out, followed by a swarm of shrieking changelings.

CHAPTER FORTY-SIX

The Jericho soldiers went right to work slaying the monsters as they charged out of the tunnel. One jumped on Betsy's shoulder. She reached back, flung it over her head, and nailed it to the floor with her dagger.

Joshua held off two at once while Taj provided him with cover from the others. Rafe, Daria, and Marissa leaped over the antique sofas, chairs, and tables, landing daggers in the tops of changeling skulls and triggering explosion after explosion of flesh and bone. Lex only had to hold out his hand at the approaching monsters, and they would erupt into flames. Odessa charged out of the tunnel chasing the horde without her team in tow.

No doubt questioning his allegiances after all he had just learned, Stephen stood paralyzed in the corner as the room fell into complete chaos.

Randy was suddenly on his feet. He grabbed a changeling's head with one hand, wrapped a bulky arm around the neck of the beast, and twisted its head completely off. Rancid blood spewed out of the gaping hole between the decapitated creature's shoulders, spraying Randy's face.

Cooper spun around on Blue's internal command. Alexander stood before him, his eyes hard and full of vengeance. A moment of reckoning saturated the air between them as the battle raged on. With a deep, cleansing breath, Blue drew on all of Cooper's power and sent it rushing down into his right arm. Cooper stared down his throbbing hand, as if it wasn't attached to him.

When he looked back up, provocation twisted Alexander's lips. "I should have drained you when I had the chance, Houngan."

Cooper curled his fingers into a ball. He drew his arm back and slammed his fist into Alexander's chest with shocking force. Alexander buckled, his chest caving in.

He found his point of entry—cutting through the black cotton fabric of Alexander's shirt with his fingers and piercing the skin above the heart. He stared into Alexander's widening emerald eyes. Blue wanted to watch the poisonous sparkle drain out of them. Cooper wanted to see it as well. He plunged his hand deeper into Alexander's chest cavity, twisting his fingers, burrowing them deep down into the cold, hard flesh like a drill.

Alexander's eyes bulged in their sockets, his body paralyzed into submission. With arms dangling at his side, a final sneer marked his lips. "Your whore was delicious." He spat the words out through staggered breaths. "Every last drop of her!"

The rage inside Cooper solidified in his muscles. Within seconds, he had submerged his whole hand into the Anakim's chest. He brushed aside the mass of thick muscle and slimy veins until he found the treasure. He gripped the dead organ and squeezed. Alexander grabbed at Cooper's hand and wailed as Cooper pulled the miry mass toward him, errant magic fueling his extraordinary strength. He wouldn't have stopped even if he had the power to do so.

Alexander's widened eyes turned from green to gray in an instant. He parted his lips and black liquid spilled out, trickling over his jaw and down his pale neck.

Cooper looked down. His hand was no longer inside Alexander's chest. It hung in the air between them, holding a dead, black heart in his open palm. The organ shrank down to the size of a golf ball and disintegrated into a pile of ash in his hand. Alexander stared up at him with dull gray eyes, the fight in them completely gone. His body crumpled to the floor with an unceremonial thud and burst into flames.

A chorus of changeling shrieks echoed around the room. Then the battle behind him fell silent. Cooper turned. All around the room, the Jericho soldiers stood panting and staring at mounds of changeling ash and ember. Stephen propped himself up on hands and knees, apparently weakened by Alexander's demise himself, but still alive.

Randy seemed to be the only seed of Alexander in the room that wasn't physically affected by the Anakim's death.

He rushed to Cooper's side and put his hands on his shoulders. "Cooper. Look at me. It's me, Randy."

Covered in changeling blood, Randy's now amber eyes were glassy and foreign to him. His touch was ice cold and shot through the fabric of Cooper's shirt. Cooper wanted to reach out to him, but Blue would not allow it.

Around him, Jericho soldiers stood shell-shocked, their

daggers still raised as if they expected the neat little piles of ash scattered around the room to suddenly reform and come back to life. Rafe and Betsy lowered their daggers first, then Odessa and Joshua eased away from the remains of their attackers. Lex had already busied himself tending to a nasty wound in Taj's side. Marissa kneeled over her twin's motionless body, covering her face in her hands and sobbing.

"What the fuck just happened?" Rafe asked, breaking the silence.

"Changelings aren't fully-formed Anakim beings," Joshua said through staggered breaths. "They can't survive without their maker's life force."

Cooper stared down at Alexander's smoldering corpse, transfixed by the dying flames. He'd done the impossible, and he could not have done it without Blue's help. But now it was time for the spirit to go.

Randy shook him again. "Cooper? Are you in there? Say something, goddammit!"

Randy's voice was different. Lower. His eyes sparkled like two drops of liquid gold. Cooper tried to touch his face and respond to him—use the deep love he felt for Randy to escape Blue's hold, like Miss Ida said. But he couldn't. The spirit wouldn't release him. Cooper could only stare at Randy through the shield of Blue's curious yet unfeeling eyes.

Blue.

The voice was soft. Sweet. Angelic. It drifted through his head like an ethereal melody.

Blue, my love. It's over now.

He turned and looked back at the tunnel opening. A vertical stream of light pulled at his insides with a force he could not deny.

You can rest now, Blue. Come home to me.

Cooper strained to focus on a translucent image forming in the light. Everything and everyone in the room fell away, and there was only her—a pale, young girl with a flowing white nightgown billowing in the chilly breeze of the tunnel. Hair the color of a shiny new penny cascaded down her back, framing a smooth face dotted with light freckles. Sally Parker.

Blue's spirit rustled deep inside Cooper as Sally reached out to him with open arms. Without a moment of hesitation, Cooper pulled free of Randy's grip and reached back to her.

Randy's voice faded behind him. "Cooper? What are you doing? Where are you going?"

He moved toward Sally, yet deep down, his soul reached back for Randy. He failed to make his limbs respond. Sally took his right hand, and radiant warmth filled him from head to toe.

Sally stared up into his eyes. *Blue. Your work here is done. It's time to let him go.*

Randy grabbed his left arm and tugged on it, but Cooper held his ground. The internal conflict ripped at his insides. He wanted so badly to turn away and run to Randy, but Blue was still in control and he wanted to be with Sally.

"Cooper, please," the crack in Randy's voice cut deep enough to draw his attention—or Blue's attention.

Randy's skin had lost its usual tanned pigment, yet it glistened under the splatter of blood caked across his heaving chest. They looked at each other. The old Randy was still in there. His eyes brimmed with light of love and tenderness that could not be extinguished by the Anakim poison now running through his veins. Cooper loved him so much, his heart ached with a dull, numbing pain. His skin sizzled with the mystic energy of the troubled spirit controlling him, pulling him to return to Sally's alluring call. Randy held out his arms to him, streaks of dark tears marring his perfect face.

Remembering Miss Ida's instructions, Cooper fought the spirit firmly rooted inside him. He focused on Randy's eyes and the love they held for him, a greater love than he had ever known or even imagined possible. Drawing up all the power he had left in his weakened shell of a body, he pushed everything outward, expelling the dread and death that filled him.

Cooper's mouth stretched open. An agonizing wail rushed up from the pit of his stomach. The room spun around him as the battle for sovereignty of his soul erupted deep inside him. He would not give in to Blue. His love for Randy was too great. With a final exhausting push, the heaviness in his stomach released its cancerous grip, finger by defiant finger, and dissipated from his consciousness.

Cooper dropped to his knees and drew in a deep gasp of air. His body was spent but purged of its domineering visitor. He looked back at the empty tunnel.

Blue and Sally were gone.

CHAPTER FORTY-SEVEN

Cooper tried to stand. His legs were like rubber and gave out. Randy grabbed him under his arms and helped him to remain upright. The room finally settled down around him, and he put a hand on Randy's chest to steady himself.

"I'm good," Cooper said. "Thanks." And he *was* good. It was over. Alexander was dead. Blue had finally found peace and his way back to Sally.

Rafe and Odessa circled the room in opposite directions, Odessa inching toward Stephen in the corner, and Rafe closing in on Randy. Alarms went off in Cooper's head. It wasn't over yet.

Odessa stood over a cowering Stephen. He bared his fangs at her and hissed, fear glazing his eyes. She leaned down and pointed her dagger in his face, grazing the tip of his nose. "I think Betsy should do the honors of ending this one."

Betsy growled at her through bared fangs.

"O!" Joshua reprimanded with a steely glare.

Though Odessa didn't look at the Manheeg, she took a step back.

Rafe edged closer to Cooper and Randy, knees bent, muscles tight. His usually rakish face was now rigid with aggression. “Let go of him and back away, Anakim.” He raised his dagger. “I know this wasn’t your fault, bro, so I’m really sorry for this.” Rafe charged.

A thunderclap of rage exploded inside Cooper once more. Without thinking or hesitation, he threw up a hand and caught Rafe by the throat, though there was three feet of empty space between them, and slowly raised him in the air.

Dangling in mid-air, Rafe kicked his legs and clawed at unseen fingers tightening around his throat, the color quickly draining from his face. Satisfied that he’d gotten Rafe’s attention, Cooper released his phantom grip with a flick of his hand. Rafe fell hard to the floor, rubbing his throat and gasping for air.

With widened eyes, Randy looked around the room from one Jericho solider to the next. Cooper couldn’t imagine what was going on in his head right now—how everything must look through those new radiant eyes.

Cooper turned and pointed at the soldiers. “Stay away from him, all of you.” His voice resonated with absolute authority. “He is under my protection.”

“That’s not how it works, Cooper,” Joshua said, his voice low and threatening. “He is Anakim now. He and Stephen must be dealt with accordingly.”

Cooper clenched his fists and took a step forward. “I don’t care if he’s Charles *fucking* Manson! You touch him and you die. Besides, *you* are Anakim. Go fall on your own damn sword, why don’t you?”

"I will, gladly," Joshua growled through gritted teeth. "*After* we have rid the earth of this unholy pestilence."

Cooper looked over at Betsy and nodded to Stephen. "So, Elizabeth Parker. Are you going to just stand by and watch them murder your own son? Your son, for Christ's sake!"

Betsy's shifting eyes betrayed her internal conflict. She looked away from Cooper, guilt resonating from every pore.

Joshua took an authoritative step forward. "Elizabeth knows what has to be done. She will not stand in the way of our mission."

Cooper shot a quick look over his shoulder. Using the wall as a defensive barrier, Stephen inched closer to him and Randy, each step a little steadier than the one before. His cheeks were streaked with black blood. Fear, defeat, and sadness pooled in his eyes. His lover had betrayed him, killed his sister, brother, and father, and lied to him about it for a hundred and fifty years. And now his own mother was duty-bound to let him die. He looked less like a vicious, murderous fiend and more like a lost child watching his world collapse around him. Cooper almost felt sorry for him.

Betsy glided forward, her eyes pleading. "Cooper, you have to leave here immediately. You have been marked now."

Cooper looked at her. "What the hell is that supposed to mean?"

"You killed Alexander," she replied.

He edged closer to Randy. "Yes. I did. And I would gladly do it again."

"You don't understand," Betsy said, only an arm's length away. "When Anakim die, their makers witness the death through the eyes of their offspring. Alexander's maker has seen your face. He knows what you did. He will come for you, seeking his revenge."

Cooper stared at her, his heart softening just a bit. "That's why you tried to stop me from killing him?"

Her shoulders sagged, and she nodded. "I did not want you to be marked for his death. I would have gladly done it in your place and bore the wrath of his maker."

He studied Betsy's usually flawless face, now dented with lines of fear and worry. Not just fear. She was terrified. "Why do you look so frightened? Who is Alexander's maker?"

Joshua's voice boomed behind her. "Once my friend and most trusted ally, he is now my sworn enemy—the supreme leader of the Anakim race and the most ruthless of them all. His madness knows no bounds, and his cruelty is only surpassed by his unquenchable bloodlust."

Cooper stared over Betsy's shoulder at Joshua, lost in his words. Comprehensive dread filled his veins, sending goose bumps racing down his arms and legs. The name fell off his tongue with little assistance. "Caleb."

Randy pressed his arm against Cooper's, centering him. Stephen was only a few steps away.

Joshua nodded and moved toward them. "Alexander was Caleb's favorite progeny. He will not take his passing well. He *will* find you."

Cooper lowered his head with the dead weight of desperation. First he'd lost Lillie Mae, then Randy had been transformed into something he could barely recognize. Now this. He would continue to be hunted, not by a monster that wanted to keep him imprisoned the rest of his life, but by one that would stop at nothing to end it.

Joshua stood beside Betsy. "Come with us, Cooper. Join Jericho and we will protect you. Your unique gifts would be an unprecedented asset to our cause. It is your destiny."

Cooper peered over at Randy, whose new amber eyes were full of loyalty, desire, and hunger. He knew Joshua's offer of protection did not extend to Randy. They would never let him live now, not Alexander's Anakim child—a descendent of Caleb.

Joshua pointed a finger at him. "If you choose not to join us, Cooper, you shall suffer the same fate as Randy and Stephen."

"Joshua, please," Betsy protested, grabbing him by the arm.

Joshua growled at her and shoved her aside, never breaking eye contact with Cooper. "We cannot allow even the possibility of your blood falling into the hands of the Anakim. That would be devastating to our cause and to the human race."

Stephen had made it over to them and stood behind Cooper and Randy, making an unlikely coalition. Cooper glanced over his shoulder at Stephen. His eyes were full of intensity as he probed Cooper's mind. This time, Cooper did not fight him, and Stephen's message was clear.

I can help you.

He had no time for thoughtful deliberation. He had no choice but to trust Stephen and accepted the offer with a nod.

Joshua, Rafe, and Odessa all charged at once.

Stephen disintegrated into a dark cloud of thick gray smoke, swirling around Cooper and Randy as if they were caught in the eye of a tornado. Odessa sailed over their heads with her dagger drawn. Rafe charged straight for Randy. Joshua lunged at Cooper, fangs extended, and a ferocious growl exploding from his mouth.

Cooper turned away and came face to face with Randy. Their eyes locked on each other, Randy slipped his arms around Cooper's waist and pulled him close. Cooper held him tight and braced for the blunt impact of the attack. The moment Cooper's feet left the floor, something sharp and hot tore into his side.

Then everything went black.

CHAPTER FORTY-EIGHT

Cooper forced his heavy eyelids open.

Long rattan blades ran in clockwise slow motion above him, the ceiling fan motor emitting a hypnotic hum. The gentle crash of low tide echoed in the distance, and a salty breeze spilled into the room, sending shivers scampering across his naked body. A dull pain gripped his side.

"Hey there." The honey-toned voice tickled his left ear, and he let his head fall in its direction.

Randy lay there, beaming at him, the side of his head sunken down into a fluffy white pillow. Cooper saw a twinkle in his once dark brown eyes, now amber and sparkly when the low light of the bedside lamp skimmed their surface.

"Randy." Cooper's voice was scratchy and thick on his tongue, but saying the name out loud comforted him.

Randy smiled and touched his face, the sting of his ice-cold fingers less unnerving than Cooper remembered.

"You gave us quite a scare there, Red," Randy said.

Cooper didn't understand what he meant at first. The

memories emerged slowly through the haze of his brain. A sudden realization hit him like a ton of bricks. They were in bed together, covered only by a white cotton sheet, the top of which rested across their lower stomachs. Cooper was completely naked underneath. Randy appeared to be as well, at least from the waist up.

Cooper scratched his head and rubbed his temples. "Well, it was a pretty scary night by most people's standards." Cooper tried not to stare at the trail of golden hair leading from Randy's flat navel to the border of the sheet.

Randy chuckled. "One hell of a first date, though."

Cooper raised his head and scanned his surroundings. The room had an upscale take on low-country shabby chic. Two old distressed doors served as headboards, crowning the iron-frame bed where they lay. A scatter of shaggy cream-colored rugs dotted a dark walnut floor. Varying shades of white covered the board-and-batten-paneled walls, a flanked ceiling, and cushy slip-covered club chairs. Faded beams of the setting sunlight broke through the intricate lace of rustling curtains, giving the room a warm, ethereal glow.

Cooper eased his head back on the pillow and looked over at Randy. "Where the hell are we?"

Randy propped himself up on one elbow, the sheet falling low enough down his rippled stomach to reveal a border of curly dark hairs. Desire stirred in Cooper's loins, causing him to shift under the sheet.

"Stephen's beach house in Pawleys Island," Randy said, looking down at him. "He brought us here from Warfield last night. He's really not a bad guy, now that he's away from Alexander the Freak. He feels horrible about all the bad shit he did. Says he was under Alexander's spell." He grinned at Cooper. "I have to admit. I can relate."

Cooper looked away, still tentative about trusting Randy's love. "Last night?" He shifted to sit up, and dull pain sucker-punched him in the side. "How long was I out?"

"Easy there, Tiger," Randy said, placing a hand directly on the bare spot of skin where the pain originated. It helped. The pain eased, or maybe his ice-cold touch just numbed it.

"You've been out for quite a while." Randy gently massaged the wound. "That bitch, Odessa, nailed you pretty good with her dagger before Stephen got us out of there. It's mostly healed now, though. Stephen said it'd be sore a while longer."

Cooper lowered the sheet so he could inspect the aching wound on his side. He didn't see any trace of one. The skin over the tender area was smooth and unblemished.

Randy pushed a lock of Cooper's hair back from his forehead. "I gave you my blood. That healed the wound. Stephen showed me how. Fucking disgusting, but effective." He pressed his open palm to Cooper's taut stomach, sending a charge of icy heat shooting through his body.

Cooper let his head sink into the soft pillow and stared at Randy. He glanced down at the bulge between Randy's legs, mounding under the sheet. "Did we..."

Randy chuckled, leaned over, and kissed him on the cheek. The light contact of his soft chilled lips felt like a snowflake landing and quickly melting on his skin. "Don't worry, Red. I didn't take advantage of you. Your honor is intact."

Warmth returned to Cooper's cheek. He didn't mind the prospect of Randy taking advantage of him, but he wanted to be fully conscious and actively participating when it happened.

"All in due time," Randy teased with a devilish grin.

A brief wave of panic shot through Cooper. "Don't tell me."

"Yep," Randy said, a quiet chuckle spilling out of his mouth. "I can hear your thoughts now. Can see your dreams too, and you had some doozies while you were out." Randy stroked Cooper's hair with the tip of an index finger. "When we got here last night, you were in pretty bad shape. The wound was really deep, and your fever skyrocketed pretty fast. Blue's possession also did a number on your body. We couldn't really take you to Georgetown Memorial, so we made do here. After I gave you some of my blood, I held you all night, using my new ass-backward body temperature to get the fever down. Miss Ida's idea. Thankfully, it worked."

"Oh," Cooper said, distracted by imagined images of the cuddling he'd missed while he was out. "Wait. Miss Ida?"

Randy reached for a damp cloth on the nightstand and dabbed Cooper's forehead and cheeks. "She stayed with you today while Stephen and I slept. The sun just went down a few minutes ago, so I slipped back in here."

A wave of grief spilled over him like a punishing waterfall. He stared at the ceiling, fighting back tears. *Lillie Mae.*

Randy stroked his cheek with the back of his hand. "I'm so sorry about Aunt Mae, Cooper. She was one hell of a woman. Miss Ida and Wayne are taking care of all the arrangements. Don't worry with that right now, okay?"

Cooper looked at Randy. He was so overcome with love and affection that he didn't know what to say. It was a dream come true. Yes. That must be it. A dream. A dreaded new reality settled in on him, disrupting his fleeting moment of peace. Randy was no longer human. He had died. He was Anakim.

"No," Randy said, a look of shame drifting over his face. "I'm afraid you're not dreaming. And yes. I am... one of them. But I'm also still Randy. Don't you forget that, Coop."

Randy's lips were cool and tender as they met Cooper's. The innocent show of affection quickly turned passionate. Randy pulled Cooper close to him, the hard mass below his waist protesting the sheer constraints of the thin layer of cotton fabric that separated their bare skin. Cooper pressed himself against Randy's body, his own hardened cock throbbing for release.

A soft, ill-timed knock sounded, and the door eased open with a slow creak. They stopped kissing. Exasperated, Cooper rolled over onto his back.

"Randy," Stephen said, poking his head in around the half-open door. Long strands of unfettered blond hair fell forward over his face. He looked at Cooper. "Oh, sorry to interrupt." A conspiratorial smile crept over his angular face.

Cooper glanced down, and heat rushed to his cheeks. He

pulled the sheet up to cover his exposed erection.

Stephen smiled at him. "Well, I can see that you are fully awake now. That's great." He looked back at Randy. "We should go now. You need to feed."

Randy nodded. "Be right there."

Stephen smiled at Cooper. "You'll be fine here until we get back. Miss Ida's still here, and nobody knows about this place. It's been my own secret oasis for years. We will need to leave soon now that you are better. Just to be safe."

Stephen ducked out and pulled the door to.

Randy sighed and lowered his head. "Sorry, Red. I'd better go." As much as he tried to hide it, Cooper could see Randy struggled with his new existence, and he had a hundred questions for him.

What does it feel like? Have you killed anyone? Can you fly like Betsy and Stephen? Can we still have sex? Just to name a few.

Randy smiled with a twinkle in his eyes. "I'll be back soon, and we can pick up where we left off. I'll answer all of your questions then."

Cooper frowned. "Dammit, that's annoying."

"And no, I haven't killed anyone," Randy said as he slid his legs over the side of the bed and looked away. "Except for Tony, that is." The pain in his voice cut like a knife through Cooper's heart.

He stroked the back of Randy's hand. "You didn't know what you were doing."

"That's what I keep telling myself." Randy ran his fingers through his mussed hair and sighed. He flashed a smile over his shoulder and then rose naked from the bed, looking like he had just stepped down from Mt. Olympus. "Thanks for saying that, though."

Randy pulled the tight jeans over his muscled thighs and perfectly sculpted ass and winked at him from across the room. Heat rushed to Cooper's cheeks. What the hell had happened to him? The boys back in Nashville would never recognize this Cooper Causey. Actually, he was just fine with that. When Cooper blinked, Randy was on top of him, straddling him on hands and knees.

Cooper flinched. "Jesus Christ, Randy. Don't do that."

Randy laughed. He stared down at Cooper, and all fun and games ceased. He closed the gap between their lips, his kiss hungry and deep, like Cooper was the only nourishment that could sustain him. He returned the passion, losing himself in the moment. His erection pressed into the crotch of Randy's jeans, the rough fabric on his tender flesh creating instant friction that he nearly lost control over.

Randy pulled away slowly. He glanced down at Cooper's pulsating girth and shot him a mischievous smile. Then, in a rustle of cold wind that sailed through the open sliding door to the terrace and out into the night, he was gone.

Cooper couldn't fight the smile forming on his lips. "Asshole!" He turned on his side and ran his hands over the soft white sheets, still cool from Randy's body. It was the first time he didn't want to slink away from a man's bed. Ever. He couldn't wait for Randy to return. Though he felt safe for the moment, his mind brimmed with anxiety-laden questions.

What would he do now? Was he supposed to just drop out of his life? School? Go on the run with his hot immortal boyfriend and his one-hundred-fifty-year-old underwear model of a gay uncle? How long could they hide from Jericho? From Caleb?

The ocean breeze serenaded him with a tranquil symphony of white noise, making his heavy eyelids droop. He and Randy would figure it out together. He closed his eyes and allowed himself to rest as the darkness rumbled deep inside him like gentle rolling thunder, lulling him into the peaceful slumber of its familiar embrace.

THE END

AUTHOR NOTE

Most special thanks to: (reader: insert your name here), for spending your money and time on my little tale. I hope it was worth it!

Heartfelt thanks to all those who cheered me on and believed in me from the very beginning of this journey (you know who you are), but especially to Melissa Chambers who inspired me to get off my ass and write the damn book. To my editors Charissa Weaks and Jerry Wheeler for helping me mold and polish it. To my super supportive beta readers: Steve, Tom, Hal, Michelle, Ray, and my sister, Monica. To all 62 agents who either rejected this manuscript or never responded to my query—all of you made me stronger (he says through gritted teeth). Finally, to my husband, Steve, who inspired me everyday with his own life journey and relentless resolve for excellence. I love you.

This story is set in the town where I was born and spent many years of my youth. If you're ever driving down to Myrtle Beach, SC, there are only a couple of ways to get there, one of which is straight through Georgetown—the

3rd oldest city in South Carolina and the "Ghost Capital of the South." I encourage you to take a few minutes to veer down to the historic district where you will find many places you read about in this book—The Strand Theater, the Rice Museum, the Harborwalk, Prince George Winyah Episcopal Church, and many Spanish moss-canopied streets lined with beautiful old homes. The place's charm was lost on me as a child and my penance for that is to share it with the world now. And if you really want the true "Warfield" experience, go stay a night or two at Mansfield Plantation, the inspiration for Warfield. Mansfield is a beautifully restored bed and breakfast now where I'm told things still go bump in the night, just as they did when I was child.

GREG HOWARD

Greg Howard grew up near the coast of South Carolina, or as he fondly refers to it, "the armpit of the American South." By the time he could afford professional therapy and medication, the damage had already been done. His hometown of Georgetown, South Carolina is known as the "Ghost Capital of the South," (seriously…there's a sign), and was always a great source of material for his overactive imagination.

Raised in a staunchly religious home, Greg escaped into the arts: singing, playing piano, acting, writing songs, and making up stories. After running away to the bright lights and big city of Nashville, Tennessee with stars in his eyes and dreams of being the Dianne Warren of Music City, he took a job peddling CDs and has been a cog in the music business machine ever since.

Now an adult with a brain, Greg finds the South Carolina coast to be a perfectly magical place where he vacations often and dreams of the day when he can return to write full time in the most tastefully decorated beach house in Pawleys Island. Greg has a soft spot for Spaniels and rescue animals. People…not so much.

For announcements about new projects and exclusive offers, sign up for my newsletter at: www.greghowardauthor.com

Trademarks Acknowledgment

The author acknowledges the trademark status and trademark owners of the following places and items mentioned in this work of fiction:

Styrofoam: The Dow Chemical Company

Pepsi: PepsiCo Inc.

Field and Stream: American Sports Licensing, Inc.

Gamecocks: University of South Carolina

Walmart: Wal-Mart Stores, Inc.

Olan Mills: Olan Mills, Inc.

Winn-Dixie: Winn-Dixie Stores, Inc.

Silly Putty: Crayola Properties, Inc.

Dairy Queen: The American Dairy Queen Corporation

Band-Aid: Johnson & Johnson

Jim Beam: Beam Global Spirits and Wine, Inc.

iPad: Apple, Inc.

Twilight Zone: CBS Broadcasting Inc.

Xena, Warrior Princess: Studios USA Television Distribution

Vanderbilt: Vanderbilt University

Men's Fitness: Weider Publications, LLC

Photoshop: Adobe Systems, Inc.

Avon: Avon Products, Inc.

Harley Davidson: H-D Michigan, LLC

Juicy Fruit: Wm. Wrigley Jr. Company

The Incredible Hulk: Cadence Industries Corporation d.b.a. Marvel Comics Group

GQ: Advance Magazine Publishers Inc.

27144488R00223

Printed in Poland
by Amazon Fulfillment
Poland Sp. z o.o., Wrocław